King
&
Raven

King
&
Raven

Cary James

TOR®

A Tom Doherty Associates Book
New York

This is a work of fiction. All the characters and events portrayed in this novel are fictitious or are used fictitiously.

KING & RAVEN

This book is printed on acid-free paper.

A Tor Book
Published by Tom Doherty Associates, Inc.
175 Fifth Avenue
New York, N.Y. 10010

Tor Books on the World-Wide Web:
http://www.tor.com

Tor® is a registered trademark of Tom Doherty Associates, Inc.

Design by Lynn Newmark

Library of Congress Cataloging-in-Publication Data

James, Cary.
    King & Raven / Cary James.
        p.   cm.
    "A Tom Doherty Associates book."
    ISBN 0-312-85870-1
    1. Arthurian romances—Adaptations. 2. Knights and knight-
hood—Fiction. 3. Peasantry—Fiction. 4. Revenge—Fiction.
I. Title.
PS3560.A3784K56   1995
813'.54—dc20   95-22692
                                                            CIP

First edition: September 1995

Printed in the United States of America

0 9 8 7 6 5 4 3 2 1

Dedication

To August and Marian Martin for their constant support; though, sadly, Gus did not live to see this book.

To the members of the writing group called the Saturday Scribbling Pigs' Society, which hardly ever meets on Saturday; to Lucy Diggs, Caroline Fairless, Mary Rose Hayes, Kermit Sheets, Katie Supinski, Liz Stewart Thompson, Marilyn Wallace, and the late Joan Cupples.

To the members of the writing group called the Saturday Gourmet Writers, which usually *does* meet on Saturday; to Steven Crane, Ed Fortier, Joan Gaustad, Walt Kleine, Barb Jernigan, Jackie Melchior, Brian Sackett, Mark Schynert, Salinda Tyson, Margaret Speaker Yuan, and Kyle Zaidan. And especially to Marta Randall, whose belief, encouragement, and persistence were essential in the making of this book.

To my editor, Debbie Notkin, for her understanding and enthusiasm.

To the staffs of the Mill Valley Library, the Marin County Library, the Library of the University of California at Berkeley; with special thanks to Harriet Goldfluss and Barbara Lekisch, then at the Corte Madera Library.

To my mother Helen, and my daughters Maya Vasquez and Sanna James and their families; to Nicolas,

Eugenio, Pablo, Nico, Lydia, and Juliana, for their encouragement and continuing support.

And most especially, for her limitless reserves of energy, patience, endurance and constancy, I dedicate this book to my wife, Elaine.

One

Once, in those times before the end, before I stood on that empty shore staggering of injury and amazement, speechless as his boat faded into the dawn, before I understood how frightful is victory, how empty revenge, and how precious love . . .

But it's a poor story that starts at its ending, and here I take a breath and begin again.

Once, in those times a certain light shone in the air and men laughed and women called from house doors as twilight fell, and children waited for the first star. Once.

And though by the evening my story begins I was a lad grown lean and gangly, and my voice wavered and I stared at village girls on market days, still that dusk I went like a child out beyond our houseyard, beyond the oaks that named us Greenfarm, and walked the furlong's edge into broad Westfield. The half-grown wheat whispered in the breeze. I raised my face to a sky of glowing orange. A blackbird began its evening song, and far across the field lights glimmered on the walls of Camelot, like stars fallen to earth.

A man sang there, at Camelot. His clear voice hung faint on the evening air like a star in the fading sky. It gave me chills, that soft far voice. He sang every evening, and though I listened alone that night, oft my sister would be there and we would stand together in the wheat and hold each other's hand, and be afraid to breathe lest we miss a note. We could not hear his words, yet she believed he sang of gentle knights and fair ladies, of adventure and chivalry and love.

She was a year older, Rebecca, and people said we were like enough to be twins, dark-haired though the rest of the family were light. Because of that she imagined us the children of other, highborn parents, and in truth there were tales enough of foundlings and fostering. I laughed at her, for in all the stories noble orphans were always raised by noble families, and our father was but a freeman on the king's demesne. And Rebecca would only shake her head and say it proved my peasant blood, that I had such small faith in romance.

The blackbird stopped. All the world lay hushed, listening to the song. A woman's voice joined him that in my fancy was the queen, and they sang together another verse, their voices weaving about each other like flowering vines. And then, like the first rumble of a storm, a faint stony clatter rang from Camelot, a distant rattle that overwhelmed their careful harmony, that echoed under the castle gates and grew to sharp thunder as the hooves of horses drummed across the drawbridge.

I was trotting homeward when my mother called. Knights rode abroad and I knew better than let them catch me after dark. The rumble of hooves grew. I could hear them shouting and cursing each other. They carried torches and galloped straight across the furlongs, five of them, unmindful of any farmer's grain, the clamor growing louder and louder till like a clap of thunder their horses vaulted our garden fence and landed in a storm of dust amid our squawking geese.

I crouched behind our house corner, frightened and excited both by their galloping power. In the flaring torchlight they were bleary drunk and one, roaring with laughter, swung his brand at our old gander and almost fell from the saddle, before their horses found the road and they galloped away.

It was this way every midsummer, John Baptist's eve. They raced to the forest chapel half a league away, with fire from the castle's hearth, and the first to thrust his brand into the stacked faggots of the bonfire won some favor of the king. Another horse, I imagined, or some varlet to clean his mail armor. They were very impartial, those knights. They had no care whose grain they rode, whose flocks they trampled, whose roof they accidentally fired. You could not call them gentle at the best of times, and we lived like people crouched against thunder under a tall tree. Lightning would surely strike. We could but pray it would not find us.

The geese still squawked and the damp air reeked of their droppings, when my father came out our house. He was a broad, sturdy man, his face sunburnt from the fields, his back stopped from the plow. I was near as tall as him already.

"By damn," he muttered, "they missed the birds?"

"Yes, father. Good horses."

He frowned at me. "Mustn't let them catch you, lad."

"No, sir."

My older brother appeared, making soft noises at the frightened geese. He was the image of our father, though yet unstooped, and his name was Harry but I thought of him as Slow. I had a way then of giving private names and though my father was only Warren, his old mother was Cluck, my mother Ruth was Worry and her father was Old Drool, and the baby was Little Drool. I kept the names to myself, all save Rebecca that I called Lark for her songs on sunny mornings.

I was Micah. But the name that fit was Raven.

In the time it takes to tell, they had all trooped out into the evening yard. " 'Twarn't like this under the old king." Old Cluck stared after the knights. "And where's Rebecca?"

"Out walking," said Harry.

"With Sam the tanner," my mother said.

"Tanner?" grumbled Old Drool. "Wat's boy? She oughtn't be seeing a tanner, there's no virtue in tanning, they're but villeins, find a freeman for her, she's a good cook, spins . . ."

"Thank you, Father," said my father. He frowned up at the darkening sky. "Nearly time for bed."

Inside our house the single room was still dim and smoky from the supper fire. My mother lit a rushlight before she banked the hearth under the cracked firepot. My father closed the thick wood shutter at the window, and we undressed and crawled together into the two housebeds.

I was half asleep when I remembered I'd forgot to piss. I unlatched the door and went to stand against the cow-byre wall. Stars hung overhead, very bright. The moon was not yet up. At the castle they had begun another song. Suddenly, from the field where I had watched there came a thick flutter of wings and a quiet scream. It was only a hare caught by a hunting owl, yet it froze my heart. I held my breath, listening. There was nothing more.

Little Drool woke me crying for the tit, and in the dark I could smell the damp night air. My father stood in our open doorway, a black shape against thin moonlight. Ruth muttered from their bed, "I told her to stay close, Warren, tonight 'specially."

He murmured something I did not catch, for I heard again the hare's scream. I climbed over Harry and out the bed.

"Who's that?" said my father.

"I'll go look for her." I found my clothes in the dark.

"Don't be a fool, Micah."

"I know where they walk, Father. The road to the village, the way to the chapel." I pushed past him out the door.

"Here," he called, "take Harry with you."

The waning moon hung lopsided in the eastern sky. Her light slanted across the night fields, and the hedges along the road lay thick black shadows on the dust. The sound of my footsteps echoed in the still night. I went quick as I could toward Ryford village, but at the turning to the forest chapel I stopped to catch my breath. Pray God, I thought, she was not so foolish to walk where the knights rode.

Somebody came trotting behind me, and I stepped into a shadow. "Micah," called Harry puffing, "Father sent me after you."

"Go on to the village," I said, "knock on Sam's door. I'll go to the chapel."

"Yes," he said, and hurried past me.

The crooked moon glared in my eyes as I turned down the lane. Eastfield glittered with spring barley to one side, each family's strip clear in the slanting light. Across the way Newfield lay dim and fallow. In the distance the chapel woods made a dark smear against a blacker sky.

My footsteps thumped steadily in the hush. I grew warm from hurrying and at the edge of the trees I stopped for breath. A man's laugh barked in the wood nearby. Other voices rumbled, slurred with drink, and I almost coughed with fright. The lane narrowed between the trees. I went on quiet as I could. The moon shone directly in my eyes. A dark figure stepped into the moonlit road and my heart thudded with terror before I recognized him.

"Sam." I could hardly whisper.

"What?" He crouched, ready to flee. "Who?"

"It's Micah, Sam."

"Micah. Oh God, they have her, Rebecca, the knights."

Their voices came again. One began to grunt over and over, more and more loudly, the same as bulls did when they mounted, and as that sound grew so did the mutter of the others until, very clear in the night a man gasped, and the others made a ragged cheer.

"Christ's name," he said, "the bitch hath bested me. I can give no more."

I could not speak, for fright and anger, and agony.

"She wanted to walk here," Sam groaned, "to see them ride."

"I will kill them."

"Micah," Sam whispered, "they are knights, five of them."

I lurched from the bright lane into a dim and moon-shot wood. A horse whickered very near and in the damp I could smell manure. I stopped my blundering and went on silently.

"Almant," cried one of them, "tie the damned horses. The bitch's ready, God knows we've warmed her for you."

"Leave her." He spoke so close it made me jump. I saw the dark shapes of horses and a man with them.

"Surely I've left her much," said another, laughing.

The moonlight came in rare splashes, enough to show four men standing in a circle. The ground between them was swallowed in shadow, yet something moved there. I bit my knuckles. I sank to my knees, trembling, wanting to cry out. I could not speak. I could not even breathe.

"Aye," said a third, "best John Baptist's I can remember." Weaving with drink, they straggled back to their animals. Harness rattled and creaked as they swung up into their saddles.

"Bastards." I had found my tongue. "Rapers." My voice cracked like a child's. "God curse every knight."

"What's that?" one said.

The horses picked their way slowly out the wood.

"Her peasant lout," said a second, laughing. "God's Name, churl, we've plowed your field aplenty."

"Damn you!" I shouted. "Hell's fire take you all."

They did not even pause, but when they reached the road cried another race back to the castle.

"Lark," I whispered.

She could not speak, though her lips moved with my name. Even in the dim moonlight bruises mottled her face. Her skirts had been ripped. She lay in blood black as the night. I knelt and took her hand, that fluttered in my own like a wounded bird.

"Sam," I called.

We got her up, though she whimpered at every move. We carried her between us. Harry and Sam's father waited at the turning of the lane and my father met us halfway home. Our hands grew dark and sticky with her blood, and my mother, waiting at our house door, screamed when she saw it.

We laid her in a bed and gave her water and at last she spoke, in a broken voice so quiet we could barely hear. "They pulled at me . . . they spread me under . . . they raped . . . over and over." She drew another breath. "Four of them, and one held the horses."

She closed her eyes and did not move. It was dawn when she spoke again, almost loud.

"I bleed again."

My mother sent Harry for the midwife. She scurried for rags to stanch the bright flow. Rebecca slept, and when the woman arrived she would not wake.

It was sunrise when Sam and his father Wat came back to our house-yard. Sam wore a bloodied rag around his head. In the night I had not noticed his wound. "Can I see her?" he said.

My father stared at him. "She's bleeding again."

"Oh Lord," Wat mumbled, "we didn't know."

"I tried to stop them," said Sam.

"He never meant it to happen," his father said.

My father nodded. "I know that."

Sam glanced away and rubbed his eyes. "We tried to get to the chapel where the priests were, but they rode round us on their horses, shouting, coarse as pigmen. They grabbed at her. I pulled one off and punched him in the face. I thought I broke his nose. They were blind drunk, you could smell the wine." He shook his head. "They had her by then. One of them hit me."

Wat shook his head. "It's been a long time, Warren, since they've done it." He showed us six or seven fingers. "And Sam didn't run away."

Inside the house our mother cried aloud.

My heart fell, dead as stone. I turned and stumbled away, blind and weeping, hardly able to breathe. After a time Harry came and put an arm round my shoulder. "It's God's will, Micah. He's taken her to Him." Damn His will, I thought, shaking my head. "Praise God you found her," he said.

The midwife stood in the doorway. "I've closed her eyes."

"It wasn't Sam's fault," Wat said, again.

My father shook his head, weeping himself.

But Old Drool thumped his stick on the ground. "Warren, you must go to the king." He stood there, dry-eyed and hard-mouthed. "We can speak, John Baptist's and Yule. Not in the manor court but to the king himself." He waved his hand toward the castle. "We speak, the king must listen." He thumped his stick again. "His knights have killed a freeman's daughter. He must pay for it."

My father wiped a sleeve across his eyes. He looked at house and yard, scratched the stubble on his chin. "They've taken her hands, her dowry, her children. I'm a poor man, I can't afford it." I saw he was trying to convince himself. "Five years past they tramped Willow fur-long like they'd had a joust in the night." He nodded at our neighbor's field. "Perkin lost half his crop."

"And Perkin complained to the king," said Old Drool.

"What did he get?" Wat asked.

My father nodded to himself. "In truth he never saw the king, but

Thomas the reeve forgave a day each week of his demesne work, for a whole year. There was a new pot for his wife's ale-making." My father straightened up, and I thought he grew an inch. "But this is not grain, this is my child. I will speak to the king."

My mother heated the water, and my father and then Harry bathed in the wooden tub. I stood beside them, complaining it was me that found her, till at last Warren said I might go, too, and I climbed into their used water. My father put on a knitted shirt and clean hose, but Slow and I had only scratchy hemp tunics, and church leggings and old boots. Wat and Sam came again, cleanly dressed though even a bath could not purge their tanner's stink. As we stood in our yard a cuckoo called in the oaks nearby, the three notes it always sang after John Baptist's. Old Drool gave us each a swig of last year's cider. For strength, he said. My eyes watered at the fire of it.

Greenfarm, that was our house and Perkin's, lay midway between Ryford village and the king's castle. I went to Ryford every week, to market or church, yet in all my life I had been no nearer Camelot than the reeve's new house, a hundred paces down the way.

Thomas would be at the castle, as it was a feast day. We did not stop at his fenced yard to ask his leave, but soon came out from the shade of the lane into the bright castle meadows. It was high summer, the air heavy with bee sound and the smell of first hay. The last buttercups gleamed in the rich grass, and beyond the level pastures the river lay still as a pond. Bright pennants, red and gold, hung unmoving above the castle roofs, and its pale walls shimmered in the afternoon haze. Seeing it so, I near forgot why we kept tight together, why we walked with such hesitant feet toward that gleaming image.

Camèlot grew till it seemed large as all of Ryford. My father, his voice hoarse, pointed the church spire and the gable of the king's great Hall, that showed over the high battlements. A broad arm of the river bent round the castle as a moat, and the outer wall, rumpled with towers, rose straight from the flat water as if stone-hard Camelot stood on its own watery reflection.

The barbican stood the near side of the moat and a lone guard, stunned by the afternoon warmth, slouched in the shade of its towers next to its opened gate. He was a son of Thomas' brother, a heavy lad I called Thick, a year older than Harry but no brighter.

When he saw us he stood up and swallowed a yawn. "What do you want?" he called.

"I come," said my father loudly, "to appeal to the king."

"Warren? What is it?"

"I have a pleading to put before my lord," my father repeated. I saw he had taken more than one swallow of the cider.

"The king . . . you can't . . ." Thick sputtered.

My father ignored him. He walked under the barbican gate and crossed the wood drawbridge into the shadow of the castle. We followed, close behind.

The guard, flustered and half asleep, called out, "Stop." His boots drummed the planks as he raced past us, and stopped at the castle gate and barred our way.

"Stop," he cried again. His voice rang in the stony arch behind him. At the far end lay a sunlit court, where one or two castle servants turned to peer at us.

"I have a pleading," my father called. He paused, as if to appreciate how well his own voice echoed on the vaults. "I will speak to the king. On the feast of John Baptist's birth, it is my right as freeman of Camelot to bring my pleading to the king."

I had no idea where he got that language. It was the way I imagined knights might talk, when they were sober. I noticed then he carried a little cloth bag.

Half a dozen servants stared out at us now. A voice rang out overhead and we craned our necks up. A knight had come out on one high tower and put his blond head over the battlements.

"God's name, villeins, what do you want?"

My father called up. "I have a petition for the king, it is my right, we may come, the feast of the Baptist."

"Damn you all." He glared down at us. "I'll fetch your damned reeve."

We shifted closer together. The castle loomed over us, its shadow grown very cool. My father smiled and nodded to himself as he paced about. I hoped the cider would last.

Thomas arrived, swearing. What were we doing, peasants on the king's drawbridge? But my father would not be frightened, and when he told our reason the reeve went pale. He went away and after a long time came back, grim-faced, and led us in.

The sun shone brighter and the day seemed warmer, inside Camelot. Sounds and voices rang against the stone, and our boots clattered on a cobbled court that looked broader than Ryford market. Servants scowled at our impudence. Grooms curried battle-horses at the stables, and cooks white with flour gossiped at a kitchen door. The stone church stood beyond, and another gate that opened into a garden with flowering apple trees. In the distance rose the king's high tower, bannered and crenelated.

I caught a glimpse of windows filled with glass, before Thomas led us under a round-headed door into an arched and gloomy space. A long stone stairway rose above us, steep as a hill, and the voices of a crowd boomed overhead. The light brightened as we climbed. At the top the air was rich with food smells, and we stepped through a doorway in a green painted wall and drew our breath at the high enormous chamber.

At first I thought the place too vast for any roof to cover, before I glimpsed the sooty trusses high above. Broidered flags hung overhead, lit by sunlight streaming through the tall windows, bright shafts in the air that smelled of applewood smoke. A hundred painted shields hung in a glittering line beneath the windows and the knights that owned them stood about in noisy groups, lit or shadowed by the sun. Knights' voices barked in my ears. The nearest turned to their faces to us, lean, handsome, bearded faces, many bearing scars. The hard faces of hard men who gazed at us as if we were uninteresting cattle. Men who stood so erect you knew at once they had never known the stoop of the plow, never felt the weight of faggots nor carried water nor milked a cow.

Thomas walked away through the hazy distance, past a great round table with elaborate chairs, toward half a dozen older men, and a cluster of ladies. We watched him go the whole long way, and bow and mutter to some old knight. He hung his head here at Camelot, not at all the self-sure reeve we knew at Ryford.

I peered about, wondering which had done the thing, but saw no freshly broken noses nor scratched faces. I had no hope of recognizing men seen by moonlight, and Sam was staring at the floor. The nearest lifted their noses at us and one of them said, "Behold, a villein come of his sheep."

"Which he hath mistook for his wife," another growled.

"Nay, thou fool, for his son."

They turned away, laughing.

Thomas had come all the way back. He cleared his throat. "Sir Ulfius will hear you."

"What?" My father blinked. "Who?"

"Sir Ulfius is chamberlain of Camelot."

"The king," my father said, his voice loud and shaking. "It is my right, I am a freeman, this is John's . . ."

Thomas took his arm. "Sir Kay that is the steward, he's not here. You must speak to Sir Ulfius. The king sits close, he will hear you."

So we made that long walk ourselves, past the eyes of knights and, at the end, the eyes of ladies. The light brightened as we neared the king, and the talk quieted till I could hear our steps on the rush-strewn floor. Overhead swallows twittered in the air, that must nest among the great rafters. Suddenly a falcon rose from among the watching knights, flashed beneath the murky ceiling, stooped, and missed the little birds.

A lean old man stood waiting for us, his white beard half covering a grand robe of red and gold. He nodded at Thomas kindly enough. Beyond him another man, his short beard red-gold and his eyes sky blue, sat a chair richer than any I could have imagined. Yet I hardly saw it, for the man himself was the sort that, once your eyes have found him they can see nothing else. Even the woman sitting near him, beautiful enough to take your breath away, had not such power over your eyes.

We clustered nervous at Thomas' back. He bowed to the old man. "Sir Ulfius, here is Warren of Greenfarm. Two of his sons. And Wat of Ryford, villein and tanner, and his son."

"Fair feast day," said Sir Ulfius, half smiling.

We bobbed our heads and mumbled at him.

"Thomas says you have a petition for the king."

My father lifted his head and spoke in a strangled voice. "I have a pleading with him, sir."

"A pleading. Yes. Well, what is it?"

"My daughter, sir. She's dead, sir."

Sir Ulfius looked at him silently.

"She died this morning, sir, the priest came afore midday but she was gone by then."

"How unfortunate."

"She bled to death, sir."

"How very unfortunate."

My father took a deep breath and shook himself. He grew that inch, again, and Sir Ulfius noticed it.

"Last night, sir. She walked out with Sam here. They hit him on the head, they took her, sir, knights, the same that raced the fire to the chapel." He took a breath. "They raped her. She died this morning."

His voice grew louder as he spoke, and when he stopped the Hall behind us was dead quiet.

"You claim . . ." said Sir Ulfius.

But the king spoke from the great chair, his voice strong though he spoke quietly. "Knights of my Roundtable?"

The power of that tongue shook us all, yet my father answered, clear. "Four of them, my lord, and one held the horses."

The king waved his hand. "We all know how it happens. Summer nights, strong drink. But it would not kill her."

"Of course not," said Sir Ulfius. "These country girls." He smiled, and laughter rippled through the Hall behind us.

"She bled to death," my father said.

"I do not think we believe you," said Sir Ulfius.

My father blinked once. With an awkward jerk he opened his bag and pulled out Rebecca's dress. Her blood had crusted and dried on its shredded tatters, very dark. The Hall fell silent. He spread it at arm's length. He turned, that king and ladies and knights all might see. After a moment the voices behind us resumed their mutter. One knight laughed, very clear.

My ears roared. My sight wavered and darkened. I shook with fury. I might expect their sneers, their hatred even, that was the way of things. But I would not swallow their laughter. I had to drop my head to hide my rage. A little table stood beside me, that held two silver cups and a glinting dagger. My hand moved toward it of its own, rock-steady despite my seething nerves, and I came within a blink of grasping that little blade, of striding to kill Sir Ulfius, of stabbing the king, even. Already I felt the pommel in my hand, the weight of it, the drape of fine cloth against my fist, the resistance of a man's chest like a stuck calf.

Harry touched my arm. He thought I meant to steal it. But I knew already that if I but scratched Sir Ulfius, they would kill us all, and our families, too, and burn our houses. After a year, after ten at most, not a soul would remember us.

My fingers touched the carved edge of the table. I stared at the king's knife and on it swore myself an oath. I would kill my sister's killers.

I raised my head again. The Hall had changed. Its vast size no longer overwhelmed me. The king that stood from his great chair no longer frightened me, though his own knights quieted under his scowling gaze.

"What do you want?" he asked my father.

Warren thrust a wavering hand at Sam's bloodied head. "Two families injured, my lord, two loyal families of the demesne of Camelot, sire. I have lost a daughter, her dowry and her children. Wat near lost a son. I ask a pair of plowing oxen, sire."

The request had no effect on the king, but Sir Ulfius could not believe it. "A pair?" The old knight blinked at my father. "Two oxen for a daughter? The boy lives, yet you ask two animals for a single girl?"

The king shook his head. "I cannot give you two oxen. I cannot give you two of anything." He gazed out at his knights and raised his voice. "But I would give you justice. God defend us, this ought not happen." I wondered if he knew which of them had killed her. "I give you a well-trained horse. You can ride him to markets, to fairs." The knights rumbled again, and again the king's glance silenced them.

No farmer of Camelot owned a horse, not even the reeve. Such an animal might cost five times the two oxen and even more to feed. A look of bewilderment came over my father. "Oh, sir, I need help for the fields, sir, you can't plow with a horse, a horse is . . ."

Useless, he almost said.

But the world shifted for me, a second time. If Lark's death were God's inexplicable will, so was this. I tugged at Warren's sleeve. "Take the horse," I said.

He growled, aside, "I can't afford to keep a horse."

"Take it. You can't refuse the king."

Something changed in his face, and after a moment he turned and bowed.

"Then it's settled," said the king. "I give you Anduin. A destrier, a battle-horse, the gift of my sister." The Hall rumbled, but he ignored it and peered at me. "This is your son?"

"Aye, my lord," said my father, half proud. "He's Micah."

"A bright lad." The king's eyes seemed to measure me. "We always have need of intelligent boys. When he's fourteen you must send him to Ulfius here."

"My lord," my father mumbled, "I need his hands, I have but one other son."

"Warren," hissed Thomas, "he'll be at the king's court."

The king pretended not to hear. He nodded to me. "When you are fourteen, lad."

"A year, sir," I said. "A year next summer."

King Arthur smiled at me. "After next summer's harvest, then."

I had never seen such a smile. It was like the sun, warm and fair and without hatred or judgment. For a quick moment that smile almost ruined my blood oath, and I had to clamp my hatred tight between my teeth.

"Aye, my lord," I said. "Next harvest."

Two

The horse Anduin was no sumpter to carry loads, nor even a riding palfrey, but a battle-horse a knight might take to war. He even stood too tall for our cow-byre, and it took a day to build a new shed against the end of the house. We cut saplings at the edge of the forest, with Thomas' permission, and leafy boughs for thatch as there would be no straw till after harvest. My father grumbled at the time it took, how much the animal would eat and what little work he might do. Nor did I know myself what to make of Anduin, save that somehow he was necessary.

In the long summer evenings Perkin and his son came to stare, and then men from the village. To stand near a king's destrier, to watch it move and judge its strength was a rare thing, and they spoke to my father with new respect, as if he were important as the reeve. Yet they glanced at him sidelong, too, amazed his daughter had been worth such an animal. They came for a month, till harvest began and there was no time for it. We reaped Westfield, all Ryford sweating in the heat and sun. We made the corn dollies and baked the Lammas loaf. We plowed fallow Newfield and took Eastfield's spring barley, and cut the straw and threshed the grain and gave our rent at Michaelmas, the end of September. And nobody came anymore, to stare at the great horse.

As for Anduin, he was unlike any battle-horse I have known since. Though big as any, his gait was near as soft as a good palfrey, and he was gentle and tolerant and easy-mannered, a thing most unsuitable for a horse of war. Surely the king knew it, that he parted with the animal so willingly.

The first week, watching him nose the green shed we had built, I saw I must learn to ride. I led him out one morning, tied a hobble round his legs, and hauled myself up on his wide back. I sat there a long time, amazed at the view. This was how knights saw the world, how they stared down at small men limited to their own petty stature, their own two feet.

I sat there on several days, till one morning I untied his hobble before I got on. Anduin tossed his head and snorted, and when I was settled began to walk across the houseyard. I felt his muscles move under me. The great strength and power of the animal half terrified me. At the road he shook his head and broke into a trot toward Thomas' farm and the castle. I leaned over his neck and gripped his mane. The wind pressed against my eyes and whistled past my ears. Familiar sights were suddenly foreign, and I could see over hedges and far across the fields, as if into a different world.

We scattered Thomas' hens as we passed. I saw he took me back to his stables, that I would ride through the barbican gate, boom on the drawbridge, clatter under the castle vaults. Halfway across the meadows I pulled desperately on his mane and cried the words we said to oxen, plowing. "Whoa, hold." Anduin slowed at once, and stopped when I repeated it. I sat a moment, stunned and elated both. The ride had set my heart beating. My command over this great animal made me dizzy with pride.

"Around," I said. "Turn, Anduin, around, go back."

The horse did nothing. His chest swelled and shrank under me as he breathed. He shook his head and looked at the castle. He switched his tail and whinnied quietly, and would not move.

"Turn around," I said. "Anduin. Around."

He lifted one hoof and put it down, and did not move.

I slid off and pushed against one wide shoulder. He shook his head and rolled his eyes at me. I worked till I sweated in the early sun, and finally, tugging at his head, I got him turned around. I had clambered up again before I saw Thomas in the road in front of us, scratching his curly hair.

"Out riding are you, Micah?"

"Yes, sir."

"You nearly killed my best hen."

"I'm sorry, sir, I didn't know what to do."

"Men don't usually get off a horse to turn it round." I felt my face go hot. "You don't have reins? A bridle?" He looked past me toward Camelot. "Mayhap I can find an old set. Now, go soft past my house, I'll take a goose of your father for every hen."

But the castle gave us nothing, for even stablemen had no like of farmers riding horses. I found, by accident, that I could guide Anduin by tapping his neck with a stick. Never have I have known another destrier that would have stood for it.

It was a sunny morning a month after harvest, that I rode home with flour ground at Ryford mill, and met a pair of Camelot knights in the road. They appeared at the bend just past the chapel lane. I stopped Anduin beside the hedge. Their elegant palfreys came on at a steady walk. Their linen tabards bore new-broidered heraldry, the thousand loops of their mail armor glittered in the sunlight, swords hung from their decorated belts, and squires in matching livery carried their pennoned lances. They went bareheaded, these knights, their beards trimmed and their hair newly washed. Their eyes glittered, cold as winter. Yet that day, sitting Anduin, for the first time my own eyes stood level with theirs. I saw with a shock these great knights were young, that each had but a score of years, hardly more than my brother.

"Behold," muttered the dark one, "the wisdom of the king."

"His first mistake." The second had bright red hair. "But God knows he is bedeviled on every side. The wizard's foolish love. His sister Morgan. The queen."

"Women." The dark knight stopped a yard away. He stared at me as if I were an ox, or a tree. "A peasant's brat atop a destrier because his bitch of a sister would not lie still."

I did not even blink, but stared at him hard, remembering his smooth forehead, his dark eyes, the short beard on his handsome jaw. His nose bent slightly, as if broken in some fight.

The red-haired knight had freckles on the back of his hands. He did not look at me at all. "Come, Briant, there's no honor in the blood of churls."

I had not forgot I was alone and facing knights, yet still his talk of blood made me clench my knees. Anduin lifted his head and began to walk. With the grand arrogance of a battle-horse he moved past Briant and shouldered his way easily between the following squires. They shouted at me but I looked straight ahead. In truth, I could not control him so well as that, and he picked his own way as always, past the knights' battle-horses and the train of laden sumpters.

Behind me the red-haired knight called, "Leave off, Briant. He comes to Camelot next harvest."

Briant. Already I had the name of one.

Rebecca's unwashed dress lay wrapped in old linen, tucked in my mother's box and never seen save when she went for something else. Rebecca's death stayed with me the same way, something hid and oft forgot, remembered with grief while doing other things. Sometimes just as I slept I felt her hand in mine, shaking. Her voice said, "I bleed again." I would lie in the black night, a taste like iron in my mouth, and listen to the others breathing, to mice in the thatch and cats fighting under the hedges and the reeve's dogs barking at a setting moon. Five knights loomed before me, tall, arrogant, one with the dark face of Briant. A red-haired figure wavered among them. I swore again to see them all dead.

Wat the tanner brought us a fine doeskin by way of apology, that my father would not accept till my mother insisted. And after harvest when the straw was cut, Sam brought thatch for Anduin's shed and helped us roof the little place.

Perkin, our neighbor, was the manor shepherd. For his help at harvest we owed him a day of Martinmas slaughter. Our breath smoked in the sharp November air and frost shone white on the fallow fields, the morning Harry and I walked out with Perkin and his son, to the penning they had built on the village common. He swung open the gate and we crowded in among the nervous animals. Steam rose off their icy wool in the early sunlight. Those where the frost melted quickest had the thinnest fleece. They would not last the winter, and Perkin walked among them and nicked their ears, and then as the day warmed we began to kill. Always at slaughter the first animal was the most difficult, and I must keep my gaze from the look in its bright eye, must ignore its quivering fright as I gripped its shoulders with my knees and lifted its muzzle to stretch the neck for the knife.

A fog soon stood around us, almost pink, that smelled of blood and flesh, the fright of the animals, the stink of bowels. It was the smell of winter, or at least of winter coming. The Church might have its round of holy days, Yule and Whitsun, John Baptist and All Souls, but the year turned truly from Candlemas and first plowing, to Easter rent and Lammas harvest and Michaelmas rent again, and Martinmas for slaughter.

The scarlet stains on our leggings were dried the color of my sister's dress when we came home at dusk. Our mother paled and shut her eyes. I wondered if the blood of knights were any different.

As the weather drew in, the beeches turned golden and the pigmen set their animals on the mast. We went into the leafless forests and gathered hazelnuts. Honey peddlers came, and my mother shouted at them angrily, as seeing Anduin in his shed they asked too dear for sweet and wax.

A square little church stood in Ryford where my family went almost every Sabbath. The forest chapel was but a place for feast days, yet that winter I walked the half league to it often as I could. A castle priest came every midday to sing Mass and I might be the only one there, save a few old widows, as he lit a single taper and muttered his Latin at the crucifix.

In the Holy Book, so priests said, God forbade murder. Only a full confession might achieve His forgiveness. I wondered if the knights confessed, or if a peasant's murder were not for them a mortal sin. It came to me that after I had killed them I must find some hermit monk to confess me, or some wandering friar that would not go at once and tell Camelot. Yet surely God knew of my plan already, and were it wrong He would keep me from it. What I had sworn, for Lark's soul, was the ruin of my own. My heart stood in my throat, afraid of it, before I swore again to never waver.

On Saint Andrew's, that was four weeks before Yule, the chapel stood wrapped by a soft and drifting snow. Pale candles burned motionless in the cold air as I touched the holy water to my forehead. The priest bobbed before the altar, muttering Latin, but in the midst of his prayer horses clattered outside. Leather creaked and harness rattled, and half a dozen knights strode in. They stamped the flagstones and shook their snowy cloaks, speaking in uncommonly hushed voices. They pulled off their gloves and dipped their fingers in the font. I watched them, wanting to remember each face. The red-haired knight was there, and a round-faced blond but little older than I.

"Sweet Lady," said the redhead, "it's cold in here." As he touched his forehead he saw me watching. His expression did not change, but he stared such a long moment the others noticed.

"What's this?" said another. "Do you know this, Almant?"

Almant. The second of them. I had heard his name that night. He held the horses.

"Are they allowed in here?" said the young blond.

"In the back, aye," said a tall knight. He was older than the rest, darkly handsome and with pale scar on one cheek. "The king hath said it."

"Methinks our lord is overgenerous, Agravain."

Agravain. He might be one of them. And the round-faced blond, for as they walked to the altar he stopped and turned. "That brat," he said. " 'Tis the one got the destrier, after John Baptist's."

Hatred lit their eyes, for the king's horse set me apart from peasants they rode past unseeing. But the priest, waiting on the steps of the altar, raised his voice in the first words of the service. They turned toward him. I went out through the door. The snow still drifted among the bare oaks.

At Yule the snow lay ankle-deep and the river had a skin of ice. Anduin suffered from the cold. His ribs showed beneath the old sacks we draped on him, as we could not spare him grain enough though we were fewer than the year before. Still, whenever I went to him, he tossed his head and wanted to go running.

"Yes," I muttered, one bitter morning, "and you would run me straight to Camelot, wouldn't you?" The horse did not deny it.

It was a little warmer in the shed, out of the wind and with the manure and straw not quite frozen. My father came in behind me. He rubbed the horse's nose. "I must give him back, Micah. I cannot keep him, and he's too fine an animal to starve."

"We could sell him."

"There's no horse market, midwinter. Besides, who'd buy the king's gift?"

"If we give him back, what have we got for . . .?" I could not say her name just then.

He frowned at me. "The king's justice, he admitted it was wrong. And, besides, you have a place in the castle." I wanted to argue that it was not enough. "I'll talk to Thomas," he said.

The reeve wanted us to keep Anduin, too. He had got the horse for us and it would look a failure if we gave it back. My father offered him the animal, yet not even Thomas could afford it, and he agreed to go with us, when we went to Camelot.

It snowed again, Epiphany morning. Anduin plodded behind us between the black and leafless hedges. The river meadows lay white under the snow. The moat was frozen, and the walls of Camelot rose over us, black and gloomy, though little scraps of white glittered where snow had caught on the sills of arrow slits. Ice glazed the drawbridge and Anduin slipped as we crossed, for he was excited now. The high gates were closed, as the king spent this Yule in London, but the guard swung open a wicket door just large enough for the horse.

Camelot seemed very empty. We waited inside the Hall door, at the foot of the stairs, until old Sir Ulfius appeared at the top. "Can't keep the horse, eh?" he called, and gave a mocking smile.

"They brought it back, sir," Thomas said, "rather than see it starve."

The chamberlain came stiffly down the steps. "How did you ever believe you might care for a horse?"

We all knew it was the king's idea. I glanced at my father, but Warren would not dispute him.

"What does a farmer even want with a horse?" said Sir Ulfius. "What can he do with it, save abuse it and starve it? And now you bring it back, ill. If it dies, the king will be very angry." He stopped three steps above us, just the height of a man on horseback. "I hope you have learned from this, that people ought keep to the station God hath allotted them."

My father bowed and shambled, but I could not hold my tongue. "We did not ask for a horse, sir, we asked for oxen to plow our fields, to increase our harvests. And our rents."

The chamberlain turned his head slowly to me. "You protest the wisdom of the king?"

"We are farmers, as you say, sir. What do farmers want with horses?"

Despite the echoing quiet of the castle, and the wry smile on Sir Ulfius' face, that moment was far more dangerous than my meeting knights in the road. He might have challenged me, forced me to fault the king, had me killed for treason. Praise God he preserved me from my own rashness.

"You are Micah, I believe."

"Aye, sir." I thought he must have a prodigious memory.

"You come on Lammasday."

Thomas glanced up, still pale from my willfulness. "The king said after harvest, sir."

"Lammas. At Terce. Do you know when Terce is, Micah?"

"No, sir."

"Midmorning, between dawn and midday."

"Lammas, sir," I repeated, "at Terce."

At Candlemas we plowed our strips in Westfield. There were half a dozen other teams out that day, plowing their own strips on the broad unfenced field under a windy sky. Harry led the oxen we always rented from Thomas, my father wrestled with the plow, and I followed spading the clods. The February soil was dark and cold, sticky under our bare feet, and smelled of winter and stones.

We had begun again, after the midday meal, when the first heralds rode past. The king came back from London and of course we stopped to watch. Knights with shields and lances rode prancing battle-horses. Loaded wains rumbled past, and then another crowd of armed knights, with squires and pages. Large roofed wagons painted blue and green trundled by, and one or two ladies peered briefly out. Dark-robed clerics passed, and falconers on prancing ponies, the hooded birds clutching their leather gauntlets, and a hundred footmen bearing scarlet banners. Finally, in the midst of another crowd of knights, their lances tipped with fluttering pennons, the king himself rode a great dark stallion. Trumpets rang from distant Camelot and then, as we had bent to the plow again, a last troop of armed knights rattled by.

"King Arthur," said my father, as if we had not guessed.

We plowed again, halfway through Lent, and sowed the barley thin, as the horse had eaten half the seed. After, I went out for weeks to scare the birds from the new seed. There were but a dozen others, boys mostly, to protect the whole wide field. The birds would arrive silent, one by one, only the rattle of their hard wings to alert us. "Raven," I cried, as I ran at them. It had been Rebecca's task, and I wondered if she had called out, Lark.

Easter Sunday the winter wheat stood green in Newfield, daffodils yellowed the sunny meadows, and the crab apples bloomed white at the eaves of the wood. Our whole family trooped the lane to the forest chapel. People came from all the villages of Camelot's demesne, everyone washed and wearing clean clothes. They clustered at the door, and shook their heads of Rebecca, before they grinned and asked about the horse. The priest rang his bell. We filed into the echoing space. The new sun blazed through the glass window behind the altar, and crowded thick together we heard again how Our Lord died on the cross, how He rose on Easter and walked the earth again.

I had always liked the story, the fright of the soldiers at the tomb, the amazement of the women, the disciples' doubts. It all had happened in Jerusalem, that I imagined a vaster Camelot, yet Jerusalem seemed very far away and Christ's death an awful time ago. Still, that year I heard the story different. Hanging from the cross, as the Jews killed Him, Christ had prayed, "Forgive them, Father." Could I believe it, that God truly forgave such things?

John Baptist's eve, despite my father's word, I walked alone down the chapel lane. The priest was come to sing Vespers. I stood in a dim corner when the knights galloped up, drunk and foul-mouthed and laughing. The redhead Sir Almant won the race, and the bonfire blazed from his torch in a roar of sparks and crackling wood. The priest gave him a little silver cross. I turned to leave but he stood blocking my way, unsteady from drink, looking like he might kill me just for sport. His voice was thick and his breath stank of wine.

"Why d'you peer at us, clod?"

I remembered not to flinch, nor shuffle my feet nor tug at my forelock. "To see the winner, sir."

His brain was thick and it took him a minute to reply. "You know 'twas me, why stare . . .?" He stopped as memory caught his tongue. "You are the churl with the horse, the brother of that screaming bitch."

"Micah of Greenfarm," I said. I looked at him straight, my fear unremembered. "Sir Briant raped her. What did you do?"

His hand clasped the pommel of his dagger.

"A year ago, tonight," I said.

Mayhap it was the wine that saved me, or boldness or luck. Or even

God's will. "A filthy varlet," he cried, "brat of a villein. Who owns not even an ox. Certainly not a horse." His voice rang with his generations of privilege. I had never heard it so clear, that no knight mourns long the death of animals, nor peasants.

"My father is a freeman," I said, out of habit. "We asked for a pair of oxen." My voice quivered, and a shaking had come suddenly over me I could not master. If Sir Almant saw, he said nothing of it, and for that small kindness I almost forgave him all the rest. And hated myself for the thought of it.

The other knights retrieved their horses and mounted. He turned and swung up, himself, and I remembered how the world seemed from the back of such an animal. "I am Almant of Damerel," he muttered, scowling down at me. "Sir Almant. When you come to the castle you must say 'Sir.' You must never forget." He paused, watching me. "And I tell you this, varlet. Beware Sir Briant, when you come to Camelot."

Three

On Lammas eve the moon rose round and white, and owls hooted in the dusk. My father and I trudged the dusty lane to the reeve's. We stood in his yard, dry and hot with harvest sunburn, while his dogs wagged their tails at us and Thomas sat inside at table with his family.

"After harvest." My father's shoulders dropped with fatigue. "The king said after harvest. I need him for the sheaves, Thomas, and the thatching straw."

"Sir Ulfius said Lammas." The reeve stood and came to the open door, and tossed a bone to his dogs.

"It's but two days." My father scuffed at the bare earth.

"Sir Ulfius is the chamberlain, Warren. His word is the king's." Thomas looked at me. "I'll take you, lad. Be here early. The old man is ill, I want to be sure he sees you come."

"The king?" said my father.

"Sir Ulfius."

We did not speak all the way home, but that night my father opened his old chest and took out a thin bundle, and unwrapped a little dagger with a carved hilt and a tooled scabbard. It was no ordinary peasant's blade. "My grandfather's," he said. "We were prosperous, once." He shook his head. "Reeves, even, in his day. There's no land to give you, lad, it'll be your inheritance. Maybe it's a blessing, your going to the castle."

"Thank you, Father." I weighed the dagger in my hand, surprised at its worth, much pleased I had even this small weapon.

I took a bath, that night. I could not sleep, and when I did I dreamed of swords and flames and galloping horses. My mother, blinking and red-eyed, woke me in the gray dawn. She gave me a bowl of gruel I could not eat, while my brother sat staring at his own, uncertain what to say. She bundled me food for the road and made me take the winter cloak that had been Harry's. But when my father called she scowled and would not hug me, nor would she watch me go, though when we stepped out into the yard she turned to snap at Old Drool, of some small thing.

The world lay smothered in fog, so thick we could not see even the tops of the oaks. Perkin and his son talked across the lane, invisible, though the sound of whetstone on sickle came very clear. A cow bawled, lost in the murk. Crows scolded in the distance. We turned down the road between dripping hedges, and the rutted way appeared five steps ahead of us, and vanished as quick behind. Everything had a sharp clarity, and every sound rang clear. I might have been leaving forever, never to see Greenfarm again, instead of only going the little way to Camelot.

Thomas' hens clucked and scratched in the dirt, when we came to his shadowy gate. The dogs came out of the mist, wagging their tails, and finally the reeve appeared lacing his tunic. He stopped and peered at my new-washed clothes.

"It's the best things he's got," said my father.

"It's not that, they'll dress him in livery anyway." He gave a tense grin. "It's the supper. Here, Warren, you carry it. It would insult the king, bringing his own food."

"I didn't mean . . ."

"I know it, man."

My father tugged the bundle from me and clamped it under one arm. Thomas lifted his head and turned toward the castle, and we followed him into the fog. A bell began at Camelot, ringing slowly. A small breeze blew off the river, that opened the mist and closed it again. My father went with us far as the barbican, but there he stopped and put his arms roughly around me. "Our Lord protect you," he muttered, his voice hoarse. "Be careful, do what they tell you, don't get above your place." He hugged me near to crack a rib and turned and vanished into the fog. I was so anxious myself I hardly noticed him leave.

Camelot stood over us like a high shadow. The bell rang very loud. A guard paced the drawbridge, trying to step softly. "Sir Ulfius," he said, making his cross. "The priests have just come from his chamber."

Inside, the castle walls kept out much of the fog, though it still murked the highest roofs. The bell clanged and echoed on the stones. Thomas led me past a cart filled with squawking chickens and through a thick plain door into a warm smoky kitchen bigger than our whole house, that smelled of baking. Cooks drew heaps of steaming loaves out of stone ovens. A heavy man looked up from kneading another great lump of dough, enough to feed my family for a week. I had never imagined so much bread.

"Will," said Thomas, "I've a lad here. Who's to be the new chamberlain?"

"Sir Kay's the steward." The baker wiped his brow with the back of a floury hand. "Sir Laramort was the old man's novice."

"Where would they be, then?"

"Not here." He bent over the dough again. "Try the Hall."

The bell still tolled, loud as ever, as we crossed the cobbled court. Inside the shadowed vestibule a crowd of boys, dressed in the blue and gold of castle squires, milled noisily about. On the steps that climbed above them knights stood in jittery clusters, muttering among themselves. I could not understand the unease that filled the air. Highborn knights faced death every day. Why was it that dying in bed made them so nervous?

Nobody gave us a glance. Thomas asked for Sir Kay. They were with the king, a squire said, knights whose names I did not recognize, all in the death chamber dressing the dead man. The door opened and two more pushed in, growling at the crush. One had black hair, a pale cold face, and narrow eyes. The second was the redhead. My heart beat suddenly in my throat.

Sir Almant frowned at Thomas. "You've brought the lout."

"Aye, sir, he told him come on Lammas. Sir Ulfius, sir." Thomas crossed himself and the knights made their sign. "I don't know what to do, sir."

The pale knight wrinkled his long nose at me. "Ulfius spoke of it." He had a high, hard voice. "What can he do?"

"A bright lad, sir," Thomas said, "quick to learn."

The knight turned his head and called a young servant. "Here, take this under your wing. Another hand to the kitchens."

The lad bobbed to him and started toward the door, but Thomas gripped my arm to stop me. "What your father said," he muttered, "I say the same."

I nodded, my mouth gone too dry to speak.

Out in the foggy court the bell no longer clanged. The boy asked my name. I managed to get it out, and then my sister and the horse.

"John Baptist, last year," he said. "I'm sorry."

His kindness amazed me. I clutched at his sleeve. "Do you know who they were?"

He turned and stared at me. "Everybody knew. We all saw them

ride out. Sir Briant won the cross, there was Sir Giles and Sir Orsain."
He gestured at the Hall. "Sir Almant and Sir Laramort."

My head swam. I had imagined it would be impossible to learn their
names, that the castle must be sworn to secrecy. Yet it was just the opposite. They did not care. What to the castle was the killing of a peasant
girl? I drew a breath, reciting their names in my head. Briant, Giles,
Orsain, Laramort, Almant. Five knights. What to them would be the
killing of a peasant boy?

"The dark one was Sir Laramort?"

"Aye. That helped Sir Ulfius with the kitchens. The others are gone
away somewhere. But they'll be back soon enough." He paused outside
the kitchen door. "They were all insulted by it, that the king gave you a
battle-horse. And now he's brought you here." He lowered his voice.
"Be careful, Micah. They can't argue with the king. You can't argue
with them."

Sir Ulfius lay in Camelot's church draped in samite and ermine. His
chain armor glittered in the taperlight beneath his broidered tabard, and
his long beard pushed out his helmet like a sheaf of white barley.

On that first night the king himself kept vigil. And I, dressed in the
king's blue livery, and in boots handed down from another boy, was set
outside the church door. If they wished anything Sir Kay would come
and tell me, and I would run to the kitchens. I watched that night, because I was newest. The servants honored Sir Ulfius well enough but
nobody wanted to lose a night of sleep; we got little enough as it was.

It amazed me. There, just there, sat King Arthur. Still, he was not
the man I had seen before. Grief lined his face and stooped his broad
shoulders, and he gave nobody his grand smile. Sir Ulfius had been
chamberlain to the king's father, and with his passing the last of King
Uther's knights died. Even the bakers shook their heads, worried Camelot would no longer be the same.

Already I had heard tales of Ulfius, and of the beguiling of the lady
Igraine, the duchess of Cornwall on whom King Uther had got his only
son, Arthur. But in truth Sir Ulfius had little to do with it. It had been
instead that most ambiguous of persons, the wizard Merlin. Who, they
said, changed the king's shape to confuse the lady. Who, when the child
was born, took him to raise and counsel till Arthur came to draw the
sword from its magic stone, and be made king himself.

I turned and looked down the long nave where King Arthur sat, next
the high bier and the clustered tapers. His hair shone red-gold in the
flickering light. There had been magic at his birth, were the tales true,
and at his coronation. Surely there would be magic at his death as well.

As for Merlin, at Camelot no one had seen him for years. Despite his great powers they said the wizard had been enchanted himself. Befuddled by love of the lady Nimue he had done what no wizard should, he had taught her his own spells. And she, annoyed at the old man or else through a beginner's mistake, had locked him away in some dark and hidden place of faerie.

I would not believe it. I was new at the castle and thought they mocked me. Surely love could never so confuse a man. Nor would a true master ever be so powerless over charms he had shaped, but would free himself and return as he always had been, shapechanger and Druid. If Merlin were captured truly, then he must be no master, but only charlatan and fraud.

But here I take another breath and come back to Camelot.

It was the darkest hour of the night. The lowering moon cast thick shadows across the court, and stars glittered above the steep roofs. It was deathly quiet; even the bats had flitted away. I sat at the half-open church door, the carved stone jamb pressed cold in my back, not even that enough to keep me awake. Inside, the tapers guttered and failed. Sir Kay slumped on his bench, though the king sat erect and wakeful.

Footsteps sounded on the stones of the court, though tonight no guards paced the battlements overhead and the priests had sung Matins hours since. The steps grew louder. I stood and yawned, and a man strode toward me, a brisk tall man wrapped in a dark cloak. I could see nothing in the shadow of his hood till he stopped and threw it back, and then the thin taperlight from the church showed a clean-shaven face of thirty winters. He did not seem a knight.

"The king keeps vigil," he said. It was not a question.

"Aye, sir." I did not know him. I knew nobody at Camelot, yet I wondered that he came at this hour.

"A great knight he must have been, to keep the king awake."

"Sir Ulfius," I said, crossing myself.

He flinched even as he made his sign. "Ulfius."

"Aye, sir. He died Lammas morn."

"A sad harvest." He drooped his head as if he wept, but when he looked up again his eyes glittered dryly. "Who are you?"

"Micah, sir. Son of Warren, of Greenfarm." I did not know what more to say. His stare made me uneasy.

Something rattled inside the church. The king stood and came striding up the aisle. He stared past me and smiled his grand smile and I thought he would speak. And then his delight vanished. I turned back. The court was empty.

I nearly jumped in surprise. I took a nervous pace and peered around.

The man might have stepped beyond a buttress, or past the corner of a tower, but when I looked I saw only darkness.

King Arthur stood in the doorway, one broad hand gripping the carved jamb. "You will find nothing, lad."

"I don't know where he went, sire." I bobbed my head, filled with a sudden fright. "He asked Sir Ulfius' name."

The king nodded sadly. "Of course he would come. They were old friends."

"He was not old, sire, no more than . . ."

"What is your name, lad?" When I spoke it memory filled his face. "The lad of the horse. He spoke to you, but not to me." His look went haggard, his mouth gaped beneath his beard, tears stood in his eyes. "To you. Not to me."

Sir Kay woke with a rumble. "My lord," he called, "I slept. I am sorry, sire."

King Arthur shuddered once, before he turned back to the church. "And well you ought be sorry, Kay, to miss so rare a visitor. Tell the boy I will have another draft of ale."

They buried Sir Ulfius beneath the floor of the church, while the bell tolled over our heads and the priests sang their chants, and the king wept. A stone carver had already begun to shape his memorial, a stone corpse in full armor, hands clasped in prayer, his shield bearing six elm leaves.

In his honor the king called a high tourney at Camelot, for the week following the Assumption of Our Lady. Soon enough barons and lords and knights began to arrive through the bright days of summer, from all over Britain. They rode palfreys and their squires led destriers, and sumpters bore armor in woolen bags, or drew enameled palanquins for their ladies. The castle had room for them all, yet only the ladies slept indoors. The knights pitched their bright pavilions in ordered rows beside the jousting field, king and Camelot knights on one side, and on the other side all the rest. Shields in bright colors hung at every tent, pennons fluttered overhead, battle-horses snorted in the paddocks or galloped the meadow turf, excited by the prospect of the joust. It made such a high display of pride and splendor that despite my oath of Lark, I began to imagine I might enjoy Camelot.

The king set another great pavilion that Sir Kay filled with trestles and made a refectory on the meadows. We had it near completed the day before the tourney, when Sir Laramort strode in. He pointed at me, his pale face wrinkled with a scowl, and called, "You, churl, get you to that tent." He pointed down the tourney field at a red and white pavilion.

Sir Kay came up, frowning. "This is my lad, Laramort. What do you want with him?"

"A mucker, for Gawain's tent. Surely you can spare him?"

Sir Kay was the king's age, a lean, bony knight with pale and thinning hair. He was famous for his black moods, and bitter nicknames, and now he turned his cold eyes on me. "Gladly will I lend you this . . . this Merdemains."

"Merdemains." Laramort burst into laughter. "Shit-hands. Damn you, Kay, you and your damn names."

Sir Kay did not smile. "Off with you, boy."

Four shields hung on the post before the pavilion. Two bore the red and white I had learned was Orkney, and the third was Sir Laramort's prancing stag. But the fourth, black with a yellow chevron, I did not know.

A knight with a thick, pox-scarred face sat inside, honing a dagger. He glanced up at me and growled, hoarse. "What do you here, lout?"

"Sir Laramort sent me," I muttered, ready to flee.

"It's Merdemains," Laramort called, behind me. "It's our mucker." He slapped my shoulder. "But you will remember him, Orsain, as the brat of Greenfarm."

The name burst in my head. Orsain was the fourth of them.

He stood so quick his stool fell over. "Greenfarm?" He pointed his dagger at me. "God's Name, where did you find it?"

"Kay has him in the kitchens," Laramort growled. "Am I the only one that remembers?"

"I remember, by God." Orsain swung his head at me, his pocked face blanched with anger. "Damn you, brat, keep from my way." His knife glittered as it chopped the air between us. "Put a finger wrong, curse you, you lose the arm."

Another knight pushed in through the tent flaps. "Is this some jest, Laramort?" he muttered. "You could have had any groom."

"Merdemains hath mucked the king's own horse, Gawain."

Here was Sir Gawain, the highest knight at Camelot save Sir Lancelot. He looked sturdy and very strong, though age lined his square face, and he ran his fingers through short, iron-gray hair. "God help you, if this be an insult to the king."

"I swear 'tis not." Laramort turned to me quick, and thrust a hand to the paddock. "Muck," he said. I took a breath at last, and went out to the horses.

Orsain. The fourth of them. And late that day the fifth came and glowered at me as I worked. He was Giles, an awkward, lanky knight with a sandy mustache and dull eyes. Stupid, I thought, and very dangerous.

The other knight in our pavilion was Sir Agravain, brother to Gawain, dark and remarkably handsome, and with a scar on one cheek that I remembered from the winter chapel. He stared at me and turned and spat, and then said nothing at all throughout the tourney. Each knight had a squire in the tent, boys but little older than I, that were themselves all the sons of knights and knights in training. They paid me little heed save for laughing at Sir Kay's name, and spent the day polishing armor, painting the ash lances, oiling tack. I lent a hand currying horses and braiding tails, but fork and shovel were mine alone.

That night I made a straw pallet in the far corner of the paddock, and had hardly slept when the knights returned from the castle Hall, laughing and noisy. Orsain's hoarse voice praised some lady's charms in such clear terms even Gawain laughed. Another, Agravain mayhap, spoke of the queen's beauty. One of them stumbled over a sleeping squire, who yelped in pain.

"Damn you," growled Orsain. "And where is the mucker?"

"With the horses, sir."

"That churl." He lowered his voice. "He doth not please me, Laramort, even shoveling manure."

"Nor I," said Laramort, equally quiet. "But think you, might Merdemains suffer some accident?"

My breath stopped in my throat.

"An accident," murmured Orsain.

"But take care. The king hath brought him here."

I woke that night every time the horses moved. Next morning, tired and muddled, I helped the squires prepare their knights. Orsain mounted and called for his lance. I handed it up. He gripped it, and let it drop.

"You stupid oaf," he bellowed.

I bent to pick it up.

"Damn you, you'll never drop another." Metal rasped above me, the sound of a sword drawn. I raised the lance quick over my head. His blade chopped half through the wooden shaft, and the force of his swing drove me back a step.

His grin faded. "Damn you," he cried, yanking at his blade.

I let go the lance and stumbled away.

Sir Gawain was suddenly there, his own lance leveled at Orsain. "Damn you, sir," he growled. "I like this varlet no better than you, but he is the king's wish. You are a king's knight. Knights obey their lords, they fight other knights, they make no feuds over petty servants."

They glowered at each other. Orsain's squire brought another lance. The rest mounted, and the four of them turned and rode together out to the tourney parade.

I stumbled back to the paddock. I could not breathe, my chest ached, it felt his sword had cleft me deep as my heart. Death had grinned at me from that pocked face. Orsain would kill me. They would all kill me. They might forget for weeks or months, but they would remember and kill me. They had swords and armor and noble blood and all the privileges of knighthood, while I had nothing save my wits, and my hatred. Tonight; they would be drunk again tonight. I would kill them in their sleep, with my grandfather's blade; Orsain and Laramort here, Giles in his other pavilion. And Almant and Briant, when they came again to Camelot.

But that night Sir Gawain sent me to sleep in the kitchen tent.

The king's tourney was two days of jousts, that were single combats between knights with lance and sword, and a third day for the melee, a little war between two sides, fought over a league of meadow and wood between the castle and the upriver ford.

Sir Gawain grumbled at jousts. " 'Tis unworthy of high knights, this Frankish fad. 'Tis but two gentlemen bowing at each other."

But in truth there was little bowing and no gentleness in the joust. Knights went heavy-armored, wearing shields and mail armor and thick iron helmets, yet a well-set lance might drive completely through a man, a sword might scar cheeks, remove fingers, cripple shoulders. The winner, as in any fight, was the one least injured.

That first morning, the battle-horses bridled and saddled, I came to watch the squires arm their knights. The two hallmarks of knighthood were the sword belt that carried a knight's bright steel blade, and the hauberk that protected him from the swords of others. The hauberk was a knee-length coat of linked chain mail, with a hood that fitted close over neck and head, and long arms that ended with mittens over their hands. Chain mail amazed me, a dense weaving of rings of iron wire, each small link looped round four others, and those round others, till the whole became a heavy metal fabric almost impervious to sword blows. I could not imagine how long it took to make a hauberk, nor was I surprised such armor cost as much as a battle-horse.

Below their hauberks knights wore chausses, mail leggings hung from a belt at the waist, that shielded legs and feet. And under it all were coats of leather or quilted linen to ease the blows, that after a strong fight on a summer's day dripped with sweat. Round helmets covered their heads, with a single narrow slot to look through, though Sir Gawain and his brother wore the newer style, with a hinged front that might be raised when not fighting.

As they dressed, Orsain shrugged under the weight of his hauberk and grinned at Gawain's helmet. How was it, he asked, that Gawain complained so of new styles of fighting, yet took up the latest armor quick as any? To battle the harder, Gawain muttered, and turned on me scowling and sent me to the kitchens for ale.

Tourney marshals set the weakest fighters early, and of our four Laramort was first to joust. When I returned with a sloshing aleskin he had, to everybody's surprise, won easily. The warming air grew thick with cheers from the watching crowd, the thunder of galloping horses, the smells of manure and trampled grass.

Orsain swung up on his destrier. He took a lance from his squire and rode out to the wooden lists to bow to the king and his older knights, and to the queen with her ladies. Heralds cried his name and his opponent's. They trotted to opposite ends of the course and raised their lances, spurred their animals and bolted toward each other. The ground shook. The hooves of the horses tore up gouts of turf. They met at near gallop, the whole thunderous force of man and animal driving their lance points against the other's shield. As it happened, both their lances shattered and they rode apart. I let out the breath I had been holding. Despite my fright and hatred of him, I had almost hoped Orsain would win.

The lists gave them but mild applause as they rode to collect new lances. They charged again. Orsain's lance drove the other clean out his saddle. He fell heavily and lay on his back, stunned a long moment before he managed to struggle up. They met in the center of the field. They hewed at each other with their swords. The harder steel of the blades dented helmets and notched shields like an ax in green oak. I could not understand how they might fight so long, receive such terrible blows, and still stand. I prayed for Orsain's injury, even his death, yet it was the other knight that wavered. Blood oozed from beneath his helmet. Orsain hit him a last huge blow, and he staggered and fell.

The king raised his hand, the horn-men blew their instruments, Orsain stepped away and raised his sword, triumphant. He walked back to the pavilion, proud and erect through the applause of the throng, but once inside he staggered and groped for a stool. He cried out softly as his squire removed his helmet, and his pale face dripped with sweat inside his mail hood; blood clotted one side of his head, bruises purpled his cheek.

"God's Name," he gasped, "another minute I'd have fallen, myself."

"A strong fight, Orsain," said Sir Gawain, happily. "You improve with every tourney. Soon you will be good as Briant."

Sir Gawain and Agravain his brother were both ranked very high. They fought after midday and won impressively. Late in the day the four knights ours had beaten limped into Gawain's tent, bruised and weary, to offer their ransoms. Many tourneys gave the winners full prizes, weapons and armor and even the battle-horse, but in Sir Ulfius' honor King Arthur had limited ransoms to armor and swords, or a sum of coin instead. Knighthood also demanded generosity, and often winners gave away half of what they won, to other knights, their lords, the king. And Gawain offered everybody drink, and once more I must run to the kitchens.

The second day of jousts our knights won again, save Laramort's draw. On the third they made a team for the melee, sworn to share victories. At midday, carrying loaves and drink, I walked up the river meadows to the wooded area marked as sanctuary.

Agravain and Laramort, wearing the blue ribbons that marked Camelot knights, were resting a minute in the tree shade. The melee still raged all around, dust blew about thick as smoke, and it was not easy to tell blue ribbons from white, the color of the other side. But it did not seem to matter. Knights shouted, cried out, laughed and bellowed challenges, and beat on whoever was closest at hand. The melee was for capture, and a knight might unhorse another that he yield, or even seize his bridle and draw him off for ransom. As I watched, a knight with a red and white shield galloped past, pursing another into the swirling dust.

"Gawain would take his third," said Agravain. He laughed and clapped on his helmet, swung up and rode to help his brother.

"*Ad Orkensis,*" Laramort cried, in what might be Latin, and followed him into the roar and clatter.

A small wind off the river briefly parted the dust. Orsain's black and yellow defeated a knight in green. Looking at it all—swords flashing in the dust, lathered horses, bruised knights, their tabards torn and shredded—I wondered how this differed from true battle. And walking back to the jousting field, I understood that knights spent all their lives at this, that I had no chance to defeat them at arms but must find some quieter and more subtle way to kill them. What that might be I could not even imagine.

At the end of the day they returned, laughing despite their weariness. They had taken a dozen ransoms between them. "Everybody wonders at our triumph," cried Orsain, as he swung down from his lathered horse. He punched Laramort's drooping arm. "Even yours, you fish."

Sir Gawain, haggard with fatigue, could only mutter, "Praise God, Lancelot did not fight. He would have beaten us all."

"He stayed next the king," muttered Agravain, scowling. "And the queen."

Orsain laughed at them both. "Today I could have beaten even Lancelot." He glanced around and saw me watching. "Don't stand gawking, varlet. Muck."

The swing of his mailed fist caught my ear, and the blow near felled me. My head rang and I had to brace myself with the shovel. I had smiled at him, forgetful, pleased at his joy, but now I saw myself grasping the shovel's rough handle, lifting it two-handed like an ax, splitting his thick skull with its filthy blade. And then Laramort's, and though Gawain might draw his sword and hack me apart, at least I would have killed half of them.

I straightened up and gripped the shovel. But Orsain, sure of his command, had already gone out again. Sir Gawain's cold eyes watched me. I dropped my head and turned away.

King Arthur held a great banquet in Camelot's Hall that night, and Sir Gawain sat the high table, so the servers told me, and Agravain and Orsain at the champions' trestle. Even Laramort's reputation had grown, from the victories of Gawain's pavilion. Next morning lords and knights packed and rode back to their own estates. Carpenters dismantled lists and paddocks, and servants struck the remaining tents, until by the end of the day nothing remained on the trampled grass save heaps of straw and manure.

The sound of Vespers bells from the castle church made me look around. There, next Thomas' hedges, stood a small cluster of peasants. I walked across the meadow toward them.

"Your cheek's bruised," said my father; "you've not behaved."

"No, Father." But I could not explain.

"You've grown," my mother said.

I laughed at her. "It's been but three weeks."

"Do they feed you?" asked Harry.

"All the bread you can eat," I said, "meat every meal. Fresh fish from the castle ponds, fast days. Always leavings of ale."

They stared at me as if I were a traveler telling lies of distant lands.

"Did you see the tourney?" I said.

"How could we?" said Warren. "There's threshing, there's plowing. We're short-handed."

"All that manure," said Harry. "Can we use it?"

I shrugged. "Ask Thomas." I had been at Camelot less than a month, yet already they saw me an overfed stranger, a watcher of jousts, a source of manure.

I took my mother's hand and looked at her lined face. "I want a piece of Rebecca's dress." She gaped and went pale, and my father sputtered at

it. "Just a bit of the hem," I said, "but make sure her blood is on it." By
their faces, I might have spoke blasphemy. "Make a little bag of Wat's
doeskin. Ask Thomas to bring it. I must remember always how she
died."

Four

In the weeks after Sir Ulfius' tourney the haze of late summer settled over Camelot like a golden mantle, as if in all the world there were no danger, nor any discourtesy. King and knights rode to hunt in the royal forests, and brought back great antlered stags. Else they went out along the river meadows, hawks on their wrists, and then the queen and her ladies rode out with them. The stags we butchered and roasted in the kitchens, but the birds from hawking were torn and shredded, fit only for falcons themselves, or the cats that appeared mewing every dusk.

Sir Bedevere was made Camelot's new chamberlain, but Laramort kept his charge over the youngest servants and would not have me in the kitchens. "We'll have no Merdemains here," he said. "The stables need you, mucker." I was not surprised.

If kitchen mornings began with carrying wood for the ovens, stable mornings began with carrying water, a heavy bucket on each end of a shoulder yoke. The smell of hay and manure hung in the cool air. We gave each of the horses a fistful of oats, bridled and groomed them, and mucked their stalls. Riding palfreys were gentle enough, but the great destriers tossed their heads and nipped, leaned to crush us against the stalls, would put a hoof on any unwary foot. They frightened me at first, so unlike gentle Anduin, but the grooms said it was only play.

At kitchens and stables both the work was much indoors, and soon enough I lost my farmer's sunburn and went almost pale, a more seemly color for life in the king's castle. But more than that, I began to lose my farmer's sense of time, of plow and seed and harvest. I wondered when

Ryford reaped the barley. The morning of first frost took me by surprise.

Morning and night the stables worked very hard, for knights went out on quests, rode the meadows to joust with padded lances, or the forests for game, and every task required horses. But there were many hours with little to do, when Anduin and I renewed our friendship. Oft the grooms let me ride him for exercise, among a troop of battle-horses trotting the drumming bridge out to the river meadows. Once I broke away and galloped nearly to Thomas' house, before something made me turn and come back again.

As the days shortened and the weather drew in, the knights turned from jousting to bladework, and Camelot's upper court would ring with swords. Else they would spar, unarmored, with bright daggers, circling and lunging at each other, cursing and grunting with pain, and would not stop till both were bloody and staggering. Even dagger scars were marks of knightly honor.

Many grooms fought in imitation, with their own small daggers. It was a skill I must learn, yet when I asked them even the youngest using but a sharpened stick was too quick for me. It took me weeks to judge the moving points, to see the difference between a lunge and a feint, and as many more to disguise my own moves. And when we began with true knives, I had to swallow my fear. Even in practice an error meant serious injury. More than once I was caught and set bleeding, and had it been one of Lark's knights and not a boy my own age, I would have sprawled the cobbles dying.

I had not forgot I came to Camelot with an oath between my teeth and, though I was but a peasant, a fierce hatred for its knights. Of course I saw some were different; Sir Gawain protected me against Orsain, Sir Kay's insults fell on every servant equally, Almant had but held the horses that night. But for those I called Lark's four, my hatred only grew. Thomas had brought the doeskin bag my mother made, that held its scrap of brown-crusted cloth. I hung it round my neck, permanent as a monk's cross, and woke each dawn to its soft weight on my chest. Each morning I recited their names, Briant, Giles, Orsain, Laramort. Each day I swore again my oath against them, as regular as the priests sang Terce in Camelot's church, and my curses became my own black and unholy Office.

There are hermit monks, so have I heard, that after years of prayer and loving meditation on Our Lord come to believe themselves no different from Him. Of course, men ought fear God's wrath, and quake in awe of His power, for He stands too high above us. Yet surely the hermit's long devotion to God's Son begins not with fear of Christ, but love instead. Fear and awe may be the proofs of difference, but love is the portent of identity. Priests might say that Christ is also God, that we cannot ever be His equal, but I believe the hermits truly love. And more, I believe all of us can only love that which is our equal, that is somehow ourselves.

Opposite bright love there stands black hate. Just as we may love only our equals, so it is with hate. Those that stand above us we can only fear, those below we can only loathe. But hatred is love's dark twin, and like love can occur only between equals. I did not fear nor loathe Lark's knights, but hated them. I hated them always, and every day I uttered my dark oath as if I imitated the hermit's bright praise. Until, at last one autumn morning and in some way I still do not understand, reciting their names, I discovered that the distance between us, that impossible, unbridgeable, God-created chasm, had suddenly vanished.

I hated them. They were, therefore, my brothers. No longer did they loom over me, made by blood and birth inevitably my superiors. They were but men, mortals like myself. I had brought them down to me, else raised myself to them. Whatever the truth, the frightful authority of their rank and privilege vanished like smoke from a dying fire. We were no different. I feared nothing of them save my lack of skill, for I had seen how good they were at battle and knew how arduous it would be to kill them.

At Michaelmas King Arthur held a great hunt, to make an end to the season for stags. Camelot rode every palfrey that late September morning, and knights even took the softer battle-horses. The wide stony court rang with the clatter of hooves. We grooms held the horses for mounting and, careful of teeth and hooves, led them out into the press of other excited animals. Sitting above us knights boasted of their skills and challenged each other to races and jumps, while the ladies whooped and giggled and made their animals prance. The king wore a scarlet cloak, a gilded oxhorn round his neck. The queen was resplendent in a fur-lined mantle, her bright hair free of wimple or any covering. At the castle gate the houndsmen waited with their packs, that were all noses and wagging tails. In the flurry I did not see who rode Anduin.

They did not return till almost dark, a line of tired horses and weary riders. The game carts rattled in. We had no time to stare, but tugged the animals into stalls and rubbed them down, gave them small oats and a little water.

Anduin was nearly the last. A squire led him in. I saw him limping, and left the animal I watered without a thought. "What is it?" I called, pushing through the crowd. "What's wrong with him?"

The squire handed me the reins. "A stone at the ford, coming home."

"Half a league, and you rode him?"

"I am not such a fool," cried a knight's voice.

Sir Lancelot du Lac stepped around the horse. I had seen him often at a distance, yet still I gaped to meet Camelot's finest knight face-to-face. Lancelot was not greatly handsome, nor tall as the king, but his brown eyes were very deep and his face had enormous character. He was immensely strong, and even when he stood easy in the noisy stable, energy flowed from him like the odor of some Orient spice, and like the king he was a man you could not keep your eyes from.

" 'Tis a good horse." He put a broad hand on Anduin's shoulder. "Stout heart, remarkable seat." He glanced at me. A small white scar decorated his left cheek. "You were not his groom this morning."

"No, sir, I . . ."

His squire barked a laugh. " 'Tis the brat of Greenfarm, sir. My lord Arthur gave him this horse."

"Aye, sir," I said, bobbing.

Lancelot's brown eyes stared at me, as if at last he saw me. "We got the stone out, but the frog is bruised. Keep him off it."

"I will, sir," I said. "Thank you, sir."

After the great hunt, Camelot's knights began to ride away, to see to their estates and collect their Michaelmas rents. Each day the stables emptied more, till of my knights only Laramort remained. One chill clear morning I took Anduin for his first run since his injury. Our breath smoked in the air as we cantered the brown meadows, and I had to curb his want to gallop. Trotting back across the drawbridge we met Laramort, dressed in travel furs.

He drew up hard when he saw me. "What do you, lout," he cried, "riding that horse?"

"His exercise, sir."

"God's love." He grabbed Anduin's bridle, tugged his own horse around, and hauled me back to the stables. "Grooms," he shouted, "damn you, this is Merdemains. Never let him on a horse. He is a mucker." Anger lit two red spots on his pale cheeks. "Get off that animal, damn you."

"Aye, sir." I slid off Anduin's shoulder.

"I would send you home to your dung heap, but for the king." He drew a quick breath. "The kitchen, scullery, slopwork. Merdemains ought muck garderobes. Anything but the Hall."

"Aye, Sir Laramort."

"If I see you on a horse again"—his voice cracked—"by God, I'll take your head." He stared at me a long moment before he turned and rode clattering out the gate.

But the garderobes had all been recently cleaned, and with Camelot half empty the kitchens had no need of help. Will the baker folded his arms over his belly and looked me up and down. "I'll not question Sir Laramort's choice. But if not Hall, there's only Ladies." He went serious and gripped my arm. "Listen to me, boy, it's cleric's sons there, you're a farmer's brat. And knights' ladies, remember, that are far above you."

So it was that Laramort, all unwitting, sent me up from the noisy lower court of kitchens and stables, through the inner gate that stood always open, into the quiet comfort of Camelot's upper bailey. Shaped flagstones and a little sheep-cropped lawn lay there instead of cobbles, eels rippled the water of the fish pool, and a stand of apple trees still held their late fruit.

And over it all stood King Arthur's great high keep, built of pale stone more finely cut and better laid up than even the great Hall, and always cool when you touched it. At the first level, up three steps, a round-headed doorway and narrow windows marked the king's audience chamber. On the floor above, glass casements opened to the queen's solar, and bedchambers for castle knights. A higher rank of windows marked the king's chambers and the queen's, and then, over everything and higher than all the rest of Camelot, crenelated battlements and high towers sharp against the sky.

King and knights ate in Camelot's great Hall, and the queen and the wives of high knights. But lesser ladies of the court had a separate place, in a new tower of the keep just inside the second gate. Beneath a glazed projecting oriel a small door opened to a narrow flight of steps, that led up to a small pantry and the chamber called Ladies. My first day I carried loaves up from the kitchen. The wide basket was very awkward in the steep way. I caught a glimpse of ladies eating in the bright chamber beyond, and when they were gone I followed the servers in. A scent like spices hung in the air. The stone walls were newly whitewashed. The polished board at the center might seat two dozen, though no more than eight or ten had eaten there that day. I walked slowly past, staring at the silver spoons and elegant cups, half afraid to touch anything. At the far end the oriel looked down over the king's bailey. I had never looked out glass before, nor from such a high window, and the view through its diamond panes almost made me dizzy. Nothing lay below, save squared flagstones that would break me, should I ever fall.

That was all I saw of the royal keep my first weeks, pantry, Ladies, a glimpse of a passage beyond. Still, I grasped quick enough the shape of life there. Nobody worked.

That was not exactly true. The knights still at the castle practiced at arms, their grunt and clang filling the mornings. Their ladies stitched or broidered in the solar, so I was told. The king held audience in his chamber, almost every day.

Better to say, nobody worried. The life of a farmer lay in my bones. Plowing, spading, weeding, harvest, threshing, slaughter, markets, rent, illness, and always weather and death. But Camelot seemed free of everything, of drought or flood or frost, of hunger or fatigue or any unpleasantness.

And soon enough I discovered another thing, how the castle lived after dark. Farmers go to bed at sundown, but tapers and fires lit Camelot every night, and tales and songs passed the hours. The singer I had heard was gone away, but there were always others, minstrels from all of Britain, from Normandy and even far Provence.

Their songs were of love, as Lark believed, though she could not have known the different kinds. Love was the heart's true yearning, they sang. Yet every marriage must encompass titles, property, and politics, must always be a decision between families, not between lovers. Knights and ladies wed whom they ought, not whom they wished. Therefore love was impossible in marriage. It must be found outside, and there were but two alternatives, chivalric love that was pure and unrequited yearning, and courtly love, all lust and passion and most especially fulfillment.

The young knights of Camelot were very arduous and little interested in chivalric love. Instead they trod the keep after dark, seeking courtly love, walking so boldly I thought they must believe themselves invisible. Mayhap they were, with only servants' eyes to see them. And the boldest and most frequent of them was that least invisible of knights, Sir Lancelot.

I had been at Ladies not more than a week when three knights rode into Camelot's court, sore wounded. They had met Sir Lancelot and challenged him. He had bested all three, and as their ransom sent them to Camelot to offer liege. Three knights, I thought, and Lancelot defeated them all. I remembered, after the long day of the great hunt, his great energy had never flagged.

But the servers murmured of a different thing. The great knight sent his vanquished knights not to the king his liege lord, but to his courtly love. And she was Lady Guenever, King Arthur's glorious wife. If Lancelot were brave and strong and always victorious in battle, he was also blind in love, besotted of the dazzling queen and she with him. Everyone knew it, they said, and when I doubted them told me of Lancelot and Elaine, and Guenever.

Years past, Lancelot, out questing, had killed a dragon and saved the life of Elaine, maiden daughter to King Pelles. Of course the girl fell in love with him, yet despite all her wiles Lancelot remained true to the queen—until, bewitched by a potion that made him believe her Guenever, he got a son on Elaine. It was a year later that she came to Camelot and the tale emerged. Guenever, frantic with jealousy, screamed and argued under the very eye of Arthur. If the king would not understand, her anger drove Lancelot mad. He fled the court and wandered lost a year, and was only brought to reason again in that same castle of King Pelles.

"How is it," I asked, "the king does not know this?"

"King Arthur," said Emrys, "is the world's most gallant knight. He believes in the purest chivalry, and from that unshakable belief comes all of Camelot, the fellowship of the Roundtable, this great assembly of proud knights."

"But she is his wife," I said. "Everybody knows."

"If it is not high chivalry, he will not see it."

I thought of my four, knights of Camelot all, grunting under the lopsided moon. "Nothing could ever blind me so."

Emrys shrugged. "But you are not King Arthur."

Emrys had made himself my teacher. He was seventeen, and slender and girlish. The other servers thought me a hopeless lout, but Emrys tried to teach me all he could, especially that most difficult of tasks, to be invisible. If I failed at it, that was not his fault. Truly I did not want to learn.

I brought food warm from the kitchen, the oldest server carved the meat, Emrys sliced the loaves, the others poured wine and passed the washing ewer. They moved silently and never spoke. The ladies never looked at them, but chattered on about knights. Their talk was always about knights, brave ones, handsome ones, injured ones, yet none ever confessed that she opened her door after dark.

I had been there nearly a month when one of the servers fell sick. It was the evening of All Souls', and with a dozen ladies there Emrys brought me out to pour the wine. A draft bothered the taper flames and made me nervous, but I spilled nothing. Thinking I had gone unnoticed, I returned to pour the second wine. As I stood beside the last and youngest lady, a hand gripped the back of my leg. The pitcher shook. I poured amiss. The hand slid up the inside of my thigh. I felt the blood hot in my cheeks. I begged her pardon and mopped the spill. I looked at her for the first time, and saw she was pretty. Her braided hair, uncovered by any wimple, was pale blonde within its jeweled net. Her breasts rose bravely beneath her robe. She watched me, unsmiling. I backed away, sore confused. Ladies never touched servers. She had no need; she must have knights enough.

It was the widow Agraine, the king's gray-haired cousin, who stopped me with her grim voice. "Who sent you here, boy? You came after Ulfius."

"Sir Laramort, madam."

"Laramort. By God, the silly fool."

I fled to the pantry. I took a few swallows of wine to ease my shaking. When the ladies rose from the meal, she who had gripped me walked away without a glance.

Emrys came and put a hand on my arm. "Be careful," he whispered. I had no idea what he meant and went to collect spoons. He shook his head and pointed me to the far door. "There," he said, "follow her. But whatever happens, tell no one."

My heart drummed. I took an uncertain step into the dark. The ladies' voices sounded ahead of me, and their lamp flickered on the white-washed wall. At Camelot the great spaces of the keep were divided by wood walls into smaller rooms, that made private bedchambers for the married knights. A narrow passage ran between them, that you might go from Ladies to the queen's solar without entering any chamber. It was down that passage I followed the glimmer of the lamp, put a hand on the painted wood and turned a corner. A servant girl seized my wrist. I nearly cried out. She pulled me quickly through a narrow door.

A high curtained bed nearly filled the space. Taperlight glimmered on the lady's hair as she shook out her pale braids. She did not even look at me, but bent to untie her garters and pull off broidered hose. She undid her sash and drew off a long blue robe, and her body shone clear and rounded beneath a thin linen shift. I felt my mouth gape, and the blood running everywhere through me. The maid went out and closed the door.

She had a shortish upper lip and small white teeth that smiled as she took a step and opened her arms and wrapped them about me, and pressed her whole length against me and murmured breathless in my ear, "Sweet Mary, thourt a pretty one."

I could not help myself. I had never felt so soft a body. I grasped her like a dying man might seize the cross. For an instant, her breath on my lips, I hung between desire and fright. And then I forgot to worry. I do not know how we reached the bed, or what happened to my clothes. I remember only her little cry as she pulled me in, and the look on her face a little after.

"I'd hardly drawn a breath, varlet," she said.

"Oh, my lady," I murmured, "wait a minute, pray, and you will have pleasure enough." And half believing my boldness, I began to make free with her, and soon enough proved myself. And then again.

I'd had a cousin once at Easter, and a village girl behind the sheaves at harvest, but never a woman, and in bed. Someone nudged my shoulder and woke me. The maid held the stub of a tallow candle and put a finger to her lips.

" 'Tis time you went, but you must be quiet."

I lay naked under the quilt. "Where are my clothes?"

She held them up, but stepped away when I reached. "A kiss for them," she said. She tasted of supper's leeks. Her tongue moved. I felt myself rousing up, and pushed her away. "This lady," I pointed to the sleeping form, "if she wakes . . ."

I climbed into the cold room, but when I turned my back to dress she danced around me, her eyes bright, and giggled. "Oh, don't hide yourself."

Holding the light, she took my arm and led me out to the passage. Our breath smoked in the cold and I was glad to have her pressed against me. She stopped at every corner and raised her lips to mine, while I struggled to remember the way. At Ladies, as she crushed me against the pantry doorway I heard a footstep. My heart stopped and she went taut herself. A knight walked down the dark passage. He carried no light, but his step was so sure in the blackness I knew he had been that way a hundred times. As he passed us his eyes glittered in the candle flame and he gave a little smile at two servants clipping in the dark. It was Sir Lancelot, going out the same way I was, down the serving stairs.

She held me tight. "You never saw him," she whispered.

"Nor he us."

She blinked at me, surprised. The flame guttered and she blew it out. In the dark she kissed me again.

"What's your name?" I asked.

"Sarah." She rubbed herself against me.

"And what is your lady's name?"

"Are you so new?" She kissed me. "Lady Sibyl, wife to Sir Edmund of Bramhill. Who is this autumn in Ireland."

"Lady Bramhill," I muttered. In her bed I had even forgot she was a noble lady. "Does she take each new server?"

"Only you. She thought it would be daring, a servant in her bed." Sarah moved against me again. "Do you refuse, young Micah? She is niece to Lady Morgan le Fay, the king's half sister."

"That witch?" This time my shiver was not from the cold.

"Oh, Micah, never say that to my lady."

I gave her a last kiss. I felt my way through the dark pantry and down the stairs. It was raining hard when I stepped into the court. A broad figure stood under the oriel, sheltered from the storm. I grunted in surprise, and Sir Lancelot turned to peer at me.

Of course he must not return wet to his chamber. "I have a small cape, sir." I began to untie it.

"That's all?" His voice was marvelously deep.

"I did not expect the rain either."

A bell rang in the church. "Matins," he said. Another door opened in the keep nearby, and lantern light flickered across the wet stones as a dark-robed monk strode through the rain.

"You could pray, sir." I waited a moment but he did not speak. "You could not sleep. The bell roused you."

He rumbled beside me, laughing softly. "I could not sleep." Then he turned and crumpled the front of my tunic with one large hand. "Do not mock the king, varlet. Nor his lady."

I could not see his eyes in the dark, but if he meant to frighten me, he failed. I kept my voice steady. "Sir, I do not."

He let me go. He stepped out into the rain and walked to the church. The door thudded shut behind him.

I was too tired to worry of Sir Lancelot. I sprinted through the inner gate down to the kitchen door, found my way to the boys' room, crept among the sleepers and fell into bed. It was narrow and very cold, but I slept at once.

It was November, and at Greenfarm they would be cutting wood in the forests, smoking the autumn's slaughter, clearing ditches and trimming hedges. But at Camelot winter meant no more than frost in the mornings and the taste of roast swans from the king's rivers. I had been there four months. Not so much had happened in fourteen years, and I had expected none of it.

When the ailing server recovered we all waited. The ladies watched me unsmiling, though even the old widow seemed less stern. I grew devoted to my lady Sibyl, to her soft body, her short lip, her little teeth that nibbled.

"I thought you too pretty for a peasant," she said. In the dark I had put my face between her breasts. "But thou art only an animal, in love."

"And what is it knights do, sweet lady?"

"They flatter, they whisper rhymes. They speak of love, they curb themselves. You are only appetite."

"Then teach me, lady."

"Why? You're but a server."

"Then would I serve you, always, lady."

She called me to her often and for two months. After the first night, Sarah returned to sleep on her own pallet inside the door. Nor would she let me go till I had kissed her, too, and very well. I began to wonder, Had I the strength for castle life?

I still wore the small bag my mother made. My lady never asked of it, and to Sarah I made it the secret charm of some old dam, to preserve me from dangers in the castle. Yet her question worried me, and one dark winter evening I climbed to the servants' gallery of the church, and knelt and prayed Rebecca's forgiveness of all my joyment of Camelot.

As it happened, next morning Sibyl did not appear at Ladies. Sir Edmund had come back to Camelot, and she sat with her husband in the great Hall. I stared at her vacant place and felt new and awkward all over again. I ached that she was gone, and the hurt of missing her took me by surprise.

The other ladies seemed not to notice, save one that stared at me, unsmiling, as she licked her lips. In the pantry I told Emrys I would be constant to my own lady. He gave a wry smile. "How quick you are at chivalry." I nearly blurted out I loved her. I could not believe it. She took me, and I served her, only for pleasure. Even when we spoke of love it was banter and mock chivalry. But now I loved her, I missed her, I ached for her. God's name, what had she done to me? How had she caught me so?

It was the week before Yule, and that evening the first storm of winter filled Camelot's court with blowing snow. I stepped out the kitchens with a platter of roast venison and bent against the wind. I heard voices rumble at the stables. A company of knights had just arrived, and though I could not see their faces I knew at once the hoarse voice of Orsain. That night I did not sleep well, and next morning as we warmed ourselves at the kitchen fires somebody said Briant was come, and Giles too. Laramort was already back. I could not stop the bowl shaking in my hands. That day I sharped my grandfather's dagger.

As he did every year, King Arthur proclaimed a feast for the eve of Our Savior's birth, the beginning of Yuletide. Another great crowd began to arrive, near as large as for the tourney, earls and barons and knights, marshals and castellans from royal castles, abbots from nearby abbeys.

They all ate in the king's Hall and Sir Lucan, the king's butler, set every server running through the cold drizzle and up another servants' stair, to a pantry large as Ladies itself. I delivered a brace of spitted ducks, and stood a moment at the wood screen, watching. The great high chamber boomed with noise. Ranks of flickering tapers lit the company. Fires blazed against the walls, under the carved mantels. Arthur and his high knights sat the great Roundtable, one seat empty as always. The queen's table stood away at the far end before another fire. Trestles filled all the rest, and knights sat shoulder-to-shoulder, eating, drinking, laughing. A score of minstrels played on the balcony overhead, while a dozen more strolled between the tables plucking lutes and singing airs.

Dark Briant and red Almant sat together. And sandy Giles bent and murmured to them. Laramort, as Sir Lucan's aide, paced nearby, his cheeks blazing from drink and excitement. But Orsain's pocked face, that had been next Giles', was nowhere to be seen. Laramort strode to me, muttering, and sent me to fetch cheeses. I pushed through the crowded pantry and down the steps. At the bottom, as I reached for the door a fist clutched my shoulder. Orsain blew his wine breath in my face. I gaped in fright. This night, of all of them, I had imagined I was safe.

"A pity," he snickered, "how this churl stumbled down the steps and broke his head."

He raised a heavy stick. I had no room to dodge nor time to draw my blade, but could only kick at his groin. I caught him well. He doubled over, coughing. I kicked him again. The club knocked against my shoulder as it fell from his hand, and he dropped to his knees and vomited.

I ran back up the stairs. "Sir Laramort," I called. "Sir Orsain has been sick, sir."

"What?"

"He's very drunk, sir."

He cursed and called an older server. Orsain had vanished, though his club lay on the bottom step and the stink of vomit nearly made me spew myself.

"Damn him." Laramort covered his nose and went up again.

I peered out the door. Nobody lurked outside when I went into the dark for a bucket of water.

"Good lad." The server sloshed the steps. "There'll be a score of knights sick tonight, and twice as many servants."

In the kitchens I grasped two of the round cheeses, one under each arm, each so heavy I staggered with their weight. Crossing the blustery court again, it came to me that Laramort had sent me to Orsain. God's Name, there he was again, barring the servants' door. He lifted his sword and swung it blind. I felt the wind of it on my face. The weight of the cheeses half nailed me to the ground. He took a step forward, but at that moment the older server came out the door behind him.

"What do you, sir?" he cried. "Armed at Yule?"

Orsain spun around. I dodged past his shoulder, through the door and up the stairs. Voices sounded below me, but I did not stop till I had put down the cheeses and drawn a shaking breath.

God protect me, four of them. Luck and drunkenness would not save me long. I must sleep that night in the Hall, among the squires and minor knights. I must never go alone into the bailey after dark, not so long as they were here.

A pantryman cut one of the cheeses. I put a large wedge on a platter and went out into the noisy Hall, as far as the queen's table. Lady Guenever sat among her ladies, surrounded by a crowd of younger knights that paid her court. I had never seen her so close. Her blue eyes looked about her with humor and weariness both, their color matched by the gown that draped her womanly form. A gold mesh caught her blonde hair above a smooth brow, a handsome nose, bright lips. Her beauty stopped my breath, but that did not explain why she so drew my gaze, nor the knights who had come for her smile. In truth she had a physical presence that set even my servant's heart afire, and I forgot to look at anybody else.

"Boy," called the widow Agraine, "leave your cheese. Pour the wine."

The ladies paid me no attention, and their husbands were impatient for the drink. A lean knight with thinning hair sat yawning beside Sibyl. I filled his cup to brimming. She did not look at me, but when I stood on her other side her hand moved on my thigh. I could but stagger away. God's Name—Orsain waited to kill me, Sibyl groped me under her husband's nose, the queen roused my heart. I wondered if I would survive the night.

I went to the pantry again, carried cheese to other tables, poured wine where it was needed. Laramort muttered with Giles, who stared at me and pulled his sandy mustache. I kept far away from them both. The feast went on, minstrels grew hoarse, tapers guttered. The queen retired, and her ladies. Barons and older knights drifted off to bed. A dagger fight flared among young knights but drew little blood, and even they began to stretch out on the benches.

Still the king sat, drinking unhurriedly, talking with Sir Lancelot and Sir Gawain. Lancelot described some combat, his hands the charging destriers, and the king smiled at the tale. Lancelot, the king's best friend, that visited the queen as often as her husband. I could not understand it, not at all.

It must have been midnight when King Arthur finally stood. He gazed around at the dying fires and snoring knights, and laughed and called out, "Happy Yule to Camelot."

I had drunk my measure already, against my fright of Orsain, and as I collected cups I drained every one. I brought a last armful from the sleeping Hall, and there in the pantry stood Emrys.

"She sends for you," he murmured.

I swear it, that I felt her hand between my legs. My head flared and I laughed aloud that even tonight she must have her hungry peasant. I forgot all notion of sleeping in the Hall. In Camelot's court snow fell out of the black night, cold and wet against my cheeks. I gave no thought to Yule or Christ's star, but felt my way quick as I could to the door of Ladies and up the dark stair. Laughs sounded behind bedchamber doors, and soft cries.

Sarah opened the door at my knock. "Micah," she whispered.

A taper flickered on its stand. Sibyl smiled from the high bed, and there lay her husband beside her, snoring. She chuckled at my dismay. "He sleeps like the dead, especially drunk."

"My lady, if he should wake . . ."

"Come, varlet." She opened the quilt. Her soft body shone in the light. It so stunned me with desire that I fell toward her unable to stop, as once I had fallen from a high tree. She clasped me and drew a sudden breath. Were her husband to rouse I might not see the morn, and even the notion of that made her more desirable. If I had been nearly broken by the fall from that tree, in bed my pain was fairer. We cried together quiet and Edmund never stirred. Still entwined and kissing in a room now dark, we heard Sarah beyond the door.

"Sir," she said loudly, "she is with Sir Edmund."

"Then why sleep you outside, wretch?" I rolled away and sat up, my heart thumping. It was Briant's voice.

"Sweet Mary," whispered Sibyl, "I put her there, he swore he would come. Micah, you must . . ." Her hands were on me, pushing me away. "Hide yourself. I will put him off."

My hands shook as I searched the dark for my robes. I crawled under the bed among the chests and baggage, where the only space large enough was underneath her husband. Sarah argued, but soon enough I heard the door open and saw the glimmer of a lamp. The bed creaked as Sibyl sat up.

"Briant," she muttered, "dear God, here is my husband."

He laughed quietly. "He never wakes, when he's drunk."

"Briant," she said. The bed groaned as he sat. Sarah closed the door again, but left the flickering lamp.

I ached and squirmed, certain he came to rape another woman.

"Briant," she said, soft as she did to me, "it has been months." I heard a noise that must be a kiss.

"I have kept myself," he murmured. "All summer I have not looked at another woman. I wore your colors in three tourneys and won great honors for you, my only love."

There was another long pause.

"Briant." She drew a shuddering breath.

I could not believe it. She promised to send him away, yet now she sighed under his kisses.

"I am your vassal, lady, do give me your sweet self."

"Briant," she said, so quiet I could barely hear.

My stomach ached, my head throbbed, the dust tickled my nose. I could not lie there, not with what was happening. Sir Edmund snorted once, and they were still for a moment. Briant murmured, and she did not protest. I slid to the edge of the bed and reached a hand up beneath the covers. My fingers touched her husband's arm. I tugged at it and pinched it. Edmund rumbled. I dug into his chest and he spoke something and suddenly he was growling and swatting. I slipped quickly back under the bed.

"Damn," he cried, "what was that?" The bed rattled as he sat up. The silence boomed like thunder and then he roared, "Briant? By God and Christ's Mother!"

His bare feet slapped the floor near my head and there was the rasp of a sword being drawn. Briant leaped from the other side. The door latch rattled.

"Damn!" he cried. "The bitch has locked it!"

Sibyl screamed, "Edmund, don't!"

Sir Edmund grunted. The door boomed under a huge blow. I peered out and saw him, still naked from bed, wrenching his sword out of the wood. Briant had backed into a dark corner. A dagger glittered in his hand.

"You cannot kill me," said Briant.

"I should kill her," Edmund cried.

"Edmund," she screamed.

The bed shuddered under another great stroke. She shrieked, but not in pain, and I knew Edmund had deliberately missed. "Wife," he cried, "this foul thing is your lover?"

Briant must have chosen that moment to make his lunge, for Edmund grunted again. His sword rang like a bell, and the door thumped as something fell heavily against it.

She shrieked again. "Edmund, you have killed him!"

"The flat of my sword. Still, mayhap his head is broken."

Under the bed, I could see Briant lying in a crumpled heap. Blood ran from his nose. One side of his face began to swell.

God's Name, I thought, how will I ever escape?

Five

Sibyl wanted Briant lifted on their bed, but Sir Edmund would not hear it. He pulled on his tunic and called Sarah to unlatch the door. Briant lay with his wounded face toward me. His eyes opened and we looked straight at each other. He blinked, as if he could not see, and closed them. I slid into the shadows behind a chest, and when he looked again he could not see me.

Edmund would have dumped the night pot to rouse him, but Sarah appeared with a water jug.

"Stand, varlet," Edmund cried.

"Jealousy," Briant muttered. He rolled on his side. " 'Tis unseemly, Edmund. The rules of courtly love . . ."

"Courtly love," said Edmund, scoffing. "Thou coxsley fool, I ought skewer you like a winded boar."

"I yield, sir." He struggled up. "You have me at fault."

"By God, so I do. For it, I'll have your stones."

"Edmund," gasped Sibyl, "the king . . ."

"The king will say what he must yield. I'll settle for nothing small." He laughed harshly. "Save that."

He must have struck Briant in the privates, for Sibyl shrieked and Briant grunted and fell to the floor again, and lay holding himself. After a pause he muttered, "I saw a face under your bed."

Edmund barked a laugh, though I heard my lady's gasp. " 'Twas thy honor, man, weeping for its ruin."

"It did not weep. It smiled."

The widow Agraine grumbled at the doorway. "Have you killed him, Edmund?"

"No, my lady."

"Pity," she said. "Stand up, sir. Get you gone." Briant got slowly to his feet again. "Bring him along, Edmund," she said, "far as the solar stairs." Their footsteps went slowly away down the passage.

"*Micah,*" Sibyl hissed. I rolled from beneath the bed. "*Go.* He will kill you without a thought. And me with you." I leaned to kiss her but she pushed me to the door. It made me stop, remembering. Briant, that raped my sister, was Sibyl's lover. But I too loved Sibyl, and Briant and I were then . . .

"*Go.*" She thrust at me, blind in her fright.

Sarah took my hand and led me rapidly down the black passage. Halfway to Ladies a light glimmered, and she stopped and pressed me hard against a wall and covered my mouth with hers. Lady Agraine came back around the corner holding a taper, and stopped and scowled at us. "Is this what you did, wench, while you ought have kept your master's door?"

Sarah hung her head. "My lady, I did not think . . ."

"Birch her, Edmund," she said to the knight behind her.

Sarah shrank against me. "My lord, how could I know?"

" 'Tis no matter, lady," Edmund said. "I'd have my revenge on the knight instead."

"If you will not, Edmund, then I must. A dozen."

He shrugged. "As you would, lady. But, hear you, girl, fetch a cat to my chamber tomorrow. It must have been a rat woke me." He rubbed his chest as he walked away. "I can still feel the claws of it."

They turned the corner. Sarah threw her arms about me and pressed her mouth to mine to keep her laughter muffled.

"You have saved me," I said, "you and the lady Agraine."

"We saved my lady. The widow did nothing for a peasant."

"I am sorry about the birch."

"I take it, for my lady." She kissed me again.

We found our way into the darkened Ladies. She pulled me down beneath the oriel and wrapped her arms about me. "Oh, Micah," she murmured, "now the widow will send you from Ladies." She kissed me. She was weeping suddenly, her face damp with tears, and there in the warm comfort of her embrace all the hazard of the night fell on me, and I began to shake.

"There are too many," I said. "Orsain would have killed me tonight, save for luck. Laramort sent me to him. Briant will remember my face under her bed." I took a breath. "There is still Giles, and even Almant if they band together."

She gripped me to her. "Sweet Mary, all of them?"

"If I stay at Camelot they will kill me."

"Oh, Micah, they cannot." I heard the ache in her voice, that astonished me. She had always been a happy girl, but now she wept and held me so I could hardly breathe. "Oh, Micah, please God they cannot kill you."

She loved me. I had not seen it before. She loved me as I loved Sibyl, and yet for months she had lain awake and listened while we made our sport together.

"Sarah." I kissed her damp cheek.

"Micah, they cannot kill you."

"How can I stay?" A thought struck me. "Emrys. His father's a vicar, he'll give me sanctuary."

"Oh yes," she said, "of course he will."

The other servers slept all together in a dark little room at the bottom of the stairs. I opened the door and called, "Emrys? It's Micah."

They grumbled awake. Somebody fumbled with a flint and lit a candle stub. I told them of my night, and they laughed at Orsain's defeat and Edmund's sword. But Emrys shook his head.

"It's ten leagues to my father's parish. On horses, they'd catch you before you'd gone one." He paused, thinking. "But they'll not injure you, sick."

"I'm not sick."

"You will burn with fever, Micah, you will vomit in your bed." He pulled on a jerkin and a pair of boots, and dug a sack from a dark corner. "I need cumin," he said, "and garlic."

"Your father's a priest," I said, "what does he know of . . . ?"

"But not my grandmother." He wrapped himself in a cloak. "Come, we'll brew it in the kitchen."

We went out together, into the blackest night I had ever seen. The wind cut like ice. The snow had stopped, but a slippery muck covered the cobbles as we felt our way past the gate and the buttress of the church. We were nearly to the kitchens when, over the noise of the wind, something rattled. I gripped his arm. A door opened just ahead. A tall knight stepped out, dark against a lantern's flickering light.

"Damn the brats, they must know where he is." It was Laramort.

"My arm is weary of beating them," said Giles. "And where has Briant got himself? Not on his squirming lady again, is he?"

I might have cried out. I don't remember. Laramort raised the blowing light. Giles drew his sword.

"Christ save us," muttered Emrys. We turned to run. I heard him slip on the cobbles behind me, but did not stop to help. He gasped as he fell, and then he shrieked, a high ghastly cry, and then again. I stopped under the church doorway, panting for breath. Emrys squirmed on the icy stones. Giles' blade fell again with an awful chop. Emrys gave a scream that faded abruptly to a shuddering cough. I had to bite my thumb to keep quiet.

Laramort bent over with the flickering light. "God save us, you've killed the wrong damn boy."

Emrys made no sound. I huddled against the damp oak door, numbed and shaking, certain they must hear my panting breath.

"I thought . . ." Giles lifted his head. "There were two."

"Two?" Laramort raised the lantern again. "Then where is he, damn him? 'Tis no longer sport." They leaned together, peering into the dark. I held my breath. Oh God, Emrys. My hand found the cold iron latch. The church was never barred; if I went in they would drag me out but I could think of nothing else. I pulled the door open and stepped inside. The wind closed it with a thud.

The air smelled of incense. A single taper flickered on the altar, and the priest who knelt below it called out, "Thou art tardy, sir, I sang Matins an hour past."

"Father." I went quickly down the aisle. "I ask sanctuary."

He turned, squinting at my livery. "This is the king's church, boy." He waved a hand. "Upstairs, the servants' gallery."

I leaned against the cold wood rail. "Sanctuary, please, father." I gripped it against my shaking. "They'll kill me."

He shook his round head. "Upstairs, churl."

The church door rattled behind me. I vaulted the rail and dodged past him into the shadows of the choir.

"In here," said Giles. His blade caught the taperlight.

The priest threw up his hands. "Sirs," he cried, "thy swords. Not in God's house."

Their boots tramped rapidly down the stone aisle. In the gloom at the back I had found a little door, that opened into a cramped space of chests and vestments.

"Sir knights," the priest scolded. "Sirs, thy weapons."

I would be a rat in a box. I left the door ajar and crawled into the shadows behind the pulpit.

"The brat," said Laramort as they came to the choir.

"Sirs, 'tis Yule, take those things away."

"We have him." Giles opened the gate rail. "There." He had seen the little room. The others turned to watch him stoop and peer inside. I slid into the gloom along the wall, thankful there was but a single taper.

"Good sir knights," the priest complained, "do not injure him, not here in God's house. . . ."

I darted up the dim side aisle, not waiting to hear the rest. Outside the wind and cold took my breath, and snow fluttered against my face again. I could not see if Emrys still lay on the frozen stones. I had no notion where to go. Not the kitchens, surely not to the servers.

Footsteps sounded nearby. A thick hatred cold as the night gripped my stomach, and for the first time I drew my knife. Another knight loomed in the snowy dark, very broad and square. Sir Lancelot peered at me, and as he did a thought came to mind. If King Arthur forgave Lancelot, he could not deny me sanctuary. It made no sense but it gave me hope. I lowered my head and sprinted into the upper bailey. Praying with my life the king's chamber would not be barred, I dashed up the few steps, turned the ring, leaned against the door. It swung in. I let out my breath.

A single fire gave the only light. The knight sitting before it lifted his head and called, "Who is it?" It was Sir Percival, his face half covered by a dark mustache. "What do you want?"

"The king's refuge, sir." I put away my dagger and strode to him. I had become fearless. This was my last retreat.

"The king's refuge?" He pulled at one end of his mustache. Behind its grand spread he was no older than my brother Harry. "You are a serving lad."

"Still I ask it, sir." I drew a shaking breath. "Of Sir Giles and Sir Laramort. Sir Orsain. Sir Briant." He tugged the other side of his mustache. "They have killed Emrys, sir, he that was a server at Ladies. They thought it was me."

"God defend us," Percival muttered.

"In the lower bailey, sir." I could hardly speak, gripped again by hatred and cold fright. "Outside the kitchen, sir."

"You are the lad of the battle-horse. Whose sister . . ."

"Micah of Greenfarm, sir."

"And they pursue you?"

"The church would not give me sanctuary."

"Ah." He had finished with his mustache. "Stay here." He strode past me and opened the door. In the dark court Briant's voice cried, "God and Christ, where is the varlet?"

I woke to the rumble of knights talking. The storm had blown away, and thin morning sunlight drifted through the narrow windows. It was a new day, and I lived. Sir Percival stood next the king's chair, and Kay and Gawain and Sir Lancelot. A herald and several clerics clustered apart, listening.

"Edmund woke to find Briant kissing his wife," said Sir Kay.

Sir Gawain laughed. "The randy fool."

"Is not Sibyl a Christian wife?" asked King Arthur, though a smile brightened his voice.

"They say she is oft confessed, sire," murmured Kay.

"Yet on the eve of Yule." The king's voice was grown severe.

It brought to me all the nights of Lancelot, and for a sudden moment I was furious at him, that he would not see it.

"And then the lad came here," said Sir Percival.

They turned and gazed at me. I got to my feet and bobbed at them, trying not to shake.

"The servant is truly slain." Sir Kay frowned at me. "Giles insists he ought not have been abroad that hour."

Oh God, Emrys. He was the second they had murdered. Almost, I hated all of them again, every knight, even the king.

"Small excuse for the death of a servant," Arthur said.

"There are witches in the boy's family, I've heard," Gawain muttered. "God's Name, how I rue Merlin's prisonment."

"As do we all." The king turned and stared at me a silent moment. "It has been very long since we spoke."

His look was the same he gave me at the chapel door, at Sir Ulfius' watch. Had that been the wizard? Had he come despite his witchment, to pay his respect for the dead? My heart froze, to think I had spoke to Merlin.

"Good sire," rumbled Sir Lancelot, "this lad . . ."

"Yes?" Arthur smiled at him.

"He would matter nothing"—Lancelot snapped his fingers—"save you made him your charge, gave a destrier for his sister, brought him here at your wish. He is under your hand, sire, you must protect him; no knight may challenge your will, nor ignore your refuge. You are the king, my lord." He stopped for breath.

"Lancelot," said Sir Kay, "what a grand speech."

"High eloquence." Gawain smiled. "Mayhap this is the son that rumor gives thee?"

"I protest for the king," Lancelot growled, "this brat . . ."

But Arthur was grown angry himself. "They have killed one servant and assaulted another. They break the peace of Yule, they ruin the peace of Camelot. I will send them away."

"Sire, this servant." Sir Kay snapped his own fingers at me. "You send away knights, yet keep him?"

Gawain agreed. "It would be high indignity, sire."

"Giles killed the boy," said Kay. "Send only him."

"But," said Percival, "this lad claimed Orsain's assault and Laramort's knowing. And I myself heard Briant threaten him."

I could hardly believe it. Not that Lancelot and Gawain argued of the king's honor, anybody might expect that. But Sir Percival took my own word, even against Camelot knights.

King Arthur drew himself up. "Five of them rode to the chapel, that damned John Baptist's eve. I send all five away, and before the days of Yule are past."

"Sire," I blurted, forgetting to be afraid, "Sir Almant has done nothing, sire."

Arthur swung at me. "Nor will I keep this lad."

"I will send him back to Greenfarm," said Kay.

"No." Arthur shook his head. "Away from Camelot."

"Winchester, sire?"

The king waved a vague hand. "Away."

My breath caught in my throat. Last night I had known I must leave. Now, in the light of day, I could not bear the thought.

Percival looked at me. "Some minstrel might take him."

"I will have their oath," the king said. "All five must swear his constant safety." He turned toward the door.

The knights followed him out, all save Percival. He looked at me again. "One thing I tell you, boy." He pulled grimly at his mustache. "Never question a king's order. Not ever."

Scores of minstrels stopped at Camelot for Yule, yet Sir Kay had no easy time finding somebody to take me. The king's anger was like a curse, that made each band protest and point to another. At last, furious, he summoned one small group.

"You are Gauls," he muttered, "foreigners that travel Britain with the king's leave. Would you have slow prison or quick banishment?"

"Ah, sir," they said, "of course we will take the lad."

They were three, bearded and long-haired in the fashion of Burgundy. Jubal the leader piped and sang with a deep voice. The youngest had a sweet high tone, and together they made a pretty sound. The lad also thumped the drum, and a thin old man named Eudes bowed the rebec.

They slept in bare chambers in the gate tower, above the guardroom, and there Sir Kay sent me until they left. Narrow slits in the thick walls looked over both the drawbridge and the great court, and when I opened that wood shutter I could see the place Emrys had died. For a moment I imagined his blood still stained the flagstones, but it was only a trick of shadows.

"We're to Winchester," Jubal said, "and then east to town and castle." He grinned at me through his curly beard. "London by Candlemas, lad. The king has set you free."

But freedom felt the bleakest thing imaginable. I had no idea how I would live. Outside Camelot I had no skill save farming, and no other place save Greenfarm would give me even a single strip within their furlongs. Nor would I believe men might live on other men's gifts, as the minstrels claimed they did.

Already I regretted not using my knife. I could have killed Orsain in his drunkenness, stabbed Briant as he kissed my lady. I could have caught Giles from behind in the church, and slashed Laramort's white face. Some knight would have killed me, but at least I would have died at Camelot, been buried beside Lark at Ryford Church. Now, even God Himself did not know where I would die.

"Well," said Jubal, "if you travel with minstrels, lad, you must earn your way." He gave me a little hand-drum, and took up a reed pipe and blew a lively tune. Old Eudes sang to his notes in a thin reedy voice, and bobbed his head in time. I followed the rhythm well enough, but could not understand the words.

" 'Tis the *langue d'oc*." Eudes gave a gap-toothed grin. "The singer says, 'I must have you, pretty lady, lest I die of your steep bosom, your round waist, your shaded field of love.' " I thought of Sibyl, and he laughed at my pained look. " 'Tis clear, boy, you have the heart for a minstrel."

I stayed with them, away from the rest of the castle, until Epiphany. I learned the drum and a half-dozen songs. But never did so few days flee so quick, and very soon one rainy morning we heard Prime in the castle church, and a priest shrived us for the road.

Sir Kay had given Jubal a tired old hackney, and I would sit Eudes' pack mule. As we mounted beneath the dripping stable eaves, I glanced back to Camelot's keep. Under the steady rain the shutters of the queen's solar were fast shut, nor could I imagine Sarah watched from the oriel at Ladies. Yet Sir Kay himself stood under the shelter of the Hall doorway, his arms folded, as if to be certain I left.

We rattled out through the gate, the drawbridge boomed under us, we turned up the muddy way toward Thomas'. It was but six months since that foggy Lammas, yet it felt a lifetime. The house at Greenfarm looked suddenly old, its thatch rotting and its walls leaning with age. Puddles filled the yard where rain fell endlessly. I nudged my animal to a stop. My father came out into the weather but the rest watched from under the shaggy eaves, and I could hardly recognize their sallow faces. He took my hand like a stranger and when I said I went away he gaped with fright.

"Away? Where?"

"With minstrels, Father. Rebecca's knights would kill me."

His eyes went wide. "Kill you?" He gripped my arm. "Oh, Micah, what have you done? God and Mary protect you, my son."

   I had got a new cloak at Yule, and a traveler's spoon of horn. Without a thought I gave him the spoon, and when he took it in both hands
to show my mother, I mounted and rode off, afraid I would weep in front
of him. I looked back, just before the road turned. He stood in the middle of the muddy way. The rain fell on his bare head. He did not wave.

Six

The rain fell in Ryford market. Villagers I had known all my life stared and did not recognize me, riding among minstrels. I had rarely been past the village mill but we did not even slow at its brimming pool. Beyond lay the ford, and a thin wood and a wasteland, and then we were among the fields of another manor. Even the puddles in the road looked strange now.

Soon enough we reached a crossroads. Jubal pointed onward. "London," he said, but I only wanted to turn for home.

The rain fell cold and steady. We rode the edges of the way out of the clinging mud, past wide bare fields and winter meadows and black forests. We stopped at midday at a priory, at a city on a steep hill they called Astolat, where even the castle on its ridge looked strange to my eye, after river-circled Camelot. Then there were more fields and villages and forests and, as the day drew in, a market town and the gray roofs of an abbey. But Jubal kept on until, with the bells of Compline ringing all around us, we clattered over a wooden bridge into a newer, larger city. The streets were laid straight and orderly and water ran in the middle of many, and the air smelled half of cooking, half of latrines. The minstrels knew a wealthy merchant's house, where we sang and played for our bowls of stew, and slept on bug-ridden pallets up under the sloping roof.

I woke, stiff from the long ride. I could not imagine where I was, and peered around shuddering with fright till old Eudes coughed and I remembered. The rain had stopped. Out in the streets a large high roof stood beyond the city houses, and though it was not the Sabbath we walked down to Salisbury's new cathedral.

Masons hammered their stone in the muddy close, and carpenters sawed and smiths worked at roaring forges. The church rose high and pale above us, tall windows, leaning arches, slender decorated spires, all very unlike massive Camelot. A wall of saplings and thatch closed the unfinished western end, but Jubal discovered a side door. Voices rattled on the stone inside, and the rasp of saws and the creak of ropes. Stone pillars thick as trees stood in rows, and their branches climbed up through the cool light to knit together high over our heads, among ranks of glass windows in colors I had never seen before. Far away east in the sunlit choir, priests began to chant, their voices like bells against the stone.

Jubal grinned at me. "God's work, young Micah."

I shook my head, stunned. Here was a space higher and more grand than even Camelot's Hall. If King Arthur had more castles than Camelot, surely God had more cathedrals than any king. God was King of all the world, but I had not wanted to believe He might be so huge and overwhelming. My mind swam as I stared up at the high gray roof. My heart beat at this sign of His power, and of the menace of His divine wrath.

Yet at that moment a workman called out, high overhead. Another answered. And suddenly I knew it was not God who built this vast and echoing space, but only men. It had been the king that gave the horse to Greenfarm, while God sent so bitter a winter we could not keep him. It had been the king who banished Lark's murderous knights, while God Himself failed even to give me sanctuary. I looked up again at the massive space and saw the workmen there, fitting glass, carving stones. I would worry of God no longer.

The rain began again as we rode up from the river valley. Water dripped from the bare trees and stood in winter fields, and the air smelled dark and cold. The way to Winchester ran straight through a darkening forest, and was old as the Romans, Jubal said.

At midday the storm began to ease. The forest retreated beyond tattered fields and the road dropped into a valley where clustered farmsteads made a little hamlet. Ahead of us a line of friars plodded down the slope, Dominicans by the black robes they hoisted above muddy sandaled feet. Jubal greeted them as we passed, but no voice answered from the gloom beneath their hoods. Friars oft shunned the luxury of baths and I could smell these very well. I knew I had reeked, myself, till Camelot made me a weekly bather, but their stench was not the same. The smell of hard labor was very different from the stink of anxious prayer.

A single friar waited up ahead, leaning against a farmyard wall, and when I came up he put back his black cowl. His hand made a cross in the air. "My son, whither go you?"

"Winchester, father."

"I would beg a ride, my son."

I glanced over my shoulder at the approaching line. "All of you? On the rump of this old mule?"

He shook his head. "Only me, my son." He was not so old as I had first thought. Thirty winters, mayhap. Stubble darkened his chin and his shaved tonsure, and drink had brightened the veins in his cheeks. A wandering hedge-friar, I thought.

Jubal stopped at the ford and looked back. "What is it?"

"He wants a ride."

"Bring him, then."

My animal sidestepped under his weight. "Winchester," he said, and I smelled last night's ale. "You ride from Camelot."

"Yes, father." I still wore Arthur's blue livery.

"The king comes to Winchester Candlemas, but you'll miss him."

I urged my mount through the shallow stream. "We will be in London. Or even Paris, Jubal says."

"Ah, fair France." He muttered something I did not catch. "What's your name, lad?"

"Micah. My father's Warren. From Greenfarm, of Camelot."

"Micah. Now, when you cross the sea, that would be Michel. And Greenfarm, well. Ver . . . Verdeur." He poked me sharply in the ribs. "Michel de Verdeur. Too fine a name for a minstrel. A knight's name, if ever I've heard one."

"Michel de Verdeur," I murmured.

"Sir Michel de Verdeur. The green knight." He laughed and ale blew around me like fog. "Well, lad, truly you are green."

The mule shook its long ears and slowed, climbing the grade. I did not understand what he meant. Though it felt a better name than Raven, I was not green. Nor was I a knight, would never be a knight, only wanted to kill knights. Once again cold hatred gripped my gut, so hard I could barely breathe. I raised my face to the thick sky. The rain fell, cold as ever. The friar's head bumped against my back.

"There is a tale at Camelot," I said aloud, "of a green knight." I felt him wake. "He rode into King Arthur's Hall, all in green armor. Straight into the Hall and challenged any knight there to cut off his head—but after a year he must bow his own neck to the green knight's sword. Nobody would accept it, till at last Sir Gawain faced him." It was not hard to imagine Gawain the bravest at Camelot, before Sir Lancelot arrived.

The friar chuckled behind me. "As it happened, Gawain's highest challenge was the knight's wife. The trial is never what you expect, lad." He poked me in the ribs again. "Could you have done it, green lad? Could you have resisted when she came to you, unbodiced, hot-breathed, her husband gone a-hunting?"

I could not answer. I had resisted nothing. But after a little I said to him, "The story can't be true. The knight rode straight into the Hall, but at Camelot that chamber is up high stairs." Somehow the notion eased my mind.

We had reached the eaves of another wood. A cold wind pushed the rain into my face. I shivered and reached to pull up my hood, but the monk caught it as he leaned against me.

"The Hall at Winchester, lad, stands at ground level. I was there. I saw it." His voice had gone cold as the rain. "Gawain hewed off the green knight's head. But the man barely staggered. He felt about like a blind man, picked up his skull, and mounted and rode away." He nudged me again. "Could you do that? Lose your head, and still live? Could you, Michel de Verdeur?"

Evening was fallen when we came to Winchester. At first I could not believe the wall, high as Camelot's nearly, that circled the whole city from the height where the castle stood, down to the meadows beside the river. The world was full of wonders.

We drew up before the western gate, and the friar slid off my mule. "Bless you for the ride, lad." He eased his back. "I'll sing Vespers at the cathedral, and find a place at the priory." He looked up at me. "It's in the city, next the church. They'd take you, if need be."

"Jubal says the castle will board us, for news of Camelot."

"Mayhap." He made a cross in the dim air. "Go you well, Michel de Verdeur. How happily that name suits you, lad." He drew his hood up, and trudged away to the city gate.

The royal castle stood outside the city, though built against its wall. We turned our animals toward its towered gate and clattered under the gloomy arch. In the narrow graveled court the castle Hall stood just opposite, a thick stone building with a high roof, its broad door one step above the court, and large enough for horse and knight. Almost, I believed my friar had seen it, the green knight and Gawain. I wondered I had not asked his name.

After our long wet day the smelly warmth of the stables was very welcome. A dozen palfreys stood in the stalls, and three battle-horses. Grooms and muckers chatted among themselves, and there sat Almant's squire with them. A spark of worry flared in my empty gut.

The castle's kitchen was almost hot. At one fireplace cooks bent over a spitted lamb, and half a dozen men sat the other, drinking. I never expected knights in a kitchen, but Almant's hair shone red in the firelight and there was Briant's dark head, and dull Giles. I clutched my knife under my cloak, while Jubal went and spoke to the cooks.

Briant stood. He put down his cup deliberately and took three steps, each quicker than the last. His sword glittered in the firelight. "By God," he cried out, "it was you, under her bed!" I dodged behind a trestle, and his blade boomed on its top and cleft a loaf there.

"Sir," cried Jubal, "the lad is under the king's hand."

I blinked and shook my head. I had dodged his attack without a thought; I had seen his swing before he made it. Briant circled the table after me. The other knights were standing, and Almant called out, "The king, you fool. You have sworn to Arthur."

I drew my dagger and thrust and missed. It was useless against a sword and now Giles strode toward us, drawing his own blade. They would have me on both sides. I bolted between them to the door just as Almant's squire opened it. "Sir," he called, "the minstrels . . ."

"Stop him," Briant shouted.

My shoulder thrust him easily aside.

Rain spat in my face as I sprinted across the noisy gravel, praying I would not slip and fall. Beyond the castle gate only a few houses stood outside the city wall, amid windblown woods and the winter night. And, God help me, the city gate was closed.

I almost cried out, till I saw the man-sized wicket open still. Knights bellowed after me. The guard shouted as I dashed in. The wide street sloped quickly down toward the river, but after a dozen steps I dodged aside into a dim narrow lane that stank of offal, that twisted down into a wider street where merchants gaped as I fled past, into another narrow way and another street, and through a narrow gate where I burst out on a broad level square.

It was the cathedral close. The massive gable of an old church stood dim in the evening gloom. Vespers murmured inside. Knights' curses rang behind me. A wall ran south from the church, its blank face pierced by small high windows, that must be the priory. I sprinted to its arched porch. The heavy door boomed shut behind me. A monk walking the lamplit corridor turned.

"Knights, father." I gasped for breath. "They'd kill me."

He eyed my cloak, deliberately. "You are from Camelot?"

"The king swore them my safety but they will not."

" 'Trust not princes.' " He spoke slowly, and still he peered at me. "Did you insult them, steal from them?"

"No, father, I swear it. Please, will you protect me?"

"You ask for sanctuary?" He paused again. My heart stopped, remembering Camelot. "Then I give it. But only in this priory."

The door boomed open, and Briant's voice barked, "Varlet, here you are." The lamp on the wall flickered. I cringed away toward the shadows as Giles puffed in behind him.

The monk turned to them. "What want you, good knights?"

"That damned churl." Briant thrust his blade and I made ready to flee, afraid there was no way out. "He is ours."

"He has been granted God's sanctuary," said the monk.

Briant stopped in mid-curse. In the long silence I let out my breath and stood erect again, and even took a step back toward them. Briant could not believe it either. "Sanctuary?" He growled and shook his head. "I am the king's knight."

"Sanctuary," the monk repeated.

"You cannot keep him always. We'll have him when he goes."

"Not in this priory, sirs."

"Thy blood, varlet." Briant pointed his blade at me, and muttered an oath under his breath, before the two of them turned and went out the door again.

"Thank you, father." My voice shook.

" 'Even as ye shelter the least of these,' " he murmured.

"I met a Blackfriar on the road, father, he said he would come here after Vespers."

"A Blackfriar?" He scowled and pursed his lips. "Not here. The Dominican house is next to the river." He must have seen me waver. "But you will want a bed. With supper, it's a silver penny."

"Father, I have no money. I have run here, you have seen the knights . . ." I opened my cloak to show I had no purse.

He looked at me, doubtful. "Well, lad, we do not deny sanctuary."

"Thank you, father. Thank you again."

He sent me up a narrow stair to a long dim chamber roofed by high trusses. Tallow candles burned at intervals, old rushes covered the floor, and screens separated each narrow cot. I could not understand it, that God might thrust me out of Camelot yet shelter me in Winchester. Still, I gave a prayer of thanks and took an empty place near the stairs. I lay down, still hardly able to breathe, and closed my eyes and felt myself falling, helpless as a leaf before a winter storm. I sat up quickly. Yesterday I had lost castle and family. Tonight I had lost the minstrels. Only my Blackfriar gave me hope, and I must find him tomorrow.

A crowd of monks murmured past me, come from Vespers. A little bell announced the evening meal. I followed them to a brighter space where, as we worked at our bowls, a brother read Scripture. The meal was simple but almost more than I could eat. Afterward, comforted by the food, I slept at once and did not wake at all, till the monks robed for Lauds.

A single candle stub lit the chamber. My breath smoked in the cold as I followed them down a narrow stair. In the cloister a thin snow dusted the frozen shrubs, but a bright sky overhead promised a fair day. In the high whispering cathedral they turned and filed into the choir, but I crossed the chill nave and went out a narrow door.

A level path ran out to a small cobbled square, and the same wide street that came down from the western gate. I could not see any knights, though half a dozen city men clustered at a smoking fire and hugged their arms against the cold.

"Blackfriars?" I asked.

They stared at my cloak. "Blackfriars," one of them mumbled. "By Eastgate, sir." I had turned away before it struck me. "Sir," he said, and had touched his forelock to Camelot's livery. Sir. I walked down the broad way, careful of thawing puddles, almost smiling.

The first farmers' carts rumbled in through the eastern gate. Nearby, a plain low building with a cross at one gable stood inside a wattle fence. I followed my nose to the refectory. The smell of food roused my stomach. They read scripture there, too. Hooded faces glanced up from their bowls. My friar was not among them.

Farmers' wains still trundled past Blackfriars and into the city. I stood at the edge of the way, trying to think. He was a Dominican and this was their house. There must be a dozen holy houses in Winchester. He might be at any of them, yet he had said the cathedral priory, sent me to Benedictines. But he was a Blackfriar.

A thick-wheeled cart creaked past. If this were the London road, I might wait here for the minstrels. If they left today. If Briant and Giles did not follow them. My head swam with fright and hunger. Free, Jubal had said. I was free, and absolutely lost.

In the press of carts a man passed, leading a burdened mule. He was dressed in black, and his dark curly beard made him look older than his two dozen years. A small yellow patch flashed on one sleeve, yet not till a walking farmer spat in the road did I see he was a Jew.

He paid no notice to the insult nor the scowls of others, though he did glance at my cloak. I had seen Jews enough at Camelot, for even King Arthur borrowed their coin and paid their usury. They had coin. I did not. At Greenfarm my father might ask of Thomas the reeve, or some other rich farmer. But here, in this city, nobody knew me. I was lost, and there were only Jews to ask, despite their mortal sins.

I took a breath and pushed into the crowd. He was easy enough to follow. I trailed behind, staying close to the houses, nervous of my knights. He went up almost to the western gate, before he turned aside into a narrow muddy street that smelled of bakers and foreign spices. He rapped on the arched door of the only house built of stone, and the gate opened and closed behind him. I paced down the street and back. I stared up at his casements, wondering at my nervousness. They were only Jews. My stomach moved with hunger. I knocked at the door.

A voice spoke through the wooden bars. "What is it, sir?"

"I have come to borrow."

The door opened slightly and he peered out at me. "You followed me from Blackfriars."

"I want to borrow."

An old man appeared beside him. White hair and white beard circled his wrinkled face, and his dark eyes glittered like an owl's. "Good sir, what do you need to buy?"

"Bread."

"The castle will feed you, sir, go back to the high street and turn right."

"I must borrow." Their slowness annoyed me. "Let me in."

The old man tugged his beard. "You wear the king's cloak."

"God's Name," I said, pushing against the door, "let me in. I will tell you of it."

After a moment he opened the door and peered about. "There is no one else?"

"No."

"Then, come in, sir."

The door closed heavily behind me. The place smelled of wool and straw. A servant was unloading the mule.

"You wear the king's cloak," the old man repeated.

"I have come from Camelot."

Though Arthur's cloak had opened their door, for a moment I did not want to explain it all. But my stomach growled, and I began with Briant at the priory. The old man shook his head. I started again, with my sister's rape and Emrys' death. When I was finished I drew a breath, and swallowed again my hatred of knights.

They listened patiently, though they glanced at each other, doubtful, when I finished. "A strange story," said the old man.

"It is true." I had not thought it strange at all.

"Of course." He led me up a stone stair into a small room with a desk and several stools, and a window that looked out to a hidden garden. "Sit down, sir. I would offer you bread myself, did not the bishop forbid you eating in my house."

"I will pay you."

"But you have no coin to pay with."

"You will lend me something."

He laughed as he leaned to finger my cloak. "Sell this."

"I cannot, it's winter." I did not want to part with Arthur's livery.
"Your knights will ask for a lad in the king's colors." He touched it
again. "Fine work, almost new."

I drew a breath. "I need another, just as good. And a month's coin."

"A month?" He rolled his eyes. "Thirty days. Two pennies a day,
three if you travel. Do you know how much that is?"

I shook my head. I knew nothing of sums. "Trade me the cloak," I
said. "Lend me the rest."

"Eight shillings." The old man stared at me. "And where will you
be when I need to collect?"

"Normandy." I said it without thinking, knowing only that the friar
had spoke of it, and I could not stay in Britain.

"And Normandy might be no bigger than Winchester."

He turned to gaze a long moment out his window. "Come," he said
at last, and led me to a storeroom filled with bolts of woolen cloth,
locked chests, and on the wall a dozen cloaks that were blue and maroon,
and one of dull green I touched in spite of myself.

"Flemish, that one." He pulled off my king's cloak. The green one
was a little large, but fit well enough. The coarse wool weighed comfortably on my shoulders. It smelled of horses.

"Your cloak was ten shillings perhaps. This one is six, at least. Four
left, but you need eight." He pointed at my knife. "That is useless, save
for cutting loaves."

"I must have my dagger." But when he held out his hand I gave it to
him anyway.

He drew the blade and weighed its balance. "Do you know what
happens to Jews who buy stolen things?"

"It is mine," I said. "It was my grandfather's. If you're afraid, you
could sell it in Normandy."

"When I come to collect my loan. What a clever lad you are." He
opened one of the chests and drew out a dagger long as my forearm, that
made my grandfather's blade very small. "This is five. Fourteen for your
cloak and blade, eleven for mine. Three, and I will lend you five, that's
your eight." I stared at him, only half believing his sums did not cheat
me. "For that you will give a penny a month. Another shilling by next
Epiphany, when you will pay six to my kin in Normandy."

"Thank you." I had put myself in his hands, and was grateful in spite
of myself.

"Now." His eyes glittered with energy. "My brother Simon lives in
Southampton, my son Aaron goes to him today. He must walk quickly,

to be there before sunset. No need to go with him." He touched the yellow patch on his sleeve. "But keep him in sight so you know Simon's house." He paused for breath. "Simon owns three ships, but they never sail in winter." He stopped and ran his fingers through his white beard. "I do not understand why I do this, young sir."

No more than he, did I understand why the old man helped me. As a servant gave me bread and cheese for the road, almost I felt annoyed that I took his help, that I must now be grateful to Jews. The old man had found two purses, one for my waist that held two dozen pennies, one that hung down my back for the rest of my little wealth. He gave me the staff no traveler went without. "All this is another shilling. Six. Seven, next Epiphany."

"Thank you," I said again.

The old man bowed. "I am Abram ben Aaron."

"I am Michel," I said at once, "Michel de Verdeur."

Aaron hugged his father, and set off with the loaded animal. I followed him out into the crowded streets. Nobody noticed me. I felt invisible without Arthur's cloak. Just beyond the city gate and beneath a winter-bare oak, a red-haired knight sat his palfrey. I prayed Sir Almant would not know me in my strange cloak. I put a hand to the pommel of my new dagger, kept my eyes on the road, and was past and breathing again when he called my name. I did not turn. He called again and I heard him trot his animal after me. I dodged aside and drew my dagger; if he pulled his sword I would hamstring his horse, and blood him as he dismounted.

He drew up and stared at my blade. "Do you threaten me?"

"No more than you threaten me, sir."

"And where go you, so busily?"

"Away from honorable knights," I said, unthinking. "God protect me from honorable knights."

"Varlet," he growled, "do not profane thy betters."

"He who breaks his king's oath is not my better." My boldness amazed him, and myself. "Will Sir Giles kill the minstrels if I am not with them? Do you send word to Sir Briant, how he ought follow me?" I could not stop. "And you, sir, how will you refute your oath to the king?"

"Damn you," he said, "I had nothing to do with this."

"And when it happens you do nothing."

His hand went to his sword then. I lifted my own blade and took a step toward him. We stared at each other. "I have no argument with you," he said at last.

I stepped back and sheathed my blade. His squire rode up, leading his battle-horse. Almant nudged his palfrey out into the road. "Do you cross the sea, Sir Almant?" I expected no answer.

"Soon as we find passage. Rouen, Paris, Troyes."

I watched them canter down the muddy road. A cold wind sprang up and dark clouds blew across the sky. The Jew had vanished beyond the next hill and I must follow, south toward the sea, mayhap even across it. Normandy, my friar had said, or France. I felt like a leaf blown by a storm, without a notion how I would ever stop.

A cool salt smell filled the air at Southampton. Aaron paced the way, just at the first houses, grumbling at my slowness. The city was new and not so large as Winchester, bounded by an earthen wall. We walked down its wide street the whole way until, just before the water's edge, Aaron turned aside into another lane and to a stone house twice the size of old Abram's.

"I must speak to your uncle," I said.

"If he is here." Aaron led his animal inside. I paced the muddy way. The air was full of shouts and the creaks of wagons and the cries of white seabirds overhead. At the end of the street the broad water was crowded with dark ships, their tall poles rocking in the wind.

Aaron came out, frowning. "He's on the quay, loading a ship. We never sail in winter."

I kept well back from the wooden edge of the dock, from the drop and the splashing water. A gang of men were loading wool sacks, and it needed half a dozen to grapple the heavy bags, slide them down the bowing plank, settle them in the rocking ship. A small dark man shouted directions, his voice blaring above the harbor noise, but when Aaron spoke he stopped and squinted at me.

"My brother seeks your passage." Simon had little of Abram's white hair. " 'Tis halcyon days, but how did he know to send you?"

I shook my head. "How much coin?"

"Five shillings." He looked at me. "For Abram, three."

I took out my purse. The bright metal discs were small and hard to handle, and I dropped several as he counted them. I could not believe such little things were a day's work, a ship's passage.

"Thirty-six," he said, the coins rattling in his hand. "The tide runs; we sail in half an hour." He pointed back into the city. "You'd best buy food, but don't eat now, take an empty stomach to sea." He turned to shout at the men again.

I bought a loaf and a little skin of ale. When I came back several ships already moved on the wide river, long oars over their sides, sails fluttering in the wind. On Simon's boat the workers stretched oxhides over the wool sacks. A lean man, sunburnt as a farmer, stood talking to the little Jew. He squinted at me and said, "Hurry, lad, get on board, the tide runs."

There was nothing but a sloping plank over the surging water. I stopped, and felt their eyes on me, and stumbled across. The boat tilted and moved so I could barely keep my feet on the rounded sacks. "There," he cried, "sit there in the stern." But I did not know the word, and he had to show me.

The ship was pointed at both ends, and he stood at the very back and grasped a long light pole. He called out, and the men took up oars and began to row. The quay beside us slipped away. The water moved, the ship rolled and shuddered, and suddenly there was a wind. The master called again, and the crew seized ropes and hauled up a level spar that raised a broad sail. The cloth snapped in the wind, and the ship trembled like a tree in a storm.

"Where do we go?" I asked. I could not look at the water heaving and unsteady all around.

"You don't know?" He laughed. "Ouistreham and Caen, if this wind holds." He gazed at the clouding sky. "Else Honfleur. Ever been at sea, lad?"

"No."

"You'll be sick. Use the lee bulwark, the side away from the wind. Don't get any on the damn wool; the Jew'll have your ass." He laughed again. "More likely your foreskin."

I crawled awkwardly across the bags.

"Winter's too rough, usually, 'tis the calm between storms today. You're a lucky young lad."

The ship rolled and pitched under us. He went on talking, and the land drew away on each side and the water broadened. I waited to be sick, but nothing happened. The sea rose and the boat climbed and shook. The sea fell and the boat slipped and wallowed. The salt spray blew into our faces. The master sat behind me, guiding his pole. The sailors crouched together at the foot of the mast, chattering and laughing, and one even played a panpipe. I could not believe anybody could be so easy, on the face of that constant watery tumble.

The sky grew darker all the rest of the day, though just at the end sunlight flared under the clouds, across the long water. I roused from a half-sick doze. We had sailed hours down a widening bay, and now we stood far out on an empty sea. There was no land right or left, and only a faint line behind us, gloomy in the failing light. The wind strengthened. The sea heaved and crested. I remembered I had not been shrived since Camelot, and now there was only water, tossing boiling crashing water beneath me, as far as I might fall.

Seven

Darkness sank heavily all about us. The ship lifted and rolled and shuddered, frail as a bubble on the heaving water. Ropes creaked and sang in the wind. The sail flapped overhead in the black night. I gripped the wet rail and my stomach lurched and I might have spewed a dozen times, and all that kept it down was my stark terror of that bleak and staggering emptiness.

I could not believe how that water always moved. I had climbed windblown trees and ridden a horse, but always on the steady earth. This ocean washed everything away. Every prop was fallen. Each new wave loomed high enough to fill the ship, beyond every crest lurked a swallowing void to draw us down to death, and all that saved us was a frail chip of wood and rope and sail.

The sailors lit a fire in an iron pot and cooked their meal. The smell of it, fitful on the rushing wind, almost made me sick. The master's lantern glinted the whole long night, though it lit only the man himself and a small bowl set before him. There was nothing else in all that hollow blackness save the pressing wind, the rolling ship, the flying salt.

Gray morning came, eventually. I could see nothing but water tossed and blown, yet for that bleak dawn I breathed a thankful prayer. A cold rain began to fall. The sailors put up a skin tent that half protected us. The day went on, the sea heaved and shifted, the rain became sleet that iced the ropes and gathered in the hollows of the wool bags. I ate half my loaf and shared my ale. Two days, I thought, no sun nor star, nor road nor anyone to ask the way. I stared ahead till my eyes ached, hoping to see hills and trees beyond the tilting waves and the slanting storm. Nothing appeared. Night came again, early.

My fright had so gone to numbness that at last I began to wonder what I might do in Normandy. I could not live long on five shillings. I might be a server at table, or a merchant's helper, or find a farmer who needed help with first plowing.

I woke, surprised I slept. The ship moved harshly, blown by a fresh cold wind. The sky shone with a clear dawn. Far ahead lay a pale line, half there and half vanished.

"Is that Normandy?" I said, hoarse from silence.

The master laughed. "Aye, so it is."

After an hour we could make out low trees atop pale cliffs, and by midday reached the mouth of a small river. A little town stood behind a curve of sand, its cluster of streets facing a narrow harbor that made me wonder where I had come. For the houses did not look like British houses, and even the bells that rang across the water were not British bells.

The wind still tugged and blustered, but the sailors let down the sail and thrust their long oars over the sides again. The tide ran inland, the master said, and all the rest of that day they rowed upriver, up to the yellow city of Caen.

Ships of every size lined the river, most covered against the winter. The shipmaster found a vacant spot along the quay, and as the sailors tied our boat he scrambled onto it.

"Come, lad, Ezra will be waiting."

I climbed up and nearly fell, for briefly the earth of Normandy moved as wildly as the ocean. A hard wind blustered along the quay, and knifed through the gate tower of the bridge. A stout church stood facing a market square, and high beyond the opposite houses there loomed the towered wall of a broad castle. The bridge, the church, the castle, even the market, all were of yellow stone. I thought all this masonry must be the privilege of kings, for Caen was old William Norman's city, the master said. He had built the castle, and with his wife put up two great abbeys whose church spires even now stood high above the city roofs.

I stopped a moment, staggering weary. The air smelled of dust. Three merchants passed, their heads bowed against the wind. Away in the west the sun dimmed beyond blowing clouds, and gloom filled the city. A cluster of old women blew toward us like dry leaves that swirled and clattered under the church porch, as the bells rang Vespers. The master took my arm and led me across the empty market. A curving way led around old William's castle, past prosperous houses to a second square where dust blew thick as fog. In a dark narrow lane beyond, men worked by the light of flaring torches, though it was Sunday. They wore black, most of them, and dark beards. We had come among the Jews of Caen.

On our way the master had said, "Ezra might give you a room, lad, but don't stay long." He shook his head. "I sail for them, they're fair enough to me but there's hard feelings in Caen. They're rich and every year their usury gets worse." He scowled. "And the Book does say they murdered Christ."

The master rapped at an iron-bound door. A servant led us through a walled yard to a high storeroom where a lamp flickered and jumped, and a hugely heavy man warmed his thick hands before a little brazier. I had never seen anybody so massive and my first thought was, How does he pass through his own doorways? Dark eyes glinted deep in the folds of his thick face. His black beard showed white at the corners of his mouth. He turned, ponderously, and raised one eyebrow at me.

"Master Simon said bring him." The shipmaster drew a leather packet from his cloak. "There's a letter, Master Ezra."

"It was a great risk to sail." Ezra's voice surprised me, high and soft as a boy's. "Simon ought not have sent you for another month."

He settled into a chair beside a heavy table. Rings glittered in the flesh of his thick fingers as he opened the packet and peered at each of the sheets. He unfolded the smallest letter. "From Abram of Winchester." He furrowed his brow. "My cousin writes the king's assurance has failed you. How can that be?"

I had a moment of hesitation before I began my story again. I told of Rebecca's death, of Camelot and Emrys, of Winchester and Abram and his son. The master gaped, but Ezra had closed his eyes.

"The man set upon by his defenders; the exile hopeless in his own land. An occasion familiar enough in Caen." He lifted the written sheet wearily. "My cousin directs me to receive your debt. He asks that I give you lodging." His thick face showed no emotion. "You have made a deep impression on Abram."

We ate the evening meal with Ezra's family. He said a prayer over the bread, and for the wine as well. His piety surprised me. Though he was rich they ate few courses, boiled beef and no cheese. There was a son Harry's age, who rattled on about the price of wool and salt and cumin. At the foot of the table sat two daughters, the older dark and very pretty. She frowned at me before she dropped her gaze, and I felt as foreign to her as Jews and Normans were to me. But her mother glared at me the whole meal, as if I were a suitor she did not favor.

I had expected to sleep with servants, but Ezra's man showed me a separate room, beneath the steep roof, and a bed to share with the mas-

ter. The shutter at the window rattled in the wind. I pulled off my boots
and lay under the quilt, and when I closed my eyes the house moved
under me like the sea.

I slept like a dead man, until a shout in the morning street roused me.
Dawn glinted around the shutter. The shipmaster was dressing, and he
went out without a word.

I had been swept away farther than I could ever have imagined, from
Camelot and Britain and even Christ. Was this God's will? Did He lead
me so very far from my knights, to this bed in a house of Jews? The
notion made me weak, as if I had been a long time ill and only now
recovered. I got up stiffly, brushed my cloak and wiped my boots, and
went down the stairs. The house seemed empty, but a servant appeared
at the sound of my steps, with a small loaf and a cup of watered wine.
Ezra sat at his table in the storeroom.

"Good morning," I said.

He nodded ponderously. "Tomorrow the wool goes on to Paris." I
had regained my appetite, and my mouth was full of bread. Paris would
be even farther from my knights. "I have nothing for you here, young
sir."

"Thank you for your lodging, Master Ezra."

His son bustled in, full of news. I watched their talk while I ate. I
thanked Ezra again, and went out to the bright cold day. The Jewish
street was already busy. In the dusty market beyond farmers ranked their
loaded carts. The sun glittered above the castle wall. House gables
caught its light in the curving street where squires and pages joked together, waiting for the noble that came yawning out of one tall house.

Empty-headed, squinting in the sun, I fell in behind them. At the
broad paved market they turned up toward the castle, up a narrow way
to a postern gate. Since Camelot, I knew very well how to enter a such a
place. I climbed the few steps carefully, raised my chin, and stared at the
back of the noble's head. The footmen at the gate did not even see me.

Old William's fortress was a single broad court spread out across the
wide hilltop, ringed by high stone walls and square roofed towers. Inside, its buildings stood about almost haphazard. Off to the right store-
rooms leaned against the wall, and ranks of stables. Several rich stone
houses stood to the left, an orchard bare with winter, and beyond, an old
Hall. Straight ahead at the upper end, three hundred paces away, there
rose a broad square keep, round turrets at each corner and a high plain
tower within.

And just before us, black-robed men filed into the side door of a
small church. My heart leaped that my friar would be here, come to Nor-

mandy before me, but they were Benedictine monks. Knights of the castle, wrapped in furred cloaks, murmured their greetings to the noble I followed. Nobody looked at me. I was a stranger in Caen, nobody knew me, yet nobody stared. It had been the same in Winchester. I lifted my hand and peered at it, and saw I had not vanished; it was only that I was not used to city ways.

I walked through their murmur and past the corner of the church. Grooms opened stable doors across the court, and led out battle-horses that tossed their heads and stamped their iron shoes. A band of squires laughed and scuffled as they hurried to the church. The first chant of Prime sounded inside, but I had no want of Mass. I leaned against a sunlit buttress and closed my eyes.

The sea moved, dark waves blown by a silent wind. My breath stopped. I clutched at the cold stone, praying I would not fall.

The winter air stood all around, blue and chill. The keep rose before me, clear in the slanting light, and a paved way led straight toward it. Two bags hung at my neck, Lark's and Aaron's, blood and money; and though my heart beat, both pressed me on. I took a step and then another. The morning air was very bright. My shadow moved before me, crisp over the rounded cobbles. The tower grew steadily. I could see the courses of its stone, the arrow slits that pierced its thick walls, the wooden bridge across its dry moat. An armed porter lounged there against the rail, and I would not pass him unseen. If I sought a place at Caen Castle I must turn back, to the stables or the kitchen.

A shriek rang out, startling in the quiet morning. A boy staggered from a stone house nearby, howling in pain. He sprawled on the gravel of the court. A knight followed, swinging a leather strap, and as the boy struggled up, kicked him down again. The lad yelped as the strap hit him. Blood already spotted his shirt. The knight hit him again.

"Varlet," he blared, "you've stolen your last wine."

The strap fell again. I felt the pain on my own back. I saw Normandy was no different than Britain, that here was a servant beaten, as servants were always beaten. Hatred lay in my stomach, cold and heavy again. The boy cried out. Knights laughed under a crooked moon, Emrys screamed on Camelot's icy cobbles, I could not breathe, and sweating in the winter air I strode across the noisy gravel.

The knight glanced up at the sound. His narrow face flared red at me. "Stand away, boy."

I reached unthinking for the strap. He drew himself up, but a little taller than I, and swung it behind him. "Damn you, boy, stand away."

I crowded in. He lashed at me. I grabbed the strap with both hands and wrenched it away. His face went even redder, and for a furious moment he could not speak. The servant struggled to his feet and took a step or two away, still bent by the hurt of his back.

"What do you?" the knight screamed. "Attack me?" He gripped the dagger on his hip. "Do you know the name of this?" The blade glinted at me. " 'Tis a misericorde, boy. To kill those who have asked to die."

I dodged his sudden lunge. I had seen it, clear, before it came. The knight slashed at my face. I dodged again. He pressed forward without pause. I swung the strap at him, pulled off my cloak, slid Abram's dagger from its sheath.

He stopped dead. "Would you truly stick me? What breed of fool are you?"

I made a feint at his belly. He did not even flinch, but answered quick. I saw his slash before it ripped my sleeve. I stabbed again. He stepped away and bent into a crouch.

Thus had the knights of Camelot sparred, that I was no match for, and now this knight bent into their same posture, took the same sidling steps. His point hovered before me like a wasp. Death waited an arm's length away.

"Come, varlet," he said, "let us see the color of thy guts."

He scythed at my stomach. I saw it coming and leaped away. He had not imagined I might avoid it and left himself briefly open. I hacked at his arm. He gave a sudden hiss of pain and charged again. I danced back, seeing what he did but unable to keep away. His pushing blade caught me across the ribs.

The sudden hurt was an enormous thorn, and when I grunted he gave a small hard laugh. "I knew you were a green brat."

"What knight fights brats?" I gasped.

"What brat dare kill a knight?"

He was right. This could have no good end. I must injure him sore enough to stop him, yet not kill him.

He jabbed at me. I saw it again. I dodged his point easily and drove my own into his outstretched arm. Once more he did not cry out, though he nearly dropped his knife. I raked his chest before he could recover. His chopping slash at the corner of my shoulder came too quick for me to dodge.

Pain stopped us both, for a moment. We faced each other, blowing our breath into the morning air like steaming horses. I felt the blood running warm down my arm.

"No style," he said, "but you're quick enough."

He stabbed as he spoke. I had already dodged away. I countered and missed. Something was very different. In the blink of an eye, even before he thrust, I saw his move. I might not dodge the glinting blade, yet the knowledge eased my terror. I feinted at his head, dodged his counter, raked his dagger arm.

Footsteps sounded, striding loud across the gravel. A sword scraped from its scabbard. I dared not take my eyes off the knight I fought, even if another came to his aid. I moved my point and took a step to one side. My opponent took an answering step. I waited for the bite of that drawn sword, and the hair stood up on the back of my neck.

The blade flashed in the air between us. *"Desistete, iste furor!"* a knight's voice boomed. We turned on him, gaping. He scowled at us, tall and hard-faced in the winter sunlight.

"Jesu," cried my rival. "I've bloodied him, Amaury, 'tis my honor now."

"Honor?" Amaury snorted. "What honor is this, Ricard? Caen is a royal castle. You break the king's truce. The castellan will have your honor as his ornament."

Ricard took a step back, muttering. Sir Amaury turned his pale eyes on me. "And who are you, boy, that you fight in the king's castle, 'gainst a king's knight?"

"The servant . . ."

"And where did you learn that knifework?"

I caught my breath. "In Britain, sir. At Camelot."

The name hung in the air between us. The knights glanced at each other and Sir Amaury frowned. " 'Tis not the livery of Camelot you wear."

"I sold my cloak to a Jew, to buy my passage."

He nodded, as if he might have done it himself. "What is your name, boy?"

"Michel de Verdeur, sir." I bowed, as squires did.

"De Verdeur," he said. "I do not know it. A fine name breeds not noble blood." Amaury raised his voice to the few knights that watched from the house. "Ought I believe him? Who has seen him at Camelot?" No one had, of course. "British knights winter at home, boy. There is no one to tell us what you truly are."

"I do not lie, good sir knight."

He stared at me. I held my breath and returned his gaze unfaltering. My life wavered in the balance. I wore a good cloak and Camelot's boots, but I had attacked a knight, and that not even noble squires might dare. My knifework had kept me alive, yet if Sir Amaury believed I was but an upstart peasant he might with the smallest effort cleave my skull, or hack it from my shoulders.

Eight

S ir Amaury stared at me so long I began to shake. His fingers tightened on his pommel and the sun glittered on his blade, but when he lifted it he thrust it back into its scabbard.

"Come," he said, "you both have wounds that want dressing."

I let out my breath. The winter air shook like a ringing bell. The solid earth moved, liquid as the sea. For a minute I forgot how I came to be in this old castle, in Caen, in Normandy. I knew only I had fought a knight and had not been killed for it.

"Amaury," cried Ricard, unbelieving, "what do you?"

But the tall knight turned and strode away across the gravel. Ricard stared and muttered, before he followed. I bent and took up my cloak and went with them, careful to walk no more than a step behind. The beaten lad stared after us, ignored.

Sir Amaury led us into the stone house where a dozen bright shields hung the whitewashed walls. Cots for knights stood to one end, and pallets for squires at the other, and a smoking hearth at the center that offered small warmth to the long chamber.

A stocky man limped toward us, carrying rags and a salve pot. "Here's the leech," Amaury said.

Three or four knights had seen the fight from the door, that now watched us pull off our bloodied tunics and murmured approval of our wounds. I looked at them as boldly as I might, and saw no hatred in their eyes, even some small admiration. I knew I had stepped, or fallen, into another world. I was no longer what I had been, but what they believed of me.

"He cut you well, Ricard," said one of them.

"But look," Ricard growled, "he has no scars at all."

Sir Amaury smiled grimly. "Shall I tell the castellan some green boy cut you so easily?"

"Jesu, no," he muttered, and clenched his jaw against the pain as the physician began to treat his cuts.

In truth I had a few small scars, of practice at Camelot, though not so many as Ricard. Remembering how I got them made me weak again. "Sir Amaury, I owe you my life." My voice quavered.

"I saved my knight, boy. Ricard would have fought till you ruined him."

"Jesu, Amaury," said Ricard.

"And I kept the king's truce."

"Who would think it, a half-grown lad?" said another.

"Damn you, Pierre," Ricard grumbled, "he has no style."

" 'Tis but poor training." Sir Pierre had a warm grin in a broad clean-shaven face, and dark shaggy curls.

"Ah, sir," I said, "my friar did not teach me."

"You've not been taught to fight?" said Amaury. "But you said you were at Camelot."

"I watched the knights, sir, we boys fought among ourselves. The king. . . ." As I began to prattle my fright increased. "King Arthur sent me to . . . to Winchester, sir. But my friar bade me sail, a ship was waiting to Normandy, I took it as a sign." I hung my head, praying the king's name might distract him. "Did I err, sir, to obey a holy man? And the servant?" I could not cease my babble. "Is not knighthood's oath to save the weak, help the poor?"

"None but a varlet defends a varlet," Ricard muttered.

Sir Amaury's voice had gone hard. "The oath of knights says nothing of servants. Do you imagine yourself a knight, boy?"

"Oh no, good sir." The words of priests came to me. "Did not Our Lord say of the Samaritan, 'Who is not thy brother?' "

"No churl is my brother," Ricard cried.

Sir Amaury turned away, his mouth grim, a bright hardness in his pale eyes. It was over. I had said too much. Other knights came that had been to Mass, stared at me and murmured among themselves. The physician wiped my cuts. His salve smelled of resin and stung like fire, and I held my breath and blinked my tears as he bound my throbbing wounds.

I drew on my tunic and walked to Sir Amaury. I knelt on the stone floor, and lifted my clasped hands. It was the gesture of a vassal. "I owe my life, sir." He stared down at me. "I would be your man, Sir Amaury.

Your servant, sir." I thought he would refuse immediately, yet his silence rang in my ears.

"Amaury." It was Sir Pierre. "He acted as the church taught him. Ought we ignore such faith?"

Sir Amaury turned, grim-faced. "Do you know this boy's family? Do you even know his name? What is it again?"

"Michel de Verdeur, good sir."

"Do you deny his skill?" said Pierre.

"King Arthur sent you to Winchester," Amaury said. "Yet by coming to Caen you denied his liege."

Still kneeling, I did not let my glance waver. "In my youth, good sir, I had sworn no liege to the king. It was my friar who sent me with God's word."

"God's word? From some wandering friar?" Still, his frown began to ease. "British knights will come after Easter, boy. They will tell us of you at Camelot."

Easter was months away. "I was but a small page, sir."

"Such skill with the dagger will have been noticed." He stood over me. "If any of this be false, I will have my knight's justice. But for now I will take you."

My heart stopped. My eyes went damp and I could barely speak. "Good sir, I thank you." The knights around us murmured their approval, though Ricard cursed under his breath. Sir Amaury clasped my shaking hands between his own, and took me as his liege.

Even now it seems astonishing. A week before I had been a Camelot servant; six months past, a farmer's youngest son, a peasant lad that so hated knights I could not keep away from them. What I had discovered of hatred at Camelot was now proved at Caen, that despite the God-made chasm between knights and peasants I felt their equal. I had entered the castle emboldened by hatred, I had fought Ricard of it, and now, if I did not quake nor show my fear, they had no idea that I ought. I was what they imagined, and how well and long that simple truth supported me.

Of course I was whipped by Sir Amaury, and with the strap Ricard had used. Not even squires might attack a knight without punishment. But, praise God, I was alive.

The castellan arrived, grumbling at our fight. He fined Sir Amaury a livre, as it had been his knight, and now his servant, that broke the king's truce. I did not know how much a livre was, but Sir Amaury did not complain.

I was given a pallet among the squires and niche to hang my cloak.

After the midday meal I walked back to Ezra's for my few goods. The heavy Jew sat his storeroom picking at a roasted chicken, and the bones were clean by the time I finished my story.

"How hazardous you live," he said. "I'd thought to send you to my cousins in Paris." He poked at the bones again. "How much do you have of Abram's coin?"

I did not want to tell him. "My knight will clothe me."

"How much is left, lad?"

"Five shillings, a little less."

Ezra shrugged again. "A month."

Not enough til even the start of Lent, if I must run again.

He sat, turning a ring on one thick finger, and after a long silence bent and lifted a small heavy box. The key scraped in its lock and the hinges moved stiffly. Silver coins lay heaped inside. The sight stopped my breath. Did he mean to tempt me? In Britain it was no real crime to take from Jews, they stole from Christians with their sinful usury. Ezra watched me as if he read my thoughts. "Abram writes I may trust you with my life," he muttered, before he took out handfuls of the little coins, counting the twenty piles, the twelve to each pile.

"A livre of Tours," he said. We both stared at the little hoard. "Not quite a British pound." This much my father paid as rent, twice a year. This much Amaury gave the castellan for my fight, without complaint.

"I cannot repay it." My mouth had gone dry. "Nor even the shillings I owe Abram."

"I do not make a loan." He lifted a broad hand. "Nor is it a gift. You will pay me, someday when I need it."

"Thank you, Ezra."

He watched me drop them, stack by stack, into my purse. "If they find you out, they will kill you."

It was true, but I could not let it frighten me. "I hope to be Sir Amaury's page. And he has but one squire."

He lifted his round face. "A page? But pages become squires, and squires become . . ." He would not say it.

I stood and paced his chamber, grimly excited. God's Name, it was the most obvious thing, and the most impossible. Squires became knights. The friar had said I was a green knight. I wore the name he gave me, as if it were already true. There was no better way for my revenge. No peasant might injure a knight, save risking his own life, yet when one knight killed another nobody thought it even unusual. It was a frightful notion, and the best disguise I might ever achieve.

"If they find you out," Ezra rumbled, "they will kill you. But if they do not, young Michel, they will make you one of them."

I shook my head. "No, Ezra. They are right. A true knight must be born a knight's son. I will never forget my own father. I will never forget who killed my sister."

Ezra did not believe me. His whole heavy frame had become a ruin of sorrow. "Heaven knows we are both fools."

The estates of Sir Amaury lay four days south of Caen, at Saint-Georges in Anjou, near the river Loire and the city of Angers. He held his lands in liege to John, baron of Craon, and if Amaury had a debt of knightly service to Sir John, John owed the same to his own lord, the king of France. Thus it was Sir Amaury, in service to Sir John, had brought his knights to help garrison the royal castle at Caen, the forty days from Yule to Candlemas.

Sir Amaury's lands were broad enough to support three other knights. Ricard de la Croix I had fought, and there was Pierre du Vallon, the knight of the dark curls, and the youngest, blond Cyril de Lande. Each knight had brought a squire, and Sir Amaury's was Bertran la Romme.

Bertran was seventeen, and would be dubbed a knight himself this summer. He was light-haired, square-faced, and no taller than I despite his age; my arrival pleased him little more than it did Ricard. His own father had broad estates along the river Loire, and owed the service of seven knights to Charles, count of Anjou and brother of the king. But Bertran was his younger son.

"My father," he said, "has the promise of Eléan, daughter of Claude de Riaille. She brings a dowry of ten manors and a knight's service to the king." He gave a grim smile. "I pray God for her, every night, lest I get my father's smallest manor and stay a bachelor at Sir Amaury's. Who can afford to be a knight, with only a dozen farms?" And once more the wealth of knights astonished me.

On my first day Bertran took me to the stables, to teach me my tasks there. I must unsaddle the destrier, help the grooms curry it, dry and polish the tack. A lad my own age, sandy-haired and strong, leaned against the stalls. His eyes drooped as if he were half asleep, or simple.

He was the servant I defended. He gave a painful bow. "I thank you, sir."

"I am Michel de Verdeur."

He knew already. "I'm Jacq. My father is Conon la Roche, Sir Amaury's reeve. Sir Amaury brought me here as a groom."

"But Sir Ricard beat you."

"Sir Ricard has a temper." Jacq straightened his hurt back. "It was true, I stole his wine."

He peered at me dully, yet I thought him quicker than he appeared. Each day for a week he bobbed and thanked me, until at last I said, "It's enough. Just don't steal anymore."

"Aye, sir, I won't sir, thank you sir."

Bertran, watching, gave me his first grin. "It will be a miracle of God, if he does."

But Jacq did not steal, the rest of our time in Caen. At least nobody caught him at it.

Each day at Caen began with Prime, sung in the church. Sir Amaury went every Sabbath, and most weekdays. I often went with him, though I must stand among the castle servants. My friar would have me do it, I said. They nodded at my piety.

After Prime we took breakfast of bread and watered ale before the day's work began, that was always battle practice. If it were dry, Bertran dressed Sir Amaury in chain armor, while I went to saddle his destrier. The animals stamped and tossed their heads and shivered with excitement. The knights came out into the winter air laughing and boasting, though each checked tack and tightened straps before they swung up on the great horses. They took padded lances and rode to joust beside the keep, the flattest place within the castle bailey. While two fought, the others would argue of the work, of the good strokes and the mistakes.

"Do you see?" Bertran said. "Sir Amaury bent left, that made Pierre aim wide, and then as they met he turned his shield, that splintered Pierre's lance."

"Luck," said Guy, Sir Pierre's squire. "My lord rides a timid horse today, the animal shied away."

"Luck? 'Twas Pierre's luck he wasn't unhorsed." Bertran saw me staring. "Friars don't see much of tourneys, do they?"

"I've seen one or two," I said, "but this is different."

Indeed it was very different. At Camelot I had been a busy servant, filled with hatred, and kept distant from the rush and crash. At Caen we all stood close to see the better, and the noise and clatter were very loud. The horses panted as they charged. The knights, practicing among friends, did not conceal their grunts and groans. It was another skill to be learned, how to hold the lance, how the shield moved, how one knight feinted or did not, how the other answered. I watched and listened hard as I could.

It might be only practice, yet it bruised and battered them, and each day one or two knights limped into the old Hall for the midday meal. I wondered how they could go on day after day, their only leisure the Sabbath. Even in bad weather, when the wind howled and sleet drove against the doors, they fought with swords, afoot in the knights' house, sweating, cursing, and never resting.

In truth, fighting was every knight's life. At Caen they all talked of the coming round of summer tourneys. Life without war bored them, they said, and Cyril even thought to fight the Moors in Spain. Yet none had taken the cross, four years past, when the French king raised a great army for his crusade. Only Sir John had gone, with six knights of Craon, Bertran told me. Yet even before they reached the Holy Land the king's army met defeat, and many were held prisoner for months. Last summer Sir John had returned with but four knights, sick and wounded himself. The king stayed on still, though Jerusalem remained in the hands of infidels.

Though I was but a servant without title, soon Sir Amaury set Bertran to improve my knifework. The squire smiled at me, without mirth, and took me aside while the knights jousted. We fought with blunted daggers, that bruised more often than they cut. Bertran was a willing teacher, never loath to hurt, and without mercy for my rawness. The other squires watched, and often several of the knights, shouting praise or criticism.

Bertran fought as did the Norman knights, and if there was much elegance to their style, there was also a predictable design. A certain sequence of foot shifts and feints with the unarmed hand, for instance, always preceded a lunge to the throat. The stable lads at Camelot had been almost as good, yet their technique was less expected and thus more difficult to counter. I learned quick, and Bertran got praise for it, and soon enough he liked me better.

In truth combat came easy to me. I was quick and strong as any of the squires. And there was that other thing, that had saved me the morning I faced Ricard, that grew each day I practiced. I could see the other's moves before they appeared. It was a thing I could not quite explain, and I never spoke of it. Bertran and the others did not seem to have it, yet I imagined it something of the air of Normandy. Still, if I might see the blows coming I did not know how to avoid them, and soon enough I carried the marks of parries missed everywhere on my body. Every day after the midday meal I polished Sir Amaury's helmet and chain mail, and cleaned his shield, as stiff and aching as the jousting knights.

I worked hard at everything. I wanted to be Sir Amaury's page, and soon enough his squire. I was fifteen already and had no time to waste in pursuit of Lark's knights. Arthur had been fifteen when he drew the sword from its stone. Lancelot had been dubbed knight at sixteen, Percival at seventeen, and that was the age Bertran would be this summer.

*   *   *

I had been there but a few weeks when Sir Amaury took us all out to the river meadows south of Caen. We rode lanes edged with frostbitten grass, beneath trees that lifted winter-black branches under an overcast sky. At the small villages he drew up and leaned to speak to the farmers.

"These are Sir John's lands," Bertran said, nodding at the broad fields. "He owns British fiefs, too, but they are in dispute with your king."

Sir Amaury had me carry a small sporting crossbow, for the quail and pheasant we raised from the edges of the fields. When he first called for the bow I had no idea what to do, and Bertran had to show me, shaking his head and muttering he had never seen anyone so ignorant. It put such a fright into me I could barely remember what he did, though it was a simple matter to cock the weapon with the lever and lay the short arrow in its groove. Amaury shot at the next covey of birds and actually hit one before it leaped into the air. Pierre and Cyril lost quarrels for nothing, and the squires tried the weapon without success. At the end of the day I carried it again, cocked and loaded, as we rode back. Just outside a village three pheasants boomed up from a roadside hedge. I shot from my trotting horse. My quarrel took the leading bird clean in the breast, and it fluttered and dropped in the fallow stubble.

They all drew up, absolutely silent, staring at the dying bird. At last Pierre laughed out loud. "Well, look you, the lad's a hunter, too."

"A lucky shot," Ricard mumbled, scowling.

I tried to swallow my delighted grin. When the farmer brought the bird, Sir Amaury let me hang it from my saddle. He said little of it, yet in the days that followed he smiled at me more readily, and gave me tasks that befitted a page.

If I learned combat quickly, and was a lucky shot, much of my life still felt a constant fright. All the squires were noble-born, yet for all that I had been at Arthur's Camelot, I had never hunted with bow or lance, never played at chess nor carried a hawk on my fist. I knew few courtly songs, and little of courtly language. It was my fostering, I claimed. I did not know my family, only the friar who named me, that had found me by the wayside. We had lived in poor houses at Winchester and Salisbury. Yet if I pleaded a life with my friar, that created another threat. Friars read Latin, yet I had not even my letters. Any day somebody might ask me of hours, or prayers, or to read a verse from the Book. Or even why I had come to the castle, when there were a dozen pious houses I might have joined, in Caen.

In truth it was not religion the squires worshiped, but lechery. They spun tales of the innumerable maids they had, and how their knights enjoyed a long variety of ladies. All save Bertran, that insisted Sir

Amaury was pure and completely innocent of women.

"I have been his squire three years, and page three years before. Yet I have never seen him touch a lady, save to kiss her hand. His father brought a dry old priest to Saint-Georges, who taught Sir Amaury only chastity and Latin." He pointed at me. "Of course he would take this one, raised by Blackfriars, their members gone black from want of use." The others laughed at the old joke. "And you all see how well he fights, for a novice. 'Tis not my training, I swear, but his purity. We must all keep him so, and worthy of Sir Amaury." He hung his head. "I fail him, and many times. *Mea culpa*. Alas, my little peasant witch."

They laughed with him again, and all together made an oath to protect me from the appetites of women. They grew quite serious, that I remain as unspotted as Amaury. I shrugged to myself. It was but another aspect of my mask.

On Candlemas, that ended Sir Amaury's service, we packed for the road—beds, clothes, armor, lances and shields. Each knight had two baggage horses, a riding palfrey, and his destrier, and every squire had his animal, too. The morning we assembled in the courtyard we were five knights, five squires, myself and two grooms, and twenty-eight horses. The air was breathless cold and smelled of snow, and the castellan, come to see us off, glanced up at the flat gray clouds and prayed us good passage.

The iron shoes of our horses clattered on the stone as we rode out the northern gate and around the castle to the dusty western market. I stared over the ranks of farmers' carts to Ezra's narrow street, feeling his silver heavy in the purse about my waist. I had not seen him since I left his house, the idea to be a knight green in my mind; it came to me that for my oath of Lark I must turn my back on everything, especially the Jews that had saved me. The street passed another market, and the abbey church of Saint-Étienne, before it sloped down to the river ford. The road beyond seemed just as muddy as British ways, and just as endless.

We stopped the night at a priory in a market town, and came at the middle of the next day to the steep hill of Domfront, and its castle high above a river valley. The thin snow that had begun the night before whitened the castle court. The castellan gave us a meal in his square keep and told us brigands had been seen in the south, and when Sir Amaury declined his offer of a night's lodging, he urged us to go carefully, that we reach Mayenne before dark, yet without tiring our horses.

"Christ's blood," said Amaury, grinning as we came out the Hall, "I could use a good fight." The others growled happily.

The knights rode in mail hauberks, and they set us unpacking helmets and shields. A few of the squires had short mail tunics, and Bertran wore an old boiled-leather jerkin. Sir Amaury had given me no armor but now he unpacked his hunting crossbow.

"You killed that bird well, lad. 'Tis very light 'gainst a man, and no honest weapon for a knight." He shrugged as he handed me the bag of quarrels. "Aim for the chest. Shoot fast as you can."

He led us on again, down the steep hill, the knights riding battle-horses now. Pierre and Ricard followed him, with the other squires and most of the animals. Cyril took the rear, with Bertran and me just in front. Our breath smoked in the chill air. Snow fell again in showers till it was fetlock-deep, and a cold wind sprang up that made us wrap our cloaks tight about us.

After another hour we crested an empty ridge where Sir Amaury announced we left Normandy for Anjou. The long empty way wore on everybody but at last, an hour before dusk, we caught the smell of wood-smoke and soon rode through a little village. The odors of cooking rose above the clustered houses. Farmers looked up from chopping wood in their yards and a woodsman with a clutch of rabbits bobbed beside the way and swore he had seen no brigands.

" 'Tis but an hour to Mayenne," Amaury said, happy.

We began to relax. The knights took off their helmets and reset their swords. I had practiced much with the crossbow, cocking it with the lever quick as I could, but now I carried it under my cloak. One of the squires began to whistle. We rode into another wood but nobody kept a careful eye. In the windless hush the only sound was the crunch of horses' hooves in the snow.

A branch shook overhead. Snow dusted on the pack horses, and a man fell squirming through the air. A voice bellowed sudden as thunder, and on both sides shouting men burst out the wood, the heads of pikes and axes glittering in the dull light.

"Swords!" Amaury bellowed. *"Ferra, milites!"* He turned his battle-horse and slashed at the attackers. *"Ereptores necatis."*

They swarmed us, screaming, points stabbing for us, hooks reaching to pull us down. One, red-faced and sweating in the cold, thrust a pike at me that I batted away with my arm. The crossbow under my cloak was still cocked. I fumbled for a quarrel, and fired without aiming. The feathered shaft stood in his right eye. He fell back, his mouth open, but I could not hear his scream above the noise of the fray.

Cyril galloped past, sword raised, driving his battle-horse straight into the bellowing mob. Screaming horses spun and reared. Riders beat away thrusting pikes, but a swarm of them had pulled somebody from his horse. Knights galloped to him, their blades red now, the horses running men down. I struggled to cock the bow. Somebody gave that awful shriek a man screams, cleft by a sword, and for a flaring instant Emrys lay on the stones of Camelot, dead as the man I had shot.

My hands shook as I fumbled for another quarrel. The thin snow had gone black and red. Fewer brigands stood. One of them lurched from the crowd and grabbed the lead of a loaded hackney just ahead. My bolt drove up to its vanes in his back. He pitched forward under our hooves. I struggled with the bow again. A horse shrieked as it fell. The thickest battle raged around the fallen knight. Something snapped at my ear like a heavy insect. Bertran yelled and stabbed at the robber beside him. Beyond them a boy bent over a fighting crossbow, pulling it taut.

He was so young I could not fire till he raised the weapon again. Our bolts passed in midair. Bertran swung again at his bandit. The boy's quarrel skipped off his leather and drove into my right shoulder, the force of it like a fist. I gripped my horse and near dropped the bow. My own dart missed the boy by a finger's width and splintered against the tree behind him. Half my mind praised God for it, before pain struck me like an ax and my sight failed.

Nine

I woke sitting in the cold snow, my back against a tree. Somebody pressed a hand against my shoulder and wrenched out the bolt, and I nearly fainted again. Sir Amaury knelt before me, a grin on his sweated face. "No barb." He held up a short, gouted shaft. "Else I would have cut it out."

Bertran pulled aside my tunic, dipped his fingers in a pot, and pressed the salve into my wound. The dark trees beyond him blurred in pain. "They'll burn it clear at Mayenne."

The smell of blood hung in the winter air, the stink of urine and failed bowels. Brigands lay hacked and bloody, and very still beneath the nervous hooves of our horses. There were a dozen of them, and more blood soaked the dirty earth than even Lark had bled. At first I could not believe it. Daggerwork had frightened me, I had seen knights at joust, but never did I think it all practice for this butchery.

A knight groaned beside me. It was Pierre, he had lost his mail hood, and his skull gleamed blue where an ear had been. Blood clotted his dark curls, oozed from his face and chest, there was no part of him not smeared with blood and when I reached to touch his hand most of it had been hacked away. Oh God, Pierre, my best ally of all of them. His squire wiped his brow and Cyril knelt before him with a cup, but Pierre could not see them. His breath came in gasps. He began to pray in quick, shuddering whispers. He called out, a woman's name perhaps. He tried to stand and almost did, and fell on his face in the dirty snow.

Cyril stumbled upright. "Christ damn them," he cried, his face white, "they'll never lie again." He limped to his horse and pulled himself up. "Don't wait, Amaury." He jerked the animal around and galloped back through the wood. His injured squire made to follow, but Bertran mounted instead and galloped off.

Ricard had taken a pike through his thigh, Cyril's squire had a chopped arm, and I had been shot, but the rest suffered no more than expected cuts and bruises. One bandit sat nearby, alive though with a broken arm. He had fought bravely, had not run away when the others fled, and surrendered only when all hope was lost. An honorable enemy, Sir Amaury said, and bound his broken arm and gave him a horse to ride. We all knew he would hang tomorrow morning in the market square of Mayenne.

There had been twenty of them, the robber said, with axes and pikes, one sword and the crossbow. "It was getting dark. We thought you were merchants; your cloaks hid your armor. We only noticed the battlehorses while we waited in ambush. We'd never have attacked, save that fool fell from his tree."

Sir Amaury might admire the robber, yet as he paced the clearing he cursed the baron of Mayenne, that did not keep his roads safe. "And damn Cyril," he muttered, "if Bertran is injured of him."

We struggled back on our animals. The pain and the motion of my horse kept me close to vomiting. It was another league before we rode out on the crest of a hill and saw the city of Mayenne below, in a narrow river valley, blurred with smoke from its chimneys. I stopped a moment to rest my shoulder. Horses sounded at a gallop behind us, and soon Cyril drew up beside me, his blond face scratched and bruised. He carried his sword naked, crusted red for half its length, and he blurted out, "I answered your blood, lad."

"The rabbit hunter?" I said.

"I never found *that* bastard. But there were four in a houseyard." He waggled the gouted blade. "One of them got away. The last ran inside the house, he had another damned crossbow." He stared at his sword a long moment. "I've never cut a man's head full off, with one swing." He blinked, seeing it again. "There was a woman, screaming. I knocked her down. I hadn't thought of it, but seeing her sprawl . . ."

I glanced at Bertran. He carried an old battered crossbow. "The spoils of war," he said sourly.

My hands began to shake. I turned away and bent, and emptied my stomach in the winter road.

Evening grayed the winter air as we clattered across the stone bridge into Mayenne. Shopkeepers peered from their doorways at the market, and townsmen gathered at a little distance and murmured at the body of

Pierre, slung over his palfrey. Pleased we had killed so many of the robbers, they brought us ale and hard loaves. The rest of our company swung down from their horses, and stretched their legs and ate. But my shoulder throbbed and my mouth tasted of iron, and the smell of the ale almost made me sick again.

A plain old castle stood the rocky mount beside Mayenne's river, where we had thought to stop the night. But Sir Amaury still muttered with anger as he rode off with Bertran and the robber, and when he returned announced he had refused the castellan's hospitality. We gaped at him and Ricard groaned with dismay, but Amaury turned his horse and led us on up through the steep town. Snow began to fall again. I shivered under my cloak, though my shoulder was afire. Beyond the city we rode a league of winter fields before the way dropped into another narrow valley. Ice blurred the surface of a small lake, and on the far shore stood the church and cloisters of an abbey, half hidden in the winter dark.

I had to clench my teeth against the pain when I swung from my saddle. Ricard could barely walk. They were Cistercians, White monks, that led us to a guest house lit by rush lamps, and laid me on a cot in Ricard's alcove, and were heating an iron to sear his thigh when I fell asleep.

Bertran woke me with bowl of morning gruel. "I must thank you, Sir Amaury says, and take care of you." He smiled and helped me sit. "That bolt you took was meant for me."

A leech-monk came and peered at my shoulder, and poked at it despite my curses, and sniffed the ooze. He did not think it wanted burning, but salved it instead and wrapped it with clean linen, and hung a loop of cloth round my neck to support my arm.

Lay brothers washed Pierre's corpse and laid him in his best robes, though Sir Amaury kept back his armor and weapons for his widow. At midday, the bells ringing Sixte in the cold air, we walked to the abbey cemetery. Under the flat gray sky Pierre's grave was but a black hole cut in the thin snow. We stood beside it, praying for his everlasting life and our own, the monks chanted their Office, the winter earth swallowed his plain coffin without a sound.

We trudged back, silent ourselves, until Sir Amaury spoke to me. "You killed two of them, lad. I am very pleased I took you in Caen."

"I am your liege, Sir Amaury. I will not fail you."

We both knew they were lucky shots, at close range, yet his praise lifted my spirits. As there were tales of noble orphans, so were there stories of youths that appeared suddenly, did miracles at arms, and were discovered to have noble blood. The abbey where we stopped reminded me of Winchester's cloister, and brought to mind my stinking friar. Normandy, he had said, or France; and though I rode to Anjou I felt he sent me there.

Still, that night I could not sleep, but lay in my rattling straw and counted the monastery bells. Vespers. Compline. My shoulder flared and throbbed, yet it was not pain that kept me awake. It was Bertran's tale of Cyril.

"I followed him back," he had said. "I could not miss the house. The gate stood open and two peasants lay dying in the yard. A woman screamed inside as I swung down. I pushed open the broken door. Cyril had her under him on the dirt floor. She squirmed and bellowed, and one of her brats whacked him with a stick. It only made him punch the harder." He glanced away. "Watching it roused me. I thought to take her when he'd done. But then I saw the man. He lay in the corner. Blood gouted the wall but I couldn't see a wound. I went to look. My foot kicked his head. It wobbled across the floor. The house stank of peasant, and I went out into the open air again."

"Did he kill her?" I could barely speak.

He had stared at me. "Jesu, she was but a farmer's bitch."

In the dead of night I touched the little sack around my neck. I heard once more the knights on Rebecca, their noisy grunts under the lopsided moon. They that killed her had slain Emrys, too. Hatred of them made me their equal, set me against Ricard, and put me here wounded in the service of knights I did not hate. For Lark's vengeance I thought to become a knight. Cyril killed peasants and raped wives, yet for her sake I must swallow the bile I tasted, clench my teeth against a wayward tongue, pretend it did not matter. I must say, like Bertran, she was only a farmer's bitch.

Deep in the black night the bells of the abbey rang Matins. I imagined the monks shivering in the cold church, the taper flames white and unmoved by their chants. God saw it all, the priests said, and found it pleasing in His sight.

A cold morning mist half hid the rolling land, when we set out again. Farmers here did not live in villages like Ryford, set amid their broad furlongs, but on scattered separate farms, each the center of its narrow hedged fields. Yet even here the dark smell of the soil came to me like a lost friend, and the winter wheat thrust up its fresh green shoots, and sowers cast the barley seed on the new-plowed earth. One family gaped as we rode past, and I could feel the mud that clotted their feet, the hunger that lined their faces. This was the hardest time of year, with the harvest eaten, the seed sown, and nothing growing in the fields. I prayed God they ate now, at Greenfarm.

The mist thickened into drizzle. My shoulder throbbed, and I dozed in the saddle. Sir Amaury hoped to reach Craon before dark, but Ricard suffered so we stopped soon at another abbey. The next day we hired a covered litter, slung between two horses, and rode beside it through a freezing rain all the slow leagues to Craon.

Sir John's castle crowned a hill, above its small town and winding river. It was built of dark stone, much smaller than Camelot or Caen, but equally rich. Every roof was slate. Carved moldings framed every door. The high keep had windows of clear glass for the Hall, and in the chapel opposite the colored image of Our Lady glinted bright among the gloomy stone. We rode up through its narrow gate and into a bailey slick with ice. Half a dozen knights came out in the weather to greet us, and Sir John waited at the doorway of his Hall stairs.

From the first I thought him very like his castle, small and dark and handsome. As I struggled from my horse I heard him ask Sir Amaury. "You bring a new lad?"

"He appeared in Caen, Sir John." Amaury motioned to me. "He served me very well at Mayenne."

"Michel de Verdeur, sire," I said, bowing.

"Welcome to Craon, man of my knight."

He had a singer's voice, deep as Jubal's. His face was pale and weary, but I hardly noticed that. I could see only the great scar that began in the dark hair above his right ear and cut a slanting line down his face, across his cheek and off the bottom of his jaw. Its width varied, as if it had been poorly bound, and in the cold rain it was dusky red against his pale skin. The top of his right ear had been cut off, too, and when I saw that I pulled my gaze away. My stiff and throbbing shoulder seemed nothing before that amazing wound.

He nodded at my bandage. "We must get you to the leech."

" 'Twas but the bolt of a crossbow, sir." I looked at his dark eyes and knew what I must ask. "And you, sir?" I touched my own cheek. "Was that . . . ?" Amaury glared and Bertran drew a breath, but I pressed on. "Was that a Saracen blade, my lord?"

John looked at me sharply, before he gave a broad smile. "There is nothing keener than Damascus steel, lad. Praise God I had laced my helmet tight."

"Praise God, sir," I repeated, amazed at such a frightful blow.

Bertran seized my good arm and pulled me away. "A servant never asks a knight of his injuries," he growled. "Wait till he speaks."

"He smiled when I asked him," I said.

"He is the baron of Craon. And you are stupid as Jacq."

We dined that evening in Craon's Hall, that lay like Camelot's up a flight of steps. Broidered damask hung the whitewashed walls, and Sara-

cen weavings carpeted the dais. Sir John had a harper, that sang tales of
Roland, and of Hector and Achilles. Sir Amaury sat at the high table
beside the baron, with steward and castellan and chaplain, and John's
wife and Denis his oldest son, who was Bertran's age. Bertran cut
Amaury's venison and I helped one-handed with the wine, and kept the
dogs off the carpets.

The lady Adele was Sir John's second wife, ten years younger, that he
had married since the crusade. Gold ribbons bound her auburn hair, and
her rich gown did not conceal her womanly figure. She had a round and
pretty face, and beneath her soft brows, eyes I had thought blue glimmered a sudden green in the taperlight. She smiled at me each time I
filled her cup. Sir John's chaplain spoke with her, but the rest at the high
table were deep in talk of Caen, of robbers, of the winter hunt.

Of course I must compare Craon with Camelot, though in my memory Arthur's court wavered between the gold of late summer and that
black murderous Yuletide night. Two dozen knights sat Craon's trestles
that evening, and talked in quiet tones and paused to hear the harper's
song. They looked to be hardy fighters, but there was no Lancelot there,
nor Gawain nor Percival. Nor was Craon's injured baron knighthood's
high king, only a man who grew soon weary. And the wife who led him
away was but a sensible woman, not some breathtaking queen. Still my
heart rested and the ache in my shoulder almost vanished, and I was
willing for that hour to stay at Craon forever.

Under a clearing sky, Sir John took his hawks out next morning for their
first hunt since winter. He had eight and a man for each, and the castellan handled his favorite. We made a large and noisy company as we rode
the crisp air, through river meadows where the thin snow was already
melting. John kept Sir Amaury beside him, and though Bertran rode
with other squires I stayed close to my knight and the baron.

"The abbot of Saint-Georges is a dying man," said Sir John.

Amaury shrugged. "He has been dying for a year."

"Craon has always appointed the abbot, but this new bishop at Angers claims it for himself."

"Steven is very ambitious." Amaury paused. "For God."

Sir John scowled. "And for himself."

Around us knights shouted as a pair of doves skimmed overhead.

"Up, send them up!" cried John. The keepers of the first pairs pulled
away the birds' hoods and tossed them in the air. They climbed on noisy
wings and circled above us but the doves were gone. Sir John turned and
motioned me close and asked of my friar.

"A Blackfriar, sir." His question surprised me. "That belonged to no
house but traveled much, preaching always the forgiveness of Our

Lord." I could smell the friar's breath, hear his voice speaking my new name, see the cross he had made in the winter air as we parted.

"Jacobins." He gazed up at the hawks. "The forgiveness of Christ. Does it truly mean a knight cannot beat a servant?"

"I ought not have attacked Sir Ricard, sir. And now he lies wounded." My shoulder ached again.

"Every knight must die someday, and better a fighting stroke than slow age." John touched the scar where it crossed his chin.

Overhead a gyrfalcon cried and stooped. We craned our necks to watch, but her prey dodged away among the bare limbs of the oaks and the knights groaned that she missed. John's squire swung the lure, and with a whistle of wings the bird circled our heads and settled on the castellan's raised fist. He seized the jesses and then hooded her. She flapped once or twice before she settled.

" 'Tis a rare lad who can quote Scripture," Sir John said to me.

His words stopped my heart. I drew a breath. "Of course I heard them, sir. Everyone has. But I am no priest."

"Our Lord's story of the Samaritan." He glanced at the quieted hawk. "I had hoped to see Jerusalem, Bethlehem, even Jacob's well where Christ drank. But God showed us only Egypt, and the coast of the Philistines." He looked away. "In Egypt we were prisoners like the people Israel. In Philistia my Saracen nearly blinded me, like Samson in Gaza."

Why does he tell me this? I wondered.

"Our Savior tells us, if a man strike one cheek we must turn the other. But I killed the Saracen who did this." He smiled at my gape. "Oh, not that same day. Months later. I recognized his arms. I drove straight for him through the battle, and he knew me just before my lance took him." He stopped to gaze away over the winter countryside. The other hawk screamed overhead. "Ought I have saved that Saracen, lad?"

"Sir." At that moment I remembered nothing of Scripture.

Beside us Sir Amaury murmured, "But on crusade, sir, you fought for Christ Himself."

John nodded. "So I did. Every man I killed, I killed for Him. Save this one. This one was for myself."

Another dove appeared. The hawk stooped and struck. Her prey burst in a cloud of feathers just above our heads, and the dead bird dropped like a torn rag to the ground.

"Wonderful," John said, laughing, "God has no finer creature than the hawk. But look, there is a flock." He gestured to his castellan. "Send up your bird again."

The unhooded falcon blinked and leaped into the air.

Sir John turned back to me, gone very sober. "What would your friar have said to me, the day I killed my Saracen?"

"Sir, I . . . I was only a boy, sir, I do not know." His gaze unnerved me. I could not understand why he tested me. If I were to be unmasked it did not need a baron to do it.

"But you were long with him, weren't you? You must think on it. Tomorrow, on the Sabbath, you will tell me what he would have said." He turned away to watch his gyrfalcon stoop and kill.

I felt my heart stop. I had known that strange and stinking friar but half a day, yet now he was become the warrant of my life.

Sabbath morning all the castle's household filled the church, and the sun lay daubs of red and blue on the stone floor and incense smoked the chill air. Tired from a restless night, I stood at the back among the household squires and listened to the priest's homily of faith. My friar's lesson had been of faith, too, for if the green knight tested Gawain's honor, his willingness to die had depended on faith's power. Still, when I came out the church with the throng of squires I had thought of nothing to say. They saw Sir John waiting, and fell away and left me alone.

"Young Michel," he said, unsmiling. "My own priest says my faith is too imperfect." He looked frail in the thin sunlight and I could but wonder that a day of hawking had so tired him.

I bowed to him, and even the knights waiting round us went silent. "Courage is everything, sir, so my friar said. And faith its most important test."

His eyes gleamed. "He sounds more knight that preacher, lad. Was he a noble before he took Orders?"

"He never told me that, sir."

"Mayhap he had a son ere he did." Did John wish me a knight's son? The notion made my head swim. "And my Saracen?" he said.

I took a breath. "It pleases God to leave Jerusalem in heathen hands, sir, despite the quest of Christian knights." I paused, struggling for thought. "It pleased God that His Son die on the cross, for without Good Friday there might be no Easter."

John frowned and his knights murmured, but the priest did not seem surprised at my words.

"It pleased Him that you be captured, sir, fall ill, receive this wound. It pleased Him that, having been wounded you should kill the Saracen, and having killed, that you should ponder." I drew another breath. "Lest you be ignorant of your own soul."

I did not know where the words came from. I was not certain Sir John understood me, or that I understood myself. But he lifted his head and smiled, his weariness drained away. "Lest I be ignorant of my own soul." He glanced at his priest. "I would have Masses sung for my Saracen, every day. And we must find this remarkable friar, lad. You never said his name."

"Martin, sir." The name spoke itself on my tongue. "Of Street, sir, near Glastonbury. Though I never stopped there."

He turned to Sir Amaury. "This is an uncommon lad. You must use him well."

Amaury stared, as though my words had unnerved him. "That I will, sir." He shook his head to collect his thoughts. "I have not your understanding of Scripture, but this lad killed two men for me." He paused again, still uncertain. "By your counsel, sir, I take him into my house, as my knight's page."

"Sir Amaury," I murmured, "thank you, sir."

And John said, "I am certain he will serve you well, Amaury."

I bowed my thanks to both of them, filled with that happy devotion each vassal ought feel for his lord. Praise God, I was his page. I would be as good a servant as any of his house. I would not rest until, somehow, he dubbed me knight.

South of Craon the sun seemed brighter and the rolling country of Anjou spread out fertile and prosperous. Ricard's litter went at the pace of walking horses and the slow leagues to La Croix took us the whole day. The city of Angers lay a league eastward, Bertran said, and I could see nothing of it from the manor house.

Ricard's father was a stern old knight who preferred his son killed, it seemed, to his son returned in a litter. And when Simon de la Croix heard of me, he growled at Amaury that he was foolish, taking an unknown lad as page. I was not sorry to leave.

The smaller estates of Le Vallon crowned the next rise to the west. The lane to Pierre's house ran under a double line of elms just beginning to show their spring color, and it felt unnatural to ride beneath their fresh green with our news of winter and death. A pair of wolfhounds greeted us at the end of the lane, barking and friendly. His young widow waited in the old Hall. She was small and finely boned and very pretty despite her sorrow, and younger than twenty. My heart beat as I looked at her. She was the most beautiful woman I had seen since Guenever at Camelot.

She leaned on her mother's arm and watched dry-eyed as Guy, Pierre's squire, set out his sword and shield, his mail hauberk and his helmet. "Thank you for them, Sir Amaury," she said.

"Of course, lady." He peered at her. "But were you not with child?"

She began to weep, and the old woman put an arm around her. "She lost the babe, sir, at the shock. And her poor son died at Epiphany of the coughs, and he only two." The old woman paused. "She has only your kindness to protect her, Sir Amaury."

Two children and both lost. My heart ached, her tears were a knife in my heart, and when Amaury took her small hand I would have held it myself. I had never been so struck with love.

"What a frightful year, lady. But you are heir to Le Vallon now. I will find you another husband."

"My lord," she whispered, "I thank you."

We trooped out to the yard. I turned to look at her, and Cyril stood at her door saying good-bye. We rode away down the lane, and Sir Amaury did not speak until we reached the crossroads. "I will take no heriot from her of Pierre's death, it was in my service. And she will need a strong guardian."

"I am very strong," said Cyril, and went immediately red.

The rest laughed at him. I turned away, angry. No such violent knight might love such a lady. Yet our first morning at Craon, Cyril had gone to kneel at the altar rail, his bent shoulders a clear sign he made confession. I knew he rued neither dead farmers nor raped woman, but did it only for his own soul, and I had hoped the burden of prayer might keep him there half the morning. Yet it did not matter. Already Our Lord had forgiven him. My own words at Craon echoed in my ears, how it pleased God that Cyril kill the peasants, rape the woman . . . My mouth tasted suddenly of ashes, and once again I wondered how any man might truly understand God's will.

"Here, Michel, this is our first field." Bertran's voice woke me. He pointed at a stone wall. "Here begins Saint-Georges."

The land had grown more level as we came west. The little streams we forded all ran southward, where now and again I caught a glimpse of the wide hazy valley of the Loire. In the separate fields the winter grain was well sprouted and the spring sowing finished, the pastured cows looked strong and healthy and the hedges well mended. A family of peasants waved from their houseyard and Sir Amaury drew up to talk with them. Sitting my palfrey, I looked at the damp thatch, the muddy yard, the manure pile. It was all very like Greenfarm. I was the one changed here, become a man of the manor, higher even than Thomas the reeve.

The lowering sun shone in our eyes as we came at last to Clos Saint-Georges, that was Sir Amaury's manor house. Its slate roof showed above a gray fieldstone wall. Inside the gate a wood barn made a third side of the court, and the fourth was stables and granaries and a dovecote. Ser-

vants crowded round us, their upturned faces laughing and happy. An
old chamberlain came with a cup of wine and they all clapped as Sir
Amaury drank.

He laughed at each of them and called their names. And then he
turned and named me, and told them of my wound. They had glanced at
me uncertain, but now they smiled and reached to help me from my
horse. I felt their touch, easy yet with that caution every servant carries
in his bones, and I knew at once it was these I must truly fear. Knights or
lords would not penetrate my mask. I need not worry of Bertran or Sir
Amaury, or even Sir John. It would be one of these, a cook mayhap, a
servant boy that would discover me, would see I was one of them, and
knowing no man ought rise above his God-given place, would expose
me instantly and without mercy.

Ten

Sir Amaury's stone-built house was ample and well furnished, and for his return his servants had strewed the floors with fresh straw, and whitewashed his narrow Hall. Bertran led me up a turning stair into the squires' bedchamber, where a shuttered window looked out over separate rolling farms, and fallow pastures, and scattered woodlots. Half a league away, on the ridge of an easy hill, stood the tower of a church.

"Saint-Georges," said Bertran. "Abbey and town. All the land is Sir Amaury's or the abbot's, both held of Craon." He went on how Sir John had come to it through the dower of his grandmother, but it was the spread of lands that amazed me, how much Sir Amaury had, how much more Sir John must have. Once again I remembered the pound that Greenfarm gave twice a year. How hard we had worked to pay it. How little it must have been to Camelot.

Next morning we sat Sir Amaury's Hall, where narrow shuttered windows let in the first rays of the sun, and a lean old priest sang Prime. He was Joachim, Bertran said, that had taught Sir Amaury his purity. After the Psalms kitchen boys set up trestles and brought us loaves and watered ale. I looked about, at a new fireplace against one wall, and the stairs that climbed the far wall to Sir Amaury's bedchamber.

Sir Amaury's father had died on the king's crusade, his widowed mother was retired to the convent of Fontevraud, and there was no lady at Clos Saint-Georges. At Craon Sir John had announced a bride, and Sir Amaury smiled ruefully of it. "The lady Clare de Neuille, that brings rich manors. Sir John insists it is a desirable union. So desirable that after the wedding I will owe him another knight."

Bertran took me in hand to show me about the manor. A narrow buttery stood just behind the Hall screen, and a smoky kitchen where Reynaud the chamberlain named the servants for me—a butler, three cooks, two bakers, a brewer, a porter, and three boys. I had not expected so many. They stared at me, curious, and I took care to be the aloof and lordly page.

We crossed the court, dodging puddles. The smell of mud and winter hay and a smoldering fire somewhere so set me remembering Greenfarm again, Warren, Ruth, even Slow, that I barely heard Bertran's chatter. "Old Reynaud has noble blood but his half-manor cannot support a knighthood, and he must serve Sir Amaury. I'd thought to get his place, till my father found my heiress."

Chamberlain. Was it that Sir Amaury had in mind for me? The notion pleased me much, though I was sworn to be a knight instead.

In the stable a farrier at his forge hammered new shoes for Amaury's palfrey, and there was a houndsman among his dogs. Grooms saddled a pair of horses, and Cyril talked to a knight I had not met, sturdy and red-faced, with a large rumpled nose and sandy hair just beginning to gray. Sir Geoffrey was the estate steward, and Cyril was his aide. "Come along," he called, "we're to the weekly round." My delight at riding all Saint-Georges had made me forget my shoulder, and when I hauled myself into the saddle the pain flared so strong tears almost wet my eyes.

Geoffrey led us down the narrow lane and out among the farms. He called me beside him and named each farmstead in his hoarse voice, and which peasant had the tenancy. Men stood from weeding and eased their backs when we came up, and laughed at Geoffrey's bawdy stories. I tried to imagine how large Greenfarm might be, all its strips together in one place like these farms. As we went I counted Sir Amaury's farmsteads and had twenty-seven before I lost my number. Even that was more than Ryford's families, and with a skip of my heart I saw again how far I had traveled from Greenfarm, and how far I might fall.

Geoffrey pointed to another and a smile creased his wide face. "That's La Roche, you've already met one of his lads."

A thick-faced peasant stood in the houseyard, talking with his three sons. They touched their foreheads as we rode up, and Jacq squinted at me with his drooping eye.

"Morning, Conon," said Geoffrey.

"Sir Geoffrey, sir. Planting's done, save Ninefarm." Conon came up to us. "New squire, sir?"

"Michel de Verdeur," Geoffrey said, "come from Britain."

"Long way." He squinted up at me. "You the squire, sir, that fought for my Jacq?"

"Yes," I said.

"Well, sir, I thank you. Though I expect he deserved the strap." He bobbed at me. "We've never got on with Sir Ricard."

"Watch your tongue, Conon," Cyril growled.

A handsome high-bosomed woman, her hair in dark braids, watched from Conon's doorway. Cyril had turned to stare at her, and when Conon noticed he scowled her back inside.

"Sirs," he said, "we've got weeding, you don't object."

"Go to it, then." Geoffrey nudged his horse and led us on. "Best reeve we have. Hardest worker. Just cleared a new field."

"And got a new wife." Cyril turned in his saddle to stare back at the house. "By God, there's a field I'd plow."

Geoffrey barked a laugh. "Go you soft there, Cyril, the man has a temper."

"Damn his temper, he's but a damned peasant."

We rode all the morning, and when we came to Saint-Georges at midday my shoulder throbbed with pain. The walled abbey sat a small hill above a spread of vines and fishponds, and the little town was four or five narrow streets and an unpaved market just before the abbey's gate. Inside, the round-headed door of the old church faced a small graveled court, and black-robed monks were filing through the cloister and into the church for Sixte. I thanked God we might sit and rest in their small refectory, and eat bread and cold meat and the abbot's own white wine.

"You've heard the dispute here?" Geoffrey asked. "The old abbot named the prior Simon his successor, and convinced the monks to elect him. But Simon is the bishop's man, and Sir John wants Paul the cellarer. It is his feudal right."

Cyril laughed. "Then we'll fight, when the abbot dies."

But Geoffrey shook his head. "Hard to imagine, war 'gainst a bishop." He gazed at me. "I hope you are quick as they say." And when we came back to Clos Saint-Georges after another long ride, he looked at me again. "We practice at arms twice a week, lad. I am Sir Amaury's marshal. We'll see how you fight, tomorrow."

I could not believe him. It had been but a week since Mayenne. Yet next morning we circled each other in the manor court, armed with blunted daggers. My shoulder so ached from yesterday's ride that I had to tuck my right hand into my tunic, and hold the weapon in my left.

Geoffrey lunged at me before I was ready. I saw it and danced away. It surprised him that his thrust missed, but he drove again, so quick I had no chance to move. I took his thrust on the ribs of my chest and jabbed his belly hard with my own blade.

"Ah," he said, hoarse, as if I hurt him. "You are dead."

"Both of us," I said.

He crouched and lunged again. I dodged away. He was quick as any I had met, and far cleverer. I fought poorly, left-handed, yet here I could see as well as at Caen, and managed to dodge most of his thrusts. If my wrong-side attack bothered him, his wiliness almost outdid me, and neither scored many touchés.

Sir Amaury came to watch, and Cyril and Bertran and Reynaud. We sparred for half an hour. My shoulder was in agony when at last, sweaty and puffing himself, he lowered his blade and stepped away. Pain lined his face, and he put a hand inside his tunic and drew it out bloody.

"Sir Geoffrey," I said, "you are injured."

He looked at his fingers. "No one has stuck me in years."

"I'm sorry, sir."

"Knights must live with pain, lad." He turned grimly to Amaury. "He matched my best, and left-handed. Even bloodied me. You were right, sir. He has a gift."

Life at Clos Saint-Georges had small likeness to that at Camelot. There were no bright days for hunting, nor minstrels at meals, nor games by taperlight in the long evenings. Sir Amaury was a knight with his own fields and vineyards, and had not the leisure of kings or barons. I was called a page but Saint-Georges had no other lad who might replace Bertran, and Amaury set me as the squire's shadow, to go everywhere with him. Together we managed Sir Amaury's chamber, helped Geoffrey oversee the stables, rode to La Croix where Ricard still lay abed, and to Le Vallon where the lady Matilde smiled at Bertran and might not even see me. I went myself each week to market at Saint-Georges, and to the abbey every fast-day eve, for the fish that were its feudal rent.

Despite my aching shoulder Sir Geoffrey soon set me swinging a light blade. He brought out a long old shield and showed how it was both protection and weapon, that you might hide behind it, or use it like a ram against your opponent. Bertran ran battle-horses at the quintain, but Geoffrey never imagined I might become a knight and kept my training to sword and dagger. Nor did I tell him of what now I called my Norman gift, but let him think, like Bertran, that my quick learning came of superior teaching.

And late each day I rapped on the chamber door of the old priest. I knew I must learn to read, though I did not understand why, save it was like learning to ride Anduin. I had first spoken of it one Sabbath meal, and Joachim glanced at me with a curious look.

"Sir John asked you of Scripture," he said.

My heart skipped a beat. "Not of me, father, but what my Blackfriar might have said."

"They say your answer pleased him," Joachim murmured, his look unreadable. "Certainly it was well-spoken."

"The words came unbidden." It amazed me he had heard of it.

"All the schools argue of it, whether faith may come from reason, or only Scripture."

I did not understand him. "My friar never taught me reading, father, but I am anxious to learn."

" 'Tis the rare knight has Latin," Joachim said, still watching me. "And you are but a page, young Michel."

"Sir Amaury reads, sir. And Reynaud, but he grows old, and Bertran leaves. I thought, if Sir Amaury would make me chamberlain I must know how to write the accounts."

"Most have clerics do it for them." He gave me a dry smile. "Of course I will teach you, lad. Every evening before Vespers."

The shape of letters was easy enough to learn, and their sounds. But my hand was used to gripping a sword or tugging at reins, and writing tiny letters with a scratchy quill I found nearly impossible. Still, Joachim praised my effort, and I worked the harder for it.

It was the Sunday before Lent that Bertran came smiling into our chamber, just before midday, to say Sir Amaury called.

Our knight waited in his bedchamber over the Hall, and when I came he held up new-sewn robes, green and blue, the colors of Saint-Georges and Craon. "Michel de Verdeur," he said, "you have been my man but three months, yet I am much pleased of you. Here, these robes of an esquire, I would have you wear them now."

I opened my mouth and closed it again, torn between pride and amazement. "Sir, I had not . . . so soon . . ." I laughed aloud. "Sir Amaury, I thank you."

"But remember, Michel de Verdeur, the grim season of Lent is upon us. In our enjoyment we must not forget the suffering of Our Lord."

The robes fit me very well, and I took the scratchiness of new wool to be a reminder of Christ's trial in the desert. After Mass, when we sat to the meal, Sir Amaury presented me to the household as his younger squire. I stared around as the servants cheered me, and my heart almost forgot its fright of them.

And when we rose from table Sir Amaury beckoned to me. "Today, Michel, I send you as herald to the widow of Le Vallon."

Spring in Anjou was an earlier and a brighter season than Britain's. I rode out on Amaury's best palfrey, warm in the sunshine under my new robes, the songs of nesting birds in the air. Yet I would almost put them all aside, than go on that errand.

Pierre's death left his widow in possession of the fief, yet Le Vallon was a knight's tenure that required a knight's service. It was Sir Amaury's feudal right to assign any knight as the widow's guardian, and if he chose a bachelor she might expect to wed him. At Clos Saint-Georges we all thought Sir Amaury would favor Ricard de la Croix. He had got a serious wound in the ambush, La Croix lay adjacent to Le Vallon, and the union would create a single, generous estate. But Amaury made a different choice that pleased me far less, Cyril de Lande.

Cyril was always amiable to me at Saint-Georges, had an easy authority over the farmers that I tried to emulate, and explained the ways of the manor with more patience than Sir Geoffrey. He had no estates at all, and Sir Amaury must soon find him a manor or risk the loss of his sword. Le Vallon would give him a well-run estate, and the lady would gain a new husband. It was all most sensible. Yet Cyril had butchered farmers and raped women, he flirted with every maid here and stared at every farmwife, and I would never believe love might exist between him and the gentle Matilde.

The league to her house took but half an hour. Under her tree-lined way, now in full leaf, the friendly barks of the wolfhounds drew her steward from the house. He was a lean weathered man the age of Geoffrey.

"I have a word from Sir Amaury." I lifted the leather case that held the letter, and he frowned, knowing well what it must be.

"My lady rides to Mass, with the lady her mother. They will be back within the hour. Would you wait, young sir?"

I rode on to La Croix instead. Sir Ricard limped from his stable. "You are brightly fit out, young Michel." He leaned on his stick and his dark face was thinner than at Caen, as if the injury wore at him. "By God, those are squire's robes. Tell me, new esquire, have you a message for me?"

"I come to inquire of your health, sir."

"You see I walk, but this damn leg cannot straddle a horse."

"Sir Amaury sends his good wishes."

He frowned. "Nothing else?"

"No, sir."

"Nothing of Le Vallon? Damn him, this leg is his matter." He gripped his stick angrily. "She would add another half, here, and a second knight. Does he fear I get too large?"

"I do not know his mind, Sir Ricard."

"No matter. This very day my father rides to Avrille." He stopped and glanced away, and I imagined he had other prospects.

Three horses walked the lane of Le Vallon, the two ladies and Guy,

Pierre's squire. They drew up when they heard me behind.

"Good Sabbath, ladies," I said.

"And to you, esquire," said the old woman.

I pulled my gaze from the lady Matilde. "I come from Sir Amaury." She put a slim hand to her pretty mouth, that so suddenly I wanted to kiss.

"We have not had our meal," said her mother. "And you must be hungry of your ride, esquire. There will be time enough when we are refreshed."

"Thank you, lady." I bowed. "I am Michel de Verdeur."

"Yes," she said.

There were but five of us in the low old Hall, the women and their steward, and myself and Guy. Their Sabbath repast was cold eels and Saturday's bread. I made talk with the steward, of rain and planting, of budding vines and new calves. I ate but little, pleading Sir Amaury's meal, but it was Matilde's beauty that had seized my appetite. Not till the end did the old woman ask of the letter. I stood and drew out the folded parchment, that they see the unbroken seal, though I had memorized what Joachim had written.

" 'I, Amaury de Saint-Georges, through my liege to John of Craon, am lord of Le Vallon. My vassal Pierre is this month dead, and buried at the Abbey of Fontaine-Daniel. I accept Matilde de Bouet, his widow, as my new vassal. By liege-right I award her guardianship, and the knight's service of the fief, to Cyril de Lande. He may take Matilde de Bouet as his wife, if she would.' "

The women looked at me without expression. After a pause the mother said, "We expected de la Croix." She reached for the letter. "Well, they say he is an energetic knight. Well set, too."

A faint smile moved Matilde's soft mouth. "Cyril de Lande." Her blue eyes gazed at me. "I did not expect this news. I must become used to it." She stood. "I will take the air. Come, esquire, tell me about him, this knight I hardly know."

Her words astounded me, exactly what I would have said to her. I wanted nothing but her company, and she must feel the same of me. What might I know of Cyril that Guy did not?

I bowed to the old woman, but already she talked to her steward. We went out into the houseyard. Sunlight fell through the early leaves thick as fog. I could not breathe, beside Matilde. She was slender and small, and fragile, and much in need of protection. I wanted to hold her, kiss her lips, feel her small breasts bare against me, lie inside her. God's Name, how quick my thought had come to that. I must beware this southern springtime, the long months since Yule and Sibyl.

She led me to a bench under an old oak, and touched the seat beside her. "They say you are from Britain."

"Yes, lady." I tried not to stare at her lips. "Camelot." The air of spring roared around us like a storm. I saw my hand took one of hers, that I bent and kissed it. "You are beautiful, lady."

She did not seem surprised, though her cheeks went pink under her fair skin. She drew her hand away. "Guy told us of you at Caen. Of the friar that fostered you, of your chivalric purity."

I could barely hear her. Love and desire thundered in my head. "I have sailed the winter sea, lady. I have journeyed a hundred leagues, to be here beside you."

She smiled at me. "Are all British so courtly, esquire?"

"Only when they are in love." My heart beat in my throat. I could not believe what I spoke, nor the power this soft woman had over me.

"Cyril de Lande," she was saying. "What think you? Is he an honest and an upright knight?" I almost choked. Cyril upon this woman, I had not seen it before. "What say you, esquire?"

"Lady."

"You stared at me all through the meal." She laughed softly. "You speak so prettily, and are such a comely lad."

I felt my cheeks blaze. "Lady, I love you more than life itself. Pray God, do not . . ."

"Every springtime fosters imagined love," she murmured.

"Dear lady, I do not imagine it. You have defeated me, my heart aches, I am overwhelmed by your charms, and those most hidden are the sweetest, the ones I most desire."

She gave a bright laugh. "I had not thought since Pierre's death ever to hear such words again." She touched my new robe and her mood went serious. "But, young Michel, so newly esquired . . ."

"Sweet lady, my tongue cannot control my heart."

"All this, so sudden, and on the eve of Lent?"

"My lady, we have still time. Two nights, three, ere . . ."

The voices of her mother and the steward rang in the warm air as they walked toward us. Matilde stood, and though she smiled to them, the face she turned to me was the proper widow's mien.

" 'Tis all most pleasant, esquire, but I have armored my heart 'gainst all such courtliness."

I rode home much perplexed. I loved her. I had loved her since first I saw her; it was not pride of my esquire's robes nor the soft warmth of springtime that made me love her. And she had led me out, sat alone with me in the thick spring air, smiled and spoke of British gallantry, before her manner closed so quick. I was but a new squire, and she the

lady of Le Vallon, betrothed to a spiteful knight. I had no time for courtliness, nor any heart for it. I drew a long breath, and touched Lark's
doeskin bag about my neck. I must armor my own heart, too. Lent was
six weeks, and after Easter were seven more till Whitsun and Bertran's
dubbing. I would keep from Le Vallon all those days.

Yet Cyril, his chin clean-shaved and his hair washed, rode to Le Vallon every Sabbath. He left after the midday meal and returned at Vespers, smiling and foolish. "She is so gentle," he would murmur, "so like
Our Lady, Christ's dear Mother, that I fear to touch her."

"Jesu, man," said Amaury, "it was Pierre that had two children on
her, not the Holy Ghost. Don't be so virginal."

Yet Cyril grew so helpless on the manor Sir Geoffrey worried our
grain would go unweeded, the fallow miss its second plowing, the early
hay stand unmoved in the meadows. "He's but a useless dreaming boy,
now she's agreed to marry him. Who would have thought it?"

Cyril's love of her had almost eased my hatred of him, made us
nearly comrades, but suddenly I was angry again. "Who would have
thought it," I growled, "after Mayenne?"

"Mayenne? But your shoulder is healed, Michel."

"It's Cyril I mean, that has never been timid of farm girls."

Geoffrey stared at me. "Jesu, 'twas but a peasant wench."

On Whitsun morn, Bertran would be dubbed with two other squires. To
honor all three Sir Amaury and the other sponsors had called a day's
tourney, in the meadow below the abbey church. Our small tourney was
but one of many that season, for heralds came from Laval proclaiming a
tourney the week before, and Saumur would hold another the second
Monday after. And Charles, count of Anjou, announced a grand tourney
at Angers, three weeks after.

The thought of his first joust so worried Bertran that after Easter he
trained every morning, sweating his battle-horse and himself until
Geoffrey made him stop and rest. "Jesu," Bertran muttered, red-faced
himself, "no knight may lose his dubbing tourney."

"You will not," said Geoffrey, "you are a fine fighter."

He shook his head. "Just good enough." He turned on me. "This
one, how is it he is so good, and but a British orphan?"

"I had the finest teachers," I said again. It did not ease him.

And then it was Rogation Sunday, two weeks ere the tourney, and
the day he returned to his father's manor. All our household gathered in
the courtyard, where his baggage was packed in a farmer's wain. He
shook our hands and swung up on his palfrey.

"Six years I've lived here, page and squire." He gazed at the stone house, the barn, the stables. "Half a lifetime, it feels. Praise God Sir Amaury is so fine a knight." He smiled at me. "But now to leave him in the hands of a fatherless esquire."

"Do not worry of Sir Amaury," I answered, trying to match his humor.

I would speak to the abbey steward of mowing the tourney field, and I rode with him far as Saint-Georges. The others cheered him out, and waved till we could hardly see them. But at the abbey I did not turn aside, and went with him through the town and half a league down the western road, before he drew up in the dusty road.

" 'Tis two leagues more to La Romme," he growled, though his voice broke.

I had to clear my throat. "It feels I lose a brother."

He gripped my hand. "Pray for me, on Whitsunday."

"I'll wager all my coin on your victory."

"Then I dare not fail."

"Till Whitsun, then." We gazed at each other a long moment, before I turned my horse and rode back toward Saint-Georges.

Eleven

We set out for Angers at Terce, Geoffrey and Cyril and myself, and it was midday when we came down the last slope to the River Maine. The city stood on the far bank and the towers of the cathedral loomed atop the opposite hill, high above the city roofs. But this was my first visit to the city, and as our ferry swung in the river current I could not keep my gaze from the great castle standing its riverside bluff, the gray stone of its high walls trimmed with level bands of whiter stone, a conical roof capping each round tower. The whole of it looked hugely strong.

" 'Twas old Fulk's castle," Geoffrey said, "that the king and his mother rebuilt, two dozen years past." He waved a broad hand. "Seventeen towers. Nothing bigger in Anjou or Normandy. They say it's even larger than Camelot."

"It's grand, Sir Geoffrey, but it cannot compare to Camelot."

"Damn you." He laughed. "You'd say that of every place."

Our horses labored up a steep street to the cathedral square, but once there the city was nearly level. At the crowded market Geoffrey bargained among the stalls and awnings for candles and cakes and a tun of Provençal wine. We rode deeper into the city, past rich merchants' houses and the gated walls of abbeys, our horses noisy in the cramped ways. Men stood quickly aside, and then we rounded a corner where half the houses were built of stone and dark-bearded men worked in the sun. I remembered Winchester then, and Caen, for we were come among the Jews of Angers.

Geoffrey drew up before a iron-strapped door. "Sir Amaury must sell his soul to these," he muttered. "Wait for us, lad, while we bicker of usury."

I sat my horse and gazed about. The men bent busily over their tasks. A pretty dark-eyed girl came up the way, and she was past me ere I remembered her.

"You are Ezra's," I called. "You are from Caen." She stopped, stiff with fright, and would not look at me. "I came on your uncle's boat, from Southampton. In winter."

"I remember you." Still she looked away.

"I mean to pay him, soon as I can."

She did not move. "They have closed Caen to us. I do not know where my father lives, or if he does." She turned to me, bitter and dry-eyed. "They burnt his accounts. Mayhap Christians owe nothing." She pointed at the next house. "That is my mother's cousin's. If you see my father, sir, please tell him I am safe here." She walked away quickly.

"I am Michel de Verdeur," I called.

In the street the men worked on, as if nothing had happened. Dear God, Ezra. Ezra, that received me in Normandy, sheltered me, loaned me coin. I remembered again that Christ upon His cross had forgiven them.

Geoffrey and Cyril came out the house, smiling as if they had got what they wanted. A small old man with a grizzled beard bobbed to them, while a younger man opened a broad door and led out an ox-cart, loaded with a stout chest. While he and Geoffrey argued the way to Saint-Georges, I bent to the old man.

"What happened in Caen?" I asked.

He glanced up, surprised. "What mean you, sir?"

"I know Ezra," I said. "I knew Aaron in Winchester."

He recovered quickly. "Caen?" His face went sour. "They burned our houses, divided our families, stole our property. A month ago. Passover. Good Friday, as you say." He lifted his head and called to the man of the cart. I did not know the tongue, but every Jew in the street stopped for a moment and stared at me.

At the abbey of Saint-Georges, Sir Amaury and I met with the old abbot who, though bedridden, seemed most unlikely to die. We spoke to the sacristan, of candles for the vigil, the reading of the service, the monks' choir for Vespers and Matins. With the cellarer Paul we arranged the morning bath for the new knights, and the high breakfast after the long night's prayer. And Simon the prior, the bishop's man, gave us the hospitality of his own table.

Whitsun eve I slept in the abbey's guesthouse, crowded among squires and younger knights. Busy with tourney matters I did not hear Mass in the abbey church, but I stood in the bright summer sun pressed about by the laughing crowd, and watched the new knights come out on the steps of the church. Dressed in white surcoats, they took their buffets from their sponsors, had sword belts bound to their waists and spurs mounted on their heels. They raised their swords, cried out the knights' prayer and, while we cheered and clapped, sprang to their draped and prancing destriers.

"By God, 'tis a wonderful thing," Geoffrey murmured. He wiped away a proud tear, and even my heart was moved.

The noisy throng began to straggle toward the lists. I had hoped to watch the knights' procession, but the leech-monk in his tent was not yet ready for the injured. The baker's cart arrived just as I heard the crowd's applause for the parade. I was showing him where to stack his baskets, white loaves for nobles and brown for peasants, when the rumble and crash of the first joust made us lift our heads. I pulled myself away and walked to the field.

New-dubbed knights had the place of honor, and over the heads of chattering farmers I could see Bertran, his colors yellow and blue, charging his opponent. They broke their lances and rode for new. The smell of crushed turf brought back sharp memories of that first tourney at Camelot, the power of the horses, the violence of the jousts, knights bruised and bleeding though they had won.

Bertran unseated the other knight. I gave a cheer, and in the crush of peasants Conon la Roche turned his red face to me.

"Fair Whitsun, sir." He touched his forehead.

"Conon," I said. On the field beyond they met with swords.

"Good sir, I'd not thanked you that you saved my calf, sir."

"I'm glad of it, Conon." I had almost forgot. At calving time I had come upon Jacq and his youngest brother, and a cow struggling with breech labor. A squire ought not put his hand to such work, but I sat my horse and told them what to do. With the calf safe Jacq had bobbed at me, and touched my leg in thanks.

Conon squinted at me, the thoughts moving behind his narrow eyes. "I wonder, sir, how you know of calving; it's not a knight's talent nor a friar's."

"I have seen many things, Conon, on my way from Britain."

The brewer's creaking wain arrived. I had to turn away and deal with it. A cheer went up from the crowd that I hoped was Bertran's win. The men struggled the heavy barrels up on new-made stands. They tapped the bung and filled a mug that I might test their wares, but before I could even swallow, a crowd of farmers pressed round us, jostling and crying out for drink.

The roar and clatter of the jousts kept on. The groundsmen carried the first injured knight into the leech's tent. His shield bore Amaury's cross of red, and it was Cyril, his face gouted from a broken nose, his teeth clenched in pain from an injured shoulder. Even our little tourney had drawn half a dozen landless knights, that made their living wandering from joust to joust; in error the marshals had matched Cyril with one of them.

Matilde waited outside the tent, frowning with worry. Her face stopped me, and struck by love I could hardly see the other lady with her, would not believe I had ever tried to forget her. "Lady." I bent and kissed her hand. It was far from a squire's right, and her cheeks went bright and she drew sharply away.

"Sir Cyril?" She peered past me. "How is my lord, esquire?"

For a moment, hearing her call him that, I could not speak. "Well enough, lady." I cleared my throat. "A broken collarbone, that will heal quick enough. By Lammas, sure."

She turned her pale eyes to me. "Our Lord's Transfiguration?"

"Aye, lady. Mayhap he will be transformed, too."

She smiled at my weak jest, and my heart floated in my chest. "I imagined," she said, "that Sir Amaury would set it our wedding date."

My heart fell like a stone. "But I pray God he will delay it for months, that for months I might see you . . ."

The other lady's laugh stopped me. "Dear Matilde, do even esquires pay you court?" She looked aside at me. "Nor would I stay, lest I hear something meant for your ears alone."

Matilde's lips were gone tight, yet I imagined some small pleasure still lingered in her look. "My lady," I said, "I have bound my heart. Yet my tongue, whenever I see you . . ."

"The esquire of my lord's liege," she grumbled, "who would vantage himself of widowhood, though even my betrothed does not."

"Lady, my love . . ."

"Who, despite such pretty words, never comes to Le Vallon."

She turned and stalked away. It left me stunned that she noticed my absence, that she was so angry of it. Once more I thought her heart must answer mine, before I saw it was but the joust of chivalry, the attraction and the repulse. I shook my head and clenched my jaw, and turned back to the tourney field, and to a combat I might better understand.

Three weeks later, the crowd of us drew up on the last hill above the river Maine and gazed across to the city of Angers. Banners flew from all the towers of the castle, and we caught the glitter of pikes on the distant battlements. Scores of rich pavilions stood the level fields south of the city, set in rows like a new and ordered town, both sides of a bright enclosure.

"You will see something now." Geoffrey had been excited for days. "Count Charles called this tourney everywhere, it's his last ere his brother comes back from crusade." He laughed and shook his head. "The good king would have us fight only infidels, but Frankish knights are the world's best, and it is tourneys that make us so. And look you," he cried, pointing, "there must be fifty tents already, and two hundred knights."

"Mayhap even British knights," muttered Ricard, "that will know our mysterious squire." But I would not worry of Camelot.

Sir Amaury had led us out, knights and squires and grooms, and we carried his own large tent and its jousting furniture, and armor and shields and bundled ash lances. Bertran had come from his father's manor to ride with us, very fine in his bright new heraldry. He had taken Guy, who had been Pierre's, as his own esquire. Cyril, his shoulder still bound, rode a chestnut palfrey and would not fight. Ricard waited at the crossroads of La Croix, and hardly smiled when he joined us.

The ferry was so crowded we had to cross in two parties. We rode up past the castle, admiring its high walls and rounded towers. A market stood at its higher corner, where beggars thrust their cups at us, jongleurs danced and sang and, as we pushed our way through the noisy crowds, joy-women leaped on tables to lift their skirts and show their dark treasures.

"Turn your head away, lad," Geoffrey said, laughing. "But no matter, you wouldn't understand any of it."

A great crowd milled about the tourney field and the count's sergeants, bright in new livery, had to bawl our way through. A marshal led us to a place among the king's vassals. Sir John's tent already stood nearby, and Amaury rode off to greet his lord.

The tourney field was three times the size of Bertran's, and already grooms cantered battle-horses across the turf. Geoffrey laughed again. "Jesu, I love a great tourney. 'Tis knighthood, chivalry, the flower of a man's life." He stopped and pointed. "By God, look there." Directly opposite stood a pavilion, blue with white flowers, and three shields at its door. "White, striped red. That can only be Sir Lancelot du Lac. Praise God, I knew it would be a great tourney. I've not seen him fight in years."

I had already recognized the colors. As Geoffrey spoke, Lancelot himself strolled out the tent, and two others followed. I did not know the taller knight, but the second had bright red hair.

"Is it Sir Lancelot?" Ricard stared across the field. "Do you truly know him?"

I did not answer. Camelot was come to Anjou. I must not shrink from it. I turned my palfrey across the field and threaded my way between the battle-horses. The British knights hardly glanced at me as I dismounted.

"Sir Almant," I said, bowing. "I did not think to see you here. And Sir Lancelot, my knight says your presence makes the tourney complete."

They glanced at one another, and the tall knight said, "Who are you, squire?" He had a long nose that stood well out from his plain face, and thick level brows above his dark eyes.

"Michel de Verdeur, esquire of Sir Amaury de Saint-Georges, sir. Once Micah of Greenfarm."

Neither he nor Lancelot remembered, but Almant's mouth gaped open. "God's Name," he cried, "the brat I left at Winchester." He stared at my livery. "You really are a squire."

I bowed again. "So I am, sir."

"Winchester," Lancelot muttered, his eyes dark with anger. "The lad you attacked, Almant, despite your oath to the king."

Almant flinched. "I did not, I swear it."

"That the king swore you to protect."

"God's love, Lancelot, he is but a churl."

"But you are not, sir." He leaned at Almant. "Your oath was a knight's oath, made to the world's best king."

"I did nothing," Almant cried, though he took a step back. "I knew nothing till the morning of Yule. But still he sent me away."

"Lancelot," said the other, "all this of a villein's brat?"

"Lambert of Denham, can you not see it either? What is a knight's oath? What is our king's honor? I tell you, had I known what happened that night . . ."

I had found my voice. "But we met, Sir Lancelot. Outside the chapel. At Matins, sir. I imagine the bells woke you."

He swung to me, his face hard.

Sir Lambert was frowning. "Does your knight know you, boy?"

"A friar gave me my name, sir." Almant snorted but I kept on. "I have said I was at Camelot."

"And your knight is Amaury . . .?"

"Sir Amaury de Saint-Georges, vassal to Sir John of Craon. That is Craon's tent, green and blue, and there they erect Sir Amaury's."

Sir Lambert nodded. "We must speak to them of you."

But Lancelot raised one hand for silence, and with his other gripped my arm and led my out on the field a dozen paces.

"Matins," he growled, quiet.

"Aye, sir," I murmured, "several times at Matins."

"I'd kill you for that." He thrust my arm away. "Save Arthur protects you, and always I defend his honor."

"Nor do I speak it, sir, to defend the king's honor."

"Churl, this is no matter of his honor."

"But on those nights, sir, you had no honor. . . ."

"No man," his bellow startled me, "no damned churl may question my honor." His dagger glinted in the air between us.

I stood unflinching, amazed at myself. "King Arthur protects me, Sir Lancelot. By your own pledge."

"Then by God and Christ your knight shall know of you."

"And of you, sir. And Sir John, too, and Count Charles."

His wrath blew at me like a wind. "God curse the knight that believes a peasant's word."

"Then I will say it."

"If you do"—he tapped my cheek with the cool blade—"I have never lost at judicial combat."

"You challenge a squire, that is a peasant? Where is the honor in that, sir?"

He saw it was true, and roared again. "God damn you."

"Sir Lancelot, hear me." I spread my hands. "It was not my father's blood that brought me to Camelot, nor sent me away. Nor from Winchester, either. Here, exiled across the sea, I am made squire. Does knightly honor drive me from Anjou as well?"

He stared at me. "A squire." He thrust his dagger into its sheath. "Well, there's small harm in that. But hear me, boy, nothing more. And never a knight. God help me, if any man dub you, the king's oath fails, I will kill the both of you."

Sir Lambert had come up. "Who would you kill, Lancelot?"

He turned, growling. "I would keep silent of this varlet."

"What?" said Lambert, his eyes gone wide.

"And you, and Almant too." Lancelot glanced past me. "Who are these?"

Geoffrey walked toward us, and Ricard and Cyril and even Bertran. "Knights of my knight," I said.

"Your silence, Lambert," Lancelot muttered.

They bowed before him, nervous as pages. I spoke their names while they gaped and stared. Even Geoffrey could but babble no man matched Lancelot's prowess, how anxious he was to see him joust.

Lancelot, as if he heard it always, put on an empty smile. "Alas, sir, this tourney I cannot joust."

"You take the cross, sir? You sail to the crusade?"

"No crusade," Lancelot murmured, "but a holy quest."

"God praise you, sir," said Geoffrey. "Even if we must miss your splendid fighting, what an honor to meet you, sir." He nodded at me. "Michel said he was at Camelot, but some of us wondered of it." They bowed again and turned reluctantly away.

I let out my breath. Lambert frowned, but Lancelot gave me a thin smile. "Your knight is a man of Craon? I've met John often, in tourneys past. I set a table at Lambert's, the last night. Sir John may come. And bring your knight if he would."

Half the assembled company had watched us, drawn by Lancelot's roar. None knew how I angered him, nor would I say it, yet knights eyed me and ladies pointed me out, all the days of the tourney. So famous was the high knight that even his fury could create renown.

As for the jousts and the melee, I had grown so used to it that the skill of battle overshone the violence, and it was all a delight to watch. Our party did well, especially Sir Amaury that won both his jousts. On the third day, making a team with Bertran and Geoffrey, he captured four in the final melee. And one of those was Ricard de la Croix.

Ricard had arrived with us, but he spent the tourney in the company of Malcom d'Avrille, and joined his party for the melee. Sir Malcolm was a banneret with a heavy face and a loud voice, held ample lands near Angers, and had but a single daughter as his heir.

Sir Amaury gave an angry shrug. " 'Tis not Ricard but Simon that holds the fief, that will be too old when next I call my forty days. Nor will I accept coin for his default. I will take it back and join it to Le Vallon, after Cyril weds the widow."

We crossed the trampled field under a pale, golden sky, the last evening, Sir John and Sir Amaury, and John's squire Fernand and myself. Knights crowded Lambert's tent, and Lancelot placed John at his high table with count and bishop, and Amaury at the lower board not far from Almant. I cut his meat and poured his wine. Soon enough he asked how Almant knew me.

"At Camelot." Almant glanced away, his face unhappy. "King Arthur had chosen him."

At the sound of famous names all the knights around bent to listen. Sir Amaury peered at me, for I had said nothing of that. "But if the king chose him, how did he come to leave?"

"I was not there." Almant scowled, not liking their stares, unwilling to speak of rape or failed oaths. "He always was a froward lad."

Amaury laughed. "And so he is, even yet."

I had gone dizzy from not breathing.

He told of my fight with Ricard, my wound in the ambush. The others smiled, always pleased by tales of battle, but Almant stared as if he believed none of it. I refilled Sir Amaury's cup. The heat and noise and the glitter of lamps blurred my head. I waited for the question of my birth. I prayed God would protect me.

"Good sirs," Lancelot called out, to the whole company. "You know I did not tourney. Tonight will I tell you why, and of God's marvels at Camelot, of the quest of the Roundtable."

The whole pavilion hushed.

"It was the week before Whitsun," he said, "that a gentlewoman came to me at Camelot. She led me out to a convent of nuns and there I met a lad, raised by the sisters, fair and strong and a man already. They begged me make him a knight, and I saw he would be a great fighter and dubbed him at once. I said to him, 'Come back with me to Camelot, King Arthur delights in brave young knights.' But he would not."

Lancelot's voice rumbled among us like small thunder, while his tale grew ever more strange. On Whitsun morn each chair of the Roundtable glittered with the name of its knight, written in gold. On the seat kept empty for the best the bright letters spelled out Galahad. No one knew the name, but as they sat to meal an old man appeared, bringing a young knight clad in red armor.

"Here was the knight I had dubbed." He stared about the pavilion, laughing. "We knew immediately he was the finest in the world." He laughed again. "It was his name on the empty chair. Galahad." His eyes shone with happiness. "And he was my own son."

Every knight in the tent clapped the board before them, and even I could not resist Lancelot's delight.

"But hear you," he said, serious again, "after Vespers we sat the Roundtable once more, the king and the twenty-four of us, and the rest around in the Hall." He looked away over our heads, and his eyes saw only Camelot. "Suddenly a tempest blew among us and though it was dusk a blaze bright as midday filled the castle and then . . ." He closed his eyes. "And then we saw . . ."

He crossed himself. In Lambert's tent no one made a sound.

"We could not speak. We could hardly draw breath. It was the holy cup of Christ's last meal. Our Lord's Sangral." Lancelot never heard the gasp we all made. "Pure samite covered it, yet in that dusk it shone of its own brightness. It moved like a bird in the air, that stopped just over our heads. We stared, frightened and comforted both. And then it vanished. It was gone. We sat speechless. At last the king stood and raised his hands and blessed God for what He had shown to us, that holy day."

In the pavilion we took another breath.

"Gawain stood, his eyes stared at its place, his voice shook like our own hearts. 'My lords,' he said, 'this thing hath roused my soul, and destroyed my ease. Here before you I make my vow, that on the morrow I will ride out, to seek without pause as long as it may take, until I behold that holy vessel clear and unveiled.' "

I saw before me Camelot's great Hall, the gleaming shape beneath its black rafters, Sir Gawain's earnest frown.

"A great spirit filled the place," Lancelot murmured. He had got to his feet. "We stood, every one of us, and made all together the same vow. Not honor nor riches nor renown, but the saving of our immortal souls. Surely there is no greater quest. A knight's best and finest act, the true reason for his life."

He closed his eyes. "Then King Arthur spoke again, and with a great sorrow we could not understand. Never, he said, had there been a quest so holy, never a quest so valiant. Yet Gawain in all his high purpose did slay the fellowship of the Roundtable. Never again would our high company sit, all of us together, at Camelot."

Tears were running down Lancelot's face. "But we had all made our vow. Our knight's oath." He paused to scrub his wet cheek. "The next morning we rode out, each of us full-armed, each to his own course." He drew from his purse a scallop shell worked in silver, the mark of Saint James. "I go to Spain, to Compostela."

We walked back across the tourney field in silence. The night smelled of dust and horses, summer stars glittered in the black sky, and the magic of Lancelot's tale, of Camelot itself, sang in our ears. Sir John stopped outside his pavilion and I thought he smiled in the starlight. "Of course this thing would happen at Camelot. God knows I envy Lancelot that vision. And that quest."

"Yet how is it, sir," said Amaury, "that Galahad the son stands higher than Sir Lancelot his father? And he a natural child, born out of wedlock?"

A young man, I thought, raised apart, clever at arms. It was another tale not so different from my own. Sir Amaury had forgot to ask of my own father, yet there would be time tomorrow. But my tongue spoke something else.

"Good sirs, it was Whitsun the Holy Spirit appeared to Our Lord's apostles. That same day the Sangral appeared at Camelot."

"How do you think these things?" Amaury muttered.

" 'Tis a question for your friar," Sir John murmured, and then he said, "I spoke to Lancelot of you." Fear burst bright as a sudden bonfire in my mind. "He says you were truly at Camelot."

"So I was, Sir John."

"There was a matter of a battle-horse, and of a girl. He was loath to say more." He paused a moment, as if unwilling himself to go on. My fright sang in my ears like hornets. "We all hear tales," he said, "of Lancelot. Of Arthur's queen . . ."

"No," I said quickly, "no, my lord. Lady Guenever is King Arthur's wife, Sir Lancelot his finest knight."

"You have heard these things?"

"I have, Sir John. But they are false."

"I am glad to hear it, Michel, you ease my heart."

I denied it for Lancelot, and for the memory of the glorious queen, and though I thought Sir John saw my falsehood, something in the way he spoke told me I had met another trial.

Twelve

Three months past I had gone out from Clos Saint-Georges, riding a fine palfrey, wearing the robes of a new squire, and through a day so green with spring I could speak of nothing but love. But on the Sabbath after our return from Angers, the fields beside the dusty road were thick with grain, I wore a summer tunic against the white sun, and my heart ached.

Matilde sat with her mother on the same bench, in the shade of the oak. I watched the old lady as I spoke, lest my tongue fail me. Sir Cyril should marry Matilde at the abbey of Saint-Georges, on Saint Michel's Day at the end of September.

"Sir Amaury himself will marry," I said, to ease my pain, "at Craon and in Yuletide."

Her mother seemed pleased of the date. She thanked me, and went to call a servant to bring us wine. Matilde had said nothing, as if remembering her anger at Saint-Georges. I did not worry of it; I wanted only to sit beside her. After a long moment she turned to me, with a new light glinting in her eye. "Sir Cyril tells us the great Sir Lancelot du Lac was at the tourney. And that you knew him."

" 'Tis true, my lady."

"Cyril had not believed you."

"I make no empty boasts, nor . . ." I stopped to draw a breath. "Nor do I speak false of my heart, that even now yearns for you." In her presence, my tongue had no restraint.

She gave me a brief smile. "Cyril," she said, "tells us you disputed the knight."

"We argued, lady. He drew his dagger."

Her eyes widened. "What said you, Michel, to so rouse him?"

"He swore to kill me, if I were ever dubbed a knight."

She put a hand to her mouth. " 'Tis a frightful curse."

"But happy would I die, sweet lady, if before it I had found the consummation of my love." I had no wish of courtly banter, yet the words came unthinking to my tongue.

She smiled again. "Esquire, you have more British honey on your tongue than many an Angevin knight." She gave a brief laugh. "Certainly more than Cyril."

"Lady," I growled, "I dread this marriage. And that it must be on Saint Michel's Day."

She looked away. "How pleasant it might be to sit with a squire that knows Sir Lancelot, that argues with him and lives. But who can attend his moods, bright flattery to sudden anger?"

"I am helpless before you, lady. I have no pleasure in chivalry. Love is not a thing I play at. My heart aches in me. All these words would distract me of you, yet they all fail."

A serving girl stood silently before us. Matilde took the cup, and the girl's eye glittered as she curtsied and turned away.

My lady took a sip and handed it to me. The wine was light and flowery, more like springtime than this heated summer day. " 'Tis true," she murmured, half to herself, "that I have small love for Sir Cyril de Lande. I marry him of the kindness of Sir Amaury, that he has chosen such a knight to protect me. And there will be La Croix to provide for our children." She looked at me sharp, for I made a strangled cough. "I cannot stay here alone. It is Sir Cyril, or the sisters of Nyoiseau."

"Lady . . ." I could barely speak, of Cyril having children on her. And of Nyoiseau, a Benedictine convent a league from Craon.

"No more than you, Michel, do I play at love." Her voice trembled suddenly, and tears wet her eyes.

I took her hand and pressed it to my lips a long minute. And when she took it back, she turned it in her lap and peered at it as if searching for some mark.

"A pleasant thing, chivalric love."

She blinked her eyes dry. Her mother came from the house. I moved away on the bench, that the old woman sit between us. She began at once on matters of the marriage, of questions I must ask Sir Amaury. I sat, trying to remember them, engulfed by love.

With Bertran gone and Cyril befuddled of his coming nuptials, my every summer day was filled with farm and manor, yet every day I thanked God it distracted me from Matilde. Still, by Our Lord's Trans-figuration the harvest was nearly finished. I rode out early that morning, and came soon to Ninefarms. There was nobody in the manor fields. I swung down and walked into the waist-high grain, silver-gold in the heating air. I counted the heads, full enough to yield five times sown. I stripped one and bit the kernels between my teeth. At Greenfarm we would harvest now. Where were Conon and his reapers?

I mounted and turned for La Roche. Conon stood in the road before me. Once again thoughts moved behind his eyes.

"Time to reap here, Conon. How much did you sow?"

"Let me think, Ninefarms manor, ten baskets."

"Then Sir Amaury will expect fifty."

"How do you know that?" He stood himself in front of my horse, crossed his arms and squinted up at me. "Been watching you, I have. Never believed you, not from the first, Michel from somewhere." He spat in the dust. "From nowhere, likely."

Absorbed by harvest worries I could only stare at him.

"Fought for my Jacq—what sneering squire'd do a thing like that?" Conon clamped his lips. "What precious noble's son can taste harvest in the seed, count the heads for my reapers' due?"

"Sir Geoffrey," I said.

"What's Sir Geoffrey know of calves?" He did not move. "I'll tell you this, you're no knight's son, you're the brat of some damn farmer, same as me."

"Watch your tongue, Conon," I growled. I felt no fear at all. "What do you want?"

"What do I want? Maybe I'd give but forty here, keep the ten?" He grinned slyly. "Think I'm a fool? Sir Geoffrey can count, you're right there." He spat again. "Tell you what I don't want, I don't want some damn villein's brat atop some damn fancy horse telling everybody he's a highborn . . ."

"Damn you, Conon." I was standing in my stirrups. My dagger glittered in my hand, though I could not remember drawing it. "God damn you," I bellowed, "shut your mouth."

He flinched, fighting a lifetime of obeying mounted men, but he stood his ground. "No you don't, you don't wave some little knife at the reeve of Saint-Georges." He gave a hard smile. "The sons know it, too."

I hardly saw him through my haze of fury. I jerked my horse around. He had to dodge as I went past him. "Harvest that damn field," I called, "else you're a dead man."

Even as I rode away I knew my anger was but fright transfigured. The storm had broken. Knights and lords had not discovered me, it had been an Angevin peasant. I had foreseen it clear enough, yet now there was another thing I had not expected. To save my peasant's revenge against murdering knights, I must now murder a peasant, myself. I did not believe I could do it.

The rest of that day stands as clear in my mind as if it were yesterday. I rode Sir Amaury's fields. I spoke to the reapers, ordering the harvest as if nothing happened. I took the midday meal at the abbey, using my dagger to cut my bread, that soon enough ought do the same to Conon. Most of the farms were reaped as I rode homeward, and the sheaves stood stacked and hooded in the fields. Thick clouds hung above the river valley. A wind smelling of rain stirred the dust in the road, as if the approaching storm mimicked my own circumstance. At the manor peasants worked the last corner of the home field, and I drew up and asked for Sir Geoffrey. A reaper named Aubin straightened up, wiped his face and pointed to Clos Saint-Georges.

"And Sir Cyril?" I said.

They stopped of a sudden, all of them, as if I had rung a bell. They looked up at me with sweating faces, and anger shook off them like waves of summer heat. Aubin spat into the stubble. "He's at the manor, sir, they do say."

I knew every one of them. Always they bobbed at me, smiling and pleasant, but in that dusty field I could smell their hatred. They might have raised their sickles and hacked me apart, and even my horse shifted nervous under me.

"What is it, Aubin?"

He spat again. The others turned back to their work. "Sir Cyril, he's killed a man, sir. Mounted the wife, sir, and they cut him, the sons, sir, they made a ballock of him, didn't they?"

"Cyril?"

He squinted up at me. "It don't surprise us none, sir, he always had a lordly prick, sir, it's just he did it to the wife and that was too much for old Conon, sir."

"Conon? Conon la Roche?"

"Aye, sir."

I spurred my horse to the manor. Cyril ballocked. Conon dead. Christ's name, what had happened?

It was exactly as Aubin said. Cyril lay bruised and whimpering and curled in pain. He had found the woman washing, her blouse open from the heat, her skirts about her hips. Conon, come back for his whetstone, heard the screams. He hit Cyril twice with a shovel before the knight could draw his dagger. The sons, missing their father, found the man gutted and dying and Cyril on the woman a second time. They had brought him back the whole distance in a hay wain. He might have bled to death, save they had done the thing with wonderful correctness.

"Damn," said Sir Amaury, sitting in his Hall. "He was so zealous of that little widow, thought her holy as Our Lady."

Geoffrey snorted as he took the ale cup. "They say he'd had a dozen farm girls the summer. Getting brats, ere it was too late."

"By Christ, I wish he'd done her, just once."

Old Reynaud smiled, but Joachim the priest shook his lean head and muttered of Amaury's impiety. I stood at the screen, waiting to call the serving lad with the first meat, still unable to grasp what had happened. Conon killed, so suddenly his threat felt hardly real. Cyril eunuched, that so revered Matilde, as if his virtue at Le Vallon might balance all the rest—Mayenne, the farm girls, Conon's handsome wife. Cyril, blind with both lust and chivalric honor, had saved me from both his marriage and Conon's denunciation.

"Damn." Sir Amaury waved the empty cup at me. "Pierre dead, Ricard strayed, now Cyril nubbed. Three knights I've lost this year. I'll hang every damn boy of Conon's."

"Sir Amaury," Joachim murmured, "remember Our Lord's word."

And I thought his sons had done no more than any son ought. "Is there nothing else for it, sir?"

"Damn me, Michel, they assaulted a knight, wounded him worse than a man ought be and still live."

"At least they didn't blind him, sir." Geoffrey burst out laughing, but Sir Amaury only grumbled. "Hang Jacq," I said, "the oldest must have done it. The others, Jules and Hugh, they'd do whatever their brother said."

"I want them all dead."

"Oh sir," I cried, "then hang them all. Hang the woman, too, for seducing him. What peasant knows anything of love? Sir Cyril might have spoke to her gentle, the courtly knight he is, but he knew only an assault could rouse her passion."

They all turned to stare at me, and Sir Amaury muttered, "Jesu, you argue like a Jacobin. Where do you get these notions?" He scowled at me. "You'd hang the one you fought Ricard for?"

"He has a point, Amaury," said Geoffrey, "least punishment is oft best."

"Three deaths for one is unjust," said Joachim, and even Reynaud murmured his agreement.

And thus on the Sabbath next Sir Amaury stood at his house door, scowled out over the peasants crowded in his court, and demanded the life of Conon's oldest son. A shudder ran through the throng, before the

men of the manor bound the lad and led him down to the old oak beside
the crossroads. He did not flinch at Joachim's shriving, nor at the rope
about his neck. Conon's widow watched at the edge of the crowd, the
other boys close beside her, and only once did she turn her dark eyes to
stare at me.

I heard Jacq wailing on the gravel at Caen, an echo half-forgot of
Emrys' scream on Camelot's icy cobbles. I could not remember how
many had died already, because of Ricard's strap, because of Lark's
knights. Dear God Father, was it all Your inscrutable Will? Was there
truly a plan that pleased You, or were we but Your playthings, here on
this Earth?

Sir Amaury took as heriot, his death duty, Conon's finest bull. The
man's brother came to assume Conon's tenancies. Cyril retired to a priory near his father's manors. And Jacq's body swung, in the heat and
rain, till Saint Michel's eve.

"Praise Mary she was saved of him," said Matilde's mother. "Who
will there be now? Bertran la Romme?"

"His betrothal is already arranged, madam," I said.

Matilde wore a darkened look. "We hear Ricard de la Croix will wed
Marie d'Avrille. Pray God she is a holy Mary, to live with him." She
raised her eyes to me. "But who will be my guardian now, good Michel?
Must I take Christ as my bridegroom after all?"

I glanced away. "I do not know Sir Amaury's mind."

Her mother smiled. "There is no one but you, esquire." I felt my
cheeks go hot, and the old lady laughed. "Oh, look at him, Matilde. Did
you know this?"

"He hides it very well, Mother. I still remember how Guy told us of
his purity."

I grew even warmer. "I will tell Sir Amaury of your wishes."

They laughed again, but her mother was suddenly serious. "How old
are you, lad?"

"Almost sixteen, lady."

She nodded. "Matilde is nineteen."

"Twenty, mother, at All Souls'."

"When will you be dubbed, Michel?"

"Bertran was seventeen, lady." I had no lands either, but Matilde
would bring me Le Vallon and there was La Croix, and almost I hoped it
might be true.

"Another year. Perhaps two." The lady shook her head.

And Matilde bent her own head and muttered, "What does God
with me, that He kills husband, sons, even my betrothed?"

I no longer had the heart to stay, and though it was rude I bowed and muttered of duty at Saint-Georges, and went out to my palfrey. Matilde followed me, and took the reins from the waiting groom.

"Lady, forgive my leaving. Your suffering grieves us all."

"Yet you will not stay to ease me of it." She moved her head a little. "Beside my door there stand the casements of my Hall. Through which, most likely, my mother watches."

I looked past her. "Yes, she does."

"And on the other hand are a smaller pair, shuttered, that are my bedchamber."

"That lead, dear lady, to the garden of my rose."

Her eyes glittered. "Get you into your saddle, esquire."

I could barely hear for my heart's throbbing. "Lady, I . . ."

She reached a finger to my lips. "Your saddle, Michel. My mother watches."

I turned and found my stirrup, and swung up.

She raised her face to me. "Now, good squire, think you it will rain, this Sabbath eve?"

"Mayhap, lady," For a moment I did not understand her, and then my hand that held the reins shook with surprise and desire. "Were I blind, lady, my heart would lead me. But, lady, though I praise God, I do not understand."

"I weary of waiting God's pleasure, Michel, I would have my own." She looked at me, barely smiling. " 'Tis the dark of the moon, it will be very gloomy at Matins. Go you well, esquire."

I could not believe it. Riding home I felt as stunned and simple as Cyril had, all that summer. Saturday night was very dark, even the stars dimmed by a soft haze, though the rain she imagined had not arrived. Her dogs me me in the lane, their tails wagging, and I had brought them each a bone. The casements of her chamber were just low enough for me to clamber over. Since Pierre left for Caen she had slept in a old curtained bed with her mother, and her maid on a pallet by the door. But that night was Our Lady's Assumption and the older lady had stopped at another manor, and the girl slept away with her lover.

Matilde took my hands without a word and pushed me upon the old rattling bed.

"Lady," I whispered.

She thrust her hands within my clothes, yet as she embraced me I felt again Lark's doeskin bag, and my desire nearly failed. I struggled to think, to say I could not, must not. "Lady, my friar, my knighthood's purity. Lady, please."

"Well," she whispered, touching me, "I see at least you do not hate me."

I could not help myself. "Oh, lady, I love you, but . . ."

Her hands paused for a moment. "Your friar is a Jacobin, a Black-friar, because his member has . . ."

"Lady." I struggled with myself.

"Yes, young Michel?"

"I cannot."

"But you cannot stop."

And it was true. She was slender and taut and very flexible, and as she moved upon me she kept up a steady murmur of hunger and delight, like the whisper of water through reeds.

"Matilde," I said. "Lady of my love."

She bit me softly on my scarred shoulder. "No one will know, Michel, but you and I. And God, who does not care."

And Lark.

For even as I lay warm and pleasured in her arms, I could not forget I had sworn to become a knight and not a courtly lover.

All that autumn I kept from Le Vallon, though each day, each Sabbath at least, I hoped she would send for me again. But she did not. I tried to think of her as Cyril had, a lady to be worshiped instead of wooed. It helped but little to ease my ache for her whispers and her kiss, and her small quick body against mine.

Then it was winter, as cold and damp as any British season, and the weather itself kept me from her. And it was Saint Andrew's, and then suddenly the week ere Yule, and Sir Amaury was grown more nervous of his wedding than Bertran of his dubbing. We fetched his mother from the convent of Fontevraud. We trekked the muddy ways to Craon through a long rainy winter day, and yet we smiled and sang beneath our dripping hoods, for such weather foretold a fruitful marriage.

Sir John's castle shone black under the rain. Just as we arrived the storm worsened, rain beat on the glass windows, and fires swirled and smoke blew. Yet his welcome was warm and generous as ever, and his Hall was bright with tapers, and noisy with laughter and the songs of minstrels.

Sir Henry, the father of the bride, sat at Sir John's right hand. Lady Adele sat on his left, and then Sir Amaury with his betrothed.

The Lady Clare had a deepish voice, a fine nose, and a slight gap between her front teeth. She wore no wimple, but bound her dark hair in a silver net. I had thought her serious, from the lines between her eyebrows, but that night the wine drew out her bright humor and made me glad she would soon be lady of Saint-Georges. I stood before them and carved their meat, and poured the wine in the cup they shared. As the minstrels sang there were courses of venison and duck, and rice made yellow by saffron, and apples baked and cloves to sweeten the breath, and ginger in honey.

When the harper began Roland's tale, the Hall hushed to the old story. But Sir John beckoned me up the table to him.

"I have seen your knight," he murmured.

"My knight, sir?" I glanced at Amaury.

Beside him Adele turned to catch his words. I had not been to Craon for nearly a year, yet I remembered well her round face, her eyes that glittered green in taperlight, her auburn hair always bound and braided in the newest style.

"Lancelot," said Sir John. "A month past."

"Sir Lancelot?" Angers came back to me, very clear. "Had he found the Sangral, sir?"

John shook his head. "He had been to Compostela, but of course it was not there. On his way back he rested at a hermitage. The monk heard his confession." John paused. "He said it did not matter Lancelot were Christendom's finest knight; because of his sins he would never see the Sangral."

"But if not Sir Lancelot . . ."

"If not he, then who?" John gave a grim smile. "Lancelot would not accept the judgment. The monk would not change it. At last, for his soul and the Sangral Lancelot swore two sacred oaths, the first 'gainst battle and war, the second 'gainst courtly love." It made me wonder of his oath against my dubbing.

Adele gave a quick laugh. "Lancelot? Truly?" Her eyes gleamed at me. "Do you believe this, Michel?"

"If my lord has said it, lady."

She nodded, yet did not take her gaze from me.

Sir John smiled, very broad, remembering. "He sat here, sad-faced, and asked my forgiveness of the defeats he gave me when we were younger."

"Lancelot?" said the lady again.

John called a page to pour their wine, and with her attention diverted he murmured, "We spoke of you. Lancelot could not understand your wit, nor your strength at arms. He imagined you were a foundling at, where was it, Greenfarm?"

My head spun, and I had to grip the edge of the table. "Sir. I never heard it." I tried to meet his gaze. "I am in your hands, Sir John."

He nodded, as if I passed a third judgment. "Then go you well, young Michel."

"Thank you, sir." I bowed carefully, and walked away.

The lady Clare peered at me. "What did Sir John want?"

It took me a moment to answer. "He had word of Sir Lancelot."
She raised her eyebrows. "Is it true you argued with him?"
"It is, lady."
"I had no idea you had such a celebrated esquire, Amaury."
"Young Michel has angered all the famous British knights."
"And some not famous." I laughed with them. I glanced again down the table. Sir John spoke with somebody else, yet his lady kept her gaze on me, as if she wondered what had passed between us.

In the night the rain changed to snow, and next morning Craon castle was a place of magic, of white and black and the red of the chapel glass. We walked a court thick with falling snow and crowded into the church. The priests swung incense and chanted Psalms in the thick air, while we took the Mass of Christ Our Savior. John's priest read out the ancestors of Our Lord, and old Joachim had taught me so well I understood almost all the Latin.

But I was much distracted. Sir John knew of Greenfarm. Sir Lancelot imagined I had noble ancestors, and I a foundling. It had been Lark's dream, that killed her and sent me here. Always I wore a mask; always I was only who they imagined. At Caen it saved my life. At Craon John had seen behind it.

The priests gave us Christ's blessing. Outside, the wind had eased and the snow stopped, though our breath showed thick in the chill air. Craon's household flowed through the court in a chattering stream, anxious for the shelter of the Hall. I ought go with them, it was midday, Sir Amaury would soon need me to serve. But I turned and walked out the castle gate, and went carefully down the slippery way.

Smoke climbed the white air over the roofs of the town. The bell of the village church rang harsh in the bitter air. Snow drifted the frozen streets, though in the market someone had lit a fire of slats and buckets and old straw, and children danced around it, screaming and throwing snow at one another. Townsmen hardly glanced at me, for a new squire at the castle was never strange to them. I walked down to the icy river and along its banks, past the last houses to the mill and its frozen pond.

The wind rose, whipping the corners of my robe. Snow fell thickly again, rattling in the bare hedges. A figure sheltered under the porch of the mill, an old man I had not noticed before.

"Good Yule, sir," I said.

"And to you, my son." Snow lay in large flakes on the fine wool of his cloak, and his white beard blew about his face. He was twice thirty winters, yet unbent by his years. "I did not know you at first, lad." A smile lit his face. "These fine robes. And you have grown."

I peered at him. "Do I know you, sir?" Something familiar sounded in his voice.

"You stay at Craon, lad?"

"Sir Amaury will marry . . ."

"John of Craon is an excellent knight," he said brusquely.

"Fine enough to be at Camelot, sir."

I had not thought that before, but the old man only nodded. "So he might. Though now he would wander lost of the Sangral, like all the rest." His voice seemed angry and sad, both, and he closed his eyes briefly. " 'Tis good you come to Craon, lad. You must stay close to John, care for him as he cares for you."

"My knight, sir, is Amaury de Saint-Georges, that is vassal to Sir John." I imagined he knew everything of myself, of Amaury and John. "But who are you, good sir? Have we ever met?"

His eyes flashed with anger and for a moment my heart stood in my throat, but he was an old man again. "Perhaps I was mistaken. Good day to you, Michel de Verdeur."

I heard the echo of something dimly remembered, yet as I wondered at it he turned and walked away into the falling snow.

Thirteen

The snow fell thick in the narrow streets of the town, and a few children still played at the dying fire. The old man had known my name, that I was squire to Sir Amaury. Despite his elegant robes something of him reminded me of my hedge-friar, yet I smelled no ale nor old men's rotting teeth. I did not understand his sudden anger or his quick leaving, nor even where he might shelter against the weather.

I shivered at the thought and drew my cloak about me. Craon castle stood its sudden hill, its dark stones half draped with white. A party of knights had just arrived, and harness rattled and horses stamped the stony court and men's voices boomed. One single bird, black as a raven, flew up from the chapel roof, beating its way through the falling snow, and without warning I shook with memory. Briant strode Winchester's kitchen, Orsain lifted his club, Laramort prowled Camelot's buttery, Giles dropped his blade on Emrys. And Lark murmured, I bleed. Stay close to Sir John, the old man had said. I had to stop on the castle steps and catch my breath, and let my heart slow, again.

Tapers and fires lit Sir John's Hall, and there were the smells of wine and woodsmoke. Melodies of rebec and psaltery echoed on the tapestried walls, and nobles' voices rumbled of hunts and tourneys and harvest. And of the crusade, for the French king was at last returned from the Holy Land.

It was Steven, newly bishop of Angers, that brought the news. He was a sturdy, broad-faced prelate, that wore a mail tunic and a short sword as if he were more knight than priest. If he came to honor Sir John at his knight's wedding, he came also to speak of the abbey of Saint-Georges. The old abbot still lingered. Each side was adamant of rights and powers. Nothing was settled, of the abbey, that Yuletide.

The wedding of Sir Amaury and the lady Clare was held at Vespers, on the day of Saint John Evangelist, that was the Sabbath and two days after Yule. Sir John dressed his chapel with boughs of pine and rowan berries, and tapers burned everywhere in the high space. The warm air smelled of pitch and beeswax and incense, and the leather and iron of knights, and the spices of the ladies. Monks sang the Mass with sweet high voices, that rang and blended on the stone vaults overhead. As esquire to the groom I stood holding sword and shield, while my knight full-armored and the lady in glinting samite knelt and took the Host. The priest called out God's blessing on the new-wedded pair, and the church filled with the answering shouts of knights and their ladies.

Out in the cold evening a fine snow fell again on the court of the castle, and the flakes sparkled in the torchlight while horn-men sounded their brassy notes in our ears. I led the couple up the castle steps to the Hall. The high space gleamed bright as the church, and as we entered the swarm of minstrels crowding the music gallery burst into song. Servers waited at the screen, bearing shoulder-high the roast head of a wild boar, the first of Sir John's enormous feast.

Amaury and his lady Clare sat at John's right. Serving my knight I must also meet the gaze of Lady Adele, and that night again her eyes were green beneath her soft brow. For no reason I remembered the old man at the mill, and then she called me to fill the cup and while I poured moved her lips as if drinking. But she was Sir John's wife. I would not imagine she meant anything by it.

The feast lasted hours, and there were a dozen varieties of meat, and fish and bread, and wines from near and far. There was dancing, even during the meal. The lady Clare retired when the sweets began. Soon after, Sir Amaury rose to follow and all the Hall cheered and clapped the tables, and he stopped at the doorway to wave to the throng. Her brother Philip waited outside her door full-armed, as he must, and would not let Sir Amaury enter till I produced the wedding contract and proved the marriage. The couple went into their private chamber, attended only by her lady's maid. Philip and I walked back to the Hall to share a cup.

Philip was four years my elder, dubbed a knight two summers past. He was more handsome than his older sister, with light hair, a high smooth brow and a squarish jaw. He laughed at everything, and claimed to love only hawks and horses.

"If I must wed the widow of Le Vallon, God be thanked she's pretty."

"She is very pretty," I said. The drink almost eased my pain of saying it.

A pale winter sun had melted all the snow save in the shadows of the woods, beside the road to Le Vallon. The old house was very warm. They were boiling soap.

"Philip de Neuille," I said. Despite her wintry seriousness Matilde was more beautiful than ever. "Sir Amaury would have you wed Saint Mark's Day, this year the second Sunday after Easter."

"The gowns are made." Her mother counted the weeks on her fingers. "It could be sooner. What does Philip have, esquire?"

"Saint-Clement, madam, two large manors, forty farms. On the river Loire, six leagues east of Angers." I drew a breath. "My lady Clare has her father's demesne, that is somewhat larger."

The lady frowned. "His father gives his son the smaller portion? Is he a backward knight?"

"No, madam." I glanced at Matilde, who sat and watched the floor and said nothing. "He is high-spirited and very happy. Yet I think, madam, Sir Philip may never be truly in earnest, of anything."

"Pray God he will be earnest in this marriage," muttered the old lady. "And will we live there, at Saint-Clement?"

"It is the larger manor, lady."

Matilde lifted her gaze, her eyes gone damp. "I do not believe I will ever wed again. I long to hide myself among the sisters of Nyoiseau."

"Matilde," said her mother.

Nor did I understand. "Lady, do you refuse this knight?"

"I have lost children, husband, even betrothed." Tears swam in her eyes. "How can I not believe God is displeased with me?"

"She has been thus since Yule." Her mother gazed at her a long moment, before she stood and kissed her cheek.

"Lady, what may I do for you?" I murmured, when her mother had gone away.

She gave a fleeting smile. "Oh, Michel, do not say that." She wiped a damp cheek. "Our single bright reprieve but makes my darkness blacker. God is angry at that, too. I yearn for the peace of the convent."

That would be the peace of death, I thought. I took her hand. "Look outside, lady. The sun shines, springtime comes." I drew a breath. "Sir Philip will make you a fine husband."

She gazed at me without expression. "He is a happy knight?"

"Very happy." I kissed her hand. "Yet you have my love always."

"A happy knight. And Sir Amaury wishes him?" She drew her hand away. "Then, Michel, I will marry Sir Philip."

Even when they met, a month later, she would only curtsy and nod, distantly. And though Philip smiled always toward her wintry look, and chatted happily with her old mother, his own heart seemed rock-hard against all her beauty. He would marry her with the same dispassion she wed him. It looked the perfect marriage, each agreed the other was acceptable, and the union very sensible. I could not understand any of it.

At Clos Saint-Georges the lady Clare brought a younger cousin as her companion, and three women as servants of her chamber. By Candlemas she had elevated the life of the manor. We drank wine at meals instead of ale, and for that feast minstrels sang in Sir Amaury's Hall. She scolded him he never taught his squires dancing, nor courtly talk, nor even elegant table manners. She showed us the steps of dances from Paris and Troyes, the moves of the chessboard, and tables and merels and hazard, and when I learned quickly she teased him I would soon be more elegant than he. She even brought several books that the cousin read to us in taperlit evenings, the newest tales of chivalry and knightly honor.

And while I learned courtly things of Lady Clare, Sir Amaury armed me with a squire's sword and my own mail tunic. Worried of conflict at the abbey, he demanded more practice at arms. Our knights gathered in the court every dry day, himself and Sir Geoffrey, and Philip who was often with us, for sword and dagger work. I served as esquire to all of them, and when they were finished, claimed my own training.

"By God," muttered Philip, after our first meeting. "Here is a squire that fights better than half the knights I've met."

"I've had the most excellent teachers."

Geoffrey smiled with pride. "There is something of Michel I have not seen before, save in the highest knights of Camelot."

"Camelot?" Philip made a face. "The smallest page of that castle has it, more than any Frankish knight?"

In truth no squire I had met had my Norman gift, nor did these knights, either. I could not believe it were a matter of Camelot; I did not remember it when I sparred with the grooms there, but only at Caen.

Despite his praise Geoffrey would not train me with horse and lance, for mounted battle or the joust. Each time I asked he had a reason to put it off, farmwork or errands at Angers, or that he had no battle-horse to spare. I understood that if Sir Amaury wished me as his chamberlain he had no need to dub me. Therefore, would I be a knight, I must somehow leave Clos Saint-Georges.

The thought saddened me, yet that spring I swallowed my protests and set myself to train hand and eye, and learn all I could of combat afoot. My skill grew so quick I soon believed I might be the equal of the knights; so anxious was I to prove my swollen hopes, I grew impatient for the mortal seriousness of battle. And thus I felt only joy when, early on the Sabbath morning before Easter, a monk of the abbey of Saint-Georges galloped in through Amaury's gates.

I stood at the manor door breathing the early air. The iron shoes of his horse rang loud on the cobbles.

"Paul sent me," he cried, breathless. "The abbot has died." He stood in his stirrups. "The old man is dead."

I took the bridle of his sweated horse. "Go wake Sir Amaury."

He sat back in his saddle. "He'll be abed. With his lady."

"Jesu, he will interrupt anything for this."

"Yes," he said, and swung down.

I bellowed to the stables for a groom. "Rub this one," I told him. "Saddle three for messengers, and then the palfreys and destriers. Bundle the thick lances."

Inside the house a crowd of servants already chattered at the Hall door. "Bread and ale for the road," I called to Reynaud. "We ride soon as we may."

I counted our knights on my fingers, Philip visiting and Geoffrey, and sent a boy to wake them. I sent another riding to the manor reeves, to rouse the farmers who owned arms, and then east to Ricard at La Croix. A third would go west to seek Bertran.

The first came back, excited now, and I gripped his shoulder. "Take our fastest horse. Ride hard for Craon, it's ten leagues but Sir John must come to Saint-Georges quick as he can."

The household clamored and swirled around me. I drew a breath, went up the stairs two at a time, and strode past the women wide-eyed in the passage.

"Is it war?" they muttered.

"Yes," I said, happy, though for one quick moment I remembered Domfront, and Sir Amaury rubbing his hands of a good fight.

"Michel," he cried, "are we ready?" He stood in his bedchamber, near naked from the bed, and his eyes glittered.

"Half an hour, sir." I laughed with him. "We have three knights and twenty men. I have sent to La Croix, sir, though I expect no answer." He frowned a moment, of Ricard. "I have asked Sir Bertran to meet us at the abbey."

Behind him the lady Clare knelt on their new bed, her robes clutched tight round her, her face drained of color.

He lifted his head, smiling. "Come, Michel, dress me."

"You must eat something," Clare said.

"I have told them, lady."

Sir Amaury had not worn armor since his wedding. I gave him the leather leggings, strapped the mail chausses round his waist. I tied on the padded leather undercoat, hung the long heavy hauberk on his shoulders, drew on the white linen tabard with its cross of red. He pulled up the mail hood and took up his polished helmet, and his eyes glittered and his face flushed with excitement, and once again he was the knight who had nearly killed me in Caen.

Footsteps rang in the solar and Philip appeared, already armored. " 'Tis a grand morning," he cried.

The lady Clare climbed from the bed, her arms wrapped about herself. "Holy Mother, look at them. See how happy they all are. This one has lost a father and that one an uncle, yet they wish nothing but to make us widows."

"Lady," said Amaury.

She shook her head. "I know, I know. Off with you, do not linger. Only leave a man to run the manor if you do not come . . ."

He blinked at her. "Geoffrey. Or Michel, here. But I cannot spare either, not today."

She walked to him and took his face in both her hands and kissed him on the mouth. "Go, my lord," she said. Her voice had grown strong again. "Go. You must not fail your lord."

We rode hard for Saint-Georges, as if we might catch the galloping shadows the early sun threw out before us. We passed farmers gaping at their doors and herds staring in the pastures. We rode the cool valley of the monks' ponds and up past the abbey's vineyard and the wall of the monastery itself. Around the corner lay the narrow market and the main portal, its gates shut tight.

Amaury leaped from his horse and beat on the wood with the pommel of his sword. "I am Amaury de Saint-Georges," he cried, before he lapsed into excited Latin. *"Vir Ioannis Craoni. Aperite portam."*

A porter monk peered out the eyebolt. *"Portam pro Stephano episcopo solum aperiam."*

"This is not the bishop's damned abbey," Amaury bellowed. *"Aperite hanc portam foetidam!"*

"Pro vobis, nunquam."

"Where is the prior?" he cried.

A stronger voice answered. "I am here."

"Open the gate, Father Simon, lest I burn it down."

We could hear them mutter inside, arguing, before the bar rattled and one leaf of the gate swung in. Simon stood with crossed arms, and the sun glinted on the dome of his tonsured head.

"I protest these swords, Saint-Georges. Here is a holy retreat, this is a funeral day and Our Lord's Sabbath."

"You know I can do no else," said Amaury.

"I will not deny Craon, but if Steven my bishop . . ."

"I bar this gate, Simon, and no man may open it without my leave. Not even to the pope himself."

"Do not threaten me, sir, the bishop may excommunicate . . ."

"Nor do you threaten me, father."

Soon after we heard horses beyond the gate and Bertran calling, "Open, damn you, I am Sir Amaury's man."

I grinned up at him as he sat his blowing horse. "I was not sure you would come, now you are another lord's liege."

He nodded, grim. "We all need a little war now and then. I knew Amaury would pay me well." He swung from his saddle and punched my shoulder. "And just look at you. Wearing mail now. The squire who loves to fight."

Bertran's arrival made us four knights and two dozen armed men. But the abbey was no castle, its gates were not strong, its walls stood but the height of two men. Geoffrey paced and grumbled we could not hold an hour against a decent attack.

Sir Amaury nodded. "Steven will not besiege an abbey."

"But his captain might. That is likely Malcolm d'Avrille."

"Ah," said Philip, "that hasty man."

Geoffrey scowled the more. "Who will bring his daughter's betrothed, Ricard de la Croix, anxious to prove his new liege." He swore under his breath. "Bishop and Malcolm and a dozen knights by midday. And we'll not see Craon ere nightfall."

There were no battlements for sentinels, and we raised a ladder inside each of the gates. We hobbled our horses on the grass below the cloister garth, bridled and saddled. If a gate failed or a wall was taken, three notes on Geoffrey's horn would be our warning, that we must ride out the south postern and through the vines, and get away as best we could. True to his judgment, just after midday we heard the noise of horses coming through the town, and the clatter as they rode into the market.

Sir Amaury climbed the ladder beside the gate. " 'Tis but six," he muttered. "Malcolm. Ricard, damn him. A dozen footmen." Somebody hammered on the gate and cried it open. "Good Sabbath to you, sirs," Amaury called out. "I hold this abbey for Craon."

"We come for the abbot's funeral." Malcolm's voice boomed over the wall. "Open to us, Saint-Georges."

"I will pass no armed men, sir."

"You would have us walk in empty-handed?"

"If you would walk in."

I had sent a man to the other gates, that when we unbarred the way we had all four knights and a dozen men there. Sir Malcolm glanced about, frowning, as if he believed this was but a part of our force.

Amaury pointed northward. "Craon will arrive soon enough."

"Steven Bishop," Malcolm said, "insists the old abbot be buried in the abbey graveyard."

"I would not delay the service," said Amaury, "but no one may attend with sword or dagger."

"Steven comes to read the service. Will you bar him, too?"

"If he comes armed."

Just before the gate shut, Amaury had peered at the knights outside. "Avrille," he said now, "you bring a man I thought my own."

"De la Croix has come with me in this matter, he believes . . ."

"Old Simon fails my call, sir. Ricard is no longer de la Croix." Sir Amaury turned and stalked to the abbot's house.

I climbed the wavering ladder and looked out over the roofs of the town. Nones rang, with neither bishop or baron. My feet began to ache from the ladder rungs. In the market below Ricard and Malcolm's knights played at mock duels with their clanging swords. At last, the sun nearly set, the dust of horses showed on the northern rise, and then the glitter of armor. Avrille's men did not dispute then, for Sir John had brought ten knights and twenty sergeants, all on lathered horses. The gate was hardly shut when other horses clattered in the market, and Bishop Steven arrived with three more knights. But it was Vespers and near dark, and Amaury would let only Steven in, and he unarmed.

The bishop led us to the abbey church, and made a brief service that praised the abbot's patience. A choir of monks sang the Office. Lay brothers carried his coffin to an orchard of budding apple trees, and there at last, in the dusk of evening, the old man found his rest.

Steven and Sir John argued half the night, but could agree only to a truce and another meeting in Angers, at the abbey of Saint-Aubin. Sir John kept his men at the abbey, but came himself to Clos Saint-Georges. Three days later, very early in the morning, we set out for the city. The day was thick with fog, and from deep in my past I remembered walking to Camelot with my father. I half expected a bell tolling for Ulfius. Bertran went with us and Philip, and though we went armored and hung shields from our saddles, we rode palfreys and expected no battle.

The castle loomed above the flowing river, gray and blurred through the fog. Mist dripped from the overhanging houses. The empty streets were slippery with mud as we rattled past the cathedral square and into a narrow lane, two abreast. Sir John and Amaury rode ahead, and Philip and John's squire Fernand and Bertran's Guy, with myself and Bertran at the rear.

High walls rose on both sides, that echoed our hoofbeats. "It is the college," Sir John said, "the abbey is just beyond."

In the mist someone coughed. Four knights, mounted and full-armed, blocked our way. We slowed and glanced at each other, and horses stamped behind us where three more knights closed the lane.

"What is this?" John called, his voice loud in the shifting damp.

A familiar voice answered, "Avrille."

"Malcolm?" said John.

"Ricard," muttered Amaury. He rode a little ahead. "You fool, Ricard, do you break another truce?"

Ricard made no answer. He and his knights sat destriers, high and strong against our palfreys. Squires waited beyond them, and the knights behind also had their squires. In that breathless silence I understood it, that here was the war we had all so wanted at Saint-Georges.

"*Milites,*" cried Amaury.

"Craon," Sir John shouted. All together we drew our swords.

"Avrille," Ricard blared. His knights lowered their lances and came at us, two abreast between the walls, and from both directions. The lane echoed with hoofbeats and shouts, and the rattle of arms.

Bertran had turned to meet those behind. I backed my palfrey and pulled it around beside him. The animal tossed his head and stepped nervously. The charging battle-horses came on, but the slippery lane was no tourney ground and their stabbing lances wavered. Bertran took the first easily on his shield. I beat the second away with my sword, and then we were a mass of shouting men and snorting animals. The knight I faced sat so high I must stand in my stirrups. My blow dented the side of his helmet. Pressed close, he could not draw his blade. He held his shield so awkward across his body I got in good blows before he backed away. I pushed my nervous horse forward. The knight fumbled for his sword. I chopped at his groping hand and he cried out. I hit him again on his shoulder, and full force on the helmet. His shield drooped and I thrust the point of my sword beneath his helmet.

"Yield, sir knight, else you die." In the roar of battle I could barely hear myself. My horse stepped and tossed its head.

He answered, strangled, "I am yours, squire."

"Get back," I cried, "fight no more." With his broken hand he could not hold a weapon.

Bertran's knight had drawn a battle-ax. "Bertran," I shouted, "save yourself!" My chop distracted the knight. The third charged, his lance driving. My palfrey, terrified now, backed and turned. Its hind legs slipped and we fell sideways in the muddy lane. I struggled to get free, under the stamping hooves of other horses. I found my sword. My animal flailed and kicked, trying to stand. A hoof drove against my thigh. I dropped in the mud, senseless with pain. I thought the blow had broke my leg.

Hoofs trampled all around, blades clanged overhead, a man cried out, a horse screamed. But clear over it all Amaury cried, *"Ad Craonum, pro Domino."*

I had forgot completely the attack to our front. Amaury and Philip chopped at their attackers. Fernand's horse stumbled, and a knight hacked the squire from his saddle. Sir John's animal fell, and as he struggled to free himself, the knight who had chopped Fernand turned and raised his sword.

I rolled in the muddy lane and clambered to one knee.

"Craon," I bellowed, without hope.

Fourteen

The cry wracked my throat, though in the crash of fighting even I could barely hear it. I stared about the muddy lane; everything moved slowly, the roar broke in waves over me, knights fought each other almost leisurely. I limped between the wounded horses, and felt no pain in my leg. Fernand lay very still, his bloody face misshapen in agony. A lance had opened the belly of Sir John's horse and its guts swarmed about its legs like great worms. John, on his knees, groped for his blade. Over him Ricard straddled the horse's head and raised his own sword two-handed. I reached the dying animal before my leg buckled; as I fell, I thrust my sword at Ricard like a spear. The point caught him in the ribs. It did not hurt him, only spoiled his aim. His stroke fell on Sir John's armored shoulder, who cried out and fell again.

I struggled to my feet, though my leg had no strength.

"Damn you," Ricard bellowed out his helmet, "I ought have killed you in Caen." I saw he would swing his blade, and could only parry with my own. My throbbing leg almost failed again. Ricard hacked, off balance himself, his feet slipped in the muck, and he sprawled backward. I chopped at him as he fell.

Before I could take a breath something hammered on the back of my head that dropped me blind into the trampled mud. I rolled aside unthinking, and coming up out of blackness saw another knight lifting his sword over me. I hacked at his knees. He cried and staggered back.

I got up, reeling. Ricard stood with his sword raised. I had no time to parry, but lowered my head and drove into his stomach. The air blew out of him. His blade fell uncertainly across my back as he staggered backward. Pain blurred my eyes but I got my footing and swung again. My sword took his neck just under his helmet. He wore no leather there beneath his mail. My blade drove the links deep into his flesh. Blood stood out in the blink of an eye, wet and red, and he fell writhing, both hands clutched at his throat.

Sir John staggered up again. Another knight hacked at him. I swung at the upraised arm. It broke under my sword, and he cried out and dropped to his knees. A squire attacked Philip. I staggered to them, my head blazing with pain though I felt nothing in my leg. My blow caught the lad's shoulder, and as he wavered Philip felled him with a blow to the head.

"God be thanked," said Philip, breathless.

"Defend Sir Amaury," I panted, for he fought their remaining knight.

One final squire came at Sir John. I hacked his shield as John chopped his sword arm. I raised my blade again. "Yield, esquire," I bellowed, and he dropped his sword. My voice rang in the narrow way. The fight was abruptly over.

In the quiet Guy called out, "Sir Bertran."

God's Name, I had left him outnumbered. I limped past Fernand, whose face was now the color of death. Bertran lay pitched like a rag against the monastery wall. He had taken a lance in his stomach, the last attack of the last knight, and he gripped its splintered stump with bloody hands.

"Bertran," I cried, "I did not mean to desert you."

I knelt and touched his cheek. His eyes opened. He tried to speak, but his mouth filled with blood and he coughed and sprayed me with it. He smiled apologetically and lifted a hand to wipe my face and choked again. Blood welled thickly over his lips and down his chin. His eyes glazed. He no longer saw me.

I stared about the lane. The first knight I had defeated sat propped against a wall. The second groaned in the mud nearby, but the third, that lanced Bertran, still sat his horse. My mind roared with fury. I strode at him and did not limp at all.

"God save you," I shouted, "today have you made an enemy you will regret."

He backed his animal and raised his sword, but was not quick enough. My blade caught his side, I beat his helmet, I chopped his sword arm. The blade staggered from his hand.

"Yield," I cried, "else I kill the horse, and you." Even as I shouted, I prayed he would not yield, that if he did I would kill him anyway. He had no weapon but his dagger and no strength to draw it, and behind him the squires would not come to his aid.

"God's Name," he cried, "I yield. Would you kill us all?"

"I would see you all in Hell," I shouted, "every one."

But already my mind had gone empty, and my rage was drained away like water from a broken bucket. I turned and limped back to Bertran. His blood made a wide pool about him. I could not believe he still breathed. I knelt beside him, awkward on my hurt leg. I touched his cheek. My own breath came in gasps. Bertran died, who was a brother nearly. Ricard died by my hand, who was no enemy. After the noise and the fury there was only emptiness.

I drew a long shuddering breath, lifted my head and got to my feet. The morning's fog had blown away. Birds sang over the wall in the abbey garden. A thin sunlight lit the street that stank of mud and horse-guts, of blood and sweat and death. Philip bent and crossed Fernand's arms. Amaury helped Sir John stand. My head hurt, and my leg and my whole body, and blood oozed down my neck from my injured skull. I limped to Sir John. "I have taken the last of them, sir." I knew I spoke too loud.

"My thanks," he said, his face gaunt with pain.

Bile rose in my mouth suddenly, and sweat drenched my face and I nearly cried out as my throbbing leg failed at last. I staggered and fell. Sir Amaury pulled me up, left-handed. His right arm hung limp and his shoulder was drenched with blood.

John stood watching us. He cleared his throat. "Sir Amaury, I would have this man of you."

"Sir? This man?" Amaury's voice was thin with hurt.

"Fernand, you see he dies. I need a squire."

Amaury blinked. "My lord." He shook his head, confused. "If you would, sir."

John stepped to me and took my shoulder, and the strength of his grip surprised me. "You saved my life, Michel de Verdeur. I am in your debt, I would have you my man."

His face wavered before me. I understood him no better than Amaury, but I had the wit to say, "Aye, Sir John."

"Then give me your hands."

I knelt before him, despite my leg. I lifted my hands and put them together between his palms. "Sir John of Craon," I said, "I, Michel de Verdeur, do wish and desire to be your man. I promise to serve you faithfully, and never injure you."

"And I take you, Michel de Verdeur, as my vassal."

He helped me stand. We kissed on the mouth. The knights around us, both sides in the battle, watched in silent amazement. Sir John, smiling now, turned again to Amaury. "Pierre de Beaumont saved me of my Saracen, and him I made marshal. Michel de Verdeur saved me of Ricard de la Croix. How ought I reward him?"

Amaury watched him and said nothing.

Sir John had gone very serious, but a light danced in his eye. "Michel de Verdeur. I have seen how you fight. We have all seen it." He gripped my shoulder. "As you are my man." He stepped to me again and lifted his right hand. His open palm hit my cheek a stinging blow. I knew before he struck what he did.

"I, John," he cried, "baron of Craon, do dub thee knight, Michel de Verdeur. Be thou always true, brave before all danger, courageous before God, honest in every word and act."

"With God's help," I said.

With my cheek afire and my leg in agony I dropped to my knees again. I remembered the responses of Bertran's dubbing. I gripped both his hands. I wept, as John pulled his hands away. "Thank you, my lord." I thought I dreamed it. Lancelot had cursed me of this. I struggled up and bowed to him, weeping still, my voice had almost gone. "Thank you, sire."

John bent over Ricard's corpse and untied his sword belt. He wrapped the thick leather round me. The scabbard banged my good leg. "This knight would have killed me. I take my ransom." He drew Ricard's blade and raised it like a cross. "Your knight's sword, Sir Michel. You have earned it."

"My lord, I thank you." I gripped the blade and bowed.

"I give all that was his." He answered my bow, one knight to another. He knelt stiffly and unstrapped Ricard's spurs, and bound the right one to my boot.

"My lord," I said. My eyes blurred again.

Amaury had stared through it all, yet now he reached to grip my hand with his left one. "God knows I hate to lose you, Michel, but this is a dubbing truly earned."

Philip took the other spur and strapped it on. "*Sir* Michel." He put an arm around my shoulder. "Praise God you don't weep so, while you're fighting."

Ricard's beaten knights straggled up and took my hand. Even the last that I had cursed, bowed to me and said, "I have met no squire who deserved it more."

I nearly wept again. We were all brothers, now.

Townsmen and students clustered in staring knots at each end of the lane. Black-robed monks brought litters for the wounded, and then Bishop Steven peered out the abbey gate. "Shame," he cried, "fighting in Holy Week. Craon? Have you lost all piety? Do you prove your strength?"

"Had I meant to prove that," John barked, "I'd have brought a score of knights and stormed you in your damn palace."

And Amaury bellowed at him, waving his good arm. "Can you not see they came at us, front and rear, and in the fog?"

The signs were clear even to the bishop. He frowned and shook his head, and then the color drained from his face when he saw Ricard's body. "God's love, have you killed him, too?"

"And where were you," cried Amaury, "when he wanted shriving?"

"I had no notion of this, Craon."

"Mayhap no," John said, "but we fought long and hard, and just over this wall, ere you heard us."

"I swear I knew nothing. I was singing Terce."

John scowled, only half believing him. "I have a knight killed and a squire, and every man injured. I have the ransoms of six knights, and one is dead. Where is Avrille?"

Steven gestured at the gate. "Inside, waiting you."

Malcolm d'Avrille was talking with the abbot, outside the bishop's door. "That is my heraldry," he cried at Ricard's litter. "Damn you, Craon, here is my new son." He glared around, pale with anger, and saw I wore Ricard's sword. "And this squire . . ."

"We came under the bishop's truce," John barked. "Your new son would have killed me, save Michel here protected me." He leaned back to stare at them, for they were both taller than he. "They bore your colors, Avrille. They attacked in your precincts, Bishop. I hold you both for it."

They swore they had done nothing, save that at the abbey and late in the night of the old abbot's funeral, Steven had muttered, "What a thorn is Craon, that I would pluck him out!"

John smiled at him, grimly. "Now, and by your hand, I will have the abbey of Saint-Georges undisputed. Every fief, all tithes, all rents, offerings, endowments, dues, everything that is abbey's or abbot's. And from you, Avrille, the tolls of your ferry below this castle." They glowered at him but he did not waver. "Else, by God and Christ, I bring my action in the king's courts."

True to his word, Sir John gave me everything of Ricard's: the leather undercoat still damp with blood about the neck, the padded leggings stiff with sweat, and the chausses that needed polishing. The heavy mail hauberk fit well enough, and when I put it on I understood at last that it was not Sir John's buffet, nor my sword and belt, nor even the sharp spurs, but the weight of that iron mail heavy on my shoulders that made me truly a knight.

Late that day I limped into the abbey's sunlit cloister. Swallows built their nests under the eaves, and early butterflies flitted among the budding flowers. Sir John sat a stone bench in the warm sun. "Come," he called, "sit with me."

I bowed to him, stiff and aching. "Sir John, I thank you again for my dubbing."

"And for my life, Sir Michel, I thank you." It took my breath to hear him say it, and my eyes swam again. "Am I a fool for dubbing you?" he asked.

"Many might believe it, my lord."

"You fight well as any knight. You sing, you dance, you even have Latin. Lancelot wonders of you, though he curses both of us." He smiled grimly. "But, Michel, you have lied to me."

"Sir?"

"We all believe Arthur is our finest king, all Christendom trembles before his repute. Yet still we hear rumor of his queen and his finest knight." He touched his scar, unthinking. "And what scandal it is, that those who know deny it."

"At Camelot, sir . . ." I struggled for an answer. "King Arthur believes wholly in chivalry, knighthood, honor. It is his faith, my lord, that blinds him to what happens, even before his eyes."

"But I can see very well, Sir Michel." He turned his frown at me. "I charge you, that you tell me if this occurs at Craon."

"My lord, as I am your man." I marveled that he had dubbed me, were this on his mind. Adele was a comely lady, but she was not Guenever. She was Sir John's wife and though he had scores of other knights, none would court his lady. And, despite her glances, I told myself he had nothing to fear of me.

Ricard had brought a chestnut palfrey to Angers, and next morning I climbed stiffly into his saddle and rode the narrow city streets. The young Jew who had driven the money chest for Bertran's dubbing squatted in the sun before his father's door.

"Ezra of Caen," I said from my horse, the name reminding me how that massive man had warned me of knights.

The young man looked quickly up.

"I have a loan of him," I said.

He stood, frowning. "Your knight owes a hundred livres."

"I am a knight of Craon, now."

"Craon?" He glanced at my sword. "Three hundred livres."

God's name, I thought, where did they get the coin? They had no manors, no vineyards, they sat these narrow streets like spiders lurking in their webs.

"Ezra of Caen," I repeated. "His daughter stays here."

He shook his head. "Ezra lives in Rouen, now."

"He gave me a livre, at Epiphany a year past. And Aaron of Winchester loaned me six shillings. That would be eight, now."

The sun in his eyes made him squint. "Why do you come with these tiny worries, grand sir knight?"

Ezra and old Aaron had saved my life. But I could not say it, especially not to this Jew.

"Pay me," he said, "I will pay him."

"No. When I see him." I turned and rode away, back to the abbey.

Good Friday, that was Christ's own death, we buried Bertran and Ricard and Fernand in the abbey's graveyard. Sir Amaury's wounds kept him from the ceremony, and soon he left with Philip, riding back to Clos Saint-Georges. On Holy Easter all that remained of our company, and Ricard's, walked the morning streets to the cathedral. Christ sat in stone above the paired doors. Inside, the high broad church was very crowded, as if all the city took the Host that Holy Day. The service went on for hours, and as I stood my injured leg ached and grew so stiff I could barely move it.

Still, for me the day was not Easter, but Pentecost. Like the apostles gathered in Jerusalem, the flame of my sudden knighthood burned upon my head, with a heat only I could feel. It was on Pentecost, so Lancelot said, the Sangral appeared at Camelot. Lancelot had committed his soul to that quest, vowed himself a chaste knight, peaceable and stalwart. I touched Lark's bag beneath my tunic. My sudden knighthood confirmed my own oath of vengeance, and in that crowded church I swore myself again to be as single-minded as Lancelot, as chaste and absolute. The prize I sought was not some bright shape seen in Camelot's Hall. It was my own Blackgral, a grim dark road, and death at the end.

Ricard's long shield, lacquered canvas on linden wood, I had painted anew. A blue field and a green tree proper, quartered with John's white dragon. And lest I forget, a large black bird upon that tree. A raven.

My own small baggage still lay at Clos Saint-Georges, and when Sir John returned to Craon we parted at the river ferry. I rode the dusty way westward, leading two sumpters and Ricard's destrier, and smiling to myself of Craon and my new life. And then I came to the crossroads of Le Vallon.

I drew up and stared down her tree-lined way. Had Philip died at Angers instead of Bertran, had Ricard not attacked Sir John, had John not dubbed me and called me to Craon, then Sir Amaury might have betrothed me to Matilde. But it was an idle dream. Sir Amaury would keep me his chamberlain and always undubbed. My knighthood could have only come from Sir John. I had known I must leave Clos Saint-Georges, yet before I went, I would see her once more, kiss her in parting, as a knight, under her mother's eye and in the light of day.

But she was not even there. The ladies had left that morning, her steward said, to visit the convent of Nyoiseau. Her marriage to Philip was but two weeks away, yet Matilde would not believe in it. As I rode away down her lane, it seemed the old trees above me showed no spring green, her fields held no early flowers, no birds sang in the bitter sunlight. The whole world was suddenly a wasteland, hollow and joyless. Even the weight of my knight's hauberk, so agreeable before, no longer pleased me.

At Clos Saint-Georges my leg had gone so stiff a servant had to help me struggle down from my mount. Geoffrey appeared, his laughter brightening my mood. "Sir Michel," he cried. "*Sir* Michel." He looked at the horses. "And all that ransom."

"Much is Sir Amaury's, of Sir John," I said. But I drew out Ricard's dagger, that I had faced at Caen, and gave it to him. "For all your teaching, Sir Geoffrey. And all your bruises."

He grinned again. "A masterful fighter, a generous knight."

"How is Sir Amaury?"

He touched his own shoulder. "I burnt it Saturday." He saw my worry. "He improves, though still he lies abed."

I met Lady Clare at the Hall door. "Sir Michel," she said, smiling. "How well do you deserve it, Michel, yet how we rue that you leave us and Clos Saint-Georges."

"Thank you, lady." I paused, half-sorry myself. "How is your lord?"

She glanced away. "Wounded. As he wished."

Sir Amaury lay within his darkened chamber, though a lowering sun through the half-closed shutters cast bars of light across his bed.

"Sir Michel, here you are."

"Pray God your wounds heal, Sir Amaury."

He shrugged, and flinched at the pain. "Geoffrey cures me."

I gave him a heavy purse. "Sir John sends his greetings, and many gifts."

"Craon is a generous lord. I am pleased for you, Michel, though Saint-Georges will miss you sorely. I had thought to make you chamberlain. Reynaud has become very forgetful."

"I would have been honored, sir."

He smiled grimly. "I do not believe you, Michel. You are too much the fighter." His servants brought in a chest of Avrille's, heavy with coin, that thumped as they set it down. Amaury waved a hand at it. "Geoffrey must choose a tithe for the abbey. Would you deliver it on your way?"

"Of course, sir."

"And take something for yourself."

"Thank you, sir." I stood a moment, anxious to be gone, yet not wanting to leave. Another servant brought in a bag of armor that clattered on the wooden floor.

"And you must thank Sir John," Amaury said. His look changed. "Lancelot knew you at Angers. He spoke to Sir John, but John would not say what passed between them."

"I was truly at Camelot, sir." Sorrowed by leave-taking, I almost knelt and clasped his hand and told him of Greenfarm.

"And why do I doubt your friar, when you answered Sir John's questions so well?"

The friar of the beery laugh, who had named me, who had called me green. "Martin, of Street near Glastonbury, Sir Amaury. I saw him again at Craon. At Yule and your wedding."

But there had been no friar at Craon, only an old man in the snow. Not till my words hung in the air did I understand. Both of them, and the midnight visitor to Sir Ulfius' watch, they were all the same, could be nobody save Arthur's shapechanger, Camelot's Druid. The room wavered before my eyes. I had to grip a post of Amaury's bed. I had been blind not to see it. He had named me, sent me to Normandy and then Craon. He had put me close to Sir John, as if he knew I would save him and be dubbed. A chill shook my spine. God's Name, Merlin. What did the mage want with me? Was I the green knight, was I Sir Gawain?

"Are you injured, Michel?" asked Amaury. "Does your leg still pain you?"

"A little." My voice shook. "My place is Craon, Sir Amaury."

He reached out his unwounded hand and clasped mine. "Our Lord be always with you, Sir Michel de Verdeur."

The road to Saint-Gorges was the same we had galloped ten days past, hurrying to war, yet now it ran through foreign country, the fields each side oddly distant, the farms unrecognizable. Even the farmers who looked up from their weeding were become strangers, so had John's dubbing transformed my life.

I reached the abbey at Vespers. The voices of chanting monks sounded at the open door of the church as I swung down, stiff and sore again. A servant came to lead me to the visitors' lodge. He was a lad of thirteen, stocky and tall for his age.

"You are Conon's youngest," I said. "Hugh."

"Aye, sir." Unlike Jacq, his hanged brother, he had lively blue eyes in a keen face.

I remembered the story, how Conon's brother sent the second son to a cousin in Angers and assigned the third to the abbey, that his own son would inherit Conon's tenancy. Sir Amaury had shrugged unhappily at it. "Conon is not my tenant now."

"Do you like it here, Hugh?" I asked.

"Aye, sir," he said, without enthusiasm.

A notion came to me. "I am a knight, I go to Craon. I need a groom."

Hugh lifted his head, his eyes widening. "I feed the abbot's horses, sir, I brush them, and muck."

"I could speak to the abbot."

He grinned. "It's Father Simon now, despite the war."

Simon stared at me in the refectory, and at my knight's cloak. "Sir Michel, is it? Well, the boy's a good worker. I cannot let him go without redress. Besides, he may not want it."

"He will go. How much?"

"A denier every day." Simon rubbed a hand over his smooth pate. "A livre and a half every year."

"I will give you three years, Father. Four and a half."

"Five," he answered.

It rained that night, and next morning as we came out the church from our shriving, Conon's widow waited under the dripping porch. She had heard, somehow, and walked the league from La Roche despite the rain. She hugged the lad a long time before she let him climb on his loaded horse. She walked to me and took my hand and kissed it, her face cold with tears and rain, before she pulled up her hood and turned away. Thus had I left Greenfarm, save Ruth would not speak to me.

I lifted my head and wished the abbot well. I led Hugh out the abbey gates and down through the little town. Past the last of the houses the puddled fields wore the green of yet another spring. Cattle drank at streams, and sheep clustered under old oaks. At the first crossroads a peasant family huddled out of our way. I saw myself through their eyes, hauberk and sword beneath my knight's cloak, bright shield on my shoulder, my hair newly trimmed. How well I remembered it, crouched at the wayside, holding my own breath till the knights were past, the mud their horses splashed not even noticed.

At the crest of the next rise I drew up and looked back. The peasant family plodded on toward the town. The abbey sat its small hill, the high bulk of its church grayed by the drifting rain. Clos Saint-Georges had vanished completely.

"Can you see La Roche, Hugh?"

He pointed a wavering hand. "It's there." His voice broke. "It's gone, sir."

I nudged my palfrey forward, and began to hum an old song.

"Can you sing, Hugh?" I asked over my shoulder.

"I whistle, sir." His voice ached with sorrow. "I pipe."

The muddy road led us on. A cool wind pulled at our cloaks. The clouds moved, the weather brightened, and the world shone new, for both of us.

Fifteen

Sunlight and shadow blew the rolling fields of Craon, lit and murked the narrow streets of the town, caught the banners of gold and white that fluttered above the castle towers. Sir John himself came smiling to welcome us, gripped my hand and clasped my shoulder. "A new knight always recalls my own youth," he said. "Welcome to Craon, Sir Michel."

"Thank you, Sir John." I saw for the first time I was grown taller than he.

"How did you leave Sir Amaury?"

"His wounds heal, sir. But I did not speak of Greenfarm." And then my breath stopped, remembering the wizard.

Sir John nodded his dark head. "It is mine to tell, Michel. You will be old as I, ere you hear the end of this."

His sons waited in his Hall, both small like their father, and in their company I felt thick and almost clumsy. Denis had a pleasant blond face. He was three years older than I, and already a knight. Gilbert, a year younger, was dark and fine-featured, gifted with a clear voice, and would become the family's cleric.

"Pouancé." Sir John handed me the ale cup. "We tourney there Rogation week. Denis and you will joust, and the second day we will play at the melee."

"Five weeks, sir?" The suddenness surprised me.

"I would have no man doubt your knight's ability, Sir Michel."

"Aye, sir." Nor doubt, I thought, the wisdom of his dubbing.

Lady Adele had come down the turning stair. The drape of her pale woolen gown marked her supple figure, she wore her hair in auburn braids, and her eyes were cool.

"Welcome to Craon, Sir Michel," she said distantly.

I bowed over her hand. "My lady, it is a great honor to be here." In truth I felt suddenly awkward at elegant Craon.

Pierre de Beaumont was Craon's marshal knight, a lean man with a balding pate and a thick mustache. He had saved Sir John's life on crusade, and having fought in that arduous war was far more serious of battle than Sir Geoffrey. It fell to him to make me a jousting knight. If I also saved John's life he was unimpressed, for I knew nothing of tourneys and he had but a month to teach me.

Craon's practice field was a long turfed strip beside its narrow river. I felt confident, my first morning of practice, till Pierre said that even for swordwork we must don helmets. Mine was Ricard's, won in Angers. Its straps and padding still stank of blood. Voices echoed strangely inside, the helmet had no moving visor in the new style, and through its eyeslot the world looked both bright and distant. I had never worn it, fighting, and when I faced Pierre I could catch only his head and shoulders, and feared I would never see his moves.

He began quick, with little warning, his attack stronger than Geoffrey's and more canny. I felt nearly blind inside the helmet, and the metal rang under the blows I could not parry. Struggling with defense I grew hot and annoyed, but even when I crowded him I could only buffet without avail, and rarely landed a solid hit. It seemed half an hour before he stepped away and lowered his blade, and I could drag off the stifling helmet.

"Young knights," he said, as if my ardor were a fault. At least he was sweating, too.

We spent four days at it. By the end I could defend myself, and land a telling blow for each two of his. He had neither praise nor censure, yet he must have been half-satisfied. After the Sabbath we began at jousting.

To my great fortune Ricard's destrier was an excellent animal, superbly trained. When first I sat him, and felt his strength and his nerves, I remembered how different was gentle Anduin. Yet true battle-horses must be like this beast, excitable, spirited, anxious to gallop and without fear of pain. His coat shone so dark it was almost black, and he wore a thin white stripe on his face and a white near forefoot. I thought to call him Sable, or even Raven, before I named him Night.

I was anxious to grip a lance and kick my new horse into a charge, but Pierre would not have it. We took up shields and heavy spears and, God's Name, walked at each other. Ardent for attack I drove my point hard against him. He moved his shield hardly at all, my lance slid away light as wind, his own rammed me to a halt.

"Look at both lances," Pierre said, "both points." Nobody can truly look at two things, yet soon enough I came to watch the place between, to see both lances moving and prepare for the collision. "Lean into it," he said.

We walked thus for three days, armored and sweating under the bright sun. At each pass he shifted his attack and would have spitted or unhorsed me, and then without a word he gripped my lance and shield and forced me to the correct position. My arm ached of holding the long spear. His endless teaching fretted me and wore at my self-confidence. Hand-to-hand fighting, and my Norman gift, made me Amaury's squire and John's knight. Yet jousting needed power and fearlessness and luck, as much as skill and foresight.

And then, were I not anxious enough, Pierre turned to the horse. He had Hugh and Denis' groom strip the animal. They must repad Night's back, hoist the saddle, fit the belly cinch and breast band and crupper. He pointed out their faults, and made them take it off and start over a dozen times, till the boys were tired and angry, and the horse stamped with impatience.

"Pray God, let us meet," I said.

" 'Tis strange," he muttered, "a knight who's never jousted." At last, the end of the second week, he agreed I might ride.

By now I knew what to expect. Astride the galloping horse, long shield on your left hand and lance in the right, you thrust the spear over the animal's left ear at the place you would meet. Just at impact you stood in the stirrups, turned your right shoulder, leaned hard into the shock. The best charge caught the other's shield high and clean, and rammed him from his saddle. Hit square, and with the power of a battle-horse at full charge, no knight could keep his seat. However, the turn of your shoulder also angled your shield. If done accurately his onrushing point would skip away harmless, his lance might even twist and shatter. Every knight knew this, of course, and at every joust you must judge the other's strength and cunning, in the instant before you meet. And more than that, though the best horses galloped smoothly, the ground might be torn, lance points must waver, and the outcome was always half chance.

That first day Pierre would joust with Denis, and then me, and then Denis and I would meet each other. Denis had fought in several tourneys the summer before, and gained draws in each. When I scoffed at draws he lifted his chin, proudly.

"There is honor enough in equal matches."

"For Denis Saint-Amadour, heir to Craon," I said. "But Sir John expects his newest knight to win."

"Three light lances," called Pierre, "blunt."

I stood in the damp grass while he and Denis fought, trying to remember it all. Night pranced beside me, excited. I checked his straps and saddle. On the field Denis rode very well. They both looked more skilled than I. When they met the last time they nearly unhorsed each other, but Denis had got his draw.

"Sir Michel," called Pierre.

There would be no easy beginning. My first joust would be at full speed. I set my helmet and swung up in the saddle. Night moved before I was ready and I had to grab a lance from Hugh. The horse cantered across the field, tossing his head. My heart thudded and my mouth went dry. Jesu, I thought, it's but a lesson.

Pierre sat his horse at the far end. I turned to him, we raised our lances, and Night charged without spurring. I peered out my eye-slot, I fought to keep the lance steady and guide Night with my heels, but the horse ran on his own. Pierre loomed up before me, between eye blinks. I stood and leaned into my lance. A huge blow hammered my left shoulder. It felt I had run into a wall. I could not breathe. My left arm burned, even as it went numb. I closed eyes for a moment, before I kicked Night to turn him. Pierre sat holding a splintered lance. Mine was whole. I had won the pass, though I did not know how.

He rode for another. We took opposite ends and charged again. My head throbbed, my shoulder hurt and my arms were afire, but I was half-prepared for the second collision. The shock had a different sound. My lance shuddered and stung my hand, and split and fell away.

Hugh grinned at me as he handed up a new lance, for Pierre's second had broken, too. The third charge, despite his teaching, I kept my point high at his helmet. He never wavered, but lifted his shield at the last moment. My lance bent and broke, and his drove so hard against me that had I not been well seated he would have unhorsed me.

My ears rang, my head thundered, my eyes blurred. Pierre raised his visor. "You can't win that way."

"Aye, sir," I said. The draw felt like a defeat.

I hoped to catch my breath but Denis was already up. My left arm ached, my lance wrist throbbed and I gasped for breath, yet I had more confidence against Denis. He raised his lance in salute and rode straight at me. His point did not waver. We met hard, his lance square against my shield. Mine found him equally well.

The pressure on my aching wrist stayed a longer moment. My point tugged sideways. Jesu, Denis was falling. I flung away my lance and grabbed the reins to pull Night round. Denis lay on his back in the morning grass. I swung down and ran to him. "Denis," I cried. Inside his helmet his eyes were wet with pain.

"Damn," he muttered, his teeth clenched. "I don't think I can move." But he sat up and I helped him stand.

Pierre walked across the field to us, the first smile in a week on his lips. "My lord Sir Denis," he said, "be not gentle with this new knight. He might kill you by mistake."

After a long month of practice my shield arm felt bruised bone-deep, I had calluses on my lance hand, and each morning must wrap its swollen wrist. Pierre had yet to praise my ability, yet now I could see how his point shifted as we met, how his shield moved. I looked to my first tourney with both hope and dread.

Pouancé would be both jousts and melee, and in the last week Pierre led us out across the fields of Craon to show how the land ought be used, in a general fight. "Always watch where you ride," he said. "Keep the high ground. Never charge uphill nor over ditches. Watch for men hidden in woods." He gave a rare laugh. "There's nothing finer than the melee, it's the true measure of a knight. Not these vain jousts." Gawain, I remembered, had said the same at Camelot.

Immersed in our weeks of practice, and my anticipation of Pouancé, I had truly forgot Saint-Georges, both Bertran's death and Matilde's wedding. I was amazed, late Rogation Monday, when a dozen riders clattered into Craon's court. Sir Amaury brought his knights and their ladies, all in high color from the ride.

I saw her at once. She sat a gray palfrey, her riding hat tied with a green ribbon. My heart turned over. I glanced away and took Amaury's bridle. "Sir Amaury," I said, "welcome to Craon."

"Thank you." He smiled at me. "Sir Michel."

I bowed over Clare's hand. "My lady."

Geoffrey clapped me on the back. Philip grinned as he swung down. Sir John came smiling to greet them, and servants moved among us, taking the horses away.

Her hand touched my arm. I could hardly breathe. "Sir Michel de Verdeur," she murmured.

"Lady." I could not trust myself to look at her. "Welcome, lady." I could not think. "At Pouancé we joust, for chivalry I need a lady's color." But of course Philip would wear it, he was her husband. I could not understand how I had forgotten her so completely. Now that she stood next me I could see nothing except her smiling lips, hear nothing but her soft laugh.

She untied her hat, draped the ribbon over my hand and pulled it slowly to her. I had to turn away, lest there in the court I seize her.

Philip was beside us, come back from greeting Sir John. He gripped my hand. "Sir Michel."

"Hello, Philip. Welcome to Craon."

"They say we will fight the melee shoulder to shoulder."

"I pray we will." I felt Matilde turn away.

" 'Tis a marvel," he said, "Anjou and Normandy 'gainst Brittany and Britain."

His enthusiasm made me smile. "We joust the first day. Pray God I am whole, the second."

"It is your first tourney." He glanced about the court. "We must find a lady, someone who treasures chivalry." His eye fell on John. "Our baron has a pretty wife."

"Jesu, Philip, the lady is too high for me."

"A true knight risks all for love."

A troop of minstrels arrived soon after, that set Craon's Hall pealing with their music. Sir John laid a generous board that evening, and I sat beside Philip, and with Matilde on his other side. It was a mistake. Looking at him, I must look at her. How could I have forgot the curve of her mouth, the turn of her small nose?

Philip was alternately gruff and shy with her, as if she were both burden and delight. He drank as much as ever, and in my discomfort I nearly equaled him. When they rose to dance I watched the pale blue of her gown among the couples. Philip led her well through the lines and circles, yet when they returned his smooth brow was damp with sweat.

" 'Tis hard work being a husband, Michel." I laughed and passed him the cup. "Sir Amaury's promised me La Croix," he said. His words came a little slurred.

"Wonderful." I said. My own head felt thick. "Two manors, you'll need a liege-knight."

"And would he were you, Michel." He glanced around Craon's Hall. "But who'd give all this up?"

"Sir John would not let me go."

He lifted a bit of meat from his trencher. "Nor his lady."

Beyond him Matilde frowned.

"Philip," I muttered, "enough."

He shrugged, chewing. "We all see how she watches."

I turned to look at the high table, and there beside Sir John the lady glanced away. For all the weeks of practice she had been polite and distant, yet tonight with other knights here, with Matilde here, now she stared again. The fumes of wine nearly made me go up to her. Lady, I would say, what do you?

The minstrels struck up a carole and Sir John called out, "Come, everyone dance." He took Adele's hand.

Matilde stood, though Philip shook his head. "Good wife, this one is beyond me." He waved a hand. "Michel will partner you."

My heart froze. "I hardly know the steps."

"Then I must teach you." She seized my hand. I could not resist. We danced the slow circles and wove the figures round the Hall. She hardly touched me, though my palm grew damp in her grip. When we returned Philip was gone. "Where is he?" I asked. She did not answer. "Fair lady, are you angry with me?"

"How you do progress in chivalry, sir." She turned and stared at the high table, but I remembered her own chivalric fancies.

"Lady, this notion of Philip's. There is nothing, she is too high, as distant as the moon." She would not look at me. "Lady, it is your color I desire."

"She stares at you."

"Can I restrain the eyes of any lady?"

One of the minstrels began a courtly lay. He had a fine voice and the Hall fell silent. Without warning I heard the blackbird's call, smelled ripened wheat, felt Lark's hand in mine. Knights galloped, the hare screamed, the moon . . .

"Do you hear him?" Philip's hand fell on my shoulder. "Could I but sing so, I would be a troubadour." He went on to the minstrels and called their cups to be filled.

"He will drink with them," said Matilde. "They will teach him songs. It will be Matins ere he comes to our chamber." She dropped her gaze. "Oft I feel a widow, still."

I remembered her quick body, her small firm breasts, her breathless whisper. I took up the cup, and saw my hand shake with desire. I imagined her mouth opened and her tongue flicked out, yet instead she stood and walked away to Amaury and his lady Clare. The minstrel began another song. Philip's squire filled the cup, again. How could I leave that woman sleep alone?

"Oh Michel," she whispered, "oh, Michel, oh . . ." Her voice slid off into that urgent murmur I could never understand. Though I ought to leave I went on, again and again.

"Michel."

I lay breathing. "I love you, Matilde."

"At last I believe you." She bit my ear softly. Her fingers on my chest touched my doeskin sack and wandered on.

My heart stopped. I could remember nothing. She appeared, she drew me like a bee hasty to honey, I flew to her and drowned without a struggle.

A distant bell rang. " 'Tis midnight, lady, I must go."

"Dear Michel, stay." She drew me to her and once again I felt nothing but her slim body against my own, and my own desire.

"Dear lady." I kissed her and she clung to me, and her mouth opened as if she would swallow me. "Matilde, lady, I must go."

"Not yet."

"But ere I do, I would have your color for the joust."

"Oh, sir, do you wrench it from me, helpless as I am?"

"I take it, and despite all your entreaties." In the dark I searched the folds of her robe and drew out the ribbon from her bodice. It smelled of her, this prize in the court of love. I tied it round my neck, there was my doeskin bag. In the space of two minutes I had forgot.

I had sworn my own oath as single-minded as Lancelot, yet how willingly I broke it now. I loved her. I could not keep from her. But it was more than love, it was the wine, the half-danger of courtly love, all knighthood's shining virility. Everything was delight, everything was frolic. Everything seduced me from my Blackgral.

"Michel?"

"My lady?"

"What do you murmur to yourself?"

"How I will carry your color to triumph on tomorrow's field."

"Make certain you do, sir. Else I close my gates."

"Then would I besiege them yet again." How easy came the courtly words.

"Oh, yes, sweet knight, please do."

How easy the words had always come. I might have been born to it all, to broidered bedclothes, to spices and rich food and bright wine, to this play of love, and sword and lance. Born of high blood, of privilege and arrogance, and not in Greenfarm's murky hut, that stank of mud and smoke and peasant sweat.

I stared into the dark. Matilde breathed beside me, sleeping. Lark's bag felt a stone upon my chest. I was a knight. I loved a lady. I had got everything I wished. Apart from virtue.

Pouancé was a small gray castle above a green river and a narrow lake. It stood in the corner of Anjou near Brittany, an estate of Étienne de Châteaubriant. The jousting field lay just outside the little village, its turf close-trimmed by sheep, and a crowd of Breton knights had already set their tents there, next a dozen from Britain. They were Outside, and our Castleside would be two score Angevins, and half as many Normans.

Pierre led us at once to the melee ground, that stretched away across rolling farms and deep valleys, and with a thick wood along one side. He warned again of ditches, of slopes and forest cover. We returned to find our pavilions set and Sir John waiting for us, very sober.

"I've arranged the matches. We've done well, save Michel."

"What do you mean, sir?" I asked.

"Any man dubbed in battle they take as champion. You are a novice, yet they rank you twentieth of twenty-nine, above us all save Pierre. A high honor," John said, while Geoffrey rumbled with worry and Pierre frowned. He pointed to a blue tent broidered with white lilies. "Lambert of Denham, Lancelot's host at Angers."

I remembered the tall knight well, and that I had seen him win both his jousts. "I will do my best, Sir John."

"Of course." He nodded grimly. "Three lances, three sword blows, three dagger thrusts. The field will be much torn when you meet. Do not let him injure you badly."

"Sir," I muttered, "I will not embarrass you."

Only then did I remember that a manor named Denham stood but a league east of Greenfarm. Were that Lambert's, then I met Camelot in my first joust. Sir Ulfius' tourney came back to me, the prowess of Sir Gawain, of Agravain and Orsain, and I spent a restless night, praying God I would not fail against Camelot.

Next morning as we armed ourselves Sir Pierre came up, tense with worry. "Remember Denis fights for the draw, Michel."

We knelt before John's priest to be shrived, and when it was done Geoffrey leaned to me. "They say Sir Lambert has lost but once, in three tourneys this season."

"God's Name," I cried, "do you think I have lost already?"

I pushed angrily out the tent. Hugh stood in the morning sun, holding Night's bridle and whistling under his breath.

"They say Sir Lambert is very rich, sir." He grinned at me. "I pray you for a fine gift, when you beat him."

I burst out laughing. "Praise God, at least somebody has faith in me."

The ladies came out Adele's tent, arrayed in bright gowns. Matilde busied herself with Philip, but Sir John's lady came up and touched the blue ribbon tied to my helmet. "May we know of this fortunate lady, Sir Michel?"

"I keep her secret close, my lady."

A brief frown passed over Lady Clare's face, before she smiled at me. "So young, and so chivalrous."

Heralds sounded their trumpets. We mounted and rode to the field, three score knights with the sun glinting on shields and helmets. Our horses pranced, excited, as the marshals paired us for the entrance, placed as we would meet. A tall knight nudged his horse beside me. His

blue shield bore white flowers, and there were the gold crowns of Camelot.

"Sir Lambert," I said, bowing.

"Sir Michel."

I smiled to hear him say it. "We met at Angers, sir."

"A squire." He watched me beneath thick level brows. "Now made a
knight. Lancelot swore both my silence and a curse of you."

I blinked at him. My dubbing so delighted me I had almost forgot
Lancelot's threat. "I see no other Camelot knights, sir."

"Many still quest the Sangral. But there is another here, Orsain of
Trundal." He saw my sudden wince. "He comes tomorrow for the
melee."

Heralds blew their trumpets again. Orsain, I thought, thick Orsain
of the pocked face. Strong enough to earn Gawain's praise. Christ be
with me. The marshals called. We donned our helmets, raised our
lances, stepped our horses onto the field. Orsain, the best fighter of the
four, save Briant. Knights in the loges cheered, and Matilde stood next
Adele and waved at each of us. Tomorrow, on the melee field, Orsain.
After the parade I stood at the edge of the field and watched how British
knights rode. The marshals had paired the fighters well. Geoffrey won
but Philip, his nose broken and one arm badly slashed, was forced to
yield. Denis managed a draw. I could not keep Orsain from my mind.

It was bright midday when I went again to the paddocks. The noise
and violence of the joust had subdued Hugh's confidence, and he did not
even smile as he handed me Night's reins. The horse quivered under me
as I took my first lance. Lambert and I cantered to our ends of the field.
We turned and saluted, Night tossed his head and leaped forward, Sir
Lambert rushed down the field. A white scarf streamed from his helmet.
My heart stopped and my mouth tasted of bile. Remembering Orsain I
had forgot today's danger. I stared along my lance at the place we would
meet. I stood. The shock nearly blinded me. His point tore away a corner
of my shield and battered my shoulder. My lance splintered as we
passed. I rode for another. Already I knew Sir Lambert was not so clever
as Pierre, and the day shone bright beyond my eye-slot and in the loges
Matilde was clad in gold. My fear was gone.

Lambert rode with his lance raised at my throat. I did not waver, but
leaned against him. His lance boomed against my shield and dug at my
helmet as it glanced away. But I had seen the twitch he would give his
shield and my driving point hit him square, the iron rammed through
his painted flowers, his head lurched forward at the impact, and then he
fell back away out of his saddle. Our passing almost tugged the lance
from my hand.

A sound rose from the loges, half gasp and half cheer. I pulled my horse around. Lambert lay on his back, unmoving.

Hugh dashed up for Night. "Hit him, sir, afore he gets up."

I swung down and walked to Lambert and drew my sword.

His own squire cried out, "Sir, stand up, sir."

Lambert climbed unsteadily to his feet, the hurt plain in his movement. Blood leaking from his chest already gouted his surcoat. My lance had split more than his shield.

"Are you fit, sir?" I said.

"Do not insult me."

The three sword-blows were without shields. I raised my blade and saluted him. He made no move to parry, and I could see his eyes closed, inside his helmet.

"Sir Lambert," I cried. His eyes opened. "Sir, I strike, else you yield."

"God defend you," he muttered. He lifted his sword.

I dropped my blade hard on his helmet. He made a staggering answer that I caught easily. I hacked a level blow to the side of his helmet that felled him on the trampled turf.

I put my sword point to his throat. "Do you yield, sir?"

"Three sword-blows," he muttered weakly.

I hit him smartly on the top of the helmet. I sheathed my sword, drew my dagger, and thrust its finer point at his eye-slot. "Now, sir, you must yield." He said nothing, though I could hear him gasping. "Yield, Lambert of Denham."

"A lucky poke. If I could but get my breath." His eyes peered out at me. "God damn me, I must yield."

The count's men came and carried him off. My lance had driven through his shield, through mail and leather both, snapped two ribs and injured his lung. "Sir Lambert," I said, at the leech's tent, "I had no thought to wound you so." He waved a hand, shook his head, and closed his eyes.

I walked back, pleased and unhappy both. I had won my first joust and a fine ransom, but I had given a dangerous wound. Sir Lambert was married. I prayed God I had not made a widow.

Tomorrow hung over me like a stone.

Count Étienne spread his evening meal in the castle court, as the Hall was too narrow for all our company. Craon sat together at a single trestle, knights and ladies beneath a flaring torch, and even Sir John with us. "We did well," he said, smiling. "And tomorrow, Sir Philip, we'll all share our melee winnings."

Philip had a bandaged nose and a blackened eye, and wore his arm bound to his chest. Matilde sat next him, her eyes downcast as befitted the wife of a beaten knight. He turned his single gaze to me. "I hear your knight is wealthy."

"Fifty livres ransom." I could not hide my pleasure. "His squire has paid me half."

"Damn." He winced in pain as he reached for the wine cup. "I've lost the same."

Sir John drew out a purse and gave us each gifts. The others who had won followed him. I had fine daggers for John and Amaury, silver crosses for Geoffrey and Pierre. I drew out a small gold ring. "Sir Philip."

His face lit up, though when he tried it, it did not fit him. "Matilde," he said, and put it on her hand.

The servants filled our cup again and we drank to each other's gallantry. Still, Sir John kept us as sober as he might, that we have clear heads tomorrow. Matilde did not look at me, yet as she turned the ring on her finger it glittered in the torchlight, and everyone might see I gave Philip a ring too narrow for his hand.

Servants came at Compline to escort the ladies back. Sir John wanted Philip to go with them, but he would not, and when we left at midnight I had to grip his shoulders and steady him.

"Good Michel." He draped his good arm over me. "What ribbon'd you wear? Some lady of Craon? Adele?"

"Don't be a fool, Philip," I muttered.

A waning moon stood over the tourney field. He raised a wavering fist and cursed it, and fell in a ditch. We got him out, muddy but unhurt, and then he insisted I lead him out on the field. He found the spot where he had yielded, fumbled out his member, and pissed on the trampled grass. "All I can do now, damn me."

"Come, Philip." I led him toward Sir Amaury's tent.

"Somebody loves my wife," he muttered.

"What?" My breath caught in my throat.

"She's dutiful," he said, "but her heart is elsewhere." He shook his wobbly head. "Fool I am, I've come to love her myself." He gripped my shoulder. "I'll kill the bastard. If you help me."

"You're new married, Philip. She will come to love you."

"Not if I lose in tourneys. Will you help me?"

"Philip, it's your imagination."

"Damn courtly love." Tears blurred his voice. "Sounds wonderful till it's your own wife. Your own lady, think what her husband feels. If he cares."

He fumbled his way into Sir Amaury's tent, where the rest already snored. His talk had nearly sobered me. If he saw Adele watch me, he must see me watch Matilde. Did he taunt me, armed by the drink? Or, dear God, had she truly another at Le Vallon?

As I passed Adele's pavilion the tent flap moved, a slender figure stepped into the moonlight, that wore a gold ring on one finger. The wine roared sudden in my head. I reached for her.

"My lady."

"Sir knight."

I wrapped my arms about her. A thundering gale filled my mind. Today had I defeated Camelot against all fears. I had won, carrying her colors. Lambert's coin lay heavy in my baggage. I gave the ring, I would take my knight's reward. Philip sickened me, all whimpers and weakness. I gripped her. I would have her.

"Michel," she said breathless, "go you easy, sir."

"Lady, I burn for you." I kissed her, very hard.

"I feel you do, sir." She squirmed in my grasp. "Michel." She tried to turn her head.

"Lady, I love you." I covered her mouth with mine. I held her, thrust my hand into her gown.

"Sir knight," she gasped, "you crush me, you tear . . ."

I lifted my head for a breath.

The moon blazed in my eyes, lopsided as the moon over Lark's wood. I dropped her. She staggered and nearly fell.

"Michel? What is this?" I could not answer. "I love you, Michel, I could never deny you." She brushed at her hair. "But here, in this field . . ."

"I forgot myself, lady." The moon glared at me.

"Michel." She leaned against me, put an arm around me. "At Craon. After the tourney."

"Lady." I shuddered against her. "Tomorrow I must fight."

The dawn sky bent overhead, bright and cloudless, though night still murked the tourney field. Grooms murmured sleepily in the paddocks where horses snorted and stamped. I stood awake at Sir John's tent and took a deep breath, of grass and manure and the smoke of cooks' fires. It would be a fine bright day. We would meet in some empty place, without judges or honor or rules, and only death at the end. Dear Rebecca, pray God I answer your blood.

Sir John and all Craon armed themselves, save the injured Philip, too excited to notice my worry. We knelt before his priest again. Young Gilbert lifted our banner, the white dragon on its green field, and led us through the throng. A dozen pennants moved in the bright morning—Alençon, Mortain, Anjou, Vendôme. Green ribbons tied to our helmets fluttered in the breeze. At the melee ground Brittany and Britain would be wearing red. I wondered how I would know Orsain. I could not remember his arms from Camelot.

The count's heralds sounded their horns. We cheered and kicked our horses forward. A clump of shouting knights passed us at a gallop, eager for the fight, and Sir John grinned after them. "The first are eager and always easy to take."

We picked our way past farmers' yards and down a walled lane. In the fields the green wheat stood high as our horses' knees. A half dozen wearing red spied our own impetuous crowd, and both sides drew swords. They charged bellowing together, but Sir John led us trotting round them like hunting wolves and not till they began to tire did he raise his blade.

We drove headlong into the brawl. Dust blew all about, thick as smoke. It was not easy to tell red from green, but it hardly mattered. We beat our swords on whoever was closest. I captured nothing, though John and Pierre each had a ransom before the red knights retreated. We circled our horses, through wheat trampled in wide circles, laughing and sweaty in the heating day. Another troop burst from nearby oaks, and John called out and rode straight at them. We met with a clatter but Night shook off their grasping hands and I drove clean through the line.

The dust was even thicker now. I turned back to help Sir John. A single horseman came trotting toward me, uninterested in the brawl. His black shield bore a yellow chevron, quartered with the gold crowns of Camelot.

I knew at once who it was.

Sixteen

Orsain drew up a dozen paces away, yet his squire came on till his horse almost nosed mine. "Varlet of Greenfarm," he cried, "you stand challenged, sword and shield, by . . ."

"Foul knight!" I bellowed. "Murderous raper." I lurched up in my stirrups and tore off my helmet. "Befouler of Arthur's freedom. Knight who fears the Sangral quest." I was Raven again, a peasant boy screaming at knights. A cold hate filled my belly. My blared words felt weightless as smoke, though the last roused him to lift his visor and reveal a pale beard too thin to hide his pocks.

"Damn you, the king had sent me away."

"Keep silent, save you can speak without a tongue." I thrust my blade at him. "I will not rest till you lie dead."

"Ere that," he cried, "you will rest among the fires of Hell."

He drew his sword. We both swung down from our horses. Hugh rode up, wide-eyed. Geoffrey broke from the melee, and Sir John, crying out, "What do you, sirs?"

" 'Tis a challenge to myself, sir," I answered, too loud. "From a knight without honor." I restrapped my helmet.

"Honor?" Orsain spat at the trampled wheat. "What honor hath a churl, impostoring a knight, dubbed by a fool?"

"Fool?" John growled. "I am that fool, sir."

"Then, sir." Orsain stared at him. "After I kill him I will avenge knighthood's honor on you."

"Let us fight now," John cried, and leapt from his horse.

I pushed between them. "Here is my combat alone, sir. Before God and Christ I answer my sister's blood."

John took a step back. "Michel, what is this?""

"A farmer's bitch," Orsain sneered, "a snotty churl. Naught to merit all this trouble."

I had not heard his sneer since that summer's night; it was this voice that said "the bitch is warmed and ready." My head flared, my hands shook with anger, I had waited years for this. He raised his sword without warning. Our weapons rang together as I parried his blow. My quickness surprised him. I swung against him hard as I could, so quick he could not parry. My blade caught his shoulder, slashed his surcoat and creased his mail. He grunted under the blow.

"Do you fight without shields?" Geoffrey cried.

Small notches glittered in the edge of my sword as I raised it again. Orsain parried quick. I attacked hard as I could. Behind his visor his eyes were damp with pain. I dropped under his guard and thrust at his gut. I hurt him, but my sword point did not pierce his mail. I swung and creased his helmet. Intent on my attack I did not see his answer.

A huge chop to my left shoulder drove the mail into my own flesh. It was the shoulder Lambert had already injured, and I staggered under the blow. My whole chest went numb. My arm felt hewn away, but when I looked both hands still held my blade. He chopped at me again, I dodged, his blade glanced off my back. My shoulder blazed. As I turned to face him, his sword fell on my helmet. I could barely lift my blade. My own eyes swam with agony. I could hardly see his attack, could barely cover myself, had no time to counter. I had lost all strength in my left arm. The blood running between my fingers made my pommel slippery. My helmet rang like a broken bell. I could not hear. I could not see what he would do next. He swung again. I half stumbled as I dodged away. Another blow bent the side of my helmet. I staggered backward. The tall grain caught at my ankles.

"Stand, churl," he bellowed. "At least die like a knight."

I could not understand him. I hacked at his helmet. Lambert had been easy, even Ricard. I had never thought to lose. Orsain's blade fell on my hurt shoulder and my knees nearly buckled. I swung, he parried easily, he hit me again. I could barely see for the pain. I stabbed at his neck, my blade slid past. He hammered my bleeding shoulder with the pommel of his sword. I gasped in agony. My foot slipped as I backed away. I fell hard.

For a moment, lying on my side, I could see only crushed wheat and the hooves of horses. I rolled on my back. Orsain stood over me, raising his sword. I lifted my own. It seemed but half a blade, broken by my fall.

My point hid beneath the skirt of his hauberk. I wrenched myself up and grasped my hilt with both hands and thrust, hard as I could. I felt my sword point drive up through his unprotected groin. My hands rode up together to the hem of his mail. His own sword hammered into my injured shoulder so hard I thought the bone snapped. Blood burst over me, and piss and the stink of bowels. A scream bellowed out his helmet. His sword fell away loose. He staggered and bent over, his fingers searching for my blade. His fall almost wrenched the pommel from my hands, as he dropped clattering beside me.

I sank back breathless, ablaze with pain. Our helmets lay so close together I could hear his ragged breathing. "Orsain of Trundal," I could barely mutter, "here is my anger."

His gasping stopped as he collected himself. "Varlet," he whispered, "peasant." He drew a choking breath. "You have killed me, churl, but others hate you as much as I."

Hugh appeared beyond my eye-slot, pale, grappling with my helmet straps. Each move was a knife into me. A bright sky hung overhead, trees moved in the breeze, knights stared down.

"Sir Michel, I thought he would kill you, sir."

"No, Hugh." The voice was not my own.

"You bleed, sir." He gripped my arm. I cried out, and Geoffrey knelt and pushed him roughly aside.

"My shoulder." I clenched myself against the pain.

"We must bind you, get you to physicians." Geoffrey put a hand under my back and made me sit. I took one shaking breath and fell into blackness.

I woke as they handed me down from a horse. A vaulted castle ceiling swam over me. A cup appeared, smelling of wine. Hands dragged off my hauberk. My mind wavered at the pain. Hands fumbled at my arm, pressed me down. I smelled heated iron, my shoulder burst into flame, I screamed at the scorch of flesh.

I woke in a litter, slung between horses, lurching down a long hill. Every jounce injured me. Sir Lambert sprawled against me, his pale face lolling on bundled robes. Hugh rode outside. Beyond him stretched a country I did not know.

Lambert opened his eyes. "Orsain of Trundal. A sturdy fighter. We ought have quested the Sangral, both of us." He gripped his chest against the jolting litter and shut his eyes.

"You have killed a great knight, sir," said Hugh.

"The first of four," I said, nearly voiceless. God's Name, were they all strong as Orsain I would not last.

One horse stepped into a deeper rut and I had no strength to hide my groan. Pain roared everywhere. I closed my eyes, and rode the foggy lanes of Angers. Ricard died, half by accident. Orsain died, half by accident. His pocked face stood before me, and behind him three, Briant and dull Giles and Laramort's pale stare. Lady Sibyl pushed herself soft against me. The night-black sea tossed, a cart bearing me to the scaffold. I throbbed with fright.

I woke. The sky had gone so pale it might be morning already. We passed a cluster of poor houses. A maid stared from the upper casements of the largest. She was very pretty. I raised my good hand to her. She made me a kiss.

"What place is this?"

"Le Gravier, sir. 'Tis but a league to Craon."

I shut my eyes. The maid blew her kiss again. I felt my sword in Orsain's bowels as if they were my own.

Sir John stood at my bed, his arms crossed tightly, his face dark with anger. "No one told me of this feud."

"Sir, it was in Britain." My head thundered with pain. "I never thought to meet him."

He gestured at Sir Lambert, that lay on a cot across the chamber. "Lambert tells me there are four others."

"Three, sir. Almant has never attacked me."

"Three. Four." He clamped his lips. "I dubbed you, I took you as my knight and vassal. I will not have this feud."

I struggled to think beyond my roaring agony. "I swore my aid and arm, Sir John, but this is my own . . ."

"I will not have it," cried John.

"Sir, they killed my sister."

"And the king gave you payment, Lambert says."

"A battle-horse, an animal we could not keep." My own voice grated in my ears. "Even that was too much for them. They attacked me at Camelot. At Winchester." I sat up, and shadows invaded the corners of my eyes. "What would you, sir, had she been your sister?"

"God's blood, I am baron of Craon."

"Aye, my lord," I said deliberately.

We stared at each other. After a long time he said, "Were Lancelot correct, she was not your sister." My head throbbed in anger and I opened my mouth to argue, but he went on. "You are the man who saved my life." He touched his scar unthinking. "For that I dubbed you knight."

"You know I thank you, sir."

"As your lord, I forbid you this feud." I knew I could never give it up. "This feud," he repeated.

My head reeled with anguish. "You are my lord, Sir John."

He frowned, uncertain what I promised. "You are my man, Michel de Verdeur." He strode out the chamber, angry still.

"Lancelot," Lambert muttered. "He refused your feud at Angers. But what is this, that she was not your sister?"

I could not answer. I could barely think through my throbbing pain. The old man at Craon's mill, he had put me next Sir John, John had dubbed me, I slew Orsain. I could not believe the wizard embraced my feud, but what did Merlin do with his green knight?

"My page rides to Britain," Lambert said. "Orsain's squire, too." He gave a cough. "Camelot will soon know of you."

Sir Pierre stood suddenly beside my cot. "You fought like a court fool," he growled. "You stabbed at him, and he killed you, nearly."

I remembered every thrust, every blow. "I hated him. He galled me, he made me blind. I forgot everything, I could think of nothing but revenge."

"Then 'tis a lesson." He put a gentle hand on my blazing shoulder. "Never fight of hate. It kills faster than any sword."

The leeches woke me from a fevered sleep, and pulled and thrust at me till I screamed at them through the pain. My shoulder bones were cracked, they said, but not broken through. The burning done at Pouancé had already begun to heal. They salved my wounds and bound my arm to my chest, and again I swore at them, my voice almost extinct from hurt.

I slept. I woke in pain, certain it would never end. A woman's voice spoke, a maid carried flagon and goblet, and there was the lady Adele. Hugh scrambled up from cleaning armor and pushed a stool at her. She frowned and would not sit.

"My lady," I said, "the stink of injury reeks this chamber."

Her mouth had gone hard and her gaze would not settle anywhere, and she might not have heard me. "Good sirs, I bring Gascon wine to ease your rest. Craon rarely shelters such chivalric knights."

Lambert roused himself. "Thank you, lady," he said, hoarse. "There is no hospitality like Craon's."

"It is my gift, not John's."

"Lady," I said, "your favor gives us huge comfort."

"And I pray God you both heal quickly." She turned and went, still awkward and unsettled.

"God save us," muttered Lambert, "a handsome lady." He took the goblet. "Nor am I so ill to miss how she looked at you."

I slept again, and woke throbbing. Sir Lambert groaned. It was night. Matilde raised her whispering lips, murmuring love. In her bed I had broke my vow. Now it broke me.

Lambert coughed, feverish. A soft wind blew in the sunlit window. Laughter sounded from the court below, the clatter of horses and, once, the scream of a falcon.

Lady Adele came again, with some potion the leeches had made for us. Sir John was anxious for his newest knight, she said, and put her hand beneath my head as I drank the bitter mull.

Yet John did not come, himself. Next day was the Sabbath and after another aching restless night I climbed from my bed. Hugh draped robes over me, and I gripped his arm down the turning stair to the Hall. A large company sat at table, that clapped and cheered me, and their noise pleased and wearied me both.

Sir Amaury was still at Craon, and Philip and Matilde, and my head swam and I glanced away from her. Sir John stood and made a place at his left hand. Lady Adele helped me into the seat, her hands soft and lingering. "Praise God our newest knight heals so quickly," she said, and Sir John smiled his agreement.

John's squire cut my meat. After three bites I was no longer hungry, but the wine tasted very good as they drank my health.

"Pray God I'll be there when next you fight," Philip said.

Sir John laughed, a little harsh. "We go to Vitré, Our Lord's Transfiguration."

I shut my eyes. Two months. I must joust again, take a lance against this shoulder. It hurt even to imagine it.

"Two victories," Philip said, "and both 'gainst Camelot knights. Few had a better tourney."

"Yet," I said, "Sir Pierre lectures me how ill I fought."

"Would he had lectured me as well, before."

"Then you ought practice with him," said Sir John. "Stay, Philip, long as you wish. You are always welcome."

I turned to look at Sir John. He was smiling. Yet Philip was no bachelor knight, but the lord of two separate estates, and high summer was no time to be absent from them.

Philip nodded. "If Michel will help, and share a cup."

"Of course, Sir Philip." I still could not look at Matilde. "You must work very hard," I said, and regretted it at once.

He laughed with the rest, but there was no humor in it.

I drank another round and ate a bit of bread, but my strength had failed. I turned to Sir John. "Pray you, sir, I would return to my chamber."

"Of course." He took my good arm and walked me to the door.

"I am sorry for my weakness, sir."

"You will recover soon enough." His voice had gone distant. "Might Pierre really teach Sir Philip?"

"Philip is very impetuous, sir." John's sudden coolness must be from my fight with Orsain. "He would be a knight troubadour."

"Courtly love, instead of battle valor?" John glanced back at the company. "Well, we must do something to help him." He looked at me and gave a thin smile. "And his pretty wife."

Lambert woke me, coughing. He coughed all the night and next morning sweat shone pale on his long face. He could not speak above a whisper. Sir John came at last, with a priest that murmured prayers. Leechmonks hung their black worms where Lambert's wound festered. By evening he could hardly stand to use the pot. I sat beside him and took his hand.

"God's name, good sir, do not leave us."

He opened bloodshot eyes. "You have killed me, Michel."

"I did not mean it, sir."

" 'Twas a fair joust." His face had shrunk against his skull, and his breath smelled of death. "A farmer's boy." He lay a minute, panting. "Surely you fight like a knight."

That night he did not cough, but when my own fever woke me a priest knelt beside him, murmuring prayers. In the morning he had grown worse. "Good Lambert," I said. He did not answer. I sat all day beside him, despite my hurt. His eyelids fluttered, but he did not wake. Two knights had I slain, and two robbers. Dear Christ, I prayed, do not make Lambert my fifth.

The lady Adele came again, without wine or potion. She put out a hand to keep me seated. After she had prayed, she touched my good shoulder. "You must rest yourself, Michel."

Sir John returned as the bells rang for Vespers, and with the priest again, that laid a hand on Lambert's brow, made his sign and began the rites.

"He has not gone," I said.

John nodded. "He fights death like any good knight."

Deep in the night Lambert cried out. A line of moonlight lay across his bed, that I imagined was his soul escaping heavenward. A huge stink filled the chamber. His squire fumbled for a rush light. A great stain of pus and blood wet Lambert's bed, and he lay pale and shrunken in the flutter of the lamp. At first I did not think he breathed but then his eyes opened. He coughed and choked, and spat a rich gob on the reeded floor.

"Christ," he said, nearly inaudible, "a man might die of thirst."

* * *

Pierre had set Philip to battle practice every morning, and soon I was healed enough to meet him in the Hall before the midday meal, for a cup of wine.

"The air of Craon fills me with strength." He sat next me, smelling of dust and horses. "And my wife with desire."

I laughed to hide my confusion. "Fortunate man."

"I thought she loved someone else." He smiling gaze did not waver. "But I was very drunk that night." He looked up as the ladies came in a chattering cluster from the solar. "Mayhap you have no need to fight for me."

We stood to greet them. Matilde sat next Philip and listened to his morning's work, and did not look at me at all. I saw her every day, at every meal, but she was always so. It had been my craze, at Pouancé.

Sir John took all his court out hawking, after the meal. I had begun my Latin again, in the weeks I waited to heal, and spent the hour after the midday meal with the priest William, that was Craon's almoner. William was a tall, dark-bearded monk, with as much patience for my struggles as Sir Amaury's old Joachim.

That day, walking back across the court with my head full of verbs, I found Matilde at the stairway door. "My lady, I thought you rode out."

Wordless, she drew me in the stair and took my face with both hands, and kissed me. Surprise and desire both flared in me. "Philip went." She kissed me again. "I said I was too weary." Her arms gripped me. "I hate it, that you are pale and injured, and Philip jealous and myself distant." I flinched in her embrace and she murmured, "Oh, Michel, I do not mean to hurt you." She took my good hand and pulled me up the curling stairs, and not till we climbed another turn could I speak.

"Lady. A moment." I held my breath that I not seize her.

"Oh, Michel, do I hurt you?"

"Lady, Sir Lancelot made a vow, that he see the Sangral." She tugged me up another step. "Matilde, I have my own vow."

"Tell me of it later."

"Against my knight at Pouancé."

"But he is killed." She pulled at me again.

" 'Tis a blood feud. There are three others."

"What?" She stopped. "What feud demands an oath 'gainst love?" She touched my injured shoulder. "Is it this? Do you believe I weaken you?"

"Only my resolve, lady."

Her eyes glittered with quick anger. "You toy with me." She backed away from me, against the curved wall. "It is some jest, of you and my lady Craon."

"I have an oath, I make my revenge."

"You loved me well enough before you killed that knight. Yet now you grip me and then fling me away."

"It was the moon, that night."

She stared at me. "There is no moon now." But she saw at last that I was serious, and her frown eased.

"Matilde." I took her hands. "You are my only love."

"Oh, Michel." Her eyes flooded abruptly. "Oh, Michel, do not say that, I cannot bear it." Tears ran down her cheeks. "Willows bend over a little stream, beside the cloister of Nyoiseau. They will remind me always of Craon's river."

"Lady, your husband . . ."

"Philip." She kissed me, softly. "Some knight will widow me, soon enough. I pray, dear Michel, it will not be you."

I had kept myself from her, yet my victory felt hollow as death. And that same week, practicing at swords on a drizzly morning, Philip slipped on a wet cobble. Denis was already thrusting and could not help the wound he gave. Philip gripped his bleeding arm. He had the injury that took Matilde from Craon.

Pierre already had me swinging a practice sword. Soon I could ride well enough, though the leeches kept my left arm strapped for six weeks of the eleven between Pouancé and Vitré. I still went to William, though oft my study brought Matilde to mind instead. After, I usually rode out with Denis or Pierre to visit the villages of the barony, until one summer day they were both occupied in castle matters and I went out alone.

It was John Baptist's. The festival had arrived before I knew it. At Craon they did not make a bonfire, but a feast for all the demesne two days after. Thinking of Lark's death and the king, I found myself at the crossroads of Le Gravier. Peasants in holiday shirts idled in the tree shade beside the ale-seller's house, swigging from their pots. They climbed to their feet and bobbed as I rode up, and my name buzzed among them. A stable boy ran to help me down and take the reins.

"Water my horse," I said. "Give him a handful of oats."

"Aye, sir. Our best, sir."

The public room was dim and murky after the bright day, and smelled of spilled ale and winter smoke. The peeling walls had forgotten their last whitewash. The owner bobbed at me, wringing his hands.

"Have you wine?" I said, and sat a teetering bench.

"Wine? Oh, no sir, only ale. Make it myself, sir, flavored with thistle and cumin. Very tasty."

"Give me a pot."

"Aye, sir."

"I saw a girl here, a month ago."

He gave a broad smile. "My wife's niece, sir. She'll bring your drink."

Flies droned in the thick air. Beyond the open shutters the farmers had resumed their chatter, and when a new one arrived I heard my name again. The girl came toward me, a large pot held in both hands. She had washed her round face and pulled back her dark hair. She was as pretty as I remembered, with plump arms and an ample bosom, and skin clear as a milkmaid's.

"Thank you," I said. "Sit down."

"Aye, sir." She perched on the bench opposite.

"I saw you at the window. A month ago."

She nodded politely, half afraid and half bold.

"A litter with two wounded knights," I said.

"Oh, sir, yes. Was it you waved to me?"

"And you made a kiss to me."

"Oh, sir." A fleeting redness lit her cheeks, and she dropped her gaze.

I drank and shuddered at the ale. "What is your name?"

"Anne, sir."

"Here, take a drink, Anne."

She frowned as she did, and wiped her lips with her hand.

"Your uncle's best, eh?"

She nodded toward the farmers. "They drink anything, sir."

I took another sip. Two long summer months it had been, since I had taken Matilde's color. Nearly one since I had refused her. I looked at the girl so that she glanced away. I felt her arms round me and her breasts against me and her lips opening in the dust of haystacks, on the old leaves of some wood.

"How much is this, Anne?"

"Half a penny, sir?"

I might set any price. I reached into my purse. I made sure she heard the coins rattle, and in truth she could not keep her glance away. I put a coin on the stained wood. I laid another beside it, and a third and a fourth. Her eyes widened with each of them. I opened my fist and three more clanked on the table.

She closed her mouth. She looked at me, unbelieving. "Sir," she said. There was greed on her face, and fright, too. She was fifteen, a pretty girl watching me, her eyes wide open. I could see her heart beating in a vein in her neck. I could see her days, her nights too, merchants leering as they grabbed at her, peasants drooling in their pots, making jokes of bulls and rams.

"Sir," she said again, as if she did not trust her tongue with longer words.

"How long have you been here, Anne?"

She swallowed. "Two years, sir, this Martinmas. Since my mother died with the baby." She still watched me, though her look was closing. She had come to grips with the coin and her want of it, and her willingness to do whatever might be needed.

I had never looked at anyone as I looked at her, and at last I saw clearly the weight my knighthood bore on the world. I pushed one coin against the pot. It made a small clink in the silent room. "For the ale." I picked up the rest. "Hold out your hands."

She stared at me, her mouth open.

"Your hands, Anne."

She cupped her hands and pushed them trembling at me. The coins ran through my fingers.

"Sir," she said.

"Wait." I dug into my purse and drew out the rest, and counted them into her palms. "Twenty-one. Keep them, Anne. Save them, for the day they are needed."

Her arms shook as if the coins were too heavy to hold.

"Sir, what do you buy?"

"A life, sweet Anne."

"Sir?"

"Go tell the boy I would have my horse."

She stared at me. "Sir, these . . ."

"Hide them. Then go tell the boy."

She held out her hands like a priest carrying the Host.

"Anne," I said, "they will see."

She clutched them to her bosom. "They say you are Sir Michel, from the castle, sir . . ."

At that moment the owner strode in. "Annie," he boomed, "have you served this good knight? Sir, do you like my ale?"

"I cannot drink it," I said, "the thistle. But I would not rob you." I picked up the single coin and gave it to him.

He eyes lit as he fingered it. "Thank you, sir, you are very kind. Has Annie . . . ?"

The girl had gone.

"She calls my horse," I said.

"Very good, sir. But listen, sir, I could keep wine for you, if you wish it, sir." He smiled at me. "Annie would be pleased to serve you, sir."

The hooves of my palfrey rang outside. I went out into the summer air. The peasants fell silent. The boy helped me up. A shutter creaked at an upstairs window. The girl clutched one hand to her bosom, and with the other wiped her tears.

I nudged my horse. He lifted his head and broke into a trot, down the dusty road to Craon.

Seventeen

The leeches at last unbound my wounded arm, but my shoulder was very stiff and when I tried to grip a shield I had no strength at all. I had no real tasks at Sir John's castle save practice at arms, and that summer meant hot and weary days spent at tourney practice, and my healing seemed to take a long time.

Summer at Craon also meant long soft evenings in the castle Hall, the windows thrown open to any breeze, a cup brim-full with white wine cooled in the cellars, the songs of troubadours. And though Amaury and the rest were gone away, that summer meant the smiles of the lady Adele, that often called me to sit next her.

"Lady," I said, "you exalt me with your company."

"Knights of Craon, Sir Michel, must know courtliness as well as combat."

Craon was a baron's castle, where every day bards recounted the histories of the heroes, and there was music every night. As Lady Clare had, at Clos Saint-Georges, Adele taught me the steps of dances, the gestures and the curtsies. And ever did she talk of knights and ladies, and especially the old court of Poitiers with its rules of love. It came to me that, were women denied the battles of tourney and crusade, they must instead delight in the combat of heart and bedchamber.

Of course her company pleased me, and the charm of her smiling gaze. Nor could I refuse her, though I worried that Sir John did not seem to care. When he came and sat with us her talk never varied, yet her lips went hard and her eyes no longer glittered in the taperlight. I was careful to speak to him as much as her, and keep my gaze away from her supple figure. Still, oft sitting near her and heated by the wine, I wondered that they had no children.

If the nights were hazardous of chivalry, at least as I healed, combat eased my days. Yet there was a morning I came back early from practice, and climbed the castle steps, aching and thirsty. Sir John stood at the top of the Hall doors, talking with his steward. "Michel," he called, "how is your arm?"

"We jousted easy, sir." I wiped my sweating face. "My shield still feels very awkward."

"It is but three weeks to Vitré, Michel."

"I will be ready, sir." Though in truth I wondered of it.

Adele had come down the solar stairs, and she walked toward us, frowning. "Ought he joust with such a shoulder, John?"

"I will be healed, lady," I said.

Sir John nodded. "Michel is stronger than anyone believes."

He turned again to his steward, and talking of some castle matter they walked away down the steps. There was nobody about save the lady and myself, and servants setting trestles in the Hall. I called one to bring a me cup of ale.

"Be not so brave, Michel," she said. "You must say it if you are not whole by Vitré."

"Lady, I will fight if my lord desires it."

"But John does not want you hurt again." She came near me, near enough to touch my injured arm and take her hand away again.

A servant brought up the cup of frothy ale. I offered her the first drink and though she shook her head, her face softened as she watched me. Troubled by her gaze, and her closeness, I took a step away. "Lady, I stink of horses and jousting."

" 'Tis the true smell of knights." She followed me, step for step. "That is always a delight to any lady."

My head began to throb, of the ale and her bright eyes. "Lady, I thank you for your worry. I will be healed by Vitré."

She watched me through her lashes. "Tis not your prowess on the tourney field I worry of, Sir Michel." I held the cup between us, as if it were a shield. She took my arm again, so close that beneath her summer mantle her breast moved soft against me. "Some whisper I am indeed your lady."

My heart drummed with fright and desire, both. I tried to lean away. "Sir Philip imagined it, lady." But it was not Philip, it was all those summer evenings I ought have kept distant.

"Whispers that soon might reach my lord's ear." She pressed against me, firm and warm. I could smell the spices in her hair.

"Lady, you are baroness of Craon, I am but . . ."

"And if he believes it, ought it not be true?"

I could not breathe. She smiled, her lips damp and her cheeks flushed, and her breath blew quick and sweet against my cheek. For a flaring moment I imagined her naked under me.

"Sir John is my lord, a fine and chivalric knight, a . . ."

Adele put a finger upon my lips. "But Michel, am I not your lady? May I not also command? You may practice chivalry each day, but are not the nights for courtly arts?" She gripped my arm to her a long moment, before she smiled and let me go.

I watched her turn and walk away. The drape of her robe moving on her hips almost made me follow. Benches clattered in the Hall, where servants were careful not to look at us. I drew a fevered breath. Once again my beery friar came to mind, and the tale of the green knight. Gawain had refused the wife, three times. I heard the wizard asking, "Could you resist her, hot-mouthed and open-bodiced, and the husband gone a-hunting?"

I pleaded the tourney, those last few weeks before Vitré, and practiced more and retired early. The lady took it as chivalric modesty, and her eyes glittered with delight. Sir John, pleased how my strength improved, might have been blind to the whole of it.

All that long summer only rare thunderstorms had wet the dusty fields, but a week from harvest the weather changed and a violent storm drenched the ripening grain. The morning we left for Vitré thick clouds pushed overhead again, a chill wind blustered in our faces, and the rain began as we forded the river into Brittany. We rode on through dripping forests, past spattered lakes and muddy villages, unhappy weather for a tourney and worse for harvest.

We were but six knights, Sir John and Pierre and Denis and myself, with two others of Craon. The weather kept Sir Amaury home, and Sir Lambert rode to Lancelot's Banioc for news of the knight and the quest. We came to the little city near the end of the day, in a pelting downpour. We rode up muddy streets past the old castle, and down again to a wood bridge over a brown and hurrying stream. Banners drooped on the sodden meadows, marking a tourney ground empty of pavilions. A gray priory stood nearby, and lords and knights already crowded the place. The monks gave us a chamber where we might sleep two on a pallet, though our squires must camp outside in the cloister arcade.

It rained all that night, and in the morning puddles had become ponds and lanes ran like streams. We sat in the refectory, grumbling, or prowled the cloister bundled against the cold. My shoulder ached so I wondered were it truly healed. At midday Sir John called us together, and we rode up through the storm to Vitré castle, on its ridge above the river. Its old walls were thick and its chambers cramped, and knights filled every space while servants slept in covered wains, ranked in the dripping court.

The baron greeted us in his dim Hall, and shook his head at the rain and the tourney's failure. He set Sir John at his high table and the rest of us thigh-to-thigh among the crowded knights. The food was ample, venison and bread and sweets, and the servers never stopped the ale. It made a grand change from the lean diet of the priory.

And when we went out again, smiling and full, the rain was stopped and sunlight sparkled in the rutted puddles. A rainbow arched in the bright air above the roofs of the town, as if a promise that the tourney might begin after all, and we hardly felt the double weight of mail hauberk and damp cloak.

"Come," said John, "we'll ride out to the melee grounds."

He did not smile, and I heard something dark in his voice. At the river meadows he stopped to send all the others back to the priory, even his own squire and Hugh. A cold wind had sprung up again and hurrying clouds hid the sun. Soon enough he turned to me. "When you came to Craon, you said a friar had fostered you."

"Aye, sir." Sir John's scar was a thin pale line against a face dark with anger. He had known of Greenfarm for a year. He had even dubbed me, mindful of it.

"But there was no friar," he rumbled, angry.

"Good sir, there was."

"I asked you a question of my Saracen. You spoke of God's pleasure, of the knowledge of my soul. You eased my heart, and now my priests read Mass each Sabbath for that pagan." He swung on me, his face thunderous. "But you spoke as Satan; there was no friar."

"God save me, sir, he gave me my name."

We had come to another stream. The swift water made our palfreys nervous. Sir John thrust out a hand. "The melee ground runs from here to that wooded rise." I had forgotten the melee. "Our Lord," he said, "once saved a woman taken in adultery."

I shivered in the gusting wind. My mind had gone blank. "A woman *taken* in adultery, sir." I knew that was not his point.

"But if we are all sinners, unable to cast that first stone, must adultery go unpunished?"

"My lord . . ."

"And what of the man with whom she lay? The Book tells us adultery is sinful." He turned his horse and blocked our way. "I have not spoke of the foolish hope my knight, dubbed of my own hand." He clamped his jaw. "By God, is Craon became Camelot? Think you I am as blind as Arthur?"

"My lord." I took a breath. "I swore to speak if such happened. It has not. My lady speaks of elegant ways, there is nothing more than that." I wondered were I the first she had been so courtly with, for he spoke of it even before I came to Craon.

He stared at me, his eyes flashing. "No one at Craon would believe you."

Damn, I thought, it was I that refused her, that had kept Craon virtuous. "My lord," I cried, "who says this? Let them accuse me. I deny it all, sir, and if you do not believe me, you must give me the justice of combat." But then my heart, that beat from anger suddenly skipped in fright. It must be Pierre that said this. Or Denis. The first might kill me, the second I dare not injure.

"Do you deny Philip's lady?" he growled.

"Sir." I stopped and gazed at him. Truth was my only hope. "I have known her, sir. Since she was a widow."

"Philip sees. Philip would train with you to learn your skills, yet he is afraid to fight you." He bent his whole form at me, furious. "But I am not afraid, Michel."

"Sir John, this charge. It is not true."

He clamped his lips. He turned his horse hard and cantered back to the priory. I rode a pace behind, wondering were my challenge accepted, wondering would I survive.

We stayed another day at Vitré. Sir John said nothing more and I kept away from him, sitting the damp church for every Office, staring at the wooden saints with only Hugh for company. The others watched and said nothing, not even Pierre or Denis. Rain fell again as we rode back to Craon, and the wind had changed to blow in our faces. The grain lay beaten and mired in the fields, and peasants stood under their dripping eaves and watched the harvest fail.

A fire blazed in Craon's Hall, yet the place felt cold as midwinter. Sir Lambert stood backed against its heat. He had arrived just before us, and John greeted him abruptly. The lady Adele came smiling to welcome us and I dared not even look at her. Water for our baths was heating, she said, where we could soak away the chill. Then she stopped, seeing our uneasiness, the way each of us stood apart.

"My lord, I expected sadness that the tourney failed. But why this thunderous anger?"

He would not answer.

"Is it this rain, my lord? The ruined harvest?"

"A harvest full of weeds and tares," he growled, and strode past her out the Hall. The others followed as quick.

She gripped my arm. "Sir Michel, what ails my lord?"

"At last, my lady, the whispers reach even his ears."

She put a hand to her mouth. Her eyes widened and her cheeks went hollow, and suddenly she looked very tired. Within the hour, surely within the day, he would confront her. I could but pray that her answer would be true, and he would believe her.

I climbed the winding stair. In our chamber Sir Lambert crouched in the steaming tub. "I've sent for more water," he said. I muttered my thanks, and Hugh took my dripping cloak and began to remove my hauberk. Lambert touched his bright scar. "I had thought Vitré would be my last tourney this summer. Now, suddenly, I miss my wife. My steward is married, my chamberlain a cleric, and I have much faith in Margaret. Still, it is time I returned to Britain."

"Would Sir John had such faith in his lady."

"Sir John seems very angry." He gave a wry smile. "I keep my young knights busy, and send them oft away. Let other men beware their wives."

"Sir Lambert, there is nothing."

He climbed dripping from the tub, and took a towel from his squire. "More's the pity, then. She is a handsome lady."

"But I am accused, and have offered challenge of it."

Lambert raised his brows. "A risky matter, Michel."

I stepped into his water. A castle servant poured in another steaming ewer, but even that sudden heat could not ease the ache in my shoulder, nor the chill in my heart.

He was dressed and gone when Hugh turned to look at me. "Another battle, sir? Like that with Sir Orsain?"

"That I was lucky to win."

"Well, sir, we've all heard talk. Sir Philip's lady, too."

"What? They believe two women of me?"

He laughed. "Valiant in the bedchamber, sir, as on the tourney field."

"Damn, Hugh, why didn't you tell me?"

"I knew it wasn't true, sir."

He began to whistle, polishing my helmet. I sat in the cooling water. A shoe scraped on the threshold. Adele stood there, her worry gone to bright anger.

"My lady." I could not rise.

"He waited for me on the stair, he pushed me into my own chamber.

Himself, Denis, Pierre." She strode across the room and glowered down at me. I tried to conceal myself. "With my own ladies there, he asked me. What could I say?" She spun and trod away. A maid lurked in the doorway.

"What did you say, lady?"

"I denied it." She turned, scowling. "He doubted me though he said you denied it, too. But not . . ." She marched back, so furious she almost spat. "But not that little bitch of Le Vallon." She shut her eyes for a wrathful moment. "When I heard it I almost said yes, it was true, we had, a dozen times. Let you fight your damned combat. With Pierre, damn him." She peered down into the tub. "Whatever you're hiding there it can't be much." She stalked out, anger swirling after her like smoke in a sudden breeze.

Hugh begun to whistle again.

I heaved myself up out of the water. "Hand me a towel," I said, "and stop that damn whistling."

"Why was she so cross, sir?" He grinned. "That she had to answer to all of them? Or that she had to answer no, again?"

"Damn, Hugh, this is no light matter."

"Sir John'll believe her, sir. Her anger'll convince him."

In the Hall two ladies playing at backgammon glanced up at me and bent their heads together. Adele was not there nor Sir John, but Lambert stood at the fire.

"Good sir," I said, "I forgot to ask of Sir Lancelot."

"Lancelot." He stared at the flames a moment, before he began.

All winter last, said his castle steward, Lancelot had been excessively pious. It was the second year of the Sangral quest, that some said was a dream, others that it never would be found. At Easter the high knight had taken ship with Sir Percival. No one knew where they went, though certainly it was not to Camelot.

"Then who defends Camelot?" I asked.

He put a hand to his chest. "I return, myself." He looked past me. "Here is Sir John. And Denis and young Gilbert."

If anger no longer furrowed John's brow, his jaw still set hard and his eyes were cold. I bowed to him, hopefully.

"Good Lambert," he said, "does it rain at Banioc?"

"It rains everywhere, sir." Lambert cleared his throat. "Sir John, with your leave, I would soon hie to Denham."

"Ah, good Sir Lambert, of course. How we will mourn your leaving, as we rue your coming, with such a wound." His gaze flickered at me. "Men of our years ought not tourney, Lambert."

"So says my wife," Lambert said, "that now I do long for. And my children. And my house, stone-built by my grandfather in King Uther's time."

Uther, I thought, King Arthur's father. Camelot rose before me. Uther, king of old Ulfius. And of the wizard, too.

"Eight good manors," Lambert was saying. "Five knights."

At Caen, Amaury and the rest of us had ridden out to the manors of Sir John. And he had others in Britain, in dispute with Arthur.

Lambert had turned to nod at me. "And I must send to Michel the half-ransom I still owe."

I hardly heard him. A notion flared in my head, like summer lightning. "Sir John," I burst out, "your British manors, I could go with Sir Lambert to win them back."

"What?" he barked, suddenly angry again.

"British manors?" said Lambert.

"British manors." John grimaced, and for a moment I thought his fury was at me. "Four of them, given by Uther's regent. Taken by Arthur, damn him, a dozen years past, as Craon is vassal to France."

Lambert nodded. "That happened to many fiefs, in those days. Arthur remade his kingdom, after his twelve battles." He nodded again. "Under British law, all lands are the king's."

I did not bother to listen. "Sir John," I cried, "I will get them for you, and return in time for next summer's tourneys."

John scowled at the fire. "He has given them to Glastonbury."

"But, sir, may not Craon object?"

"Craon objected, God knows. And my cousin Olivier, who held them. Letters, arguments. I should have gone myself."

"Father," said blond Denis, "if you send an envoy, surely it must be me."

But Lambert said no, that Denis was Craon's heir, that his going might threaten John's vassalage of the French king.

"Well," said Sir John, "ought I truly send Michel?"

Lambert paused before he spoke, and would not look at me. "They will remember him at Camelot, Sir John."

For the briefest moment I did not know what he meant, was startled by his doubtful tone. Certainly I was still Raven, I bore the bird on my shield, I prayed for my Blackgral. I had lived so long among knights I truly believed myself one of them. I had forgot how Camelot remembered me.

"Sir John," I said, "I am your vassal, truly dubbed by your hand."

"This sudden urge to Britain." He stared at me. "I have denied your damned feud."

Lambert put in his counsel. "King Arthur gave you justice."

I took a step back, grown quickly furious. "Sir John, I am your vassal. I went to Pouancé only at your wish. I did not seek out Orsain of Trundal. But when he found me I defended myself." I heard my voice boom in the Hall. "As for the others, they too will find me. As easy as he did, even here in Anjou. When they do, sir, must I run away? Desert my arms for the shelter of a cloister? Yield, that they kill me without a fight? Would you forbid my sword? Would you forbid my knight's honor?"

The Hall had gone dead quiet. Knights stared, players paused in their moves, the harper no longer tuned his instrument. My voice even brought the lady Adele, though its anger stopped her midway to us, and she put a hand to her mouth.

"My lord Sir John," I said, "let me serve you at Camelot."

Adele called out, "Good sirs, what is this dispute?"

John might not have heard her. "At Camelot," he repeated. As he stared at me his frown eased and a smile lit his face. "Battle is a knight's life, Lambert, no one can refuse him that."

The knight shook his lean head. "He must not challenge them."

"Good Sir Lambert," I said, "I would those knights were as polite as you."

Adele came toward us, pale, as if she believed this dispute was of her. "Can we know this matter, my lord?"

John still watched me. "My British fiefs," he said, "in Blackmoor Vale." He did not notice her surprise. "Michel would seek them, at Camelot. Where is the harm in trying?"

"In Britain?" Her voice had an angry edge.

"He would travel with Sir Lambert."

She turned and stared at me, a sudden hardness on her cheeks and a dark glitter in her eyes.

"I will send letters patent," John said, "and William as my cleric, that has read law at Angers."

"British law," said Lambert, "is not Angevin law."

John smiled at him. "But another problem you must help us with, good Lambert."

We sat to the meal then. William sat with Lambert and spoke of manors, of pleadings, and of Britain's law, all through the meal. I listened, only half understanding them. It came to me that Pierre, who had charged me and Adele, was not there that night. Hugh had said, she must say no, again. Servants always knew everything, and suddenly I knew it was Pierre she had flirted with, the other knight who saved John's life; that was why John had spoke so to me.

I turned to gaze at her, sitting next Sir John. She did not look up. She said nothing, and left with her ladies soon as she might. Sir John rose soon after and then I went, unafraid who might see me, and climbed the curling stairs to her solar.

She sat at a little fire with three of her women, broidery hoops in their laps. They looked up at me, surprised.

"My lady." I bowed, filled with hope and fright. "May I speak aside with you?"

She stared a long moment, before she stood and walked to another chair. She sat with her back to the firelight, and pointed a low slow stool for me. Looking up at her shadowed face I could see only the lit edges of her auburn hair, and the resentful angles of her body.

"My lady," I said again, "before I leave . . ."

"I am the baroness of Craon." Her voice still held its edge.

"Yes, lady."

Her fingers twitched at the folds of her robe. "I would not mind this love of Philip's silly wife," she muttered, "but that when I spoke, you flushed like a sparrow under the hawk." She bent toward me, exactly as a falcon stooping. "And now you flee to *Camelot.*" She spat the word as if it were a mortal failing.

"My lady, you are baroness of Craon, and I am a landless bachelor. But you are also a beautiful woman, and were the distance not so vast I would court you every day, plead 'gainst your refusals, urge you with all the songs of troubadours." I could not read her shadowed face, but the angle of her shoulders eased. "Yet even then, lady, I would be loath to sit the horns of cuckoldry on my lord's head."

"Tonight at table." She leaned away, and turned her gaze from me. "Tonight he told me of you . . . what was it, Greenway? I was not surprised. Peasants that live with animals know only animal lust. Courtly love is impossible, for a peasant."

I sat a moment, stunned, before I held up both my hands. "At Camelot Sir Kay named me Merdemains." I clapped them on her knees. "Do they still stink, madam, here at Craon?"

She flinched, but did not pull away. "I am baroness of Craon," she muttered. "I am the daughter of Louvigny, they are my manors at Caen." She had gone very still. "Do you know, in the Book, the tale of Joseph and Potiphar's wife?"

"Yes, lady." When Joseph would not love Potiphar's wife, she falsely claimed assault and her husband thrust him into prison. I lifted my hands and drew them away.

"But you love Sir John?"

I peered at her shadowed face. "Sir John is my lord, he made me knight. . . ."

"Yes, yes, I know." She stared at me. "And you are his loyal vassal. As are all his vassals loyal." She reached and took my face and kissed me on the lips. "Would my kiss might make you as loyal, to me."

Eighteen

The dawn was gray and cool, and the blustery wind smelled of rain as we filed into Craon's chapel. Our company for Britain was Sir Lambert and his squire, the priest William and his page, myself with Hugh, and René du Plessis, the dark, quick-witted son of a knight of Craon, to be my own esquire. Sir John had told them all of Greenfarm, and then of Lancelot's notion of my blood, and against any man's doubts took care to send with me a squire of clear nobility. As for René, he believed God made no mistakes, that if He allowed my dubbing I could be nothing but a true knight.

We heard Prime and knelt to be shriven. Walking back up the aisle Sir John drew me aside. "My lady Adele denies the charges against her," he murmured. "There is no challenge of you, Michel."

"I am pleased of it, my lord." Had he forgotten it was I who made the challenge? "I would not flee the matter."

"Did you understand the Latin of the Psalms?"

"Much of it, sir." I wondered what he meant.

" 'The Lord hath raised me up from the gates of death.' " It was what his priest had read. "And so He has with me, and I am healed of my Saracen wound." His voice was cool and distant. "It was William once said my faith was too weak. But now I send him with you and will need another almoner, mayhap some wandering friar."

I heard his doubt very clear. "On my life, Sir John, there was a friar. I had seen him at Camelot, at Winchester, sir, I met him again by Craon's mill in the Yuletide Sir Amaury was wed."

"You saw him here?" His head turned quick, and his glance was dark with anger. "Michel, why did you not bring him to me?"

"He walked away, sir, into the storm." I drew a breath. "He told me I must stay close to you." For a moment I did not want to say more. "My lord, he was Camelot's druid, the wizard Merlin."

"Merlin?" Sir John's eyes narrowed in disbelief, yet even a baron's voice must stumble at the name. "But Merlin is witched and caught, so everybody says, and no one sees him."

"Yet, I have, sir. And so did King Arthur, at Camelot."

He frowned again. "I'd sooner believe your wandering friar, Michel, than Camelot's wizard."

"He was the friar, sir, and the old man, too." The friar who named me. Who warned me, if I might believe it, of the lady Adele.

"And now," John muttered, doubtful, "he sends you to Britain?"

"No, sir. God help us both, it is you that send me."

He paled briefly, and turned and stared down the aisle to his Saracen window. "Then 'tis well I send William as your chaplain."

In Craon's stony court our horses stamped their hooves and tossed their heads, and the wind tugging our cloaks half blew our words away. John shook all our hands and wished us Godspeed. He gave me another quick frown. "If your friar truly . . ." He seemed unwilling to speak the name. "What does he say of Camelot? Of the queen and her knights? Who will it be that casts the first stone?"

"My lord, I do not know."

"Then, Michel, you must find the answer."

The rain began as we rode out Craon's gate. Vitré and its castle were gloomy as ever under its steady fall, and we stopped the night in the same gray priory. By morning it had eased, and the cold wind that buffeted our cloaks scoured the sky of clouds.

I thought of Matilde all that day, how much I loved her, yet how it was love that gave me strength to keep from her. After she had left, that summer morning, I heard her voice in the chatter of Craon's Hall, in the morning songs of birds. Even the wind smelled of her spices. And then Adele had smiled, as if she offered courtly love.

The lowering sun was setting in a clear sky. There, out beyond reedy marshes and a narrow sea, stood the astonishing rock of Saint Michel. A little crowd of pilgrims clustered at the water's edge, and half a dozen merchants on loaded hackneys, but the abbey stood out on the sea, unreachable.

"Sir Lambert," I asked, "where is the ferry?"

Those close by laughed at me. "It ebbs, young sir," one of them said. "We'll be there afore Vespers."

"The tide," said Lambert, smiling too. "Half the day you can walk dry-footed."

Though I could hardly believe it, already the sea retreated before us. The merchants pushed their horses carefully into the water, and we followed through waves never higher than our animals' knees, and soon clambered up into the narrow town. High above the roofs of crowded houses, the setting sun lit the abbey gold.

"Jesu," William murmured, " 'tis God's holy castle, more splendid than I had heard." The rest of us had no words at all.

We clattered up the turning street to a slanting square. Empty wains leaned together next stable doors, as the way beyond was too steep for horses. The monastery lay up a hundred steps, and since we were neither poor nor pilgrims the porter sent us up again, to a hostel almost at the top. Tall casements looked back to the Norman coast, so high above the sea I almost feared to step into their deep embrasures. We heard Vespers in the echoing church, and down another stair found the great refectory, where glass set between stone pillars filled one whole wall and made the place brighter than any cathedral. Far below us the darkening sea was a thousand paces out, the drop more worrisome even than from the hostel, and as we sat our trestle we glanced silent at each other, half unwilling to believe the marvels of this magic place.

The next day was the Sabbath. I walked down to the stables to look to our horses. It was a brisk sunny morning, and the smell of baking loaves that blew up from the town tugged me down the narrow street, through crowds of pilgrims climbing to the abbey. The baker stood at his door, rubbing floury hands. He bobbed at my knight's robe and showed me a little room with a few benches. Despite the crowds outside but one other person sat there, a lad my own age with lanky blond hair. He wore a dagger lean as himself and watched me with hard eyes.

The baker offered me a pot of ale with my bread. I took a swallow and broke the warm loaf.

"Are you a pilgrim, sir?" the lad asked.

"Knights, traveling. We stop for the Sabbath."

"And where go you tomorrow, sir?"

"Britain," I said. "Camelot."

His eyes lit at the name. "They've found the Sangral?"

"No."

"No? Then they never will."

His certainty annoyed me. "Do you live here?"

"With my uncle. My father lives over, in Weymouth."

"Fishermen?"

"Traders," he said.

Smugglers, more likely, I thought. I chewed my bread.

"I would cross, sir." He touched a little purse at his belt and coins rattled. "Can you take me?"

"We have horses and much baggage, and sail from Granville."

He frowned. "Then have you care, sir, of boats and the sea."

Something in his voice woke a memory. "Who are you?"

"David. My father's Samuel."

I peered at him and knew he lied. "God's name, who are you?" I stood and strode to him, saw he would take his blade, and grabbed his wrist. He drew as quick with his left. I pushed him backward and dodged his thrust and drew my own.

"You are very quick, Sir Michel de Verdeur."

He sheathed his blade, took up the last of his loaf, and stepped past me. I knew him very well, that he was no simple boy, yet that knowing so lamed me I could not speak till he stood in the doorway. "Sir, what do you with me?"

He turned. "Why go you to Britain, if you are Craon's man?"

"Sir John sends me." His greenest knight, I thought abruptly.

He nodded. "Then in Britain you must be Arthur's man."

He was gone. I stumbled after him. Of course he had vanished in the crowds.

He came as a lad, an old man, a drunken friar. What would he be next? A woman? A Jew? He sent me to Caen and Amaury, to Craon and Sir John. Now he said, be Arthur's. Yet Arthur had Gawain and Lancelot and all the Roundtable, and no need of me.

A crowd of pilgrims burst in the room, clamoring for bread.

The sands of Saint Michel's Bay gleamed red under the sunrise as we rode to Avranches on its hill, and then north along the coast. Over our shoulders the abbey stood once more upon its waves. Clouds darkened the sky again and a squall drenched us halfway to Granville. When we reached the town the waters of its harbor still tossed, yet the rain was blown away and evening lit the sky.

"We'll stop," said Lambert. "I must find passage." We sat our horses on the wooden quay, and the wind tugged our cloaks and ships swung their masts in crazy circles. He came back smiling that he had found a ship for a good price, that sailed the morning ebb.

The *Bluesea* was a newly painted cob, wide enough to carry all our animals in her open belly. It was cold out on the morning sea. If I had forgot the fright sailing put in my heart, at least I had been afloat. Of the others, only Lambert and his squire had ever seen the ocean. As the waves grew higher Hugh turned a green face to me. "When you paid the abbot, sir, you never said it'd come to this."

I watched the gray water slide past. The rain began again, and the cabin but half sheltered us. A dull low coast stood on our right all day, and over the noise of flapping sail and creaking ropes sailors called the names of headlands and harbors, and worried of sands and tides. As we settled for the night, I remembered Aaron's boat, and the little pot that master had steered by. The *Bluesea* did not have one. William said the Hours for Compline. I slept fitfully, cold and damp, and dreamed of Philip and a woman holding him, that I could not tell were Matilde or Adele. I woke in black night, the sea gone very rough. The ship had turned, and it struggled against the rain and wind.

"We've cleared the last of Normandy," said the master. "Chop the whole way now."

The horses, tied in their stalls, neighed and whinnied in the dark. Hugh stumbled across my feet and the sound of his retching nearly made me sick. I woke when we turned again. The sky began to lighten, but nothing was visible through the gray rain, even when we crested the highest waves. Lambert's squire opened a sack and cut slabs of salt mutton, though most refused it.

The horses had quieted. Hugh and William's page clambered down the narrow ladder to look at them, and Hugh's head reappeared at once. "There's water, sir."

The master shrugged. "There's always a bit of water."

Lambert peered down the ladder. "It's fetlock-deep, it will ruin their feet."

"Ah, damn this storm." The master raised his head and cried out. "Bail! Every man bail, damn you!"

The crew spilled out of their shed. They brought wooden pails and from the way they worked it was clear they had done it before, on the *Bluesea*. After an hour they were exhausted but the water had hardly retreated. We took our places in the bucket lines. The master put William to steering and bailed, himself. The rain did not stop, nor the whistling wind, yet we forgot the lurching of the ship save to time our movements with the sloshing buckets. The crew relieved us after another hour. When we began again the water had risen half to our knees, and the horses rolled their eyes and tossed their heads.

"God defend me," Lambert cried, "a dozen animals. I'll have this damn boat if you've ruined them."

"Bail," the master cried. "And damn me, the wind's shifting against my tack." He rushed to take the steering bar, and the sail flapped noisily overhead, and the ship shuddered from the stronger waves. The storm had wet us all to the skin, the salt stung where the cord handles wore our hands, our arms were so tired we could hardly raise the dribbling buckets. Even William bailed now, and Hugh leaned on the steering bar.

"It's gone down, hasn't it, sir?" he asked.

"I think not, Hugh."

"Will we drown, sir? I can't swim."

Neither could I, and the fear in his voice stirred my own. " 'Tis not far, they say we'll land by dark."

But at nightfall the sea was still empty. Even the sailor who climbed the waving mast could see nothing ahead. Darkness made bailing more difficult. The horses grew nervous again, and tugged at their bonds and stamped their hooves.

"If they put a foot through . . ." the master cried.

"It would not leak the faster," I shouted back.

At that moment the rain stopped. The wind fell. In the sudden quiet the ship wallowed in the tossing seas. A pale light came and went in the clouds, and a half moon shone out overhead.

Another sailor clambered up the mast. "Land," he cried out. "There's land. It's white, it's chalk, sure."

The sailors glanced at each other and the master called up, "It's Purbeck we need."

"Too far, I can't tell."

Lambert barked at him. "Don't you know where we are?"

The master glanced at the moon. "Aye, sir. It's Weymouth you want and we'll make it afore dawn."

But as he spoke the wind came up again, blustering and sharp from the other side. The sail cracked and fluttered, and the ship rolled, slow as a dream. We grabbed each other in fright, the master bellowed and the crew ran to pull the spar around.

The new wind bore the scent of land. The ship labored against the waves, and shook and creaked. We began to bail again. The sailor below me muttered, "It's come up half a foot."

The master leaned over and swore at the sloshing water.

"There," cried the lookout overhead. "End of the chalk, it's Chesil, sure."

"What's Chesil?" I asked.

"Damn me," barked the master, "Lyme's straight upwind, and it's damn twenty mile round Portland Bill—we'll never make it ere the morning ebb."

The sailor below me had stopped work. "So we go in."

"We'll wreck?" I said.

"Keep bailing," cried the master. "We'll run, sir, we've a fresh breeze."

But even as he spoke, the wind altered once more, swinging round till it blew almost to the land. He cried out to the crew to shift the sail

again. By now the water was deep enough to splash the bellies of the
horses. They snorted and heaved and lurched toward panic.

"This sieve'll never make it," said the sailor below me.

"We'll wreck," I cried to the master.

"Ah, sir, don't worry. Chesil's shingle, I'll go in easy, we'll be fine
and the horses'll swim."

"But the chests."

"Well, sir, save your coin or save your souls."

Overhead the lookout called, "There's surf."

The moon had set, but soon enough we could see breakers in the
starlight, and hear the grind of the sea driving ashore.

The crew shortened sail. René and I carried John's chest across the
ship's open middle to the front, and crouched next a sailor and watched
the line of surf come steadily closer. The ship lurched once.

"A stray bar," the sailor muttered. Then he stood and shouted, "It's
quick shallow. Turn, turn, back the sail."

A noise like breaking stone rang out under us. The ship drove up
like a heaving animal and nearly threw me out. Timbers groaned and
splintered. We slewed and tilted, grinding on the bottom, floated free a
moment, and then drove in with another heavy lunge that sprawled me
on the deck. There was a thunderous, snapping crash, as the mast shattered and fell. The sail billowed over the ship, thick ropes fell on me as I
staggered up, a man screamed over the cries of the animals.

I felt my way down among the rearing horses. "Calm," I said, and
slapped their shoulders as I dodged their feet. I drew my dagger and
careful under the water hacked away leg bindings. The ship lurched
again, and floundering animals nearly trampled me and then the sea
crashed in among us. I cut Night away, and a second. They kicked and
staggered as they struggled out into the waves. The sea was up to my
waist. I freed my palfrey and another, and there was Lambert in the middle of the rolling ship.

"I've got four," I shouted.

The ship lurched again. A horse fell, and in the dark the master
screamed, "Oh Christ Mary God my legs."

We got the animal up. Lambert put an arm around the master and
dragged him over the side. I clambered to the front again. John's chest
had gone. The ship lurched and splintered under me and I had no choice
but take a breath and jump. A drenching wave knocked me against rolling gravel. I struggled against the tugging water and got my head out.
Another wave pushed me off my feet, before I clambered up the steep
and rolling slope. Drenched and cold, coughing and shaking with fright,
I knelt and made a prayer of thanks, that God had spared me.

The sailors had hauled their master up the sloping beach. A wave came in over his legs and ran out again, black with blood. "Christ God," he screamed, "give me your dagger, good knight."

René came struggling out of the water, and William and Lambert's squire. Horses fought in through the breaking waves, snorting and whinnying. There was Night, and when I called he trotted up to me. I had nothing to dry him with.

"Where's Hugh?" I asked René.

He shook his head. "He was in the back, pushing horses."

We went back down and waded nearly to the wreck. I called a dozen times. Jesu, had I brought him all this way to drown him?

"We've lost two others," said René as we climbed back up the beach. "William's page, under the mast, and a sailor."

"And the master," I said, "who said it would be so easy."

The man no longer screamed. The sailors began to turn away, and one of them bent and took up a handful of the round gravel.

"Abbotsbury," he said. The others nodded.

"What do you mean?" I asked.

"Sand at the west, cobbles at the Bill." He rattled the stones in his hand. "This be acorn size, acorns be abbots."

"How far to the abbey?" said Lambert.

"Mile, sir, maybe two or three. Best wait till light, sir, see which way to go."

All that night the grounded ship gave out loud groans. We hauled what baggage we could find up the gravel slope and sat leaning together, trying to keep warm. The gray dawn showed a rolling ocean and a sky of torn clouds. The dark shapes of two horses lay on the beach, but the sailors pointed at something smaller, like a log floating, and ran down to it.

Our baggage lay scattered far along the beach. Lambert's chest lay half-empty but John's, nearly buried, was still bound firm. As René and I dragged it up the beach, a voice called from the wreck. Hugh lay under the sail, caught by a tangle of ropes. The falling spar had broken his left arm; save that he was as well as the rest of us.

The drowned horses had both been Lambert's. The corpse in the waves was William's page. We could not find the dead sailor.

Abbotsbury lay in a sheltered valley, hidden from the sea. The monks of Saint Peter's bandaged us and set Hugh's arm. We asked them of Camelot, of the Sangral and Sir Lancelot, but they knew nothing. Nobody had heard of Gawain or Galahad or Percival, not for a year. King Arthur stopped at Caerleon, they said, and soon returned to Camelot.

In the bright morning we buried our dead in their cemetery. We borrowed an ox-cart and recovered much of our baggage, and all our armor save my sword of Ricard, and Sir Lambert's shield. Half asleep in the sun-warmed stableyard, we oiled tack, washed our clothes of salt, bandaged the animals.

"Damn," grumbled Lambert, "I'll take the wreck for my horses."

"And I need a sword."

"The Jews at Winchester will have the best."

Aaron had my grandfather's dagger, that I must retrieve soon. But Britain still held three of my knights and I dared not travel, even in Lambert's company, without a sword. He thought the monks might have some poor weapon, and when I asked the cellarer he led me to a dim storeroom beneath the dormitory. Three old swords hung inside the door. Their dusty scabbards swung under my touch.

"Our abbot was a knight, ere he took Orders." The monk touched the longest one. "Saracen, from the Holy Land."

I took it down. "It's very heavy."

"Christian souls weigh much on it."

I drew the sword. Only a few spots of rust marked the bright steel, and lines of heathen writing squirmed all down its length. I stepped outside, raised the blade and slashed the air. Its weight vanished as it moved. I had never held so fine a weapon, and I looked away and swallowed to hide my desire.

"What would you have for it?"

"It is the abbot's. You must ask him."

We found the old man in the garden next his house, sitting in the shade of a tree. A long white beard lay on his chest and his thin face showed every bone beneath its skin. He scowled and thrust out a knobby hand. "That is my father's sword." His voice was very clear. "Brought from Outremier."

"Good sir abbot, I would buy it of you."

"The shipwreck, sir," said the monk. "He lost his own."

"Then it has pleased God to disarm you."

I heard the echo of my own words to Sir John of his Saracen's blade, and half turned away, of fright. Yet my tongue spoke itself. "Disarmed, sir, that I might have this finer steel."

His mouth puckered with distaste. "How clever are the young, always."

"I'd give ten pounds, sir." Lambert owed me twenty-five.

The displeasure had not left his voice. "Only that? For all those souls?"

"Twenty, sir?" It was much, even for so fine a blade.

He closed his eyes, and for a long minute he looked like a snake asleep. A bird sang in the tree overhead. Impatient, I made ready to offer thirty, whatever he wanted, for this blade.

His eyes opened. "What is your name, young sir knight?"

"Michel de Verdeur, sir. Knight of John, baron of Craon. In Anjou, sir abbot."

"I know where Craon is."

I waited through another silence. "Sir abbot," I asked, "how did your father gain this? Did he kill one of Saladin's knights?"

"Always the young have questions." He reached for the scabbard and drew the blade half-out, and his eyes went dark and even the bird hushed. He traced a bit of the writing with his thumb. "Here is the name of their heathen god, young sir. Would you carry such a thing?"

"If Christ and His Father saved me from the storm, sir abbot, I fear no Saracen idol."

He thrust the blade in. "Then I give it to you."

"Sir?"

"It will cost but one small thing. Each man it kills you must confess. And every day thereafter you must pray for each dead soul. And when you are finished you must bring it back."

I stared at the dusty scabbard. I could not pray for Briant, nor Giles or Laramort. Almost I said, I will not take this heathen thing. Almost I said, They have murdered, let the saints pray for them. But it was such a glorious blade.

"I will pray, good father. I will confess."

I was afraid to ask how he knew it would all be finished. It came to me he might be the wizard, but then I was certain he was not. He was but an old man, that made a sign I took to be the cross, took up his beads, and began to mumble again.

As we walked back I asked the monk, "What is his name?"

"The abbot Geoffrey. His father was Caerdius, his uncle Constans." He spoke the names as if they had great meaning, but I did not know them.

"Here," I said to René, "polish this with all your care."

He drew it and stared, and even Lambert gaped. "God help us, that is a fine Saracen. What did you pay?"

"More than I wanted," I said.

At Vespers we offered thanks again, that we were delivered from the sea. The chanting voices of monks echoed in the stone nave, while the sun set and the church grew dim as the sleep of death.

It was in the middle of the night, lying abed and thinking of Matilde and Adele, that I felt a sudden emptiness on my chest. I sat up in the dark, my heart beating. The leather thong lay about my neck, but in the wreck I had lost Rebecca's little bag. I had traded the soft leather of her bag for the hard steel of the abbot's sword; was this, too, the mage's bidding?

"Wake you," cried Lambert, rousing us, " 'tis sunrise, I'd be home to Denham by nightfall."

We rode out through the slanting light, past reapers bent to the ripe grain, and were soon beyond the last field. A silent wind blew soft and urgent down the empty valleys, birds we could not see sang in shadowed woods, the green lane ran up into empty hills where sheep nibbled the grass, where fog still draped the ridges and coiled round ancient barrows. The whole country felt strange and witched to me, as if Anjou and Normandy were lands of light and clarity, while all Britain lay wrapped in the magic of wizards.

We rode the whole day, till an hour from Vespers Sir Lambert cried out, "Here, these, 'tis Denham here." He gestured at rolling pastures and broad fields, where peasants stared up from the harvest and waved at him. But he would not stop until, at the edge of a little valley he drew up and laughed aloud. "Home," he shouted, and pushed his horse quick down the way, to the village among its fields and a fine stone house under its shading elms.

I could not follow him, but sat and stared westward out over the broad level country. The late sun hazed the air. I shaded my eyes, unsure where to look, and caught a glint of water far in the distance. There like a shadow of oaks stood the battlements of Camelot. And there, nearer, Ryford village. And Westfield, its harvested strips plain in the lowering sunlight. There was the wood with its chapel and there, those trees, that was Greenfarm.

I, too, had come home. I could see it all in a single glance, the limits of my childhood. Sudden as a thick hand on my neck I felt the lifelong burden of peasantry, and knew they felt it still, Warren and Ruth, Harry, Old Drool, all the rest. I woke again in that dank house, my father stood at the black doorway, the moon flared lopsided. Lark called and died.

My palfrey shifted under me. My knight's hauberk sat heavy on my shoulders, my heathen sword hung at my side. My own esquire waited, holding my shield. My groom led a hackney laden with coin. Had Lark not walked out that summer's night I would be there still, reaping the last furlong, my face burnt by the harvest sun, my mouth dry with dust, my fingers torn from binding sheaves.

I raised my hand and stared at it. It was pale as any knight's, and smooth and uncallused save as a sword wears. It had done no work in years. My eyes blurred. I felt tears on my cheeks. Beside me Hugh murmured, "Where is it, sir?"

I could only point and turn away.

Nineteen

Dogs barked and servants laughed in Lambert's court, and a gray-robed cleric lifted the welcome cup to him. His manor house was larger than Amaury's, and there under the arch of his door waited his wife, a good-faced lady with a bright smile, and round-bellied with their next. A small son stood on one side of her and two little daughters on the other. Lambert stooped to kiss each child, and then he embraced her a long time. The warmth of his welcome surprised me. In all his months at Craon he had rarely spoke of Denham, yet now his eyes were damp with joy.

"Dear Margaret." He turned and gestured to me. "Here is the knight whose stroke brought me to the doors of Purgatory."

I bowed to her. "My lady, I had no wish to widow you."

"Praise God you did not," she said. "But this knight will ever tourney."

"No more, dear wife," said Lambert. "I promise it."

"Truly, husband?" She smiled and took both our hands. "Never regret your stroke, Sir Michel, if it gives me back my lord."

Servants showed us to a clean, well-fitted chamber, where William and I would share a high carved bed, and there were pallets for René and Hugh. Maids brought us steaming water for our bath. We heard shouts and laughter in the Hall as Lambert's knights gathered, and when we went out half a dozen were already at the wine. Most were young, though an older knight that must be Denham's steward stood among them. He turned and stared at me, and they all fell silent, the smiles dying on their faces. Tension sang in the air like wasps, and even the dust motes in the slanting light stopped their dance.

The youngest, round-faced and fair, curled his lip. "God defend us. 'Tis the damned varlet."

I had seen him years past, at Camelot. In a moment I would remember his name. He wrinkled his nose and turned away. "Sir Balen," I called. The name stopped him. "God's peace to you, sir. And all of you. I am Michel de Verdeur, man of Craon."

"Greenfarm," growled another, "fit out in sham heraldry."

"By some treacherous Frank," sneered Balen.

Here was my welcome. I had expected it, yet still I ground my teeth. "A finer knight," I called out, "than any I see here."

My new sword lay in my chamber, but a dagger hung at my hip, and when I saw Balen would take his, my blade glittered already before his eyes. "A finer man than any here," I said again, "saving Sir Lambert."

"Sirs," cried William, "peace, pray you." We did not heed him.

"Beware this whelp," the steward muttered. " 'Tis Orsain's homicide."

"That doth ever stink of byre and cott," growled Balen.

His own dagger glinted. I saw his thrust and lunged first. I caught only his sleeve, and as I spun away his driving point seared my ribs. Already I hacked at his retreating wrist. The pain distracted him, I slashed at his chest, he grunted at it, chopped my sleeve, and stepped away. Bright blood stained his tunic front.

I crouched and swung my point, watching the rest. "A finer knight than any here," I repeated, half breathless. Praise God my Norman gift of seeing was not lost on the Norman sea.

"Good sirs," cried Sir Lambert, "what is this?" He strode in the doorway. "Defending my honor, Balen?"

"Sir." He put a hand to his oozing chest.

Lambert stood between us, frowning. "By Christ, it's good the rest kept your knives covered. This is the knight that bested me, that sent Orsain to a priory graveyard."

" 'Tis but a knave, sir," said Balen.

Sir Lambert lifted his head and looked at them all. "I hold in high honor John of Craon, and so, too, this man he knighted. As you all are my men, you will not fight Michel de Verdeur." He gave them a grim smile. "Not for his safety, damn you, but your own."

Servants brought cloths and water and bound our cuts. Lambert set Balen scowling beside me at table, and the knight's mood lifted as the food came and the wine flowed.

He flexed his bandaged wrist. "You are quick enough."

"I am a knight," I said.

"At Camelot you are a farmer's brat."

"Then Camelot must see me different."

Balen gave a hard smile. "It was the eve of John Baptist's that Sir Lambert's page arrived. I was the one that rode to Camelot with the news of him. And Orsain. That night we had small heed for fields or fences." He touched a small cross at his neck. "I came first to the chapel."

I stared at the trencher before me, my hunger gone, my head throbbing. I saw the house afire, my mother beaten, my father crippled. Clear as yesterday Rebecca bled and died. "And what did you at Greenfarm?" I muttered.

He had begun to gnaw a bone. "An old goose trampled, an empty horse-byre burnt." He shrugged. "But we injured the king's demesne and thus the king himself. So said his newest counsel." He tossed his bone to Lambert's dogs. "Damned arrogant knight."

"Forty pence he fined us," a knight grumbled across the board. "Each of us, for a peasant's stinking thatch."

Unforgivable as a battle-horse for a peasant's daughter. The wine in my cup was gone so sour I nearly spat it out. "For that you cursed me?"

Balen's gaze did not falter. "Greenfarm had slain a knight."

"Then why did you not attack me, all together?"

"Six against a single churl? Where's the honor there?" He took another bone, "Still, 'tis a pity Sir Lambert stopped me, before I killed you."

I broke my bread and put a bit in my dry mouth, and let his arrogance pass. "I was a dubbed knight when I slew Orsain. Now I come to plead Craon's manors."

William spoke up. "We bring letters patent."

Denham's chamberlain, the gray-robed cleric of the welcome cup, had just sat down with us. Sir Lambert pointed a hand at him. "Brother Francis has oft argued before the king."

The monk nodded his tonsured head. "We must discuss your petition, before you plead it." He had a deep, rumbling voice.

"But who can argue the king's new defender?" grumbled Balen, and the others muttered among themselves.

"Who is this knight?" I asked.

Sir Lambert frowned. "Youngest brother to Gawain."

"Come soon from Orkney," Balen said, "ever giving wisdom, never jousting." He scowled at me. "Knights ought not repay peasants' byres. I drew my dagger for that, much as the other."

"He upholds Greenfarm?"

"He upholds anything useful for himself."

"He upholds king and Roundtable," muttered Lambert. "Chivalry and honor, he says. But were true Roundtable knights at Camelot, this upstart would have no place."

Balen still scowled at me. "It was years past they met you at Winchester, yet still he keeps Giles and Briant from Camelot. For the king's honor, and who may dispute the king's honor?"

Though his news of Briant pleased me, I felt suddenly uneasy. "The king banished me along with them. May I now go to Camelot?"

"You are Craon's man," said Lambert. "I will take you."

"Thank you, sir. Again I am in your debt." I looked about at their angry faces. "But, sirs, who is this new knight?"

The place fell silent, save for the dogs cracking bones.

"The king's nephew," said Balen at last. "Mayhap."

I stared at him. "Why mayhap?"

"All Orkney is dark-haired. Only he has the king's color."

"King Lot of Lothian and Orkney." I dug into my memory. "His lady is Morgause."

Francis rumbled the lineage. "Morgause, that was daughter to Tintagel and Lady Igraine, the same on whom Uther got his son."

His son the king. God save us, this were no matter of consanguinity, of cousins too closely related. If Morgause were Arthur's half sister, then her fair son was half incestuous.

"Tomorrow." Lambert cleared his throat. "King Arthur comes to Camelot tomorrow. You must have a gift for him."

"And for his nephew," I said.

Lambert nodded. "Mordred, prince of Orkney."

The sting of my new wounds was almost agreeable as I dressed the next morning. The weight of my mail hauberk sat pleasantly on my shoulders. My tabard was newly broidered with green tree and black bird, and I strapped on my heathen sword, hung my polished shield on my shoulder, and dropped my best rings into my purse.

Lambert's grooms had tied little bells on our bridles, that made a bright sound as we rode in the hazy sunlight. William and Francis, just behind me, already argued of my petition.

"Uther's regents," said William, "gave the fiefs to Craon. They were held by Gerard, brother of the baron. And then by Gilbert, Gerard's son." William loved to recite history.

"But when Gilbert died," Francis rumbled, "King Arthur took them of Olivier, Gilbert's son, as the price of vassalage."

"He needed no such relief," said William. "In France . . ."

"In France kings have done so a hundred years."

We went jingling through the shade of a small wood, forded the stream, and came among the fields of Ryford. The village church looked stooped and tiny, to my eyes, and the market square no bigger than Craon's courtyard. Yet I recognized every tree now, every doorway and hedge and stile, each the same and yet all completely changed. Out beyond the clustered village houses every family stooped to harvest Westfield's grain.

"Gilbert married very rich in Cornwall," William was saying.

"All Britain knows it," Francis rumbled, "that Arthur fought twelve great battles. Yet Gilbert brought knights only to the last. The four manors are because of that."

We rode past the lane to the forest chapel. I could not look down its dusty length. The white sun beat hot on my head, the air felt thick, my ears sang like bees swarming. There, just ahead, there lay Greenfarm, house and byres newly thatched.

"Craon protested," said William. "Sir John sent letters."

Francis chuckled. "Craon, vassal of the king of France."

Over the hedges I saw they reaped Willow furlong. I knew my father's stoop, Harry tying sheaves, Perkin and his son. Harness and armor rattled in the thick air, bells tinkled so I could not think. Hardly knowing what I did, I tugged my palfrey aside into the houseyard. The others straggled to a halt. A goose honked nervously. The dust of our progress drifted against the house.

My mother's face appeared at the door. "Oh, Holy Mary," she muttered. "Go," she called inside, "tell your father." A small tow-haired girl emerged, staring. "Run," Ruth cried, and Little Drool bolted for the fields. My mother took a nervous step. "Good sirs." She bobbed. "I have naught to feed you." She stared past me, her face in agony. "So many of you."

"It's me." I swung down from my palfrey and strode to her and reached my hand. "It's Micah."

"Sir?" She shrank back, hugging herself with fright. "Micah? Oh, good sir, Micah's gone, years away." She held up several fingers. "They say knights killed him, sir."

"Mother." I took another step. "Ruth." She gasped with panic, blind to everything but my knight's armor.

Harry dashed around the shed. My father puffed behind him. They stopped dead at the sight of us, but after a moment my father bowed and shambled toward me. His broad face shone with harvest sweat. He tugged his dusty forelock.

"Good sir, what would you?"

"Damn you," I growled, "I am Micah."

They all flinched at my knightly tongue. I took a breath and went on, softer. "I left a spoon of horn, well polished. You stood there, Father." I pointed to the road. "It was raining. You watched the minstrels as we rode away."

A light flickered in his eye. I swore he knew me, yet he glanced at the knights behind me, at the clerics and squires sitting palfreys, and his eyes went dead. "I'm a poor farmer, sir, so was my son." He gestured. "See how great a knight you are."

His blank stared chilled me, there in the August heat. I looked at Ruth, at old Cluck bent in the doorway, at my brother gaping beside the shed that knights had burnt, two months past. They were right to be afraid.

"Then you must keep the spoon. 'Till he returns."

"Oh, good sir, thank you." He wiped his sunburnt face. "If my son lives, sir, if you meet him, kindly say we'd hope to see him soon." He bobbed once more, as well as he had ever done.

I swung up on my palfrey. Its little bells rang in the hush. The others were already moving through the thin shade of Thomas' hedges. I felt a fool to have stopped, yet I could not have gone past. The reeve's hens fled squawking before us. One of his dogs, white at the muzzle now, barked and wagged his tail.

And then the way blossomed, as it did always, out to the broad green meadows. And there stood Camelot.

"Jesu," William murmured, "and I thought Craon beautiful."

The soft breeze barely moved the banners on its towers. The wide moat lay mirror-smooth and the stone walls stood up from their own reflections, the color of peaches under the summer sun. A crush of wains, first of the king's baggage, blocked the barbican gate, where a young knight astride a roan palfrey shouted at the drivers. His linen tabard bore the white and red of Orkney, yet his red-blond hair made me see him a younger Arthur.

"Sir Lambert," he called out. "Here you are, and whole again." His laugh sang in the summer air. " 'Tis wonderful you return today, sir. The king comes, we dine after Vespers."

"Sir Mordred," Lambert answered, with only a moment's pause. "Happy will I be to bow once more to Arthur, king."

Mordred laughed again. "How Angevin elegance ornaments your words." His gaze stopped at me. "And who is this young knight?"

I nudged my palfrey forward. "Sir Mordred, my honor, sir. I am Michel de Verdeur, man of Craon."

"The king's honor, sir. Welcome to Camelot." His smile faded. "It was you defeated Lambert?"

"It was, Sir Mordred."

"Then you have seen Camelot before." He looked at my shield with a careful eye. "A green oak, the dragon of Craon. How very apt." If he noticed the raven he did not speak of it. I could not understand Lambert's distaste of him. I had never met a finer knight save Gawain, his brother, and Lancelot. Even were Sir Mordred the spawn of incest, I would not afflict the son with his parents' sins.

He turned and shouted the drovers to make way. The drawbridge drummed under us and the gates of Camelot echoed over us as we entered the castle. And there at the Hall doorway, exactly as the day I left, stood the lean figure of Sir Kay. The years had taken more of his hair and cut deeper lines beside his mouth, and he frowned when Lambert spoke my name.

"Michel de Verdeur? But surely this is Micah of Greenfarm, sent from Camelot years ago."

"I come, Sir Kay, as knight of Craon, to petition the king." I heard the echo of my father's words, that fateful John Baptist's.

"A rainy Epiphany, as I remember it." He gazed up briefly at the clear sky. "Sent from Camelot by royal order." His voice went hard. "If some may know the king's mind before he speaks, I am not among them. The king banished you. Therefore, I arrest you."

"Sir Kay," barked Lambert, "this man hath mine honor."

"The baron of Craon sends him," William sputtered.

Even Mordred growled, "Damn you, Kay, what do you?"

He ignored them all. He raised his lean head and called the sergeants from the gate. I watched his brittle eyes, and wondered why I had believed John's dubbing would protect me in Britain.

"I would plead Craon's manors before the king," I said.

Kay shrugged. "When he comes."

"This will not go well for thee," Mordred grumbled.

"Your sword." He spoke as if Mordred did not exist, but as he took my belt and sword I saw his eyes flicker at the weight.

The oak door thudded shut behind me, and the heavy bar dropped. The dim round chamber stank of mold and dust and prisoners' fear. At least it was no dungeon underground, but a high prison just beneath the battlements, where thin bars of sunlight shone in through arrow slits. Peering out one I saw, far below, drawbridge and barbican and moat. Out the other was the lower bailey and there, just in the shadow of the kitchen, Giles had killed Emrys. It was the same tower where the minstrels stayed, that murderous Yule. I had returned, dubbed a knight, yet Greenfarm could see only bright armor, and Camelot nothing save a brat of the king's demesne, a servant exiled.

A broken stool lay on a pile of last year's straw, in a corner that smelled worse than the rest. I sat carefully and leaned against the cold wall. The narrow sunlight crept across the floor, revealing unpleasant stains. Voices drifted up, and the smell of baking bread, and I remembered they opened the ovens an hour after Terce. I closed my eyes, certain I would never sleep.

Trumpets woke me, blaring on the battlements overhead, and were answered from afar. I leaned my cheek on the cool stone of the outer slit. The king returned. A crowd of knights boomed in over the drawbridge. Bright-painted wagons rumbled beneath me, ladies waving from their windows. There was a company of dark clerics, and falconers on prancing ponies, and sumpter wagons heavy with plate and coin. A crowd of footmen bearing scarlet banners reminded me of all the progressions I had seen from Greenfarm. And here was the king himself, riding a great pale stallion, laughing at the noise of the horns. Out the other arrow slit Sir Kay bowed in the court and King Arthur laughed as he swung down, pulled off his cloak and shook his red-blond hair. The queen and her ladies, hooded and wimpled, trailed into the upper court. Knights pressed into the Hall. Squires and servants scurried to unload baggage, and soon enough there was no one about save two grooms sweeping manure.

A rear guard clattered in, armed and bannered. Their leader was Edmund of Bramhill, Sibyl's lean husband; remembering her I was at last afraid, at Camelot. Kay sparred with Mordred of the king's favor, while the rest grumbled or took sides. Greenfarm was an embarrassment. The king passed over everything, and would see my petition as a nuisance. I was of no importance, like a pawn at chess, useful mayhap, but soon sacrificed.

A cloud passed overhead. Thunder rumbled in the distance. The smell of meat roasting came up from the kitchen. I sat, and woke again to chill rain blowing in through the arrowslits. The stones of the court below gleamed under servers' torches. The wind brought faintly the strains of lute and sackbut; they would be eating in the Hall, they would be telling Arthur of me. Footsteps passed my door without stopping. Men called overhead, it was the guard changing. I sat in the dusty straw and hugged myself against the chill. Nobody came.

I woke at dawn. My stomach ached of fasting and my mouth was dry. Rats slept curled in my lap, four of them, that opened their eyes and stretched fearlessly. A boy whistled in the damp court below. I paced to warm myself, and when I heard footsteps outside I took up the stool and beat on the door.

"Water," I shouted, "bread."

After a pause the bar rattled and the door swung carefully open. The guard held a short sword, and he blinked at my armor.

"What do you here, sir? Nobody said of you."

"I am Michel de Verdeur. Sir Kay put me here. You must tell Sir Lambert. And Sir Mordred."

"Sir Mordred?"

"And send my squire, I haven't eaten for a day."

He shut the door, and a little later I saw him crossing the bailey to the kitchens. Eventually the bar moved again and Sir Lambert strode into the chamber, and behind him René, with a pot of ale and half a loaf.

"Thank God you've come, sir," I said.

"Damn Kay," he muttered, "damn Mordred. And the king would hear nothing of it till this morning."

Arthur held his court in Camelot's high keep, in that same chamber Sir Percival had given me sanctuary so long ago. He sat a great chair, with Mordred and several clerics at his shoulder. Two knights argued some matter before him. The rest, in a murmuring crowd, nearly filled the place. Their talk stilled as we entered. The faces that turned to me were as hard as they had been, the first day I had ever come to Camelot, yet even as they stared their frowns eased. I was a knight, I wore a hauberk, they must see me as their equal.

The king raised his rich voice and gave his justice. The knights bowed to him. Sir Mordred came to lead me to Arthur.

"Sire, here is the young knight I spoke of."

I bowed. The king's handsome face turned and I saw he remembered me, for he pressed his lips in an angry line and his eyes flashed. "Micah, son of Warren of Greenfarm," he muttered, and tugged his red-gold beard.

"Michel de Verdeur, my lord. Knight of John, baron of Craon." I drew out my best ring. "A small gift, sire."

He frowned as he fingered it. "Methinks Craon doth insult Camelot, sending a villein."

"Sire, I am a dubbed knight. I bring letters of it, that are with my clerk William."

It was clear he did not believe it. "Then we will see them."

His cleric sent a herald. While we waited, Sir Kay came in, and Mordred thrust an angry hand to him. "My lord, your steward prisoned this man yestermorn."

The king nodded. "I know it, Mordred. I will speak of it."

William bustled in. He gripped his leather box and gave me a worried glance. "Sire," he cried, too loud, "William of Fournil, almoner to Sir John of Craon." He bowed deeply.

"The letters patent," said the herald.

"Yes, sir." William drew out the parchment and raised it to show John's seals. "*Ad Arthuris regis Britanniae . . .*"

But the king lifted his hand, and one of his own clerics took the sheet and read it out, article by article, first the Latin and then his translation, of my knighthood and of John's claim.

When the cleric finished, Arthur's gaze found Sir Lambert. "Do you know this man, Lambert of Denham?"

"I do, my lord. At Craon's request I brought him here."

"And you swear he is knighted?"

"So have I been told, my lord. By men of high honor." He gestured at the cleric. "As do these patents, sire."

Arthur lifted his head and gazed about the chamber. "What a marvel have we here." His voice rang with irony. "Micah of Greenfarm, that we sent away a peasant boy, is returned a dubbed knight. Or so he claims. But who can tell us of him?"

Behind me René cleared his throat. "Sire, I am René du Plessis. My father is a knight of Craon." He raised his voice and told of Sir Amaury, of the ambush at Mayenne, of Angers where Ricard died and John dubbed me. He spoke of the tourney at Pouancé, of Lambert's wound and Orsain's death. It made such pleasant listening I nearly forgot my danger, here at Camelot.

"A great fighter," said the king, "who has defeated Camelot's own. Or so says his squire."

René flared with anger. "I do not lie, my lord."

"My lord," said Lambert, "I swear of my tourney with him. And his defeat of Orsain of Trundal."

I kept my eyes on Arthur's face, and barely heard the rumble that name created. René's story had diverted him, but still he pressed his lips together. Each time I came I brought mischance.

"I would honor John of Craon," he said at last, "and the surety of Lambert of Denham." He said nothing of René, nor Sir Mordred's aid. "I do not complain of Kay, for I had truly banished him." He gazed over our heads, thinking as he spoke. "He comes as man of Craon, knighted for battle valor." His frown eased. He had reached a decision. "But Camelot knows him as a peasant, with no right to our court, no right to sue for lands, no right to sword, hauberk, or heraldry." He smiled as he turned to me. "We shall have the justice of trial by combat."

He looked very pleased with his verdict, and the knights in the chamber murmured their approval. But my heart stopped. Trial by combat. It was trial by God's hand; he that won proved in the right by God's own Providence. If God would not allow an ill-dubbed knight, no more would He allow a wrongful victor. No matter that judgment went always to the strongest. No matter that for honor the loser must fight to his death. Trial by combat. Lancelot had muttered of it, at Angers. So might I have fought Pierre at Craon, of the lady Adele. Almost I fought Orsain thus. Yet, truly, God had allowed my dubbing. And Orsain had truly died.

The king lifted his head, smiling. "Well, my lords, who will be my champion?"

They muttered and shifted behind me. After a heavy silence one of them growled, "Sire, 'tis but a villein's brat."

"God's beard, then he will die the sooner." Arthur rose glowering from his chair. "I call for a champion." The silence echoed. "Must I wait for a Sangral knight? Gawain? Lancelot?" His face went red. "Must I fight him myself?"

In their hush one knight called, "Sire, I will defend you."

Arthur swung his head. "Edmund. Edmund of Bramhill. But, good sir, you are married. And a new father."

"Since Easter have I been your guard, sire. Do you refuse me now?"

Arthur's gaze swept over them all. "God defend us, is Camelot so barren of chivalrous knights that only this fine man . . . ?" He stared at Mordred. "We all know and believe God protects the righteous."

Edmund came forward to bow to the king. Age had marked him, too, with deeper lines on his high forehead and the first gray in his thinning hair. He was more than a dozen years my senior, and tall enough to overreach me, save for my new sword. I could but wonder at God's will, that at my return to Camelot I must either die, or widow my lady Sibyl.

"Broadswords and shields," the king announced. "Daggers if you would. Afoot, in the upper bailey, as soon as you each are ready, for as long as you may."

"My lord," we said, bowing.

"Kay," Arthur cried, "call a priest for their shriving, the brewer for their drink. Sand the stones of the court, that their feet not slip." He was full of energy again. "Squires shall fetch their arms. All others here shall put away their weapons, that only these two be armed."

Twenty

E dmund and I trod full-armed down the long nave of Camelot's church. The priest that would shrive us for combat was the same who had refused me sanctuary, and after he confessed Edmund I knelt and muttered at him, "I have never forgot that Yule, father."

A frown creased his pompous face, grown even fatter. "No serving boy ought enter Our Lord's holy choir."

"Though God would not, Sir Percival gave me sanctuary."

"Curb thy tongue."

"Forgive me, father," I murmured. "I have sinned. I have lain with Sir Edmund's wife and now must fight. . . ."

"*Deo gratia,*" he barked, before he quickly lowered his voice. "Perjure not thyself in God's house."

"Father, it is true."

He muttered Latin I could not catch, in a voice that made me wonder were it prayer or curse.

Edmund waited at the doorway, frowning with concentration.

"Sir Edmund," I said, "I bear you no spite."

He nodded soberly. "The king hath commanded us. God gives victory to the righteous." He had set a leather cap on his head, and now he pulled up his cowl of chain mail.

"As we are knights," I said.

"As I am knight and you . . ."

"Sir Edmund, I am truly dubbed. I fear this will not go well with you. And the king said you were a new father."

"Do not imagine you distract me," he growled.

"But your lady . . ."

"My wife rests at Bramhill. She has given me a new daughter, and a son of two years. And I shall father more, by God." He turned, gripping his helmet, and strode out into the court.

A boy. I counted the years. A boy, born the summer after I left. Who but I lay with Sibyl, that sweet autumn? Ought I confess that, too?

All around me Camelot glittered with a sudden light, and the servants chattering at the inner gate stared at my sudden laugh. In the upper bailey knights lined the walls, muttering impatient for Edmund's victory. Arthur sat a chair at his doorway, Mordred and Kay at his side. A casement at the solar above caught the light where the blonde head of the queen moved among her ladies.

René, pale with worry, brought up my shield. His hands shook as he strapped my helmet. "God knows you are knighted, sir."

"Pray He does," I muttered, fumbling with the mail of Ricard's hauberk. No worse, I thought again, than the fight with Orsain.

My heathen blade glinted in the sun, and the watching knights murmured with surprise. Edmund and I saluted each other. He attacked in a rush but I saw his stroke and caught it on my shield. He swung, quick and very hard, six times at least, as if he knew he must end it soon. His shield boomed under my reply. I pressed him hard, searching for an opening. He countered well, jabbing me with a corner of his shield. We traded blows, hard and noisy, and he retreated slowly, to make a stand in the little grove of apple trees. Our blades slashed among the leaves and distracted us both.

I backed away. Edmund came at me hard. I saw him clear and parried every blow, save one that rang on my helmet, and another that hacked a gash from my shield. My answer made him step away. I pressed him back. The knights called a warning, and as he dodged the fishpond his guard faltered. My blade hewed a split in his shield. His counter came too quick to parry. He crowded in. I saw his attack but could find no answer. With each exchange our shields splintered a little more. I had hoped Edmund's age would tire him, but it was my shoulder that throbbed, my sword arm that ached, my vision that blurred under his blows. Sweat stung my eyes and my breath labored inside my helmet. I stepped back, exhausted.

He gave a blow that split my shield, and drove the mail into my arm. The bright hurt purged my weariness. I shook off the tattered wood. I caught his next on my blade, two-handed. I parried several, but now he could not prolong his rush. My two-handed strength drove him back. His shield split. The dangling weight distracted him, and I swung with all my strength and the blade cut deep into the top of his helmet. He staggered. I hit him twice again. He dropped to his knees. I hit his helmet once more, my blade opened a broader gap, and he sprawled face-down on the stones.

I barely heard the noise of the watching knights. I stepped away, panting for breath. Edmund struggled up. Blood oozed from under his helmet. He flung away his shield and drew his dagger. Waving both blades to confuse me he charged headlong. I met him with a blow to his battered helmet. He faltered. I dropped my sword on his left shoulder like an ax. The dagger spun up and away, a cry rang inside his helmet, and he curled against the pain.

The blood of victory roared in my head. My heathen blade cut through helmet and mail. His left arm hung useless. I beat him down and let him rise, and beat him down again. After the third I stepped away, blowing. Around us knights shouted and groaned. Edmund climbed up, his sword a crutch.

"Sir Edmund," I said, "do you yield?"

"Protect thyself," he gasped, "worry not of my small hurts."

He raised his blade. I hit his helmet, his shoulder. His sword clattered from his hand, and he fell to his knees again.

"Do you yield, Sir Edmund?"

I could barely hear his answer. "Do not spare me."

"My lord," I called, "must I kill this knight?"

Sir Lambert cried out, over the crowd's noise. "The issue is clear, my lord. Sir Michel has won this combat."

It brought a louder rumble from the knights. "Let them finish, damn it," cried one.

Edmund had got his sword up again. He dropped the blade against my shoulder. His blow had no strength at all. I stepped back. He pursued me, staggering.

"I would not kill you, sir," I said.

"Then you must yield to me."

"Leave off," cried the king at last.

Edmund swung his blade again. My answer dropped him like a stone. I knelt and drew my dagger and cut his helmet straps. Blood covered his face. His lips moved without a sound.

Sir Kay was at my side, gripping my arm. "The king," he shouted, "would have him safe."

"Nor would I slay him, sir."

I stood, shaking. I could not catch my breath. My head reeled and all else throbbed with pain. René unlaced my helmet. The world blazed bright as fire. The thing was done. I was proved.

"My lord Arthur," I called, loud, wanting them all to hear. "See you, I am truly a knight of Craon, and Michael de Verdeur."

In the knights' tower Camelot physicians washed my bloody face and salved my wounds. Sir Edmund lay in an alcove, breathing heavily. I took his injured hand and praised his valor. He did not answer. Sir Kay sent me clean robes, worthy of the king's Hall. Hurt flared everywhere as I climbed the long stone stair, where years ago I had followed my father. For a single moment that dread loomed over me again, but René went with me now, smiling, and at the top Sir Lambert gripped my hand and murmured his praise.

And then King Arthur's herald stepped out in Camelot's Hall and cried, "Sir Michel de Verdeur, knight of John, baron of Craon."

I pressed my lips together, fighting my smile. I lifted my head and stared at all their watching eyes. Orsain's death might have been a rumor, but now before their eyes I had truly beaten Edmund, and with him Camelot itself. I walked in through their silence and bowed stiffly to the king.

Arthur stood from the Roundtable. He gave me wine from his own cup. He raised his voice to them all. "Welcome, Michel de Verdeur." Fatigue lined his brow as if my victory had exhausted him. "I give you the freedom of this place, and all my realm."

"My lord," I answered, strong as I could, "I thank you for your favor, and your liberty. My lord, I thank you for the honor you show my lord Craon."

Still, though I was proved, they sat me at a trestle far from the king, where young knights glanced at my battered face and murmured among themselves, and only Balen spoke.

"A pity Edmund was no match," he growled.

"God's hand defeated him," I said. He had no answer. I ate, though I had small appetite. I praised God for my victory, regretted I had so injured Edmund, and wondered how many years would pass till Camelot accepted me.

Once briefly through the crowd of diners I glimpsed the queen watching me. Her gaze felt almost a shock. I was sore and aching weary, and caught in my moment of high honor, yet of a sudden Adele pressed against me, Matilde murmured, Sibyl lay soft abed. Guenever herself smiled, that black Yule night. Jesu, her beauty and her seductiveness. I looked again, but could not see her.

We had finished the second course when, over the chatter of the company, iron-shod hooves tramped the stones of the castle court. Knights around me lifted their heads, murmuring. Footsteps sounded on the stair. The figures that paused at the screen were so weary it took a moment to recognize them, but then the whole company sprang cheering to its feet.

"Gawain," cried the king, leaping up. "Praise God, you are come back. And Ector and Lionel. Welcome, welcome, all of you." Gawain shut his eyes at the acclaim, yet Arthur spread his arms. "Where did you find the Sangral? Have you brought it with you? What news of Lancelot? Galahad his son? Percival?"

Gawain stumbled forward, bent against the applause as into a storm. Tears streamed down his cheeks. "Alas, my lord," he cried out. "Alas, my king."

Camelot fell silent as an empty wood.

"What do you mean?" Arthur said.

Gawain could say no more. The knight next him shook his blond head. "My lord. We have failed."

"Good Sir Ector, what do you mean?"

"We found nothing. Nothing save mischance, danger, frightful accident, awful forests, murderous battles against knights we loved, priests who reviled our sins." He spoke in a rush as if quicker told were quicker rid. "A whole year bleak as winter."

The king stared, unbelieving. "Surely you found something."

Sir Lionel, on Gawain's other side, lifted his lean hands. "Nothing, my lord, save in madness I slew a holy monk, and a pure knight, and would even have killed my brother Bors."

"Bors?" Disbelief rang in Arthur's voice. "But you are all my noble knights."

Gawain had collected himself. "It was worse than that." In our breathless silence he lifted his gaze to the sooty rafters. "How well do I recall that Pentecost, my lord. How certain I was, the finest knights of the finest king . . ." He shut his damp eyes. "Christ's greatest boon. Yet, Our Father's virtue . . ." He staggered and half knelt. "Oh, my lord, on my knee I pray you forgive me that oath, and all your knights I have led to their death."

"Noble Gawain." Arthur took his arm and pulled him upright. "You were forgiven, sir. Even that day. Sit you and rest."

But Gawain could not stop. "Though I rode to Christendom's highest quest, I slew good knights and in my turn was injured sore." He pushed his fingers through his grizzled hair, that half covered a new scar. "The Holy Sangral stands too high, my lord." Gawain wept again. "It demands the sinless man. But for the lesser, for he who has any sin at all, it is His greatest curse."

"Dear Gawain," said the king, and led the knight to his seat.

We turned back to food and drink gone flavorless. The young knights around me blinked and shook their heads, and would not meet each other's gaze. "What befalls the world?" one grumbled. "Peasants defeat knights, the Sangral's boon is death. Ought we expect fire and earthquake? Are these Our Lord's last days?"

Even I, knowing well the sins of knights, could not believe Gawain had failed. He was Camelot's finest, save Lancelot. I could only think that the Sangral required some other form of virtue than chivalry and knightly valor.

Distressed by Gawain's tale, the king would not hold court nor hear my plea of Craon till the morning after the Sabbath. Lambert and I rode in from Denham, with William and Francis. Arthur's chamber was crowded again, but now Sir Gawain stood frowning beside the king.

"This is he that defeated Bramhill?" he muttered.

"Sir Gawain of Orkney." I bowed. "Michel de Verdeur."

His mouth made a bitter grove across his clean-shaven face. "Laramort's mucker?" he said in a hard voice.

"Once, sir." It surprised me he remembered.

Gawain turned away. "The world is truly upside down."

If I had come to Camelot a day later, or Gawain returned a day sooner, I would have fought him instead of Edmund. I could never have defeated Gawain, yet as I drew a thankful breath I wondered, Was this, too, the wizard's work?

"My lords," I said, "I bring news of Sir Lancelot." The chamber hushed, and the king leaned to me. "He made pilgrimage to Compostela, sire. On his return he spoke to my lord Craon. He, too, had met hard ways and dark judgments." I saw Gawain close his eyes. "For his soul and the Sangral, Sir Lancelot swore an oath 'gainst fighting."

"Lancelot?" cried Arthur, "against battle?"

"And another, my lord, 'gainst courtly love."

The king stared at me, and did not seem to notice the knights' murmur. "Lancelot? God's blood, this is an awful quest."

Sir Lambert spoke, of his own visit to Banioc, of Lancelot's piety and the ship he took with Sir Percival. Arthur sat silent, staring away over our heads.

At last I lifted my voice. "My lord, I bring petition of Craon."

The king brought his unwilling gaze back to me. He peered at the arms on my broidered tabard. His eye fell on the pommel of sword. "If you are Craon's, why is that weapon familiar?"

I drew the blade. Once more the heathen letters squirmed on its bright steel. Gawain stared, and Arthur sat up, pointing. "How came you by that?"

"Abbotsbury, sire. I had lost my sword by shipwreck. The old abbot gave it to me."

"The abbot?"

"His name was Geoffrey, sire. He said it was his father's."

Arthur might not have heard. "Gawain, know you this blade?"

" 'Tis the Saracen your grandfather won at Acre." He turned at me. "Geoffrey was cousin to King Uther."

I could not believe it any more than they, that the king's relation gave me a sword of the king's grandfather.

"Had I known that blade sooner I would not . . ." Arthur paused, staring at me. "The old abbot, had you ever seen him before?"

"No, sire." I knew well what he meant. "He was not the man at Sir Ulfius' vigil. I am certain of it, sire, for I have seen him three times since and . . ."

"Three times?" Arthur's eyes sprang open.

"Though each a different shape. I swear it, my lord."

"Three times," he muttered, almost angry.

Again the talk had strayed. I raised my head. "My lord, I come for John, baron of Craon. To plead his manors in Blackmoor, sire, that you took of his cousin, Olivier."

Arthur seemed lost in thought. Beside him Sir Kay lifted his voice. "The king gave them to the abbot of Glastonbury, to be a chantry for King Uther, the prayers for his father's soul."

Behind me William cleared his throat. "All four manors, sir?"

"Uther Pendragon was lord of all Britain."

"But," said William, "Uther's regents gave the manors to Craon. If my lord Arthur wished relief for vassalage, he ought take lands Olivier held of him, not what Olivier held of Craon."

"That is a matter of Craon and Olivier," said Kay. "Let Olivier give your baron four other manors."

The cleric Francis stepped up and boomed his opinion. "Nay, sir, they are still Craon's. Let Olivier give others to the king."

"Nor was Craon consulted ere they were taken," said William.

Clerics might argue the whole day, but I knew the king would do as he wished. I stepped past them and bowed again to Arthur. "My lord. With this sword am I proved a knight. The wizard speaks to me. I come for Craon . . ."

"The wizard?" barked Sir Gawain.

The king nodded. "I have seen him, too." He stood restlessly, as if he wanted action. "Edmund has earned his ease and our high debt." His voice stopped the clerics' argument. "You will see him safely home, Sir Michel. Stay at his wish, see him healed. But come you to Camelot ere Michaelmas, for then we go to Winchester."

"Sire, I do it gladly." I drew a breath, pleased and unhappy both. "But, my lord, I am Craon's man, I will never rest of pleading his lands."

"Nor ought you." He smiled his warm smile, that I had not seen for years. "As you are a true liege man."

Far more than his greeting in the Hall, this escort of Edmund showed the king's belief in my combat, and his favor of me. My place at Camelot altered at once, and every knight knew me and even ladies smiled.

And Balen sat the bench next me, at the midday meal. "What is this we hear of Lancelot?" He gave a wry smile. "Who can believe he might never lift a sword again? Nor a lady's skirt?"

"Balen," said another, glancing at the queen. "Take care."

"Sir John," I said, "told me he was much distraught."

"God knows he must have been, to so deny himself." Balen half frowned at me. "And Camelot has a tale of you."

"What do you mean?"

"They whisper you are not truly of Greenfarm, but are bastard of a great lady, fostered all unknown on the king's demesne."

"Damn them," I muttered, suddenly angered.

"The king himself was nurtured by a parent not his own." He gave a shrug. "And you are dark, though all Greenfarm is blond."

"My sister was as dark," I spat out. "Damn you, who do they say was mother to us both?"

"The lady Morgan le Fay."

"That witch?"

"The old abbot was her uncle, that gave you the sword that defeated Edmund. The lady is the king's sister, the only dark child of King Uther." Humor and spite both glinted in his eyes. "As Mordred is the only fair prince of Orkney."

Twenty-one

That legend of Morgan le Fay confirmed my position at Camelot, made my knighthood as clear as any philosopher's argument of premise and conclusion. Knights were truly knights, not by battle skills nor the ceremony of dubbing, but by their station of birth and their noble blood. Judicial battle, God's infallible proof, had confirmed my knighthood. Therefore, I must have noble blood. There was no other possibility.

And who better to be my noble parent than that dark and wayward lady, known both for her lovers and her willfulness? It was such an attractive notion I wondered at it myself, half hoping it were true. Yet in truth I felt both anger and a kind of bitter joy, that once again it was the belief of knights, their own faith in chivalry, that upheld me.

With William's help I wrote a letter to Sir John, of my battle with Sir Edmund, of the king's denial of the manors yet of his pleasure at me nevertheless. Arthur had left the matter unresolved and I asked John's leave to stay longer, to make my petition again. I did not write of the wizard, for I did not understand how I might be Arthur's man yet keep my feudal loyalty to Craon.

Sir Edmund's steward soon arrived, with a litter for his lord. We set Edmund in it, his face purple, his arm bound, and rode out with three of his knights through the haze of early autumn. The way to Bramhill led upriver, across the ford, and into the gloom of Camelot's ancient forest. Some at the castle said Merlin lay enchanted there, yet we saw nothing stranger than a swineherd and his animals, come too early for the beech mast. After a dim woodland league we rode out to open country again, but not till the sun was half down the western sky did we reach Edmund's broad fields and rich manors.

The wounded knight struggled up in the litter and waved to his farmers, that watched from fields and houseyards, dour and almost silent. Bramhill's manor was built of old stone, with a narrow stream like a moat along three walls. As we rode toward his gate a well-set knight came out, shaded his eyes to peer at us, and galloped away.

"Damn," growled the steward, riding beside me.

"Who was that?" I asked.

"Good Sir Edmund serves his king, fights his battles, receives his wounds"—he spat aside—"while that one . . ."

Jesu, did Sibyl still entertain Briant?

Certainly she showed nothing of it when we rode into Edmund's court, but stepped without hesitation from her circle of women. Her hair was still flaxen pale beneath its linen wimple, and motherhood agreed with her, deepened her bosom and rounded her face. At the sight of Edmund's wounds she put a hand to her mouth, that mouth with its short lip and small white teeth.

Two nurses waited behind her. One carried a red-faced infant, and the other held the hand of a small boy. My heart leapt to see him. He was Harold, Edmund had told me. His face was round like his mother's, his hair dark as mine. I could not keep my gaze from him, and when he gaped at Edmund's battered face and began to wail, I had to harden myself not to take the lad in my arms. His nurse picked him up and carried him inside, yet he stared bleary-eyed over her shoulder the whole way.

Servants lifted Edmund from his litter, and I followed Sibyl and the steward up the worn stairs to a dim solar and a curtained bedchamber. Only after they laid him on a high bed did the wounded knight open his eyes.

"Wife," he said, hoarse with pain, "I rue this homecoming."

"My lord," she said, "God be thanked you come to your chamber, and not your tomb."

"Here." He waved his good hand weakly. "Sir Michel."

"Sir knight," she said shortly. She did not remember me.

"My lady, it pains me I have injured your lord."

Her gaze swung back, as if my voice roused memories. "The king required it," she said flatly. "But how is it Camelot could find no champion save my husband?"

"None offered themselves, madam."

Not till the Sabbath did Edmund rise and limp through his solar to the little chapel. After, he sat in the sun at his narrow oriel and bade me talk with him.

"Praise God you heal, Sir Edmund."

"You did not kill me."

"I had no want, sir. . . ."

"A lad we thought a peasant on the king's demesne." He spoke as if talk wearied him. "Yet despite all, the king's relation." He gazed away. "Mayhap. I would not have fought had I known. Each year comes yet another knight, young and proud, to brighten Camelot's eye." He had closed his own eyes. "Yet why do I feel that Camelot fails?"

He was injured, I thought, and tired. And much older than thirty. "The king wished me to serve you, good sir."

He nodded. "I have hawks that want training, hounds that have not coursed for months." He drew a breath, his long face pinched with pain and fatigue. "A knight rode from my gate." He did not look at me. "But a man cannot easily put aside a wife who is distant cousin to the king. Or brought so fine a dowry."

"Sir Edmund," I murmured, "where does this knight live?"

"Marwood lies two days northward, a long ride beyond the abbey at Malmesbury." He turned his bruised face to me. "But, sir, it is my own matter."

I wondered if he knew of my own quarrel with Briant. Out his leaded glass I saw Sibyl crossing the court. "They say, Sir Edmund, that King Arthur approves of courtly love."

"Else for chivalry will not believe it when it happens."

Sibyl and her ladies chattered up the stairs. "My lord," she called, "you will tire yourself."

"And it is for that," he muttered to me, "Camelot fails."

"Husband," Sibyl murmured, "enough. Come, sir, help me."

I did not believe that Camelot failed, nor that Arthur wavered as high king. It was but the horns of his own cuckoldry that angered Edmund. We each took an arm and led him back to bed. He sighed as he lay down. "Michel, speak to my steward of birds and hounds."

"My lord," Sibyl said, "rest you." She pulled the chamber curtain closed behind us. "Your name is Michel, sir knight."

"It is, lady. Michel de Verdeur."

"They say you are a natural son to Lady Morgan." She smiled, showing again her small white teeth. "I am her niece, by marriage." She was still very attractive, but I told myself I wanted nothing of her now. "Have we met before, sir?"

"Some years past, lady."

"Oh?" Her gaze flickered. "Where was it?"

"Camelot."

"Camelot." She leaned her head, and suddenly her cheeks flushed and she cried out, "It can't be." Her ladies, sitting to their broidery at the solar window, rustled at her voice.

I took her hand and kissed it. "My soft lady of Yule."

She snatched it away. "I can't believe it." She stepped away, her hands curled into fists. "I am near a widow of you."

"As I was once near dead of you. And of Briant, too."

"By God," she whispered, "you must say nothing of that."

I lowered my voice, though I could not hide my grin. "How fair to be a father." I counted on my fingers. "Harold cannot be Sir Edmund's. And who else had you, that long sweet autumn?"

" 'Tis a lie," she muttered "But if this be true, of Morgan . . ." If it were true of Morgan, then were I almost nephew to the king. And her son, almost grand-nephew. Even as Sibyl spoke the name, her face smoothed of anger.

At Bramhill, Sir Edmund and his dour steward kept me busy till the last Sabbath of September. It was a narrow household, austere and quiet, and only my obligation to the king held me there the whole six weeks. Sibyl I saw only at table, where she was always pleasant and always distant. Not till my last morning did I climb the solar stairs again. A lady sat to one side of the glass window, bent over her broidery. Young Harold skipped about, humming to himself, while Sibyl suckled her daughter and looked again the single brightness in all this gloomy house.

"My lady," I said, bowing, "I come to ask your leave."

"Sir Michel." She moved the child to her other breast and left the first uncovered. I pulled my glance away, unused to such domesticity. "You are for Camelot, then?"

"I come to thank you for your welcome, lady."

"The king wished it." She glanced at her son. "Come, Harold, say your greeting to this knight."

The child walked to me and bowed. "S'Mic'l."

"Harold," I said, and touched his dark hair. I had seen him much, but from a distance and with his nurse. To touch him and speak to him made me proud as a cock. Here was my own son, out of my loins. "A sweet child," I said, happily. The lad walked away, carefully stepping over the cracks between the floor boards.

"What dost thou think, Mary?" Sibyl murmured.

The lady smiled, ere she bent over her stitchery again. "I'd not speak against Sir Edmund, but there is favor between them."

Everybody at Camelot must have made their counting. The child was not Edmund's, clearly. If he thought it were Briant's, there must be some at Ladies that suspected it mine. Mayhap the tale of Morgan had begun not among knights, but in the queen's solar.

Sibyl gazed at me as if she read my thoughts. "Sir Uriens, husband to Lady Morgan, is my uncle. I am her niece by marriage." Her pretty smile did not waver. "We are but five removes in blood, Michel. Some might believe the child's soul in danger."

I turned to look at Harold, who stood at the narrow window watching the autumn sky. "Surely he is baptized against it?"

"God's love, of course he is." She shifted the infant to her shoulder, and drew at last a shawl across her bosom.

"The lady Morgan," I murmured, thinking I ought visit her, ask the truth of this rumor. "My lady, do you know where she dwells?"

"Castle Chariot, oft enough." Sibyl made a vague gesture with her free hand. "A half-day's ride. My steward will know the way."

I had expected some castle in Wales, or far Scotland, and the thought she was so close made hope and fright both flare in my mind. I drew a breath. "May I say you sent me, lady?"

"Of course, Sir Michel. But surely she will remember you."

If Sibyl's faith in Morgan eased my own fright, still Bramhill's steward paled when I spoke to him. "God's blood," he muttered, "you would seek *that* woman?"

"May I not visit my mother's castle?" I dared not waver.

He scowled and stepped a little away, as if he were suddenly afraid of me, and dread tightened his voice. "Well, sir. Three leagues west is an old straight way, Roman-built. Her valley lies southward, lost among trees, the path hidden. A holy abbey stands another league farther on; it's there you must be by nightfall."

"Sir Michel," Hugh said, "ought we not go back to Camelot?"

"The king expects us," said René.

"I must speak to the lady." Their fear had hardened my resolve.

"Pray do not, sir," muttered the steward. "A dozen men have loved her, they say, and all are perished."

"But think you." I grinned at their worried faces. "If one were my own father, then what have I to fear?"

I turned my horse the way he pointed, westward down a narrow, overgrown track. René and Hugh rode after me, reluctantly. It was farther than the steward said, else the way had grown rougher, for we did not reach the old road till past Nones. Following its line of tumbled stones, we came after another hour to the gnarled and ancient trees of a thick forest. Our easy way quickly became a rutted passage, twisting down into a dim, steep valley. At the bottom a narrow path branched away, that I turned up without a thought.

"Sir Michel," Hugh called. "Is she truly your mother?"

His question re-woke my own misgivings. I drew up, and turned on him with an angry frown. "Surely she will give us welcome."

"Sir, our heraldry is Craon's," said René, "not Camelot's."

"There are tales aplenty, of her arguments with Camelot."

" 'Tis late, sir," Hugh said, "let us come back tomorrow."

René nodded, anxiously. "With somebody who knows the way."

"The abbey is but a league distant, sir."

"Then go, both of you," I cried, afraid their worry would bolster mine. I pulled my horse around and trotted quickly up the way. Behind me they argued briefly, ere they spurred to catch up.

The narrow path was as clean and smooth as if men traveled it every day. We came to a side parting but I kept straight on. Soon after was another parting, and then a third, and all the while the old forest grew dim about us, as if clouds covered the sky beyond the trees. Suddenly the way turned, and we came out onto the verge of a small lake, its still face bright with orange from the evening sky overhead. I could not believe the day had passed so quick.

"Look, sir," René whispered, "there."

Across the lake a hundred tapers glimmered in the forest.

"There," I said, "Castle Chariot. She waits us."

"But where is the way, sir?" Hugh muttered.

For our path ended at the water, and on each side stood reed swamps or stony cliffs. They glanced at each other again, and René whispered, "We met nobody, sir, how can she know we come?"

"We will ride around." I pointed at the lights. "It's not far." I turned my horse toward the dark wood, and there at last they would not follow.

"A dozen men have gone lost of her, sir," said Hugh.

"Forgive us, sir," René called. "We go to the abbey."

They rode off at a canter, the sound of their hoofbeats swallowed quickly by the forest. The evening fell silent, and in that hush I suddenly remembered the lady was not my mother, that it was Sibyl's hopes and my own unspoken wish that sent me here.

I put a hand on the pommel of my sword. I nudged my horse ahead, but if I thought to come easily to her lights I soon lost my way among the old trees, and only the cry of a waterbird led me back to the lake. The day had nearly failed. I had come halfway round, yet her lights still flickered exactly opposite. It was true. She was a witch. There was no castle. Or else it was a castle unknowable, the way to it running straight through the water, with not even a sword's edge to bridge it. Nor did I hear people, or feasting and song, nothing at all save my palfrey cropping the thin grass. I unsaddled him and let him drink, and sat against a tree. The night deepened. Stars appeared overhead, flickering like her witchly tapers.

And then without warning there came across the mirrored water the voice of the singer of my boyhood. I scrambled to my feet, my heart thumping. My heathen blade grated from its scabbard. I peered into the night, alive again to that summer's evening, the sky, the song, Lark's blood sticky on my hands. I stared across the water. Tapers and stars both glimmered on its face. I had expected a castle, a Hall, and within a lady who would say no, or yes. Morgan le Fay showed me only lights flickering, as they had on Camelot's walls. I heard only the voice of the singer, as I had that evening. Briefly my heart froze, waiting for the hare's scream, but it never came.

She knew I was there, and this was her answer, neither yes or no, but once again the start of it all. The wizard might appear and point me onward, but this lady sent me back to the beginning, to that first and fatal night. I drew a breath. I pushed my blade into its scabbard, the sword I had got from her uncle. If Merlin said be Arthur's man, Morgan would have me Lark's. I had only my feudal honor to remind me I was also John's. I sat against the tree again. The singer went on for several songs, though I could not make out his words. When he stopped the forest was silent as a wilderness.

Not till the end of the following day did we ride clattering under the gates of Camelot. I had found René and Hugh at the abbey, afraid to go back for me, afraid to go on. The monks were certain I was dead. When I arrived they crossed themselves, and my two paled and glanced away. We rode the whole day almost silent, and even when we came to Arthur's darkening castle they had hardly lost their fright of me.

Flaring torches lit Camelot. Wains crowded the court and porters shouted and squires cursed. The king would leave in the morning, and everything but beds ought have been packed. I climbed to the Hall. That great space was nearly empty, too, though the king sat one bare trestle with Mordred and a dozen others.

"Sir Michel," he called, "how fares Sir Edmund?"

"Well, my lord. I left him nearly healed."

"I am much pleased to hear it."

"I am a day late returning, sire." I stopped, half afraid to speak of it, the memory more frightful than the happening. "I lost my way in the forest of Castle Chariot."

The knights around him stared and drew in their breath. The king scowled, very dark, before he muttered, "My sister hath small love of me, nor my knights." And then he lifted his head and pondered me. "Merlin. And now Morgan."

"There is a rumor of myself and the lady." Of course he must have heard. "I saw lights, but could find no way to her castle."

Still he watched me. "My sister is a cunning lady."

"Lights?" said Mordred, astonished. "It was after dark?"

"I stopped the night in her forest, sir."

"Christ and Our Father!" he barked. The others muttered to each other, nearly as frightened as the monks had been.

But Arthur was not distracted. "She did not speak to you?"

"No, sire. I did not see her at all."

"Not at all," he repeated. It seemed to ease his mind.

The royal train that set out for Winchester was nearly the same I had watched enter Camelot two months before. Only Guenever had left a day earlier, with clerics and ladies and a dozen knights. The king smiled on me again, and set me with a half dozen more, to ride to her at Salisbury.

Three of them were the younger Orkney princes. Agravain I remembered, tall and handsome, a pale scar on his right cheek and a stiff, half-wooden manner. Gaheris his brother, that Kay named Beaumains for his generosity, was lanky and angular. Gareth the youngest save Mordred, had a soft, boyish face, though under his hauberk his shoulders were as broad as any. They were all, as Balen had said, dark as Gawain. And there was blond Ector and stout Lionel, of Gawain's Sangral quest.

Only Agravain had seen my fight with Edmund, and as we stood at the stables he spoke of it, and my heathen sword. I drew the blade for them, and their eyes lit at the squirming letters.

"From the king's grandfather?" said Ector.

"From the uncle of your mother?" said Gareth.

"Geoffrey of Abbotsbury." I shook my head. "I heard nothing of the lady Morgan till I defeated Sir Edmund."

Agravain gave a grim smile. "I remember you a varlet but God help me, 'tis not possible you are a farmer. You fight too well. And the lady preserved you."

They had all heard of my night in her wood. It was another proof of our relation. I would not argue their judgment.

Once more we rode under Camelot's echoing gate, out to a day of bright autumn sunshine. We passed Greenfarm at a quick trot. The whole family worked in Newfield, spreading manure on the family strips, and I must look away from their stooped forms. We overtook Arthur's train beyond Ryford, and stopped at Astolat's high castle at midday. And with the bells of Vespers ringing in the cool dusk, as they had rung so many years before, we clattered across the bridge into Salisbury.

The unfinished front of the cathedral still wore its cover of thatch. We rode past to the bishop's walled palace, where lute and psaltery played in a Hall shining with tapers. The queen sat at the high table. I had forgot how beautiful she was. I could not see Gawain beside her nor the bishop on her other side, for the clear line of her cheek, her high smooth brow, the smile with which she greeted us. Once again her bright presence recalled my every love, though each in my memory stood pale and wan beside her.

"My lady and my queen," murmured Agravain, bowing.

"Good Sir Agravain," she said, her voice low and musical. "And your brothers. And Sir Ector, Sir Lionel. And here is . . ."

"Michel de Verdeur." I did not want to take my eyes from her, even to bow. "Knight of Craon and your servant, lady."

"Michel de Verdeur." Her mouth went hard. "Morgan le Fay's bastard."

"I pray you, lady, if it be true, think not the less of me."

Her gray eyes were very cool. "Such elegant language, sir."

"I am a knight of Anjou, madam." I bowed again. "You bring it unbidden to my tongue."

A brief smile moved her lips. "Welcome, then, Sir Michel."

I found my place at a lower table, between Gareth and a cathedral priest. As René cut my meat he murmured, "Jesu, she takes my breath, the same time she stirs my . . ."

"Thy tongue, boy." A frown creased Gareth's soft brow.

"He meant no hurt, Sir Gareth," I said. "What did you, when first you saw her?"

He did not answer, but nodded toward Sir Agravain. "My brother will hear no ill of the lady, and I support him in it."

On my other side the priest smiled into his cup. "Bright as sun and moon," he murmured. "And as true as both of them."

Gareth's face went red. "That holds for clerics, too."

The priest might not have heard. I saw, very clear, bees swarming round a bright rose, stinging each other in their haste.

The queen went not to Winchester, but northward to her favorite nunnery at Amesbury, and we rode up from the city past old Sarum Castle standing its grassy hill. After three leagues of open upland we came to the crossroads above the little town, where another lane led us down into a market crowded with booths. Peasants gawked at us and gave a ragged cheer when they recognized the queen. Beside the narrow river the slate roofs of a rich abbey stood over a high wall. An old groom hobbled the gravel court to take our horses, and servants showed us quarters in the ample lodge, though Guenever and her ladies took chambers inside the abbey cloisters. Here at this convent, all the sisters were of noble families, and her arrival seemed more a meeting of equals than the advent of Britain's high queen.

We were a score of knights with her, our number for honor more than any danger. Still, Gawain decreed every daylight hour must see an armed knight at the crossroads above the town. He set the hours from Prime to Nones, and Nones to Compline, and the youngest shared the task, myself and Gareth, and Patrise, a sandy-haired bachelor recently come from Ireland.

The queen was very kind, and sat the midday meal in the visitor's refectory with every knight save the guard. Gawain was her oldest friend and clearly her favorite. But dark Agravain brooded on her, and grumbled if any but Gawain sat close, or even received her smile too often. In truth there was always about her some tension that made her the center of everyone's eye, though as she was the queen, each tried to forget it.

The same morning we left for Amesbury, King Arthur had gone east to royal Winchester, and called a tourney there, for Saint Luke's Day. We all practiced for it, at Amesbury, and the stable court rang with swords and we galloped to joust in the abbey's fallow fields. I had not ridden Night thus since Craon, and the thundering charge and the strain of collision excited us both. I wanted fame at arms, that it aid my petition of John's fiefs, and be a threat to Lark's killers. I watched the queen's knights close, and saw they were all able fighters. Yet I thought I might beat any of them save Agravain, and of course Sir Gawain.

Despite the tourney, the queen would still need her knights' guard. Winchester was but a short day's ride, and Gawain decided that only three of us need stay. He drew lots. Ector's was the first name out, and he grumbled how ill fortune pursued him still, before he stopped and muttered of the honor of it. The second name was young Patrise.

"I would stay for the third," said Agravain.

Gawain did not even look at him, but reached into the pot again. "Michel de Verdeur." He smiled at me grimly. "I had hoped to meet you on the field, sir."

"And I as well, Sir Gawain." In truth I had no wish to battle him, yet I rued I must give up this last tourney of the season.

The day they left Ector gave me the morning's guard. The queen had the others at her midday table, and when I returned she sent for me. She sat her chamber apart from her ladies, staring out an open shutter to her cloister. A cleric read from a book of Trojans and Greeks, of Circe and her haunted isle.

I bowed at the door. "My lady."

"Sir Michel. Come and sit." She pointed to a stool beside her. Her smile was as beautiful as ever, yet in the daylight a weariness lined her face. "I regret you cannot tourney, sir."

"I am repaid, madam, being your servant."

The energy I had felt of her before was become a soft and vulnerable air, and my own desire but a wish I might ease her pain.

"You have news of Lancelot."

"Nothing more than I told the king, madam."

She did not take her gray eyes from me. "I would hear it from you myself."

I did not know how to begin. "I saw him at Angers. His tale of the Sangral amazed us all."

"He was so certain of it," she murmured. "I wonder I speak to Gawain. It was he that proposed that awful quest." Her face had gone bleak as winter. "But 'tis Lancelot I rue."

"He came to Craon before Yule, madam."

"A year ago?"

"Almost." I began again the amazing tale, of the pilgrimage to Compostela, of the priestly hermit, of the knight's vows against battle and love.

"I cannot believe it," she said, her love of him plain in her voice.

I told of Lambert's visit to Banioc, and of the ship Lancelot had taken. After, hoping to draw out my time, I spoke of my folly at Angers, and Lancelot's anger. She did not seem to hear, but stood and paced her chamber. We all watched her, silent, till she waved a hand at the cleric. "Good father, read more." He resumed his drone. She paused before me. "Do you guard the high road tomorrow morn?"

I stood up. "No, my lady."

"Then you will ride with me," she said, and paced away.

"Lady, you do me honor." But she had not heard, again.

We gathered at the stables after Terce, heavy-cloaked against the morning chill. René would ride ahead with a page, and the queen with me, and then her ladies and a younger cleric.

Dark smudges lay beneath her eyes. My heart ached for her. "My lady, are you well?"

"As well as ever, sir." Yet as we rode out the abbey gate she murmured, "What think you, Sir Michel? Ought I take Orders, and never leave this sweet place?"

Matilde had said the same, nearly. I could not understand this fondness for the cloister. "Lady, your king . . ."

"Ah, my king." She turned her horse toward the river. "My grand, poor king. That finest and most blinded man." She was wading her horse through the ford when she lifted her head and muttered, "Truly thou art Morgan's brat, there is a spell of you that has me speak heedless things."

"Madam . . ."

"I have ladies, I have confessors, why do I need some green knight's ear?"

The road left the wood and ran up between stubbled fields. Behind us her ladies laughed as the cleric flirted with them.

"Think you he will keep his oaths?" she said.

I knew she did not mean the cleric. "Would you have him fail the Sangral?"

"Ought I pray his salvation, then?"

"Mayhap it is beyond your prayers." I spoke unthinking, and my face went hot. "Lady, forgive my plainness."

" 'Tis nearer rudeness."

"My foreign manners," I said, and immediately regretted that.

She looked at me, her mouth compressed, all trace of sadness gone. "I understand well how you angered him, young sir knight."

And I understood how Lancelot loved her, despite her moods or perhaps because of them. Each showed another side of her, more engaging than the last. Closeness but made her more attractive, till I could not keep my eyes away, nor be too far. Lancelot had sworn his soul against her, but now I doubted even a knight of Lancelot's strength could turn away from this lady's gaze.

A chill breeze gusted across the hilltop. Grassy tumps, the graves of old pagans, lay thick around. She pointed to the next rise, where a huddle of stones leaned against the wind. "The Giant's Dance. That Merlin in his youth brought from the west, so they say." She nudged her palfrey to a trot, down the slope. "Though now he finds himself bewitched."

"Captured by love," I called to her. "As any man may be."

"Yet the king saw him at Ulfius' funeral."

"Aye, my lady. He asked me the knight's name."

She nodded. "It was for that King Arthur gave you exile, instead of death."

I gaped at her. "Madam, I had not known it."

"Nor is Merlin oft so friendly with your mother."

"When I rode the lady's forest, she hid herself."

She gave a hard smile. "Mayhap 'tis beyond your questions."

We crossed a grassy bottom and came up to the stones. They were set in a rough circle and though some had fallen, others still carried lintels at their tops, high above our heads.

"My lady," the cleric called, "beware this pagan place."

"Ah, Padric, I would not walk on wizards' ground." She glanced to me. "Think you this is Merlin's work?"

"I am certain he builds better, lady."

She gave a quick smile. "It was my father gave the king his Round-table." I had always thought it Merlin. "The wizard was much distressed by it," she said, "that knighthood and chivalry became Arthur's enthusiasm, and not his dark, ambiguous magic." She had walked her horse into the circle, and she leaned to touch one rude upright. "See you, Michel, how it was a great pavilion. A court of kings older than the Romans." She made a wide gesture. "A Camelot without walls, for knights who did not battle, nor seek inconstant visions, nor give up love at whim."

"My lady," I said, "there never was such a time."

"So unlike our own days, we might call them blest."

"Lady, they were but savage pagans."

"As were we all, ere the coming of Our Lord's Word." She dropped her head. "Yet I believe those days were brighter, the knights finer, the ladies more . . ."

She broke off. Without another word she turned her horse back toward the abbey. We had crested the last ridge before she drew up and turned to me, her face sorrowful. "And yet I know women were unhappy then, as well. Women wed to men they could not love. Women caught by love without hope. Women bound to nunneries for unanswered love."

"Madam, pray God you may forget this vision."

She lay a hand on my arm and at her touch my heart nearly stopped its beating. "Oh, good Sir Michel, may I not pursue it? As all my knights do chase their own phantasms?"

Twenty-two

Sir Gawain had taken a dozen ransoms at Winchester, and the king acclaimed him winner of the tourney. He brought back to Amesbury fine winter cloaks, for each of us that remained with the queen, and of course we thanked him and praised his generosity.

On the day after, as we all sat the midday meal, his brother Sir Mordred strode smiling into the refectory. "High knights, fair ladies," he cried, "wonderful news. Sir Lancelot has landed at Dover not three days past. King Arthur calls his whole court to London, to greet his return."

While the others cheered him, I saw again Lancelot on the field of Angers. His dagger glinted in my face, he growled his curse. I had known he must come. I could but pray his oaths of the Sangral annulled his oath of me.

When we rose from table I went to Sir Mordred, who gave me a bright smile and murmured his regret I had missed Winchester. Despite Lancelot, I would petition the king of Craon's manors again. But King Arthur, said Mordred, was most impatient of the knight, and if I would entreat him I must ride at once to Winchester, or follow him to London.

Tomorrow early, I thought, and called Hugh out to look to our horses. Just as we finished Patrise rode into the stableyard, come from the crossroads with a face reddened by the autumn wind.

"Wherefore this clamor?" he called, squinting down at me.

"Sir Mordred brings news. The king goes to London." I found it hard to say. "Sir Lancelot has come to Dover."

He did not smile. "Lancelot."

A sudden wind blustered about us, that flung the rattling leaves in circles about corners of the court. It was winter, come early. I pulled my cloak about me. "They are all delighted."

"They are all fools." He swung down angrily. "Can no one see it— that the queen and that knight will ruin Camelot."

"Pray God you are mistaken."

"Pray God," he muttered.

I turned back to the sisters' cloister. A lady waited inside the gate. "Sir Michel," she called out. I stopped and stared at her, and my heart leaped in my chest, seized by love. "The queen would speak with you, sir." The cold wind tugged and fluttered her green cloak, yet I thought her graceful as a summer willow.

"The queen?" Her look benumbed me, that and the line of sunlight on her cheek, the curve of her lips, the turn of her head.

"She waits in the abbess' garden." Her voice sang in my ears like some half-remembered minstrel's air. "Sir Lancelot comes."

"Lancelot?" Watching her I had forgot even that.

"My lady is much joyed." She had walked before me into the cloisters, and now she paused under an arched portal. "But do you not see it, sir? How in these last years King Arthur hath seemed a noble monarch, and Guenever his true lady." I could see nothing but her pale and lidded eyes. "Yet now the king hies him to Sir Lancelot. And brings his lady as if we did not all remember . . ." Her cheeks flushed, but I could remember nothing save her bright gaze. "Oh, sir, were it all to begin anew."

I tried to think. "Sir Lancelot took vows, lady."

"Vows are easily forgot." Her voice had gone almost harsh. "Sir Michel, you must see it, how this matter disturbs Camelot."

She took my arm to lead me on. Not even the queen's touch had so confused me, and we crossed the second cloister before I found my tongue again. "Lady, what may I do?"

"Good knight, you have her ear." She slowed, for there beyond the next arch Guenever walked with the abbess. "Sir Michel, you see the wizard, you are son to Morgan, Camelot marvels at you." Still her hand lay on my arm. "I pray you, speak for the king. For Camelot and all of us."

"Lady, I do not know your name."

"I am Naime, sir. Daughter of Corbin." She smiled, and pushed me gently, yet I nearly stumbled into the abbess' garden.

"Sir Michel?" The queen frowned in the autumn sunlight. "What do you here?" Thyme and lavender scented the bright air.

"Madam." I bowed. "You called me."

"I did not."

"That lady." I pointed, but Naime had gone.

"I see no lady." She held herself stiffly now, and much apart. The news of Lancelot's coming had closed her look, made her cool as some cathedral statue. "Well, you are here, what would you say?" She turned to pace the gravel path.

Even my desire of her was vanished, for if she could think only of Lancelot I could see only Naime. "I would go to Winchester, lady, to plead Craon's manors before the king."

She shrugged, as if the matter meant nothing to her.

"I thought to ask your leave, madam."

"Sir Michel, of course you have it."

But I cried out, "Jesu, it was him!" I turned, staring across the garden. Naime had vanished, nobody saw us speak, she had said near enough "be Arthur's man."

Guenever frowned at me. "Forgive me, madam," I said. "The lady that brought me, it was the mage, disguised."

"Merlin? Here?" Her voice went hard, and she hunched her shoulders as if the sudden breeze announced his presence.

"The lady Naime."

"What lady?" cried Guenever. "You came of yourself."

The abbess glanced down the paths at us.

"He said Sir Lancelot ought not be too near you." I pressed on, though anger paled her face. "That you ought love the king. . . ."

"He is the finest knight in Christendom."

"Ah, madam, which do you mean?"

For a moment her wrath wholly stopped her tongue. "I am the queen," she muttered, "no one speaks thus, I will not hear it, the king . . ." She stopped, her face rigid and her fists clenched.

"My lady, 'tis for the king I speak." We both knew it, that in this matter she could ask nothing of the king.

She glared at me so furious I could barely catch her words. "Gawain. He will challenge you. Tomorrow. At Terce. Sir Gawain will slay you, easily."

"Yet when the king asks of his challenge, madam, what will Sir Gawain say? That I said Sir Lancelot ought obey his oath?"

Her right hand swung at me, the back of it hard and loud against my cheek. My face flared with pain.

The abbess hurried up. "What is this, my lady?"

"This knight." Guenever could hardly speak.

"Do you insult her, sir?" said the abbess.

"Good mother, let her speak it." But Guenever would only shake her head. "Dear lady," I said, "we all love you, it gives me no pleasure . . ."

"Thy tongue, sir." She raised her hand again, but caught herself. "There was no lady, no wizard, naught but petty deceits."

The road to Winchester had gone to mud under the winter rains. I pulled up the hood of Gawain's cloak, that smelled of new wool gone quickly wet. He had said naught of challenge when we broke our fast in the gray dawn, and only wished me well on the road.

God knew I regretted my hasty speech, that I must leave the queen, and my new lady unwooed. I could not believe Naime were truly Merlin, though she spoke exactly as the wizard might, and carried in her lidded gaze such witchment as only he might muster. All the way she stood before me, clear as some vision of churchly meditation, or else of fever. We reached Winchester as the day drew in. The crunch of gravel in the castle courtyard brought back my first night there, Briant's attack, my flight to the priory as the mage had told me. Was it possible she was truly Merlin?

The castle seemed half empty. King and high knights had left for London that morning, even as I left Amesbury, and the rest of his court would depart tomorrow. I took the evening meal in the great Hall, where thick stone pillars held up a timber roof blacked with smoke, over a central hearth that gave small light and less warmth. Here it was, said the mage, that Gawain had faced the green knight, and with a courage that still amazed me. I sat among knights boasting of their tourney, or chattering of London and Lancelot. I thought at first to follow them, yet the king had departed so quickly, of his pleasure of the knight, he would not speak soon of the manors of Craon. This winter I would go to Glastonbury and its abbot, and to John's cousin that lived in Devon. And Lark's knights would know I was in Britain, and would regret it.

In the dark night outside the rain had stopped. René took up a torch and we went out the castle, through the wicket of the city gate and down the cobbled street to the Jewish lane. I expected Aaron at the door, but a huge, heavy man opened it to me.

"Ezra," I said. He blinked at me. "Ezra of Caen. I thought you were in Rouen."

"No, sir." His boy's voice still astonished me. He lifted his lamp and peered at me, and at René behind me.

"Michel de Verdeur," I said, "that came on Simon's ship."

He stared another moment, searching his memory, ere he cried out, "By heaven, is it you, you are grown, are you truly a knight?"

"Truly, Ezra. Almost one of them."

"Well," he said, "perhaps I am not surprised."

"When did you come to Britain?"

"Last summer. All save my wife. Who . . ." He cleared his throat. "Who died last winter." His scowl could not hide his sorrow. "A natural death, praise heaven."

"I am sorry, Ezra."

He led me up to old Abram's little chamber. Aaron was gone to Southampton. A mob had burnt a ship of Simon's tied at the quay, and they could no longer get men to sail for them. He shook his great head. "Simon will come to Winchester in the week. I will go to our cousin in Astolat."

I did not know what to say. It was the way of the world. I could but praise God I had been born a peasant, and not a Jew.

A dark and very pretty girl came into the room, bringing ale. She stopped dead when she saw me. "Oh, I thought, Father, I did not know it was a knight."

Ezra smiled at her. "Set down the pot, dear." He nodded at me. "Do you remember Micah, from Caen?"

"I saw you in Angers," I said, "but you were not so pretty."

She frowned and smiled together, as if unable to decide were she pleased at my words or offended, and gave me a quick little curtsy as she left.

"There is a young man in Astolat," Ezra said, "of whom we have hopes."

"He will be a lucky man, Ezra."

I took out my purse and counted the pennies I owed old Abram, making their stacks on the table. Ezra nodded, pleased I knew my sums. He brought my grandfather's little dagger out of Aaron's strongbox. I began to count his livre, from Caen.

He lifted a massive hand. "It was no loan, young sir. Be not so anxious to relieve yourself of it." He gazed at me. "Perhaps you are not yet one of them."

"They say," I muttered, "that the lady Morgan le Fay is my mother." His face paled in the lamplight. "I must be noble. They can believe nothing else, and almost they convince me."

He reached to roll the damp wool of my cloak between his thick fingers. "Such a fine garment nearly convinces me."

"It was a gift," I said.

"A gift? Good heaven, 'tis worth . . ."

"Five times your livre." I dropped his coins in my purse again. "You must tell me, Ezra, when you want it."

Sir John's cousin had his manors at Brucombe, that lay to the west six cold and rainy days, far past Denham and Camelot. Unlike the baron,

Olivier was a tall man with a broad face, reddened by wind and weather, the very image of a rustic knight. His wife, whose generous dowry had let him abandon John's manors, was nearly as large and as thick. They had a brood of energetic sons that tracked mud into every chamber of the house, and with manners at table that reminded me of Greenfarm. It surprised me how attached I had become of the order and cleanliness of castle living.

I told him of the combat that proved my knighthood, and of Morgan's silence at the rumor of my noble blood. The tales diverted him, yet when I spoke of John's manors he lifted his thick shoulders in a shrug. "I can do nothing. The king required them for my liege. I have two dozen I will not risk, for those four."

"But John of Craon is your close cousin. Your grandfather received those manors from the baron that was his grandfather."

Olivier shrugged again. "John is a vassal of the French king. I was born of a British father, and live in Britain. I can be no other than Arthur's man."

Arthur's man. The words gave me pause, and briefly I lost my argument. "But by feudal law a lord may defend . . ."

"Then where is Craon's defense? John sent naught but letters when Arthur took those lands. Now, a dozen years after, there comes a single knight, with cloudy antecedents, to dispute the matter." He opened his thick hands. "Is this a vigorous defense?"

"You should have given British manors, not those of Craon."

"By damn, Sir Michel, I gave what he asked."

At Glastonbury the abbot sat behind his thick table, pressed his fingertips together, and shook his tonsured head. "Those manors are the livings of a dozen priests, and a long-established chantry. Even if you paid their rent in coin, we need the tallow and wax for candles, the sheep-hides for parchment."

"But could you never give them back?"

"If the king asked. If he had others for his father's prayers. Even then I would oppose him, and so would my bishop." He watched me a moment. "If it were old Uther he might do it, despite our disapproval. But King Arthur is very pious."

The winter that had begun with rain kept on that way. I spent a wet Yule at Lambert's Denham, where Margaret had given him a second son, Andrew, born the saint's day. I had hoped to find an answering letter from Sir John, but the hazards of winter travel delayed it. William and Francis together had found no help of law for the Blackmoor manors. The manors were Arthur's gift, that asked his father's chantry in return.

Gifts to the Church were gifts in *mortemain,* the hand that held it truly dead for rent or service. To take back such a gift was always possible, as the abbot said, but never done. The best they could suggest was that Craon be recompensed by other manors.

"But Sir John sent me only for them," I said to Lambert.

"Then argue the king again, Michel. This matter of Lancelot distracts him. He will come to Camelot in the spring."

When Arthur came so would the queen, and Lancelot with his anger. And my lady of the cloister, with her lidded gaze.

I rode out again, after Epiphany. I went heavy-armed, and took René and Hugh both equally equipped, for with the turning of the year I thought again of my Blackgral. Laramort's manors lay closest to Denham, north and east two days' ride through driving sleet, though when we reached his little village the weather eased, and the sleet became an easy rain. The single street, faced with well-kept houses, lay between broad puddled fields. His manor house stood at the end of a lane, next a stand of trees and a little church. Smoke rose from a new chimney in his Hall. As I drew up, muddy peasants that cleared his ditches stared at me.

"Is your lord at home?" I asked one of them.

"Aye, sir." He stared at the heraldry on my shield. "And his old mother, my lady Winifred."

It surprised me. I had never thought Laramort might have a mother. I thought to ride in and show him my face, tell him my name. Of all of them, I was least afraid of Laramort. He had been no fighter at Camelot and I did not believe he would challenge me. Yet if he did, and if I killed him . . . But I could kill him, there before his mother. And it would betray Sir John's refusal, and destroy my plea with the king.

"This is one of them, sir?" asked Hugh, scowling.

I nodded.

But René spoke, and in a careful voice. "Sir Michel, you are a dubbed knight of Craon. The son mayhap of Lady Morgan."

"Yes," I said. I turned my palfrey toward Astolat.

Sir Clegis, castellan to royal Astolat, stood at his blazing fire, laughing that King Arthur returned to Camelot at Candlemas. He was delighted I would take them word, and the next day, as if the king's coming changed the weather, we rode out under a clearing sky and a brightening sun.

It was midday when I paused at Denham's crossroads. I sent Hugh off with Night that Lambert might stable my battle-horse, and went on to Camelot with René, almost carefree in the bright day. After half an hour we came to Ryford's stream. There, at the edge of the winter wood, a knight and his squire sat their horses astride the rutted way.

"What is this?" I muttered.

"Knight-errant, sir, full-armed," Rene said.

The knight wore a thick sandy mustache, but his blue shield showed no devices and at that distance I could not recognize him.

The squire trotted his horse up to us. "Sir knight," he called, "you must give ransom, ere you pass."

It was something out of the old tales, this seizure of a ford, and I could not believe him. "Who denies the road to Camelot?"

"You will know his name, sir, when you yield."

"King Arthur," I said, "hath decreed that we fight only in tourneys."

" 'Tis but a tourney of two, sir. Or shall I say you yield?"

"I do not yield," I growled. I wore my mail armor, had sword and helmet and shield. But I carried no lance, and Night would be chewing Lambert's oats by now.

"Then defend yourself, sir."

The other knight mounted his battle-horse and grasped a lance.

René set my helmet. "Is this some country fool," I muttered, "or a rogue hasty for money?"

"Money, sir," René murmured. "That squire eyed your cloak."

"Then arm yourself, and watch my back."

The knight raised his lance. I drew my heathen blade and kicked my palfrey into a trot down the muddy road. As we closed, my horse grew nervous and shied away at the last. The lance glanced off my shield. I stood in my stirrups and as we met my sword chopped his helmet. The blow rang through my gauntlets.

As I turned I saw his squire draw a blade. "René," I called, pointing, but his was already out.

The knight turned and charged again. The crease in his helmet was very clear. My palfrey tossed his head and skittered. Once more the lance point slipped off my shield. My backhanded chop nicked the rear of his helmet. He was no very able fighter, and I wondered that he risked such challenges.

On the third pass I saw he judged my palfrey's flinch. I took his shaft so it splintered. I swung down, thinking he would fight afoot, but he dropped the broken lance and drew his sword. It shone in the fading sunlight as he charged again. Grasping my own with both hands I leaned left but at the last dodged right. It was an old ruse, that put his sword on his far side, yet he did not expect it. As he turned, his shield moved and left him unguarded. I hit him full, my swing increased by the rush of his horse. My blade caught his eye-slot, and drove a crease deep in the face of his helmet. His arm sagged, his sword fell from his hand, and when the horse slowed he slumped from his saddle to the muddy road.

"Sir," cried his squire.

But I came first to the fallen man, and parried the squire's blow. René rode up behind and dragged him away by his cloak.

The knight struggled to his knees in the mud.

"Yield, sir," I cried.

He grasped for his sword, but it lay too far away. He stood, wavering. Blood streamed beneath his helmet.

"Yield," I cried again.

He drew his dagger. I saw his lunge. My sword dropped him in the mud again. I rolled him on his back and cut his helmet away with my own dagger. The stroke that unhorsed him had broken his nose and hacked his forehead. Blood covered his face. One eye might go blind. But I saw none of it.

For I saw the face of Giles, Giles of Pennard, Giles of the large and crooked teeth, of the sandy mustache clotted now with blood. Giles who had slain Emrys that Yule so long ago; who had come at me in Winchester's kitchen.

The blade in my hand began to quiver.

His eye stared blank as ever, as if some half-shrewd beast lurked within. He coughed, dribbling blood. "You are a quick fighter, sir. 'Tis no dishonor that I yield to you."

I could not speak. I stood and drew off my own helmet.

He squinted up at me. "I do not know you, sir,"

"Michel de Verdeur." I had to clear my throat.

"I might have heard that name."

"Do you still rape peasants, Giles of Pennard?" His good eye blinked at me. "I killed Orsain, in Anjou."

"God's mercy," he muttered, " 'tis the damn yokel." He tried to rise but I put a knee on his chest, and when he struggled, slapped him with my mailed fist. He did not feel it.

"Sir," said René, "do you know this knight?"

"I yield," said Giles, suddenly. "I yield. Anders," he called.

"Sir?" answered his squire.

"You hear me that I yield?"

"I do, sir."

Giles raised a hand to wipe his bloody eye. "The sworn honor of knighthood protects a man that yields. I yield horse, weapons, purse to you, what is your new name?" He smiled beneath his bloody mustache, certain of himself.

My hands begin to shake again. "I have killed Orsain," I muttered, "you are the second."

"But sir," said René, "your oath to Sir John."

"An oath?" Giles grew more certain. "An honorable knight."

I lay my sword aside, sat on his chest, and ignored his groan. "You forget, Giles of Pennard, that peasants have no honor. They are mindless as the beasts of the field. 'Tis no more to rape a peasant girl than pull the legs off a fly."

He rolled beneath me.

"Lie still, damn you." I showed my dagger to his good eye. "The king said nothing when you killed my sister."

"He gave a horse," he said, coughing, "he made you a Camelot servant." He rolled again. My dagger nicked his cheek and he flinched, despite his greater hurts.

"Sir," called his squire, "he yields, do not injure him."

"You weight grows heavy," said Giles.

I stood off him. With my dagger I cut away his sword belt.

He stared at me, one-eyed. "I have yielded."

"Much good may it do you, this yielding to a peasant."

He sat up slowly, watching me. "You are a knight now."

I bent to pick up my own blade. In one quick move he rolled to his knees, grasped his dagger, and stood and slashed at me. But already I lifted my sword with both hands. I dropped it on him, hard, at the angle between his neck and shoulder. His mail hood had fallen back and my Saracen blade chopped through it like some poor wool, and a hand's span into his chest. His blood erupted, spattering even my hands and face. He gave one high scream, the echo of Emrys that bitter Yule, and dropped twitching into the mud.

"Christ and God," cried his squire, his speech slurred by fright. "He had yielded. You truly are a peasant."

A brave lad. I waved my gouted sword at him. "A knight who attacked after he was beaten, a thief, my sister's murderer."

"He had yielded," he repeated.

I drew a breath, and my heart slowed again. "Are you a knight's son, esquire?"

He blinked at me. "Robert of Wayland."

"Anders of Wayland, how come you to these robberies?"

"My father set me as squire to Sir Giles. But the king banished him from Camelot, and his own father disowned him for the shame, and his manors were too poor . . ."

"What honor takes your father from this knight's robberies?"

Anders glanced away. "He does not know."

"Then for your father's honor I will not kill you, too."

A taste like rusted iron had come into my mouth, a taste like cumin and thistle mixed. I stripped Giles of armor and sword, of shield and horses and coin, and left his squire to bury the unshriven corpse. Three or four peasants stood watching at the wood's edge. I knew it well, that for them one knight killed by another was but the way of the world. The sky had gone dark again. A quick wind rattled the bare trees. Ryford village smelled of wet manure. The rain began as we passed the lane to the forest chapel, making quick circles in the roadside puddles.

Giles of Pennard. Orsain of Trundal. I might believe it was God's will that sent Orsain to Pouancé's tourney, that today had set Giles on my way to Camelot. God's will, mayhap. Save that all of them dead would not bring Lark to life again.

My father, covered by a straw cape, chopped wood in the houseyard. He glanced up at the sound of horse, the ax held uncertainly. I pushed back my mail hood. "I have killed the second, Father, beyond the village ford." The rain had nearly washed Giles' blood from my hands, as I made my cross.

Under his dripping hat he gave me his old squint.

I swung down and walked to him. "They are saying at Camelot my mother was Morgan le Fay." The rain dribbled down my face.

He did not smile. "Who can know these things, good sir?"

"Did you see Micah born?"

He coughed and spat. "The midwives always chase us out." He nodded at the door, where Harry my brother watched under the low eaves. "A bright summer's day. They brought out the baby, sir, beetle red and crying."

The two leather sacks I untied from Giles' palfrey made the sound of coin. He backed away. "Sir, I'm but a poor farmer."

I growled and pushed past him. Harry flinched away at the door, and I heard my mother's gasp inside as I bent under the eaves. At first I could not see for the gloom and smoke, but the smell had not changed and in an instant I had never left. A little blaze flickered at the hearth. Everything was small and dirty and old. Little Drool cowered away in a corner. A dry rattle came from the house bed, where old Cluck complained, "Who'sat?"

"Hush, Mother," whispered Ruth.

"Lark's second knight lies unshriven beyond Ryford." I walked to the fire and set the bags beside the old chipped firepot. "There's fifteen pounds, at least."

"Warren," my mother gasped, "who is this knight?"

My father squinted at me. "They'll say we stole it."

"Would you have the battle-horse instead?"

My mother's hand flew to her mouth. The others did not move, save their mouths fell open and their eyes went round. At last they knew me. After a moment my father nudged at one sack with his foot. "I'll bury it, sir."

"Micah?" said my mother. "Is it you?" She stepped toward me, her hand still at her mouth. "Dear Mary, you've grown so, you stand so straight. This fine cloak. This armor." The tips of her fingers rested on my iron mail briefly, fearfully. "The king sent you away. We thought you were dead."

"Ruth," said my father. "We'll bury that, too."

Tears flooded her eyes. "Are you truly my son?"

"Ruth," said my father, again. She took a step back, staring.

In the doorway René cleared his throat. It made them jump. "Sir, it's raining harder, and near dark." They were the first words he had spoke since Giles' death.

I pointed at the coin bags. "Take care with this. Do not be greedy. I'll have no tales of a new stable, a matched ox-pair, a slate roof."

"Oh, no sir," my father said. "A bit more seed, the rent of another strip . . ."

I followed René out into the cold wet evening. We mounted and pulled our cloaks about us, and rode on through the rain.

I had promised the old abbot a prayer each day, for each death by his heathen sword. I had known the cost would be high, but it truly vexed me that I must now think every day of Giles, and though the prayers were not difficult, still I must go, in the gloom of Vespers usually, and mutter for his blighted soul.

At Camelot I asked the stables of the horse Anduin. The king had given him away again, to some Irish noble. Nor was the servant Sarah in the keep, but had become a lay sister in the nunnery at Chewstoke. Anduin galloping an Irish moor seemed a perfect thing, but I remembered Sarah's arms about me and grieved for her, that she must be bound to the cloister.

Candlemas it snowed. The king did not come, and on the morrow Sir Kay sent me out to meet him, with gifts from Camelot. The storm had stopped when we set out with a castle groom, and leading three pack horses. Drifts lay against every hedge, and at midday the wind sprang up and soon the snow began again. It was dark when we came to Astolat, and the guard at the castle gate would not open it till I gave him a penny for each horse.

"King's not come, sir," he said, "but all the great knights sit in the Hall."

I shook the snow off my cloak in the narrow court, and pushed in through the door of the Hall. A harper sang beside the fire. Sir Gawain sat the high table speaking to the castellan. Sir Mordred was on Gawain's other side. And there sat Lancelot.

Lancelot. I stopped, almost ready to turn and leave. Yet I drew a breath and raised my head and strode in past the trestles. "Sir Clegis," I called, "I bring gifts for King Arthur, from Camelot."

"The king stops at Sarum Castle. But here." He made a smiling gesture. "Here is our great knight."

"Sir Lancelot," I bowed to him, "what an honor to greet you again, sir." He nodded absently. Age had begun to line his broad face, yet still that remarkable energy sprang from him. "Michel de Verdeur, knight of John of Craon. We met at Angers, sir."

"Angers?" His brown eyes flickered. "Craon? Then you are . . ."

"A year past, sir, I saved Sir John's life. He dubbed me for it, as reward."

"You are made a knight?" He stared at my hauberk and my sword. "Jesu, I swore to kill you for that." Astolat's Hall went deadly quiet. He stood and leaned at me, both fists on the board. "I swore your death," he rumbled, "and any knight that dubbed you."

Twenty-three

"But Sir Lancelot," Mordred said, "everyone has heard it, that his mother was Morgan le Fay."

"Morgan?" Lancelot gave a snort. "That shrew?"

Sir Clegis lifted a hand. "She is the king's sister."

"Jesu, am I to believe this is the king's nephew?" He glowered around. "Has anyone asked the lady?"

"Sir," I said, "I went, but I could not find her."

He swung back to me, thunderous angry, yet something of his manner made me certain he already knew. He thrust his dagger in its sheath. "Come," he growled.

The others sprang to their feet, hoping for a fight, but Lancelot shook his head. "We will speak apart."

I did not worry after that, for if Lancelot intended to kill me he would invite them all to watch. He led me silently across the dim snowy court to the church, pushed open the door and peered at me by the taper-light.

"I did not know you," he muttered.

"It has been two years, Sir Lancelot."

"A long two years." The memory seemed to weary him. "Did you think I would forget?"

"I knew you would not, sir. But think you of my part. Sir John dubbed me for saving his life. Ought I have refused, of fear? Must Sir John be always afraid?" He raised his brows, surprised. "I will fight you, sir, if I must."

"Yes," he rumbled, "I believe you would." His gaze seemed to measure me. "And you are proved 'gainst Edmund of Bramhill." He led me down to the chancel rail. Despite the taper-flames the narrow church seemed colder than outside. "I made an oath 'gainst battle." His words came reluctantly, as if he could not believe it himself. "For my knight's honor. For my immortal soul." He glanced at the crucifix. "For the Sangral."

"We all believed you would achieve it, sir."

"I almost saw it."

"Wonderful, sir."

"No. I was kept away, despite my vows. As if they meant nothing." He stared at the cross again. "I swore 'gainst courtly love as well, and then . . ." He shut his eyes a moment. "And then she came to London."

I remembered her at Amesbury. "She is very beautiful, sir."

"For my immortal soul." He shook his head. "I try to keep a distance. She believes my love fails, that I have another somewhere." He gave a bitter laugh. "Compostela, mayhap." He turned to stare at me. "Jesu, there is truly something of Morgan about you, that I prattle so."

"I could find only lights in her wood, sir."

"She can be elusive as the mage."

"But I saw him, sir. At Amesbury."

He pressed his lips tight. "Merlin would never take a woman's form. Thy jealousy is the same as Morgan's." The queen had told him everything.

"Good sir, how can a small knight be jealous of the queen?" He would not kill me, and the notion had made me almost giddy. "Praise God you honor your oaths, sir. I remember yet your protests at Angers, of knights without honor."

His mouth went hard. "Damn you, I too remember Angers, and your insolence. Take care, lest I kill you for it yet."

"But your honor, sir . . ." I could not help myself.

Anger shook from him like heat. He reached for his dagger. The church door creaked behind us and a single priest brought in a swirl of cold air.

"Good even, sirs," he called, " 'tis Compline."

"We would hear your Office, father," I called.

Lancelot stared at me, ere he put his blade away. We stood together at the rail, and knelt for the prayers. After, while he had made his cross I stayed on my knees, praying for Giles. He asked of it, and I told him of the fight, and though it was proper to kill a robber, still he muttered it might be my feud.

"I have his battle-horse at Camelot," I said, "that I would give to you."

"You buy my honor?" he growled, though his frown eased.

"I know well, sir, no earthly thing may buy that."

He stared at me, another grimace on his lips. "You are as insulting as the shrew your mother."

I kept my gaze steady. "But I strive to be like you, sir, loyal, generous, valiant." I stopped before I said *honorable.*

That year Easter would come early, and when the king arrived at Camelot it was already the Monday before Lent. The day after, Holy Tuesday, the evening meal was rich and savory, as it was the last before the long weeks of fast. And that night, as a fitting start to the barren season, another Sangral knight came back to Camelot.

Bors de Ganis stood in the Hall, his great blond frame haggard from travel. Like Gawain, he told a story of accident and chance. Yet his face shone with an uncanny light and his eyes gazed far away over our heads. At first we did not know why.

In a hoarse voice he described leaving his cousins Ector and Lionel, and then of finding Percival. He told of Percival's sister and her death, and their brief meeting with Lancelot. With Percival and Galahad he came to Castle Carbonek, that faced the western ocean. Its king was Pelles, a knight of high chivalry, and rumor held he bore a wound that, unlike Sir John's, never healed.

Bors said nothing of that, but told instead how the three of them sailed from Carbonek to the city of Sarras. Its king imprisoned them without reason. Yet soon, ill to dying himself, he set them free again. At his funeral the city acclaimed Galahad their king, and on the day following his coronation, that was the Sabbath . . .

Bors paused and shut his eyes. On the day following, as the three of them knelt at Mass, the Sangral appeared.

A noise rose among us in Camelot's Hall, half groan and half sigh. Bors gazed around, tears streaming his cheeks.

"The Sangral," he said, "clear and blinding."

Galahad, his life fulfilled by the vision, gave up his soul that same day. Percival entered a monastery and died soon after. Bors buried them, side by side, and came sadly back to Camelot.

"God preserved me to tell the story." He wiped his eyes. "The Sangral amazed and delighted me, yet I cling to this hard, unyielding, sinful world. I am a knight, and I will die a knight."

Camelot was amazed. None could understand how modest Bors, and not famous Lancelot nor sturdy Gawain, had come to stand among us, the Sangral still bright in his eyes.

King Arthur rose to his feet. "Oh, God Our Lord," he cried, "praise

Thee that Bors has come back to us. But, oh God, will Thy highest call-ing ever demand the lives of our finest knights?" Bors scrubbed his cheeks with a fist, and the king turned to him. "Good Sir Bors, every knight here honors you of this holy vision, and praises God the Sangral was achieved. For here together are the knights who gained it, yourself clearly, Lancelot distantly."

But Lancelot shook his head, frowning. And Gawain sat nearby, his head buried in his hands.

"Tomorrow begins Lent," said the king, "our memorial of Christ's trial in the desert. For many the Sangral quest hath seemed Camelot's own desert season. Yet we know He will rise again." A smile lit his face. "And therefore, to honor every questing knight, I call a royal tourney."

All around us the Hall rang with loud approval. Every knight was eager to put behind both the Sangral and its unnatural ending. The king had to raise his voice. "Forty days and ten. The second week after Easter I call you all to Winchester."

Balen grinned and punched my shoulder. "Fifty days is too long to wait, till I unhorse you with my first lance."

"You'll wish it were a hundred, when they carry you off."

"I only regret you are so poor, Michel, that I must gain fame instead of wealth."

Patrise, that I had sparred with at Amesbury, gave him a grim smile. "If you fight this knight, sir, you had best practice all of Lent."

Balen made a rude noise at us both.

"But what of Lancelot?" asked another beside us.

Balen shrugged. "I fear the queen doth over-fatigue him."

"He speaks with many ladies, now," said Patrise, "and the queen frowns of it. Mayhap he keeps his oath of courtly love."

"Ah, Patrise," said Balen, more sad than ironic. " 'Tis plain he hath forgot oath, Sangral, everything." He shook his head. "And who would not, in the light of her eye?"

A letter had finally come from Craon to Denham, and William helped me read the Latin script. Sir John was dismayed that Arthur refused the manors, although I thought it did not surprise him. If the king would not respond to arguments of feudal ownership, I must offer him coin, promise ten pounds for each manor, for each of the next three years. One hundred pounds and more, and I wondered were they truly worth it.

I had paid much of my way with Lambert's ransom, and there were forty pounds, nearly, left in Craon's chest. "Tomorrow," I said to Wil-liam, "we will speak to the king again."

But at Camelot, listening to his cleric read John's letter, Arthur set his mouth. "It is not a matter of coin, Sir Michel. I gave them to Glastonbury, they are my father's prayers."

"Sire, they were a gift to Craon that you took without counsel or compensation."

The king put his hands together, as lords do when they take liegemen. "Sir Olivier is my vassal. He gave them freely."

"Could you not take others, sire? British lands?"

"God save us!" he barked. "They were British ere my father's regents gave them away."

For the first time my petition had angered him. I heard in his voice something like a door closing. "My lord," I said, bowing, "thank you for hearing my petition. Craon will not be pleased of your reply."

He did not answer but looked past me, at another knight come to plead some other matter. I bowed and went out to the upper bailey, where a blustering wind troubled the stand of apple trees. "If we plead him every week," I said to William, "he will not budge." The priest nodded unhappily. There seemed nothing for it but go fruitless back to Craon, back to Adele's courtly amusements and John's jealousy, to Matilde's love and Philip's mockery. And leave my lady of Amesbury, that might be but the wizard's vagary.

Knights crowded the lower court before the stables, noisy after a morning of tourney practice. Bors and his cousins were there, and the Orkney princes. Gawain called out, "Sir Michel, do you not practice for the tourney?"

"Alas, sir, the king will not hear my petition. I must return to Anjou, soon as I may."

"But I would meet you, sir, on the field at Winchester."

I stared, amazed that Guenever had him challenge me now. "Sir Gawain, the queen . . ."

"The queen?" He glanced about. "My lady has nothing to do with it. 'Tis my own notion, to test each young knight that comes to Camelot. Yet, sir, if you do not meet me, all Britain will wonder at your bravery. And Anjou as well."

He stood there among his brothers, smiling, certain I could not refuse. And it would be high disservice to Craon, I told myself, to leave with his challenge against me.

I bowed to him. "At Winchester, then, Sir Gawain."

He laughed. "At Winchester, Sir Michel."

After that, the weeks of Lent passed very quick. Long practice of jousting and swordwork, in warm days or damp, soon restored my confidence and my Norman eye. In truth I enjoyed nothing more than the clash of blades, the thunder of hooves, the meeting of lances. Even the aches and bruises of combat. I hoped for victories before I met Gawain, for it was clear he would best me easily enough. Still, winning more than I lost, I might return to Craon with honor.

We paused in the work for Holy Week, but Easter Monday Patrise and I galloped our battle-horses along the river. Coming back we met the Orkney princes riding all in a group, and trotted together along the grassy edge of the moat.

"King Arthur will be Castleside," Sir Gawain was saying, "and Orkney must fight beside him."

"Who are the marshals to pair us?" I asked.

He burst out laughing. "Praise God, it will be none of your polite Frankish jousts, but a grand melee, Terce to Nones." He pointed at us. "You two, Anjou and Ireland, you must ride Outside."

"I would not fight 'gainst the king, Sir Gawain."

He grinned at me. "But, sir, I would fight against you."

"And will Sir Lancelot tourney?" I asked. The knight had told us his holy vow stood only against true war, and had practiced hard as any. But now he had been ill a week with tertian fever.

Gawain frowned. "No affliction will keep him from the field."

"But I do wonder," said Gareth, his voice mild as his face, "if the Sangral makes Bors a better knight than Lancelot?"

Gawain barked a laugh. "What has the state of a knight's soul to do with his fighting strength?"

We turned under the barbican. Agravain, who had scowled at Gawain's humor, suddenly cried out, "God's Name, must we be so polite?" His voice rattled on the arched gate. "Everyone knows Lancelot stays to dally with the queen."

"Hist, brother," Gaheris murmured.

"We are all Arthur's knights," Agravain growled. "The king's sworn vassals. And more, he is our uncle, our kinsman. Ought we not protect him within his castle, as we would outside?"

The hooves of our mounts drummed on the wooden bridge. Gawain pushed his fingers through his gray hair. "I would not abuse my queen, brother, nor attack Camelot's best knight."

"Best knight?" cried Agravain. In the shadow of Camelot's gate his scar shone pale on his flushed cheek. "The best knights, brother, were they that achieved the Sangral. Percival. Galahad. And Bors come back to us. Bors de Ganis, brother." His voice echoed on the stone. "Not famous Lancelot du Lac, that glimpsed it but afar. That now, as if holy oaths had no importance, breaks his own against love with the queen, and every day."

"God's blood, brother." Gawain scowled and thrust a finger at me. "Keep this to yourself."

"Sir Gawain," I said, "the whole world knows. My lord Craon asked of it, in Anjou."

"Ah, brother," said Agravain, "you swore it was secret." He gave a sharp laugh. "The whole world."

"Christ," Gawain said, "in Anjou."

"In Jerusalem," growled Agravain. He drew up hard at the stables, and swung down so abrupt that his horse started and reared. "Damn him," he cried, "this pious knight. 'Tis time the king was told."

Gawain seized his arm and shook him. "Damn you, be quiet." And Gareth glanced at the grooms.

Agravain stepped back to stare at him. "Is this knighthood's honor? Silence? Bowing and scraping?" He shook off Gawain's grip and stalked away. "Christ save me from it."

Knighthood's honor. So Lancelot himself had argued, at Angers. Why was it so elusive, so difficult?

"Sir Agravain loves her," I murmured.

Gawain nodded. "The fool is a menace, of that love."

"We all love her," said Gareth, "but we love the king, too."

"And Lancelot," said Gaheris.

Mordred had said nothing, but at last he roused himself. "Of course we love them. But Agravain is right, Orkney must stand for the king."

Adultery against the king was treason, and the penalty for treason was death. John had asked who would take up the first stone. The wizard had said, *be Arthur's man.* But that day I did not want to stand against the queen. Nor even Lancelot.

We rode out for Winchester in the king's progress, a hundred knights astride our palfreys, and under flying banners. King Arthur traveled with little haste, and he stopped several days in Astolat before going on. It seemed Agravain had been mistaken of Lancelot, for Lady Guenever joined us at the castle there, on the second day, though the high knight was nowhere to be seen.

The tourney was set for the river meadows below Winchester, a mile and more of new grass where willows showed their red buds, daffodils made broad yellow swaths upon the green, and skylarks sang over the hills. Loges of new wood rose at the center of the field, for king and older knights, and the queen. Courtly pavilions stood in bright ranks beside the city walls, where Sir Gawain added his own, white and red, and with his usual chivalry offered me a corner. It was all very grand, and much different from the farms and rough forests of Pouancé, and almost I forgot to worry what I might lose.

The tourney day dawned with the thick smells of trampled grass and anxious horses in the air. We were armed and shrived when Gawain came scowling back from the king. "Sir Michel de Verdeur," he grumbled, "you are Outside."

"Of course," I said, "and you are Castleside."

He shook his head. "He says I must not fight. That I must be a marshal, a watcher of other knights' battles, a reckoner of other men's victories, damn me." He spat in frustration. "But there are others anxious to cross lances with you."

Agravain, beside him, peered at my shield. "Green oak, white dragon. Black bird." He nodded, grim. "I'll remember it."

"Is there news of Lancelot?" I said. Gawain shook his head.

The knights of Outside were gathered at the lower end of the field where Patrise took me to our leader, Northgalis. He shook my hand bleakly. "Pray God you are a fighter, Sir Michel," he muttered. "We are but fifty to their fourscore. The king has given us the sun at our back, but still it will be a long day."

A herald bound a green band on my right arm. Night pranced and snorted under me, and René stood nearby, grinning with nerves. "Stay close," I said, "if I break a lance, bring a new one quick. If I make a capture, hold him till I have his name and promise. If I fall, pull me out. I will avoid high knights long as I can." Gawain had challenged me, but honor did not require I meet his brothers, and I could battle for ransoms only.

The horns of the marshals echoed in the warming air. We swung up and went off at a canter, several lines spread wide across the grass. I found a place a little to the rear. The first lines broke into a gallop and met with a thunderous crash. Knights shouted, lances broke, horses cried and milled about. The second line passed through almost unharmed. One bore down on me. I set my shield and lance and nudged Night into a run. Seeing his lance would waver, I drove mine straight at him. Our meeting, that half stunned me, broke his saddle-girths. He slid over the rump of his horse and fell on his back, his feet still in the stirrups.

I turned Night and thrust my lance point in the grass beside his neck. He made a gesture of surrender as René ran up and bent over him. "William of Rhoad," he cried, barely audible over the clatter. Our collision had not injured him, but in falling his shield had bent his left arm under him. He stood gripping it in pain, till his squire came to help him away.

"Good ride, sir," René cried, "but beware."

Camelot knights rode in hunting circles, and a second drove at me. I had no time to set myself but he was hasty himself. His point barely nicked my shield. I pushed onward, my eye on another that dodged and hit me with his sword. I circled round and after several encounters had unseated a second.

Two, I thought, as I caught my breath. All over the field green-ribboned knights were being driven into little clusters, two or three against a half dozen of Camelot. A tall knight drove at me. His heraldry, red and white, was not Orkney's. His horse broke into a gallop. His point wavered but not from lack of skill. We met with such a crash it felt my shield had broke, and as he drove me out of my saddle I saw him falling, too.

I hung a moment in midair, and when I fell I could not move. Not since practice at Craon had I been so cleanly unhorsed. I struggled up, dazed. He was up as quick. I caught his sword on my shield as I drew my own. I could see his attack well enough, but my head throbbed and I moved slow as a dream. We fought for long minutes. I lunged and creased the top of his helmet. It stunned him, yet I left myself open. His answer caught me, clean. I chopped at him. He hit me a huge blow that felled me, and before I could move he had a foot on my chest and his sword at my throat.

"I yield," I cried, and let go my blade. He took my hand to help me up. "Michel de Verdeur," I said. My ears rang inside my helmet.

"I know," he answered. "Bors de Ganis."

"Sir Bors. Alas, I had prayed God to avoid you."

He barked a laugh, and turned to mount again. Certainly it was a high honor to be beaten by the Sangral knight.

While we fought, Castle knights had driven the Outside far down the field. Riders battled now with drawn swords, a harder and a noisier business. A dozen surrounded our leader at the center of the crashing fight. I rode in and battered helmets, and collected blows myself, yet though I injured several they all managed to dodge away. Suddenly two new knights rode on the field. They both carried the white shields of novices, yet they drove like the wind straight through the melee, battering Castle knights with their swords. Having served notice, they returned with lances.

The larger of them, that wore a red sleeve on his helmet, unhorsed five knights in quick succession before his shaft broke. Both sides paused and drew apart, amazed at his display, and when he returned with a new lance all Outside rode cheering to join him. Weary and outnumbered, still we took such hope from the knight's energy that we drove Castle steadily up the field.

I swung my heathen sword two-handed, Night moved under me without fear or hesitation, and there on the field of Winchester, dust and sweat and horse-stink in my nose, my ears deafened by the roar of battle, my face bruised, my shoulders aching, there at last the brutal and wonderful delight of war broke in on me. Nothing could compare to battle, especially a winning battle, led by such a magnificent knight. Oft I paused to watch him, how he held the lance, how he ran his battle-horse, how he worked with shield and blade. Every charge was exact. Every blow fell as it should, so powerful only the strongest could withstand it. If I might delight in my own ability, I knew I would never battle so well.

Yet in the middle of it, somehow Bors found the knight isolated, and while Lionel and Ector distracted him, attacked and drove his lance into the other's side. It unhorsed him, and though it was a grievous wound, the brave knight would not yield. He leapt up on his mount again, defeated Bors in turn and fought on.

By Nones I had taken four more ransoms and Castleside was driven against the city walls. The marshals rode among us, blowing the horn of lodging. We drew apart and sheathed our blades. All that could, rode to the unknown knight and crowded round him, praised his chivalry and asked his name. He was but a knight-errant, he said, come late to tourney. Blood soaked his tattered surcoat, and the pain of the wound wracked his voice. He bowed at our admiration, begged our leave, and cantered away with his companion.

"I have never seen the like," said a knight beside me. "Surely he was Lancelot." He wore Orkney colors and when he pulled off his helmet, soft-faced Gareth grinned at me. "Sir Michel, 'tis a pity you fought Outside, you had no chance to yield to that great knight."

King Arthur declared the unknown knight champion of the tourney. He had beaten, the heralds reckoned, thirty knights. "But where is he? A knight ought reveal his name, and claim his ransoms."

"He would not stay," said one knight.

"He was sore wounded," said another.

The king stared about. "And no one knows where he lodges?"

"My lord," cried Gawain, "I have taken my ease all this day. I will ride out and discover him."

Twenty-four

Knights with bruised and dusty faces laughed among the bright pavilions, and staggered not of drink but long fatigue. I sat exhausted in Gawain's tent, while René pulled off my hauberk and chausses, salved my wounds and brought me cooled ale. My sword hand shook with fatigue, my shield arm was bruised numb, I ached from hours in the saddle. But, praise God, I had won six ransoms.

The king had set the prizes at hauberks and blades or twenty pounds coin, and soon Bors pushed his tall blond head into the tent, come to collect his winning. He took up my sword and stared at it a long moment, and then swung it in the air. "A wonderful blade, Sir Michel, that I would be glad to have. But I know better than take an abbot's boon." He laughed at my relief. "I'll have the coin, instead."

I shook his hand and thanked him. We walked out together to collect our other ransoms, and though there was much gaiety and bragging tales, there were those who could not afford the losses, who were as broken in purse as in body. I remembered Cyril at Saint-Georges. And then Matilde, and for a moment all this seemed aside from Sir John's petition, and my own dark oath. Yet then another brimming cup was pressed into my hand, the ale flared in my head, and I laughed among Camelot's knights.

Of my winnings I sent gifts to my Outside leader, and to Gawain and the king. Late in the day we rode in a crowd up to the castle. I was stiff and full of aches. The steaming tub in the knights' chamber did little good, nor could I could hide my limp crossing the graveled court.

In the old Hall, knights' shields hung in a glittering rank round all the walls. My own, scratched and battered as the rest, hung near the king's dais. Sir Grummore, Winchester's castellan, came and led me through the company, past trestles where knights called out praise or laughing threats, all the way to the champions' table. I lifted my head as I walked, and smiled with huge pleasure, and every weariness fled away.

I sat between Bors and Gaheris, and with a dozen others who had done as well. A herald stood and called out our exploits, to the applause of the whole Hall. Fatigue and wine made them all noisy, but the admiration in their eyes was very clear. Even Arthur, on his dais with high lords and ladies, drank our health and praised our valor. I proved myself against Edmund, and was rumored kin of Morgan, yet that day I had triumphed, at last, in the one thing that truly mattered, combat in the field.

Servers brought our courses. Minstrels sang of tournaments and courtly love. We chattered how we had won this fight or that, beaten some knight, lost to another. My own mind grew soft under the wine, and I told how I might have defeated even Bors, had I been quicker. He rumbled with laughter and offered to meet me, at any tourney I chose.

Gawain strode into the Hall then, and all our chatter died away. He had found no sign of the champion, and we glanced at each other, sobered, for we all believed the knight had been Lancelot.

"No one else ever fought like that," Gaheris said. "Pray Christ he hath a good leech."

"God knows I rue that stroke," said Bors, "and to my uncle."

"It was chivalry, Sir Bors." I peered through the fumes of wine at his broad face. Alone in all the world his brown eyes had looked on the Sangral. Blinding white. God's boon, they said, yet how many had died of it.

Bors glanced toward the royal dais. "How good it is," he murmured, "to see the king and queen together."

"Sir Bors," I said, "do you stand always by Sir Lancelot?"

"He is my kinsman." But he knew I meant another thing.

"The king's nephews, though unhappy, stand by the king."

"You two may mutter all the night," a knight cried down the board, "but pray God pass the cup. Tourneys make me thirsty."

We laughed at him, as if we might forget it all. We drank and laughed again. When the meal was done knights crowded round to shake our hands and praise our deeds again. We were the champions at Winchester.

Balen leaned against me, muttering thickly, "Can no one remember the brat of Greenfarm?"

And there in that royal Hall I smelled dung, again, and smoke and mud and rotting thatch. Knights reached to touch my hand, yet I saw instead the dim house, the rainy yard, the long dusty roads, the stubble of reaped fields. The king sat me in royal castles, among the noble knights that were his champions, yet I was but a peasant lad in disguise, like busker in a mystery play, strutting the aisles of some Yuletide cathedral.

I turned on Balen. "I'll have your damn tongue," I growled.

" 'Tis no use to me," he mumbled, and his grin disarmed me.

At the door Edmund of Bramhill seized my hand. "How well you fought today, Sir Michel." A broad smile softened his dour mien, and beside him Sibyl's round face glowed with pleasure.

"I must weep and argue," she said, "to keep him from the field."

I bent over her hand. "And how are your children, lady?"

"Very well." Her smile revealed nothing. "You must visit us again, good knight. Bramhill is always open to you."

She walked between us, holding both our arms, as we crossed the court. Torches flickered on the broad stair, and tapers lit the king's chamber. Over the chatter of the throng the songs of minstrels rang from the music gallery. Edmund went off, but Sibyl made me sit with her in a window brasure, touched my hand as she spoke, and was rude when other ladies came to me with compliments.

"These women," she said, "they know we are old friends." Do they? I wondered. "But you wore no lady's color, Sir Michel."

"I was too modest to ask for yours, lady." It made her smile. "Sir Edmund seems much recovered." To ask of Briant would spoil my mood. "I could not find Castle Chariot."

"You will not see the lady till she is ready." She spoke so certain that for a moment I imagined she knew Morgan's mind, that it were all true.

Edmund soon came to lead her away, despite her complaints. She waved from the door, but three ladies already circled me, their eyes bright, their lips smiling, each pushing in front to pledge their admiration. How pleasant it all was, being a champion. The widow Agraine appeared, bent by age and gone very gray. We had hardly spoke since that Camelot Yule, so long ago.

I stood and bowed. "My lady."

She waved a wrinkled hand at the others. "Go away." She eyed me as she sat. "My lady Bramhill was very attentive."

"And very attractive." I could not help my smile. "And so are those that you chased away."

"Ladies flit round famous knights," she muttered, "like moths at a taper-flame. And burn their wings as easily."

"Still, 'tis very pleasant for the flame."

She nodded sourly. "The queen would speak to you."

"The queen?" I glanced at the crowd around Guenever.

"And here is someone you must meet."

Even as Agraine spoke, before I saw her, I knew who she was. The breath stopped in my throat. My lady of Amesbury walked toward us, tall and slender and clad in deep blue, her pale eyes smiling under their lids, her brown hair in a mesh of gold.

"Lady Corbin," said Agraine, "daughter to King Pecchere."

"My lady." I stood clumsily and gripped her hand, half certain she was a phantom. "Lady, I am Michel de Verdeur."

She smiled. "I remember you, sir. I am Naime."

"And beautiful enough to have enchanted Merlin."

She laughed as she drew her hand away, and my heart fluttered. "Oh, sir, that was Nimue. A distant cousin. But, sir, how well you fought today."

"Would I had worn your color, lady."

She flushed and dropped her gaze. "I cannot promise that, Sir Michel." She turned quickly away.

"A pretty girl," said the lady Agraine.

"Very pretty, my lady." I drew a breath, my head befogged. The daughter of even a small king stood as distant as the sky.

Agraine clutched my arm to help her stand. "The queen would speak with you." Her old eyes watched me. "Young Michel, an aged lady's advice. Keep to your own bed tonight."

"My lady," I said, startled, "I thank you for it."

Agraine was gone, and another lady smiled beside me, marveling how well I fought. "I am Michel de Verdeur."

"Oh, I know, sir." Her dark eyes sparkled in the taperlight. "I am Anne, lady of Rhoad." Her full lips smiled in a comely face, and the drape of her robe revealed a fine bosom. Despite Agraine's advice, my fingers ached for the plucking. Were this Camelot, I would know exactly which door to knock.

"I met Sir William on the tourney field, lady." I looked around. "But I do not see him here. How is his arm?"

"Broken," she said, smiling.

"I am sorry for that."

She took my own arm close. "How hard he practiced, and then to meet you first. He sleeps with the castle leeches." Her eyes glittered at me, her mouth opened again.

"Alas, my lady Rhoad, the queen sends for me."

"The queen." Her brow creased, and she nearly flung my arm away.

"Then you must hurry to her." Alas, I thought, now she will hate me and poor William both.

At the circle around Guenever I watched her a moment in the taperlight, seeing how her beauty had gone distant and cool. It was Naime's face I cherished now.

"Sir Michael." The queen gestured me closer. "Everyone speaks of you tonight."

I bowed. "Sudden fame, madam, doth vanish as suddenly."

"Not for those who deserve it, good sir."

I ought have delighted in her praise, yet I said, "The wounded champion overshadows us all."

She gnawed her lip, worried and angered both, and then shook her head to put the thought away. "There is a lady I would have you meet." She nodded, and I turned to see that Naime stood next to Agravain, laughing at something he said. "Her father had sent her to us, that day at Amesbury. And though she went to him for Lent, now she is one of my own ladies." The queen looked at me intently. "She is not who you imagined."

"She is not, my lady." I bowed, and would turn away.

Guenever lifted a hand to stop my going. "The wounded champion. You fought beside him, sir. Did you know him?"

"We all believe he was Sir Lancelot."

"Yet he wore a lady's color." She stared away. "Red."

Over the surrounding chatter Naime laughed again with Agravain. Jesu, Agravain, what did she with that angry jealous fish, so besotted of the queen? I had known it was she, before I saw her. The thought sent a chill up my back.

"Red," Guenever repeated.

The gabble of empty voices rang in my ears. I remembered, as I bowed to her, I had never seen the queen wear red. "My lady," I said.

"Sir Michel," she murmured absently.

The lady Rhoad still watched me. There were others who might not thrust me from their bed. But Naime's laugh pierced my heart, and I strode through their chatter, past their eyes, down to the castle bailey. The cool night smelled of spring, the black sky wore its twinkling stars. Winchester meant the wizard and his beery breath, Gawain and the green knight. But now it was Naime, who leaned as close to Agravain as Lady Rhoad to me, so close he must smile with pleasure despite his infatuation of the queen.

Jealousy hewed my heart, as if it were a woodsman's ax.

* * *

Winchester's audience chamber was not so broad as Camelot's, nor lit by ample windows, yet up its worn steps bright tapestries hung the walls, and new rushes strewed the floor for Arthur's morning court, as the herald announced me.

"My lord, once more I come before you, pleading the manors of Blackmoor and Craon's right to them." I spoke again of Sir John's offer, the coin and the rent.

The king smiled, even as he shook his head. "Sir Michel, I will never give them. Though I praise your constancy."

"Then, sire, and my lords," and I bowed at Gawain and his brothers, at Bors and Ector and the others, "my envoy fails. I have no other task here, I ask your leave to return to Craon."

But Arthur raised his face and smiled around at his knights. "Good lords, I am much loath to lose such a champion."

"And," cried Gawain, "I would meet him yet, in tournament."

"Craon," I said, "did not send me for the pleasure of the joust. Thrice have I pled his manors, and am thrice rebuffed."

Arthur gazed at me, undisturbed by my rudeness. "Who might believe a young knight's prowess, if he fight but one tourney?"

"Tanebourc," Gawain said. "Northgalis calls us to his castle, Whitsun week."

"All Camelot will fight together, as Outside." Arthur smiled again, and it was very clear he wished me to stay. " 'Tis but six weeks, Sir Michel. Cannot Craon spare you that?"

"Sire," I murmured, bowing, "if it be your wish."

"Good. Now, sir, you must attend me when we hawk today."

But when he rode out after midday so many wanted his ear, and others came to praise my tourney, that not till we came back to the castle, gamebags full and the falcons calmed, did the king turn in his saddle and call me to him.

"Sir Michel," he said, walking his palfrey. "I see how you enjoy the stoop of hawks. You ought have birds of your own."

"My lord, so I will. When I have lands."

He frowned, as if he could not imagine a knight without lands. "How well it pleases me, to see such tourney valor in a young knight." He waved absently to a crowd of men cheering at the gate. "Only a brave knight would seek my sister in her forest. Even I have been lost there."

"It was more foolish than brave, sire."

He nodded. We rode in under the castle gate. He swung off his horse in the gravel court, and though I could hardly believe it, led me through the crowd and up the turning stairs to his own apartments. New panels of unpainted wood lined the walls, and a glass window stood open to the evening air.

A page waited with a cup. Arthur took a swallow and handed it to me. "You will stay til Tanebourc, then."

"I will, my lord." The wine did not confuse me more than this sudden intimacy.

He stared out the window. His knights' escort had followed us, and they gathered quietly outside the open door. "I thank God for tourneys, when we may be true knights again and not questers of the Sangral." He shook his head. "What a pity Lancelot was so injured. My lady has become very doleful." He spoke as if I were not there. "And I worry of him, that he cannot be found." He waved his hand at a chair, but I would not sit before him and he paced about. "To think he did not see the Sangral. Since his return I feel a distance between us. He came disguised to the melee. Now, wounded, he keeps himself away."

Clearly Lancelot was become the life of both queen and king. "Mayhap," I said, "he would not show himself, crippled."

Arthur turned and studied my face. "A wise young man. Was it that Merlin saw?" He gave a quick sad smile. "Praise God I sent you away, Sir Michel, that you might return such a fine fighter."

"I came to Britain, my lord, for the manors of Craon."

"Nor do I forget it." He lifted his head suddenly. "But I pray you call Gawain, I have an new idea where Lancelot might be."

I went down the turning stair feeling almost blessed. A new young knight, interviewed by the king in his own apartments. And at Winchester knights and ladies watched me, and sought my smile, as if it might reflect to them some of the king's high pleasure.

At Greenfarm my family stood in the muddy yard, smiling happy in the rare sunshine, for the skies had been seldom clear that spring. They shrank away when I rode in, before my father recognized my heraldry. I had sold my tourney ransoms to Aaron at Winchester, and Harry nearly dropped the bags René handed him, surprised by their weight.

"Which of them you kill this time, sir?" Warren asked.

"Nobody. 'Tis part of my winnings at Winchester."

"Part," he muttered. "And you wear a new cloak, and ride a fine palfrey." He frowned at the bright new robes René wore. "We have more than we need here, good sir."

"Camelot believes I was fostered here." I saw my mother put a hand to her mouth. "I give you twenty pounds for it." They gaped, unbelieving. Twenty pounds had been one knight's ransom at Winchester, but at Greenfarm it was ten years' rent. "I give it openly, in case the lady has forgotten."

"Oh, sir, so she has." My father grinned, his wits returned.

"Buy what you want." I waved a hand. "Iron pots, a yoke of oxen, tenancies, if they're to be had."

"Truly, sir?" His voice hushed. "Old man Benton died in the winter, he had no sons, it'll near double what we have."

"Twenty pounds," I said.

"Aye, sir," He raised the bag as if it was weightless, though behind him the rest of the family leaned together.

On his way east to Winchester the king had stopped at Astolat. Coming back to Camelot he followed a different route, yet Sir Gawain and his brothers, still searching for Lancelot, passed once more through the little city. Rumors led them to an old banneret's house, where they discovered Lancelot had been a guest before the tourney. He had left his own shield and heraldry there, and gone on to Winchester wearing novice's white. The red sleeve was from the banneret's young daughter, though not even she knew where Lancelot was, or even if he lived.

Orkney rode into Camelot breathless with the story. It made the king distraught, and sent Guenever to her bedchamber. And the castle knights, uneasy at these strange events, lost themselves in tourney practice, every day that rainy spring.

I practiced with them, at the king's wish. I wrote again to Sir John, of the tourneys I could not refuse. Drawing my name at the end, I saw Matilde's saddened face, and with it how much I had forgot Craon. I thought now only of Naime; I saw her every day and though she always answered my greeting, she never smiled. Seeking anything to change her glance, I thought to ride to Bramhill. I would ask Sibyl for her color. Mayhap it would make Naime jealous.

It was Whitmonday that I set out, the day before Arthur's court rode for Tanebourc. We left under a steady rain, but the weather soon eased, and when we reached Edmund's village a thin sunlight lit the chestnut blossoms, and a rainbow arched the brightening sky.

I called out to a farmwife in her muddy yard. "Good woman, is Sir Edmund at home?"

She shaded her eyes. "Nay, sir, he's to Frome three days."

"Three days." Something darkened in my mind. "Damn," I muttered, "with Edmund away Briant might creep in again."

"I'll take his horse," said René.

"I'll take his stones," said Hugh. " 'Tis an old family custom."

We rode in, quiet as we could through the open gate. No porter greeted us, though two saddled horses waited at the stables, and a squire with them. My mind had gone numb. I swung down and drew my sword and strode to the manor door. A cry rang out behind me as Hugh and René attacked the squire. I took the stairs two at a time. At the top a servant darted away and her ladies turned from the window, gone pale at my naked blade.

"Good sir," cried the lady Mary, "in this house, oh sir . . ."

Briant had heard his squire's alarm. He stepped through the curtained doorway just as I reached it. I swung at him two-handed. His hauberk saved him, though my blow drove him backward into Edmund's chamber. Sibyl screamed inside. I stabbed at the curtain as I pushed through. His parry smacked my armored legs. The curtain tangled my blade as I swung again, and it was the flat that smacked his head. He dropped to the floor, his scalp split and bleeding.

On the bed Sibyl hugged a furred robe and looked ready to scream again. "Oh, my God, it's you." Her hair blew bright all around her. "Is Edmund here? Oh God, see him, he's bleeding."

Blood streamed down his handsome face. Briant. The third of them. I pushed the point of my heathen sword at his throat.

"Stop," cried Sibyl.

"I have sworn it, lady."

"Stop." She clambered off the bed. "Edmund let him go, once."

"This is not for Edmund," I said. My sword moved.

"Stop." She gripped my arm. "Sweet Mother, you took him by surprise, he's but half-armed, oh God, please Micah, you cannot kill him."

She clung to me, tears streaming down her face. I lowered my blade. She had said, *Micah.*

"Oh, praise God, thank you. Here," she cried to the servants, "move him, be careful."

They took him out to the solar. The ladies washed and bound his head, though blood soon oozed brightly through the cloth. I stood and watched, my sword dragging in my hand.

Sibyl was smiling again. "Thank you, Sir Michel."

But she had said, Micah. Micah, who had loved her. Micah, who was sworn to kill this man. Micah, who was Raven.

Plain as yesterday, Lark died. And Orsain and Giles, and now Briant, here. I put a hand to my chest, but I had long since lost that bloody scrap. I had this heathen blade instead. I elbowed a servant aside, thrust my sword at him, the point scored his cheek.

"Oh God, Michel," screamed Sibyl.

But the blade would move no farther. I could not believe it. I must not let him go, lest I never find him again. I must not let him wake, lest he yield. I must stab him, thrust my point through his neck to the wall behind, watch the blood erupt.

Instead I stared at him, and Sibyl gripped my sword hand with both her own, that were slippery with fear. Her tangled hair hid her face but her voice came very strong. "If you slay him, Michel, you must slay me too."

"This man killed my sister." I drew a breath. "You are wife to Sir Edmund. You are mother to my child." She dropped her head. "How is it you are so loyal to him?"

In my roaring ears her voice came very clear. "I love him."

Once I had loved her.

He grunted in pain. One leg twitched. I had heard him grunting over Rebecca before she died. Surely he had grunted over Sibyl but an hour before.

Oh, God, just put the point through his neck.

I could not believe it. I stepped away. Oh, sweet Rebecca, forgive me. I thrust my blade into its sheath, pushed through the gaping servants, half stumbled down the stair.

In the court René stood over Briant's wounded squire. "Did you kill him, sir?"

"I did not."

"Oh, Christ, sir," said Hugh, "why not?"

I pointed at Briant's horses. "Bring those with us."

Twenty-five

Tanebourc Castle seemed as old as the steep rock from which it grew. It was small as Astolat, without room for all our tourney knights, and once again Gawain offered me a place in his pavilion. He gave a mock frown that the king called us all to his Outside, that he and I could not meet on the field. At least there would be worthy foes, as Bors and his cousins joined our host, Northgalis.

Again there were no jousts, but a daylong melee over a rough commons and a dozen manors, uneven land that made us fight in smaller groups. Ransoms were set at full equipment, horse, armor, and blades. For the higher prizes every knight was less willing to yield, and gave and received more grievous wounds. That day I gained five ransoms. That night I sat again at the champions trestle. In truth I had fought all the tourney in a blind fury. I had deserted Lark at Bramhill. The sword I was given had gone unused. It did not matter were it for some memory of love or the honor of chivalry, I had failed my oath. I raged at myself of it, and through the whole day each knight I faced had been Briant that I must destroy, and then the next. Only that evening, as the second cup came round, did I remember that Patrise had defeated me till Gawain drove him away, that I had chased a crowd from Agravain, that Bors and I met again and broke lances before others assaulted us both.

My shoulders ached and my arms were sore, and Patrise's last blow to my helmet had bruised my face and blacked an eye. Gawain grinned at it, and Bors rumbled, " 'Tis an ugly sight."

I lifted my head and gazed one-eyed around the Hall. Fewer knights had the strength to celebrate, after this tourney. Our trestle stood just below the dais, and there sat Arthur, smiling with our host, and the queen with her face drawn and sad, and among her ladies Naime, beautiful in the taperlight.

"Lancelot did not fight," said Gawain, "even in disguise."

Bors shook his blond head. "Jesu, if I have killed him . . ."

"Were he dead," Gaheris said, "Camelot would know of it."

"But were he healed," I muttered, angry, "he would be here. With the queen." Agravain lay in Gawain's tent with broken ribs. I could not understand why I took his part.

"Can we not forget this thing?" murmured Bors.

"He wore a maid's sleeve at Winchester. Mayhap the queen . . ."

"Enough," said Gawain. "We are champions tonight, this is the feast of Northgalis, it is our hour of triumph and pride."

We ate silently. My own betrayal made it worse. If I failed Lark, I failed Craon as well, and even myself. The courses came and the cup passed. I watched Naime. Despite myself her beauty eased me, and when the minstrels began to play I got up, stiff from my hurts, and walked to her.

"Lady," I said, "you are fair as moon and stars together."

"I am warned," she said, "of all such Angevin courtesy." Yet she smiled and it comforted my heart. "I rue your injury, Sir Michel, though it gives you a place among the champions again."

"I wore no lady's color."

"Everyone remarked it, sir."

"There is one I seek, yet it alone is denied me." The wine swam in my flaring mind. I gestured at the other ladies in the Hall. "I have but to stretch out my hand, lady."

"And what is this, sir? Your famous Angevin modesty?"

I bowed and turned away.

William of Rhoad had fought today, but again tonight his pretty wife sat alone with other ladies. "My lady Rhoad," I said, beside her trestle.

"Sir Michel de Verdeur." Her voice was very cool, for she had seen my talk with Naime.

"How pleasant to see you again, lady."

"And to see you a champion again, sir." Her mouth softened as she gazed at my bruised face. "Everyone regrets your injury."

"Ah, lady, it was given by a sturdy knight." I smiled despite the hurt. "But tonight again I do not see Sir William."

"He broke his other arm, today."

I coughed to hide my laughter. Poor William. I stared at her, and almost felt her full lips on mine, her high bosom against me. Almost I stretched out my hand to take her, lead her away, a moth to my flame. And then I saw the inn at Le Gravier, its pretty maid that was also Anne. She I might have bought. This lady would give herself free. God's Name, how I had climbed above myself. And always I forgot Lark.

"My lady," I growled. She blinked, frightened of my tone, as I bowed and walked away. Damn me, that I had not killed him. Damn me, that I remembered not the mud of Greenfarm but the silken pleasures of Camelot, that I thought myself Michel, not Raven.

In the narrow chapel of Tanebourc, lit by a single taper, I knelt and prayed for Giles' soul. Damn me, it would have been no harder to pray for two.

King Arthur's court set out again for Camelot on a bright May morning. Briant lived, Glastonbury still held Craon's manors, the lady Naime encouraged Agravain. Yet that day the sun gleamed in a soft sky, trees wore their new green, and the cuckoo's song echoed in the dancing air. I gazed about at the king's company astride fine animals, at the wagons of the ladies, the lumbering wains that carried coin, furniture, pavilions. There was even a little troop of minstrels, piping and singing around the queen, coaxing her to smile in the warm sun. I shook my head against my wintry thoughts, and spurred my palfrey to ride beside the king.

"My lord," I called, " 'tis a grand day for your progress."

"So it is." He smiled at me. "And what a handsome eye you wear, Sir Michel."

"Thank you, sire." I had half forgot it.

"I call a tourney at Camelot," Arthur said, "in four weeks."

I counted on my fingers, it was the week of John Baptist's. The light went abruptly harsh. Damn me again, that I saved Briant. "Sire," I began, "I came to Britain for Craon's manors. At your command I proved my knighthood. At Gawain's challenge I jousted at Winchester. At your desire I came to Tanebourc."

His voice went cold. "You win ransoms and fame, sir. All Britain marvels that no one may best you."

"Save Bors, sire, and Gawain's aid. Yet my lord's relief . . ."

Ahead of us riders cried out. A herd of deer, the great stags still in velvet, sprinted across our way. We spurred after them down a long meadow, but the king drew off when they vanished in a wood. It was too early for the chase.

"After Camelot," Arthur said, "after my tourney will I call a great hunt. Days in the forests against deer and, God willing, boar." And he began to laugh of forests and hounds.

As we rode on, I remembered that the first stag killed was butchered in the field, its joints divided out among the hunters as their portions. But first they cut the tail of the chine and threw it away into the thicket, a portion for the greenwood, something that might protect them, or bring them luck. That little scrap they called the raven's fee. Damn me, the fee for this raven ought have been Briant's death. But I had refused it.

"My lord," I called. "Craon sent me, 'tis my liege-duty to persist of Blackmoor."

Arthur hardly glanced at me. "I would have you at Camelot's tourney, Sir Michel. Outside, that Gawain meet you in the field."

"Aye, my lord." Once more I saw no way to refuse him. Nor could I avoid Gawain forever. "It will be my honor."

That night we stopped at Castle Tauroc, another small fortress with a Hall too narrow for the crowd of us. In the soft summer eve the castellan spread his trestles in the court. Minstrels sang under a darkling sky, and when the queen called for bright tunes we all clapped to see her dancing with the king. At the ronde I bowed to Naime, and sitting among Guenever's ladies she could not refuse.

We traced the figure of the dance. She did not speak till near the end and then she whispered, not looking at me, "You are very good at dancing. For a farmer."

" 'Tis the chivalry of Anjou, lady." But I had missed the rhythm and took a dozen steps to find myself again.

She watched her feet. The music stopped. I took her hand and led her away from the torchlight. She went reluctantly.

"Pity Agravain," I said, "who must stay behind and heal."

"Mayhap," she muttered, "he has met the lady Rhoad."

I could not stop my bitter laugh. "Lady, Sir Agravain is a monk, given to the queen. You need not worry of him and that lady. No more than me." Among the shadows her beauty almost stopped my tongue. The minstrels began another tune. Dancers moved brightly in the shifting torchlight. "Lady, forgive me, but why do you so pursue that knight?"

She glanced away. "Because he is so ardent of the queen."

I did not understand it, but I could never think next to her. "Dear lady, I have been your vassal since we first spoke. But at Amesbury the queen had not sent for me."

She turned her lidded gaze. "Yet she spoke to you, Sir Michel. Though you were foolish enough to anger her."

"I thought you were the mage, the shapechanger in his most comely form." Her brief smile lifted my heart. "Your cousin's spell takes every power of his, but shapechanging."

"My very distant cousin," she said.

"Very near cousin, lady. For you have caught me as strong as he is seized. Like him I seem to walk abroad, yet my heart is tight imprisoned."

She could not help another smile. "How pretty is this Angevin courtesy." She put a quick hand on my chest and leaned and kissed me, once. "Though I believe nothing of it."

Praise God, how that kiss both stirred and eased my heart. It softened my jealousy of Agravain, my failure of Sir John, even my hatred at saving Briant. Almost it made me her chivalric knight, resigned to seek and never to achieve.

Our company came to Camelot the next day. All save Arthur, that, excited by his notion of a hunt, took a dozen knights and rode his royal forests to speak with woodsmen and count the game. At Tanebourc I had given away half my winnings, yet I had the rest of those large ransoms, Briant's palfreys I took from Bramhill, gifts other knights offered me. I shared a cart to carry it all, and at Nones I sat Camelot's knights' tower sorting it, when the clatter of horses came up from the courtyard.

" 'Tis Gawain," cried a knight, peering through an arrow slot, "and Bors. And, praise God, here is Lancelot."

He and the others rushed to greet them. Though I felt small pleasure at Lancelot's arrival, I went to the slit and watched him smile to the greeting throng. A short new beard covered his chin, and he looked strong and vigorous as ever. He waved at them all, before he strode away toward the king's keep.

Half an hour later I walked the inner bailey myself, and climbed the turning stair to the queen's solar. It surprised me to find Gawain there, pacing the room, while Bors peered nervously up the farther stair to the queen's bedchamber. Guenever's voice echoed down, and if we could not hear the words, her tone was very angry. The ladies leaned together, murmuring and nervous.

"Where did you find him, Sir Gawain?" I said.

"Near Winchester." He paused in his stalking. "Praise God, he is completely whole."

Footsteps came down the stair. Lancelot's cheeks blazed red. "She'll not see me." He sounded strangled. "She is ill."

"Oh, sir," said a lady, "she is but tired from travel. We are all pleased at your return, Sir Lancelot."

He did not answer nor even look at them, but plunged on down the stair. Gawain and Bors followed him. In the nervous silence old Agraine called, "Is that you, Sir Michel? What do you here?"

"I would speak to the lady Naime."

"She is with the queen, sir. Come, sit with us."

They all knew I was Camelot's newest champion. Hoping to forget Lancelot and the queen they made a pleasant flurry over me, and I was playing at merels when Naime came down the stair.

"Oh, lady," cried my opponent, "here is thy suitor."

She gazed at me. "This is no suitor of mine."

I stood and bowed, and said for them all to hear, "Dear lady, I ask only for a sign."

"That you ask, first. 'Tis what follows I am wary of."

The whole chamber laughed. She walked past me to an open casement. A spring rain had begun and the smell of it blew softly in. She raised a hand to touch the leaded panes.

"Lady, I did not know the queen was ill."

"She is not."

There on the path below us, sheltered beneath budding apple trees, Agravain shook Lancelot's hand.

"The queen's rivals," I muttered, despite myself. "Hath not your cousin some potion for you, for Sir Agravain?" She blinked eyes suddenly gone wet. "Lady, forgive me." A tear ran down her cheek I ached to touch. God's Name, how I loved her.

She turned to me, as if her damp eyes gazed into my soul. "There is no rivalry. There is naught but a train of fools."

"And I am the last, dear lady, that cannot forget your kiss."

She scrubbed her cheek, and after a moment went on. "The queen hates Sir Lancelot, for the lady of the red sleeve. With whom he hath spent these last months."

"But that lady lives at Astolat. And Lancelot stopped at Winchester, grievously injured. He must have a deep scar." I did not wish to argue Lancelot's part.

"Ought he show that to the queen, as proof?"

"I would," I said, and she gave a little laugh. At last we smiled at each other. "Dear lady, pray remember me. Despite Sir Agravain."

"Of course, Sir Michel."

I took her hand and kissed her fingers. The ladies behind us gave a sigh we hardly noticed.

Yet that evening she stood again with Agravain and spoke to him with many smiles. And he answered distracted, his eye ever on Guenever. Because he was so ardent of the queen. I did not understand her. I could not watch. I could not go away.

It was another week before King Arthur returned to the castle. Lancelot, daunted by the queen's displeasure, was already gone away. The king, gratified the high knight was well healed, still seemed much annoyed he departed without leave. But it was more than that, for Arthur now strode through Camelot with a cold abruptness.

One midday I found a place at table beside Patrise, that had ridden in the king's company. He wiped his blond mustache and smiled at me. "Your eye's still purple. Everyone says 'twas a rare stroke."

"So it was," I said, touching it. "Did you find his deer?"

"Enough for the hunt. But it was Castle Chariot delayed us."

"Chariot?" I gaped at him. "Truly? You stopped there? What was it like? I found only Morgan's lake. Did anybody ask of me?"

Patrise laughed. "No," he said, before he stared away. " 'Tis small, a most elegant place. The king sat much with his sister, but would not speak of their talk. He has been dark, ever since."

She spoke of me, I thought, that I was not her son. Yet as the days passed and the king did not denounce me, nor hardly saw me when we met, I knew it was some other thing. There was a tale that Morgan had once imprisoned Lancelot. What might she tell the king, but what we all knew of that knight and Guenever?

Yet presently his brow cleared, he laughed again at table, and spoke happily of the coming tourney. Two days of jousts, he decreed, that each knight display his prowess to all the court. And a day of melee for those who would practice war. He sent heralds to all Britain, to Wales and Scotland and even across the sea. The week before John Baptist's, bright pavilions rose once again on Camelot's meadows. Amid all that glitter and pageantry Lancelot did not appear, though Bors and Gawain had seen him but a week before. Camelot waited, almost breathless, as if the tourney could not begin without its most famous knight.

I had swallowed my anger of the date. The tourney would be the saint's festival and Camelot held no chapel race that year. As I must be Outside I found a place with Étienne of Châteaubriant, that years past was our host at Pouancé. On the last evening I stepped from his tent into the summer night. Songs and laughter sounded on the gentle air. At the bottom of the field the moon rose white and round, while in the dusk around me the ranked pavilions glowed, each a great dim lantern illumined by scores of tapers. The queen's own tent stood next the loges and though Guenever remained in the castle, knights and ladies filled the place. A smell of wine and spices hung in the taperlit air and Naime, clad in pale blue, sat laughing with Camelot ladies. Agravain was not there.

I bowed to her. "Lady, how fares thy heart?"

She smiled at me brightly. "Sir Michel, come sit with us." She made a place beside her, and I could not hide my own pleasure. The others greeted me, and one lady asked the essential question. "What knight do you meet tomorrow, sir?"

"The marshals place me after Sixte." They murmured I was ranked so high. I looked at Naime. "I meet Sir Agravain."

They burst into applause, and another laughed and said, "How wonderful, that the field doth mirror the court."

Naime knew already. "He said Orkney will win every joust."

"All save one," I said. "Does he carry your color, lady?"

"Yes."

I had expected it, but still I ground my teeth. Damn, I thought, I will break his head, I will . . . The lady on my other side touched my arm. "Good knight, I have no champion."

"Dear lady, I thank you. But we saw at Winchester what befalls a knight, if he wear the wrong lady's color. Even if she be fair as you. Or the maid of Astolat."

Naime glanced away, her cheeks gone red.

The others laughed, though the lady next me gave a sour smile. "Never have I received a more elegant insult. Still." She gripped my hand. "I will cheer for you, Sir Michel. Until Sir Lancelot appears."

We made a splendid parade, two hundred knights in polished mail and new-broidered tabards, helmets shining and shields glittering under a warm and cloudless sky. But after, I could only pace the field and watch the combat, impatient to meet Agravain, wondering how I might defeat him soundly, yet not cripple him.

It was Sixte when Huge brought Night from the stalls. René gave my heathen sword a last polish. "I give you the best lance first, sir. The second is good, but the third is weak and twisted. Be very careful of it."

"I will, René."

"Orkney has won three jousts this morning, sir. Even Sir Mordred." I nodded, busy with my gauntlets. "Sir Agravain is younger than Sir Gawain, yet just as strong. Full ransoms, but after Tanebourc you can afford it, sir."

It took me like a slap in the face. "Damn you," I cried. "Do you believe he will best me?"

He did not blink. " 'Tis high honor to be matched 'gainst a prince of Orkney, sir. Had you forgotten that?"

"Get me a drink of water." My hand shook with anger as I took the leather bottle, but I saw he was right. "René du Plessis," I muttered, "I am in your debt."

Night ran without urging, accurate as always. Agravain wore a pale blue scarf. We met with a crash that broke both our lances. With my second I rode at him again, spurring Night. We met very hard. The impact half unseated me, but my lance drove Agravain out of his saddle.

We met with swords. He was very quick and very sure. We traded blows for long minutes and though he was an fine swordsman, I saw his attack clear as I ever had, and my Norman gift eventually overcame him. His knees faltered. The pale blue scarf hung in tatters, and I cut it away completely. He did not even see my last blow, but stumbled heavily and lay unmoving. I raised my sword to Arthur and all the cheering crowd, as Agravain's squires came to carry him off on his shield. Among the ladies around the queen I could not find Naime's face.

The jousts went on, each now a contest between famous knights. At Gawain's tent Agravain lay groggy and bleeding. We shook hands, though he did not speak. Gareth scowled at me. "A mark against Orkney. Praise God it came by a strong hand."

And Sir Gawain, armed for his joust, muttered at me. "Today's winners meet tomorrow. I pray I draw you, Sir Michel."

But next day the marshals gave me Lionel de Maris, that unhorsed me at our the first pass. We fought very long afoot and injured each other much. I was spent and battling for a draw when he faltered, and I caught him clean. Again I lifted my blade to the king. Naime stood among the clapping throng. Her smile much eased my hurts, though inside the tent I groaned as I sat. And René scowled at me. "Must I insult you, sir, before every joust?"

I looked at him. "Mayhap, René, till I learn it for myself."

"That, sir, will take a great defeat."

And who might give it, I wondered, save Lancelot himself?

The melee, as oft happened, became a contest for answering losses at joust. Weaker knights had rested while the strongest, that had fought twice, were tired and battered. All day I kept away from Orkney. I had no want to answer Agravain's loss, nor Gawain's challenge. Once again I sought ransoms, and by day's end had won four. I was riding for sanctuary when one last knight charged at me. He raised his sword and gave my shield a massive blow. His own red shield carried no arms and at first I feared he truly was Lancelot. But he was not so fine a fighter. I saw his attack well enough to cover myself and my blade was quicker. He was Gawain. His heavy blade battered me, his strength wore at me, and if I could not defeat him quick, I must fight till I dropped, for he would do the same. Mayhap this was my great defeat.

We fought on till, praise God, the horns finally blew. I backed away. He raised his sword, that I caught on my shield. He raised his blade again, as if he would not stop. The horns sounded nearer, and he paused and lowered his weapon.

"Damn," he muttered, inside his helmet.

"Sir Gawain," I cried, "we must leave off."

We both tugged off our helmets. Blood crusted one side of his bruised face but he did not look tired at all. "Did I strike after the horns? I am sorry, Sir Michel."

"I would never question your honor, Sir Gawain."

He looked at my tattered surcoat and my own bruised face. "You have taken blows aplenty, this day."

"And four ransoms."

He reached to shake my hand. "We will meet again at the champion's trestle."

We rode together back to the pavilions. At Étienne's tent a gray-haired esquire sat his palfrey; he swung down and bowed to me. "My lady would speak with you, sir knight."

I did not recognize his arms. "Do I know you?"

"I am not of Camelot, sir. Nor is my lady."

"I have ransoms to collect."

"Sir, I will do it for you," said René.

"After a day of battle I ought bathe."

"I am to bring you at once, good sir. And alone."

"Then let us go." I turned to walk down the field.

The old man made a vague gesture. " 'Tis far enough, sir, that you must ride." And when Hugh brought my palfrey he led me past the tents, away from the castle, to the river ford.

"Where do you take me, esquire?"

"Are you afraid, sir knight?"

"Of course not." Still, when we forded the shallow water and rode into Camelot's dark forest, I put a hand to the pommel of my sword and wished for shield and helmet.

He turned down a thin track I had not noticed before. The forest seemed very dim. A wind I could not feel rattled the tops of the trees. After half a league we came to a clearing where three elegant pavilions stood the grassy sward, under spreading oaks. Well-dressed grooms took our mounts. Squires in spotless robes made me welcome. I was sweaty and tired, and a steaming tub stood inside the smallest tent. Pages undressed me, and without the weight of chain armor I settled gratefully into the water.

"Who is your lady?" I asked the old esquire.

"You will meet her soon enough, sir."

"Do all her knights tourney?" The only sword I had seen hung at the waist of a young cleric.

"No, sir," he said, and nothing more.

He brought clean robes, and when I was dressed led me to the largest tent. There sat a dark-haired woman, handsome as a queen.

"My lady," I said, and bowed before her. Under her dark brows her eyes were deep as night. I could not tell her age.

"Sir Michel de Verdeur." She had a husky voice.

"You know my name, good lady. May I know yours?"

"I am sister to the king," she said.

"Lady Morgan le Fay." I bowed again to hide my nervousness.

"Sit you down, good knight."

A page brought a decorated cup. Ladies in bright gowns came to sit around us. The armed priest stood behind her. I waited till they quieted and then I waited in their silence. She stared at me. She had high cheeks, one brow faintly higher than the other, one side of her mouth turned slightly down. All added to her beauty.

"Sir Michel de Verdeur," she repeated, as if announcing me. "A young knight, a splendid fighter. Six ransoms at Camelot, five at Tanebourc. Six at Winchester, with but a single defeat."

"Thank you, lady." I wondered how she knew all this.

"Yet is he not Micah of Greenfarm, that calls himself my son?"

I sat up. "Lady, I do not. I have never said it." Her deep eyes did not waver, and at last I had to glance away. "Though many at Camelot believe it, lady."

"And you, sir?"

I forced myself to look at her. Surely Rebecca had those same wide cheeks, those same dark eyes.

"What say you, Sir Michel?"

"I do not know what the truth is, lady."

The others rustled and murmured, and Morgan took a sip from the cup. "A wise and modest young man, as well."

Again I waited in her silence. Servants talked outside, setting trestles for the meal. I had seen no kitchen, yet I smelled roasting meat and baking bread. Hunger moved my stomach.

"My lady," I said, "though I delight in your company, I wonder you brought me here but to ask that question. Surely you knew the answer already."

She did not smile. I thought she never smiled, though now and again her eyes lost their knife-edge glitter. She was beautiful, and had enormous force of will. Of course she had so many lovers. If she were to bend that gaze at me, call me to her bed, I myself might not resist her.

I drew a long breath. "Are you my mother, good lady?"

Her look went dark as night. "You ask for truth, sir? In this world of fancy, of rumor, of imagination?"

I glanced away, shamed I wanted to believe it. I stood and bowed.

"My thanks, lady, for your kindness to a peasant's brat."

"Sit you down, sir." Her eyes glittered. "You see Merlin."

It took a moment to clear my mind. "Yes, lady, I have."

"In several guises, and despite his witchment."

"Yes, lady." Once more I wondered how she knew.

"But why should anyone believe you?"

"The king saw him. At Camelot."

"Merlin would save my brother's throne. On that matter I agree with him." She stared at me so ardent I could not meet her gaze. "A young man, knighted against all odds, too fine a fighter to be a peasant. I wonder what the old man does."

"I made my own way," I blurted, angry.

She put back her head and gave a long, unbelieving laugh.

And I was at Winchester that first night, seeing Briant's swing before it fell. I was at Caen, at Angers, seeing every blow. My Norman gift, my seeing, a small thing but enough to make me champion, I had got it from my beery friar. I had got it from the wizard. Christ and Our Father, what *did* the old man do?

"I tried prisonment," she was saying. "The Sangral kept him away a few years. Now comes a new knight, bearing an old and heathen blade." Her gaze grew dark as midnight and I shivered, remembering it was her uncle gave the sword to me. "Who must he fight with it?"

My heart stopped. I knew very well who she meant. "Lady, I cannot defeat Sir Lancelot." And in my fright I remembered Gawain's courage, bending his neck to the Green Knight's sword.

"I do not see what else will do." Her eyes glittered. "Even now he lies nearby, in a hermitage, wounded by accident."

Twenty-six

Sir Lancelot?" I stared at Morgan. "He is injured again?"

"Mistaken for a stag." She gave me a quick ironic smile. "A small thing, an arrow through his thigh, but he cannot ride his destrier. It kept him from Camelot's tourney." Her gaze was gone somber once again. "And from the queen."

"We all wondered."

"The hermit that shelters him is my man. Tonight he will give a potion, that Lancelot not wake till after Terce. You must sharp your blade, sir."

"Lady," I cried, "think you I am an assassin?"

Her eyes went cold as winter. "I think you know what is necessary."

Lancelot. God's Name, she was right. Agravain was right, and Mordred. Even Edmund, wounded, grumbled of Camelot's decay, this courtly love of knight and queen. I shut my eyes, and there in Morgan's tent I saw Camelot fail, the castle ruined, thistles in the courtyard. But I could not murder Lancelot in his sleep.

"I have killed knights in battle, lady, but this . . ."

"Spare me your little vengeances, sir. This is for the king."

One stroke, to save both Arthur and Camelot. Why did I still resist? "The king would never do it, lady."

She frowned, knowing it was true. "More fool the king." She turned her full gaze to me. "Yet are you not Arthur's man?"

I gaped at her. She spoke Merlin's words as if she knew his mind, but the wizard would not have me do this. I must debate with Lancelot instead, sway him from his ways. I would seem to agree with her.

"Surely we must save the king, my lady."

Morgan's look had closed, her mouth become a narrow line.

"Where lies this hermitage?" I asked.

"Half a league away."

"Than I must leave at dawn."

"You will be waked." She gazed at me beneath her dark brows. "All Britain will thank you, Sir Michel de Verdeur."

I lay that night in her smallest tent, restless and vexed. She had knights, even an armed cleric. Would none of them kill a sleeping knight? An owl called in the night forest, and Naime's eyes smiled at me. I wondered Morgan had not witched me of this, offered herself if I would do it, left me unable to refuse. But she brought me here, and that was witchment aplenty.

Lark's death, and Merlin's gift, had made me knight. The wizard had said be Arthur's man, not Lancelot's slayer. I saw it clear, that if I killed the knight asleep, I failed both mage and sister. Who might believe it, that born a peasant I would so cling to chivalry and knighthood's honor? All about me the noble-born forgot most easily. Even Lancelot followed desire against his Sangral oaths, as if honor were a word his tongue uttered, that never touched his heart. Knighthood's honor was Camelot's highest boon. Its failure had killed my sister, and I would not fail it again by murdering Lancelot abed, even if that death saved Camelot.

I had feared Morgan would not wake me, but in the gray dawn her servants roused me and helped me arm. I stepped out into the cool morning. My palfrey stood saddled and waiting, and nearby stood another horse, also ready.

The gray-haired squire bowed to me. "Good morrow, sir."

Behind him the priest came out the next pavilion, armed himself.

"Who will show me Lancelot's hermitage?" I said.

The squire shook his head. "My lady would have you return to Camelot, good sir." He pointed to the path we had come by.

"Camelot? Why?" The priest mounted and rode off another way.

"She doubts your resolve, sir."

"That priest," I shouted, and ran to my palfrey.

"If you follow," the old man cried, "you will lose your way."

The priest glanced back at the noise of my gallop and spurred his horse. We rode hard. I gained on him. He turned aside into a thicket. I followed him in. There was no trail, but I could follow his track of broken branches. And then in that mass of young trees there was nothing. I drew up to listen for his passage. There was no sound at all save my winded palfrey, and one bird calling. Damn, I was a fool, still she toyed with me.

It was nearly sundown when I found my way at last into another clearing. I took a deep breath, thankful of the opening after a day of trackless wood, and saw it was the same I had left at dawn. There, under that broad oak, had stood Morgan's pavilion. There I had spent my uneasy night. Yet there were no marks on the turf, nor any narrow way to lead me out.

My breath stopped for a moment. I shook my head to clear it, and swung down. My stiff legs still ached with tourney bruises. At least my pains were real. The aged retainer that brought me, the lady Morgan, surely they had been real. All the rest now felt of witchment, like her lights in that other forest. Yet I had no fear of danger. I was here under her protection. I paced the clearing, the light faded much as it had beside her lake, my stomach rumbled with hunger. I unsaddled my palfrey and let him graze. I unbound my sword belt and, though the place was not sacred ground, I knelt and prayed for Giles, for Arthur and Camelot, for Lancelot and the queen, and even Morgan.

At dawn the narrow path again lay clear before me. Soon enough I found the forest road and then the river ford. I stopped that my horse might drink. The road forked, and almost I turned to Lambert's Denham, and to Craon. Yet there, a league away stood Camelot, dreamlike in the summer haze. And Naime.

Beside the tourney field the king's loges were but half removed, and carpenters stood about, muttering. At the castle barbican a guard stopped me with his spear, and would not let me pass till his sergeant came, armed and belted, and recognized me.

"What is it?" I asked.

The sergeant shook his head. "The queen, sir."

I rode through the echoing gate and into the wide bailey. Servants stood in whispering knots and did not see me. Even the groom was slow to take my horse.

"What is this of the queen?" I asked.

The boy frowned at the keep. "The king hears it, sir."

I could not imagine what had happened. If it were something of her and Lancelot, surely they would speak his name. In the upper bailey a cluster of knights grumbled outside the door of the king's chamber. A herald within called someone's name.

"What is it?" I said. They shushed me quiet.

I turned back, and went through the servants' door to Ladies. Upstairs in that chamber cups and knives still lay on the board, the remains of a large dinner not yet removed. My boots echoed down the empty passage. Ladies shrank with fright when I strode into the solar. I pressed down through the throng on the stairs, till I could see into the king's chamber.

Arthur sat in his great chair, his face thunderous with anger. A herald thumped a staff on the stone floor.

"The king calls Gawain, Prince of Orkney."

Sir Gawain bowed to the king.

Someone moved beside me. A hand touched my shoulder and it was Naime, and for a moment I forgot everything. "Lady," I murmured, "what is this?" She shook her head, but left her hand on my shoulder.

"What happened, Gawain?" Arthur growled.

"My lord," said Gawain, slowly. "Last evening my lady the queen gave a dinner. Twenty-four knights, my lord. At the end a basket of apples was placed before us. Early apples, sire, of which I am very fond. A fine round one lay on the top, but before I could take it Sir Patrise reached out his hand." Gawain put out his own, and drew it back and crossed himself. "He had eaten nearly all when the cramps took him."

Dear God, I thought, Patrise. She has killed my champion.

A king's cleric lifted his voice. "Did the queen bring in the apples, Sir Gawain?"

"The queen's servant." Gawain raised his head. "I am certain the poison was meant for me."

"The queen would poison you, Sir Gawain?"

"No, God help me, nor did she poison Patrise."

"Who would kill you, Gawain?" said Arthur.

"Pinel." He thrust an arm out toward a knight standing in one corner. "Pinel le Sauvage, cousin of Sir Lamorak whom I and my brothers slew . . ."

The cleric cut him off. "Can you show proof, sir? Did you see him bring the apple?"

"Of course not, he put it there before . . ."

"But it was offered by the queen, or rather by her servant?"

"She did not do it."

I turned to Naime and whispered, "What of the servant?" She closed her eyes. I wondered if I had known him.

The king cleared his throat. "Do you swear all this is true, Sir Gawain?"

Gawain raised his voice. "So I do, on my knight's honor."

The inquiry had begun with Sir Kay and Sir Aliduke. After Gawain the cleric questioned Bors. He said what Gawain had, the queen's servant, the apples, Patrise's death. When the herald called Mordred I turned and pushed my way back up to the solar.

Naime followed me. "Where were you, Michel?"

I told her of the lady Morgan, of Lancelot, of my nights in the forest.

But she hardly listened. "The queen invited you, but as you were not here she called Patrise." She gripped my arm and the color left her face. "Dear Mary, it might have been you."

Her worry so pleased my heart I nearly forgot I had no great love of apples, that had I been at the queen's supper Gawain would have eaten the poisoned fruit and died. Was it the knight of Orkney that Morgan rescued?

Mordred's voice sounded up the stairs, defending the queen. Naime stared at me, still frightened. I took her hand to kiss it, but she pulled away.

"Lady, if the queen be not guilty, why the trial?"

"Sir Mador has accused her. He is Patrise's cousin." She gave a bitter smile. "Mador had Sir Lancelot's place."

Neither king nor clerics could find a way to disprove the charge. After an hour of trial, Arthur decreed a judicial combat, though he refused Mador's demand that it occur at once. "Fifteen days, Sir Mador de la Porte." His voice boomed up the stairs. "Come you ready to battle the queen's champion. If you prevail, her life shall answer the death of thy kinsman."

"Where is Lancelot?" whispered Naime.

"I told you. In Camelot forest. Dead mayhap. But, lady, can only Lancelot defend her? Are there not others? Gawain? Bors?"

She wrung her hands. "This is the queen's life, Michel."

"Then will not God protect her of this combat?" I stopped, smiling grimly. Now, even I believed in God's chivalry. "Think you, if Lancelot defends her it will begin their matter again."

She blinked her damp eyes. "You must find him, Michel."

"Lady, have no doubt of my love for the queen. But as I would not kill him sleeping, I will not bring him awake to Camelot."

"And you think to serve Camelot?" Her sudden anger surprised me. "The queen's death will ruin it."

I bowed to her. Almost I said, so might Guenever alive.

My nights in Morgan's forests, the prayers I gave for Giles, my inability to kill Briant, all now showed me how to honor my sister's death. At Camelot I had armor, horses, and coin, ransoms from both Tanebourc and the king's tourney. I collected my rattling bags of coin and took them to the priests of the castle church, and though they grumbled and sputtered at my notion they could not, in the end, refuse me.

I rode out through the haze of a summer evening, across the castle meadow, past the house of Thomas the reeve, and drew up yet again in the dusty yard of Greenfarm. My brother Harry looked out a new-built byre, larger than the one before, where a calf butted its head against the udder of a new cow, and a pale ox stood chewing its cud. He carried a wooden pail of milk, that he almost dropped when he saw me. My father came at his call, and recognized my palfrey and my arms.

"A new byre," I said as I swung down.

"Aye, sir. We thank you every day."

In the dim house the smells of my childhood assaulted me once again. My mother stood up quickly from the firepit, and in the housebed old Cluck coughed. "Who'zit?"

"The knight," said Little Drool, staring.

"We thank you, sir, for all your kindness." My father still bobbed and shuffled at me. "I've old Benton's strips, that's the best in Newfield. And his cottage in the village, I rent it to the miller's son." He laughed. "Spring, we'll add another room here."

"He spends too much," my mother grumbled. "I worry that the summer is so dry, if there's no rain we'll . . ."

"Ruth," he said.

I cleared my throat. "I have founded a chantry." They did not understand. "At the forest chapel."

Here in this dim and smoky house the memory of it all nearly took my voice. Once more I heard the hare's scream, saw the lopsided moon. If I failed her blood, if knighthood kept me from killing the last of her slayers, at least I might succor her soul, and bring her name each day before God.

"I have given the church at Camelot coin to buy a priest's living." They gaped and muttered, hardly able to grasp the thing. "A priest will come, every day. He will sing a Mass. At Vespers. For Rebecca. For her soul."

My mother gave a little strangled cry. She stood and came and put her arms around me, still frightened of me yet knowing I was her son. "Oh, thank you, sir." Her embrace half unnerved me. She pressed her weeping face against my armored chest. "I will go, Micah. Every day. Oh, praise God, sir, you have not forgotten."

"And I will come," I said, "John Baptist's eve, whenever I am in Britain."

The day of the queen's trial, I had gone to Arthur and told my tale of Morgan and the forest. Sir Gawain gaped at the story, and clattered off in a rush in search of Lancelot, forgetting in his haste to ask the king's leave. Arthur stared after him, his face dark with anger. Bound by his own laws, the king could do nothing himself to preserve his wife.

Bors agreed to be her champion, as the rest seemed frozen with distress, and erected his pavilion in the castle meadows opposite Mador's. On the fateful morning all Camelot trooped out to watch their combat. Bors delayed his appearance so long that only Mador's complaints brought him out, after Terce, and just at that moment another knight rode out the woods beside the river. He wore plain armor and carried a blank shield; he cried to Bors to stand away, and on his first charge neatly unhorsed Mador.

Lancelot had carried a blank shield at Winchester. There, too, he had come unheralded out a wood. I muttered his name, and though the knights standing near me laughed in agreement, I felt almost dismayed Morgan's priest had not slain him, after all. Mador climbed to his feet. They battled for an hour, and we marveled how Mador stood so long. At last he fell. Lancelot grabbed for his helmet, but Mador rolled aside and stood, and drove his blade into Lancelot's thigh. Lancelot roared with pain and anger. He chopped Major down with a huge blow, and the defeated knight cried out his yielding.

King Arthur came down from the lists to embrace Lancelot, and praise him for the queen's defense. He had litters brought to carry them to the castle; he invited both to stop there while they healed. Mador, vanquished, would not stay. Lancelot ought have left as well, for after that day the king showed him only a hard coolness. But Lancelot saw none of it. Beside Arthur the queen bowed her thanks, and smiled as if she saw only him.

In the days that followed there was no coolness at all, between knight and queen. They were always together, at table, in the solar, walking the upper bailey with Lancelot limping on a stick. Guenever seemed to forget her fears and jealousies. Lancelot abandoned his old discretion. It was as if, having forgotten his vow against battle in the queen's defense, he might now forget his vows of love, as well.

The queen's combat had delayed Arthur's great hunt, but soon he set it anew, two weeks after the battle. The morning after the proclamation I climbed the knights' tower, up the turning stair to Lancelot's chamber. He limped about, pain still clear on his face, while a page waited on him. Bors and the others had gone to break their fast in Camelot's Hall.

"Sir Lancelot," I said. "Pray God you mend quick, that you may hunt with the king."

He stared at me, unsmiling. "I cannot ride in two weeks."

"Did you know it, sir, that as you lay wounded in Camelot's forest the lady Morgan was nearby?"

"No." He sat heavily on a stool, rubbing his bandaged leg.

"She called me to her. The hermit would give you a draught, and I might kill you asleep."

He swung his head up. "There was a morning," he muttered, "that I could not wake. Nor was the hermit about. Damn that shrew." He peered at me. "Did you imagine you could kill me?"

"Were you asleep, sir, the least boy might. But I held you a knight of honor, that kept his holy oaths." His eyes flashed with growing anger. "I would not dishonor you, sir, nor knighthood. But I was mistaken. You forget everything. All oaths, all honor, all chivalry. I see it, and so does all Camelot."

"Damn you," he roared, and lurched up on his wounded leg. "When I am healed." He thrust a finger at me. "In a month, damn you, bastard spawn of that black bitch."

I bowed to him. "A month, sir." I counted my fingers. "August, sir, the Assumption of Our Lady."

Halfway down the curving stairs I had to stop and grip the wall to let my shaking pass. Yet my mind stayed very calm, for I had the wizard's gift, and if it did not suffice to save my life, it would ruin Lancelot's manhood before he killed me.

I took no pleasure in the king's hunt, though much of Camelot practiced as if it were another tourney, coursing the forests, leaping streams, riding with spear and bow. Nor did the king speak to me, save in brusque passing. It was Nones, the day before the hunt, that I went up to Camelot's Hall and found Sir Gawain with his brothers, come back from riding and already blurred with ale.

"Sir Michel," he called, "come join our cup."

It had been ere Winchester's tourney I had been with all five, the day Agravain railed of Lancelot and the queen. Now once again, as they thrust a cup at me, the same rancor warped his handsome face.

"Tomorrow," Gawain was saying, "the king leads us out. Has anyone seen deer in the forest?"

"None at all," said young Gareth.

"We must ride far as Tauroc," said Gaheris.

"Even Morgan's castle," Agravain muttered, indistinct.

I looked at them. "Something happened at Castle Chariot. The king has been different, since."

"It was nothing," said Gawain.

"Nothing?" Agravain said. He slapped a hand on the board. "She told him what we all know, that Lancelot lies with the queen."

"God's beard," Gawain muttered, "keep quiet of this."

"Sir Agravain." The drink sang already in my own head. "Do you say adultery, sir?"

"Mayhap 'tis the custom in Anjou, damn you, but not in Britain."

I let his gibe pass. "But think you, sir. Adultery against the king is treason. The punishment for treason is death." Had not he thought of this, I wondered. Or was he so pure he could cast the first stone?

"Don't you see it, brother?" Gawain muttered. "Your charge would kill her, and never injure him."

Agravain frowned into the emptied cup. "I'd kill any knight I found upon the king's wife." Behind him Sir Lucan appeared at the serving screen, talking with someone. "Tomorrow he'll not hunt," Agravain said. His voice had grown loud. "That little wound will keep him here with the queen."

Sir Lucan turned at his voice and there was the king with him.

"Hist, man," Gawain muttered, "he will hear."

"So he should," cried Agravain, "his own wife."

Arthur swung his head and stared at us.

"Fool," Gaheris whispered, "he's there behind you."

Agravain went suddenly white. The king walked to us. "My lord," we murmured, standing.

"Sit you." He frowned at Agravain. "What of my lady, sir?"

Agravain had gone dead sober. "Nothing, my lord."

"Something of my wife," Arthur repeated, his voice hard.

" 'Tis but the ale, sire," Gawain said.

"Then I would know what it is," Arthur barked, abruptly angry.

"God's leave, sire," Gareth murmured, "let it rest."

The king stared about, grown more furious than I had ever seen him. "God defend us," he cried, his fists clenched, "you are my kin, my liege knights." His voice turned the head of every knight in the Hall. "By the oath you swore me, your hands in mine, I would know this matter of the queen."

It came to me that Arthur already knew. For years, in his high faith, he had been unwilling to believe it—that chivalry might fail through desire; that knightly brotherhood might be crippled by lust; that the oaths of vassalage made by high knights could ever be despoiled by passion. Now, as he glared at us, his anger was also shame and sorrow. Those who failed him were his wife and his finest knight. All that he had tried to avoid must happen now, the death of his knight, or even of his queen.

Gawain climbed to his feet. He bowed carefully before the king. "Good sire, as you are my liege and I your vassal, I swear nothing but injury will come of the telling of this thing."

Arthur went deathly pale. His eyes blazed. "Sir Gawain, I might have your head. This is high contempt."

Gaheris stood up too. "Then you must kill me also, sire."

"And I," said soft Gareth. They bowed together, the three of them, and walked away out the Hall.

"Damn you," cried Arthur after them.

It was time I stood, myself. "My lord, I am neither liege nor kin, yet I too beg you to leave off."

His gaze fell on me like a stone. "You have nothing here but my pleasure, sir. And now that fails."

"My lord." I bowed and walked away.

Behind the screen, Gawain was muttering furiously. "Damn you, Agravain. Mordred, leave. Damn you, why do you stay? What more is there to say?"

"Agravain loves the queen too much," I said.

"And Mordred," said Gareth, "loves the king's honor."

"Honor," Gawain muttered. " 'Tis for that honor, God save us, that we are all doomed."

"God's Name," Sir Lambert muttered at Denham, where I had fled the king's wrath. "And Arthur calls me to his hunt."

"You must go," I said. "Do not anger him. If he dislikes my stopping here, I will go away to some abbey."

I waited til Nones the next day, and the king well away in his forests, ere I returned to Camelot. The castle felt almost empty. Walking the upper bailey I met a single page, a letter in his hand, that asked had I seen Lancelot. Only a few aged ladies sat in the queen's solar. Old Agraine smiled up at me. "Not hunting, Sir Michel? You miss the king's sport?"

"He seeks another sport," said a second, and they all cackled.

"Alas, good ladies, the king is much displeased with me."

"The king is much displeased with everyone, these days." Agraine patted the seat beside her. "As is the queen." She held out her broidery to peer at the pattern. The others went very quiet, and Naime stood before us, weeping.

"Oh, child," said Agraine, "what does she now?"

"Sends a letter for Lancelot." She daubed at her eyes. "And when I said she ought not, the king away, she cursed me."

"May she not see him?" said Agraine.

"After Compline?"

"Sweet Mary."

Naime sat between us, wiping her eyes. "She said it was no matter

for me, nor any lady. She said I was a shrew, that I might leave her, were
I so unpleasant." She glanced at me. "Where have you been?"

"At Denham, lady. The king frowns at me."

Agraine spoke, half to herself. "What does the king? He set a date
Lancelot could not hunt. He stays from Camelot a week. Neither Mordred nor Agravain go with him." She frowned at me. "Nor do you."

I saw the two of them, murmuring with Arthur after Gawain's argument. I stood quickly. "I will find them, lady."

Climbing the knights' stair I met Agravain. I asked for his brother,
and he frowned and said Gawain, in spite of their dispute, hunted with
the king.

"I would visit my lord's cousin in Cornwall, sir." The thought came
to me unbidden. "But the king is not here to give me leave. Nor Sir
Kay."

Agravain waved a hand. "Of course. Go."

"Sir Mordred hath the king's ear, and I thought . . ."

A door opened just above him and Mordred peered out. "Sir
Michel?" He wore his mail hauberk.

"Give him leave to travel," said Agravain, hurriedly.

I stared at him. "Sir, why go you armored?"

" 'Tis no matter of yours," Agravain growled.

"Ah, brother," said Mordred, " 'tis a matter for every knight that
honors chivalry and liege fealty." Several others appeared behind him,
Scottish cousins of Orkney, and also armed. "He goes to her tonight."

I understood at once what they did. "Good sirs, the knight is a for-
midable opponent."

"May he defeat a dozen and he soft from bed?" said Agravain.

A dozen of them, against Lancelot unarmed. It would be bad as killing him asleep. "Sir Mordred, by chivalry you ought not . . ."

He turned away abruptly. "Go you well, Sir Michel."

I walked slowly back to the keep. I saw Lancelot butchered, the
queen brokenhearted, the king speechless with sorrow. Morgan had not
killed him, yet Orkney would. The world shuddered around me, yet I
could not see what path to take.

Agraine's old face wrinkled with pain when I told her. Naime put a
hand to her mouth.

"I will speak to Lancelot," I said, "you must tell the queen."

But the old lady had other worries. "I see the king's clear hand in
this. Ought we frustrate his wishes?"

"I will tell her," said Naime, standing.

"Child." She seized her hand. "Sit you, and think. The king, or at
least his cousins, takes a fateful step. The queen, if she know, will send

that Lancelot come armed. Lancelot, armed, will sorely injure Orkney."

"But we cannot let him be murdered," Naime said.

"It is his death," I said. "Or the queen's, for adultery."

"Sweet Mary," whispered Naime, "he will kill her after all."

"What do you mean?" I asked.

She slumped against me and closed her eyes as if defeated. "Agravain," she said.

I put an arm round her. That much, at least, came of tragedy.

Less than a dozen knights dined in Camelot's Hall that evening. Mordred and his brothers did not appear, nor Lancelot and his kin. I understood my course at last. As I would not kill Lancelot at Morgan's urging, I could not let him go unknowing to his death. Still, I drained another cup of wine ere I climbed to his chamber.

Ector answered my knock. "Sir Michel. Good even, sir."

I looked past him. Lancelot had trimmed his beard and his hair, and looked very fine in new-broidered robes.

"Sir," I called, "Sir Mordred and Sir Agravain go armed tonight. And their Orkney cousins."

"Do you hear?" cried Bors, and stopped his pacing. "Have we not warned you?"

"They will attack you, sir," I said. "You must not go."

He strode to me, his limp nearly vanished. "Do you imagine I am afraid of them?"

I could but curse my tongue. Of course, if I spoke of battle, it would only rouse him. "She is the queen, sir. It is for her sake that I pray you keep away."

"You see what it comes to?" said Bors. "God's Name, will you not remember your oaths? To God? To the king?"

I took a breath. "Sir, this adultery . . ."

Lancelot leaned at me, his anger sudden as a furnace wind, and his hand gripped my robe. "Damn you, I will have your blood of that word." Then he turned on his nephews. "Damn you all. My lady calls, I go, we speak. Nothing more."

I could not understand why he denied it, nor how he might imagine nobody knew. Was it some notion of the queen's honor?

Bors came up. "God save us, uncle, where's the reason in this? I will go to her, say you are ill or something."

Despite all our protestations we might have stood silent as trees. Lancelot ran a hand along the edge of his beard, adjusted his robes, and thrust himself past me.

"Christ help you, sir," Bors cried after him, and then, "Damn his thick head."

I followed him down the turning stair. A long summer evening still colored the sky over Camelot. "Sir Lancelot," I called, though I had no idea how to stop him.

"What, damn you?"

"Do you remember Angers, sir?"

He stopped and turned. "I call you to Astolat, the day of Our Lady's Assumption. It is two weeks. I will kill you then."

"I will remind you, sir. One rainy night, Matins had rung, you hid in the church. You remembered it, at Angers."

"I did not hide, damn you."

"And the Yule night I was attacked, you were there again at Matins. Who might believe you but spoke with her all those hours?"

He raised his bearded chin. "Jesu, I will not wait. Tomorrow will I kill you."

"Tomorrow?" I cried. His guise of innocence at last enraged me. "Tomorrow?" I drew my dagger. "God's name, sir, let us fight now. Tomorrow you will be dead."

He watched my blade, but did not move. "You are very brave, Sir Michel. 'Tis a pity I must kill you for knightly honor."

"Honor?" My cry echoed in the darkening court. "Honor? What honor hath a knight that invades his king's bed? Whose damned prick is always more upright than his knightly honor?"

His own blade glinted in the dusk.

"Good," I cried. "You may kill me, sir, but I swear you will regret that killing." I drove my point at his groin.

He dodged my thrust and took a step back. "I do not fear you, sir. But the queen calls."

"This," I cried, and thrust again, "this is no matter of fear or bravery. Nor of that honor you so prattle about. Camelot's greatest knight is but a randy fool."

But he stepped back another pace, pushed his dagger in its sheath, and strode away.

Drawn by the noise of my arguments, cooks were clustered at the kitchen door and grooms at the stable. They shrank away as he passed. And I, once more nearly dead of bravery, faltered after him as far as the church, shaking of fright and anger both.

God help me, I was a fool. Would the mage gave me the gift of fair words, instead. Had I spoke of the queen's danger Lancelot might have heard, but news of armed men was like a trumpet of war. It was not love that led him to Guenever, but a mindless groin. Once again I saw him butchered. I drew a breath, remembered my prayer for Giles, and then sat waiting in the silent church.

After long hours a priest came to sing Matins, and if he wondered at me, he said nothing. We walked together back up the aisle. Outside the door a waning moon lit the vacant court, and the scent of flowers from the upper bailey made me think of Naime.

A sudden scream rang from the keep, a blade that cleft the silence. Men shouted, swords clashed, there were cries of pain.

"Christ Our Lord," the priest whispered, "what is that?"

"The king's will. Get you to your bed, father."

He glanced at me and scurried across the court. The night had fallen silent again. Lancelot was killed. But then the battle rang out again, louder and more violent. It went on and on, filled with the screams men give, hacked by swords. How many did he take with him, into death?

And then, sudden as it began, the noise stopped. The cries died away. A single figure stumbled from the keep. It was Mordred that limped past me through the moonlight. He cried hoarsely at the stables for a horse, shouted open the wicket gate, and rode away hard over the drawbridge.

After a long moment a second man appeared, that staggered and wheezed in pain. It was Lancelot, armed in somebody's hauberk, carrying someone's sword, the blood that smeared it black in the moonlight. I did not move, but he saw me watching and stopped and leaned on the sword. "Good even to you, Sir Michel."

"Sir Lancelot."

"The stupid fools." He lifted the sword and waved it, puffing. "Even more stupid than I, wise young Michel."

"Have you killed them all?"

"They came at me down a corridor. One at a time." He laughed, breathlessly. "Had they got me here, out in the open . . ." He banged the sword point on the cobbles and staggered away.

King and hunters rode into Camelot at midday, their horses lathered from long galloping.

Lancelot and his nephews had left just after Prime. He had taken with him a goodly number of knights. Some owed him liege, some swore him friendship or admired him above all others, some thought the ambush vile or hated the Orkney princes. But all had long since lost their love of the king.

At first light I went to the corridor outside the queen's chambers. Blood gouted every wall and puddled on the stairs. Swords had hacked the wood partitions, and hewn the very paint from the stones. Lancelot unarmed had killed one, taken his sword and mail, and butchered a dozen more. Their mangled bloody corpses stuffed the way like trees felled by a violent storm. The last few had been chopped down fleeing;

the narrow way that limited their attack also hindered their escape. In the midst of them sprawled Agravain, his mouth open in death's scream, his head split by a huge blow.

Like trees felled in a great storm, I thought, the first storm of a winter that soon would batter Camelot. A storm I had done little to prevent. Caught up by a zeal for my own knighthood, I had forgot to be Arthur's man. Once in Morgan's forest I had imagined arguing with Lancelot, yet last night my words only warned him, made this slaughter certain. In truth I doubted that any man might do it, might find the one thing that would defend both Arthur's chivalry and Arthur's Camelot. I glanced again at the mangled face of Agravain, my eyes blurred, I had to turn away.

By the time the king arrived, Sir Lucan had the bodies laid out on trestles in the arched chamber beneath the Hall. Maids scrubbed at the blooded passage floor. Masons daubed whitewash over the stains. Armed sergeants stood outside the queen's door.

For a second time within the month, Guenever stood trial. This time there would be no question of challenge, nor of champion's defense. Arthur had the evidence of Mordred, of the dead knights, of Lancelot's flight. Adultery against Britain's king was treason against Britain itself. There was but one penalty: burning.

Twenty-seven

rthur walked the battered corridor and spoke with the queen an hour. He called his oldest advisors to his private chamber, where they sat the rest of that day and all the next morning. At last, after the bells had rung for Sixte, he came out on the steps of his keep. His face had gone haggard and his eyes were sunk in his head, but he raised his voice and cried the verdict himself.

"Guenever, daughter of Leodegrance, king of Camelard, wife to Arthur and queen of Britain, is charged with treason by adultery." He paused at the murmur of the waiting throng. "Today she is found guilty, before this king's court." The listeners groaned. He waved a hand toward the river meadows. "Three days hence at the hour of Terce she will be given to the flames." He leaned a moment against the sound of their distress, before he went again inside.

Sir Gawain had been among the jurists, and Gaheris and I waited till he came out. I murmured my sorrow at Agravain's death, but Gawain only nodded, tight-lipped. "The fools, they brought it on themselves. Lancelot . . ." He glanced away. "I have owed him my life a dozen years, of Carados of the Dolorous Tower."

"And now he owes us Agravain." Gaheris stared at him. "Could you not save the queen?"

"I tried, I argued that nothing was seen, that . . ." Gawain was not a knight to weep, yet the tears ran freely down his face. "The king would not listen." He wiped a cheek. "Now Arthur commands Orkney escort her to her fire. I told him if she dies he will lose my vassalage. I will abjure my fiefs, return to Orkney, see Camelot no more." He touched his brother's arm. "Since Agravain, you are the oldest, after me."

"God help me," barked Gaheris, "I will not do it."

"You must, brother." Gawain swung his head to me. "And you with him, Sir Michel, lest you lose the freedom of Britain."

"I thought I had lost it already," I said. "But, Sir Gawain, ought we not search for Lancelot? He cannot be far, we are enough knights at Camelot to seize him."

" 'Tis not the king's will."

"What?" I could not understand him. "Who killed those knights? Who killed your brother? God save us, is it easier to burn a lady than challenge a knight?"

"Sir Michel, pray you watch your tongue."

"Is Camelot but a place of fools? King, knight, adulterer, all are willing to kill the queen." My voice broke.

"By my knight's honor . . ." Gawain rumbled.

"Honor?" I shouted, defeated at last by the word. "Christ's blood, your brother dies and you defend his killer. The king's wife dallies and you defend her seducer. God save me of such honor."

He thrust a sudden dagger at me, but I had dodged aside.

"Brother," Gaheris cried, "you know he is right. Save your anger for Lancelot."

Be Arthur's man, the wizard had said. Yet I could see no reason in it now, nor any virtue in Guenever's death. The burning of the queen promised the end of everything.

At Lambert's Denham I sent William packing for Anjou. "Tell Sir John," I said, "the king holds in his own hand the first stone." The cleric nodded, understanding the Scripture reference. "And I send René back with you." The squire frowned and argued, and for a time I wondered were he not the steady counsel I might need. But I told him, "Britain is no place, now, to learn knights' chivalry."

Hugh and I rode back to Camelot. He turned his round face to me and gave a wry grin. "Sir Michel, I wonder at my high favor, that you keep an orphan peasant with you."

"Do you wish you were back at the abbey of Saint-Georges?"

He gave a laugh. "Well, sir, knightly life is very risky."

"God knows it is, Hugh."

The wooden loges, erected for the king's tourney and then the queen's defense, stood again on the castle meadows to see her burning. The bonfire was stacked a yard high, a post at its center to bind the queen. I drew up beside it. A man nearby bobbed at me. "Good day, Sir Michel." It was Thomas, Ryford's reeve.

"A better one than tomorrow, Thomas."

"Aye, sir. They say you are her escort."

"Though the king's justice pleases few of us."

"Aye, sir," he said again. "We've had to search a league round for the wood." He pointed to the river forest, below the castle. "Found hoof-prints there aplenty, sir. Well-shod horses."

It could only be Lancelot, and when I told Gaheris he nodded his agreement. Mordred and Agravain had taken twelve against him. To-morrow we would be twenty-four. We could but pray God Lancelot would not bring as many against us. Damn the king, for not pursuing him.

I slept the night fitfully. At Prime Gaheris led us all, full-armed, into the church to be shriven. One knight made a joke of Lancelot's weakness, now he was not with the queen. The rest of us remembered the clutter of corpses outside her door.

"My brother Gawain," Gaheris muttered, "insists Lancelot's honor forswears an ambush."

Guenever appeared, clad in a gown of gold and satin, trimmed with ermine despite the summer. Her ladies came out with her, weeping, and Naime would not look at me. We walked to the stables through a press of servants that made a low and steady moan like a winter wind in dead trees. The queen sat a white mare and her confessor a gray donkey, both animals very short beside our destriers, and the servants' wails increased as we led her out through the echoing gate. Gaheris and I rode on each side, bareheaded in her honor, though all the rest strapped on helmets and gripped swords and shields. King and nobles waited already in the loges, and Camelot's sergeants kept the staring peasants away at the meadow edges. We came soon to the bonfire. A small flame burned next it, the smoke rising pale in the sunlight. I peered toward the river wood, but nothing moved in its summer green.

"Sir Michel," said Gaheris, "do you assist the lady."

I swung down and helped Guenever from her horse. Her pale face was drawn and unwell, yet still she was beautiful. "My lady, it pains me to do this."

She stared at me with dull eyes. "Sir Michel de Verdeur. Bearer of false titles. Greeter of false wizards."

The priest beside us murmured, "Would you be shriven, lady?"

"Aye, father. Pray for me." She knelt in the rough grass and mut-tered her confession.

A swirl of smoke blew about us. Gaheris held a torch, his face gone blank as stone. "Stand you, madam, and remove your robe. You meet your end a plain and treasonous woman."

Guenever untied her robe and let it fall, and stood in a thin linen

smock that barely concealed her strong bosom. I clambered on the pile
and reached a hand that she took at once. Only then, atop the bonfire
that would kill her, did she stagger and open her mouth in gasping fear,
and clutch my arm with both her hands. Hardly believing what I did, I
drew out the rope to bind her. Horns rang on the field and men cried
out. Our guard, mounted in a circle round us, turned to meet the charge
of a dozen knights.

"It is Lancelot," I cried. The queen did not seem to hear. I took her
by the shoulders and sat her down.

Lancelot rode straight at us, his sword gleaming. I stumbled off the
pile, he was upon us, Gaheris lifted his torch, Lancelot's blade hacked it
aside and fell on his bare head. I shouted for Night. My destrier tossed
his head and galloped away, as straight as if I rode him. I drew my
sword. Lancelot's company unhorsed four of our guard and turned to
charge again. A knight dipped his lance at me. I leapt away and stabbed
his horse's gut as they passed. Blood roiled from its belly. The animal
cried and fell. I hit the rider two-handed across his shoulders.

Something enormous and heavy hammered the back of my head.

I woke to voices over me. I could see nothing but bloody trampled grass.

"Here," called a gruff voice, "here's the last."

I lifted my head. The world throbbed with pain and glare.

"God's mercy," the voice cried, "this one's alive. Call Sir Kay."
Boots trod the grass next my ear. "Sir." A hand gripped my shoulder.
"Sir."

I woke coughing from strong ale dribbled in my mouth. Arms held
me. I nearly vomited at the pain and dizziness.

"Sir Michel." Kay's face swam before me. "God help us, you are the
luckiest man alive."

I did not understand. I remembered Guenever. I remembered Lancelot. I remembered gutting the battle-horse.

"Lancelot." I did not remember my own voice.

"He killed them all," said Kay. "Every damned one, without quar-
ter, exactly like that night. Damn the butcher." He bent over me. "He
thought you dead, you are so covered with blood."

"The horse," I muttered.

He put an arm round me. "Can you stand?"

The world swam and shifted. Every move sent agony rattling
through my head. I leaned against Kay. The sergeant gave me another
swallow of ale.

"Sir Michel." Hugh grinned up at me. "They said everybody was
killed."

"I need your palfrey, Hugh."

"Aye, sir." He dashed away.

Climbing on the animal was agony. Riding to Camelot was high punishment. A sergeant led the horse and Hugh walked beside to support me, and I could hardly keep awake for the pain. Servants gaped at me, for my bloody surcoat wrapped my head and my armor was red, drenched in horse's blood. Sir Lucan led my mount into the upper bailey, to the door to Arthur's keep.

I woke to the smell of brewed herbs. Naime sat beside my bed. The king stood behind her, frowning.

"Sire." I tried to sit up. The chamber dimmed, and she put a hand on my chest.

"Good Sir Michel," said Arthur, hoarse. "Ease yourself."

"They took the queen, sire?"

"Nor hath our chase arrested them." His look went darker. "I have called my every liege knight. In ten days I will besiege Lancelot at his castle, Joyous Gard." He gave a grim nod. "I have sent especial for Olivier of Brucombe, that the son not avoid my service as the father did." I could hardly remember what he meant. "Sir Michel," said the king, "ask that when you are recovered, you join me at Joyous Gard."

"My lord," I said. I closed my eyes, weary of the talk, weary of Camelot. When I opened them again the king had gone, and Naime held my hand.

"They thought you dead. Truly."

"Dear lady, one glimpse of your face will heal me."

She gave a worried smile. "And I believed you were dying."

"Only for your love, dear lady."

I shut my eyes and opened them again. She was still there. How wonderful to imagine she wished only to sit with me till I was whole again. If once I thought her the wizard, surely she had a craft I had never met before. She fed me soups and teas and bitter herbs; she attended me with gentle hands, a ready smile, eyes bright with concern. I loved her more each day, and hoped that she loved me, though she would only murmur, "Good Michel, you must rest yourself."

I slept three days, hardly waking. On the fourth I stood and walked, without dizziness. After three more I rode my palfrey, and but a fortnight after my injury I made ready to travel, to Joyous Gard. The king had asked for my arm. I pondered it long, and I saw I could not refuse. I must go, for better or worse, to be Arthur's man.

It was bright harvest time, yet my leaving made the sunlight seem thin as winter. I walked to the apple trees in Camelot's bailey, plucked one ripe fruit and brought it to Naime. "Since we met at Amesbury, dear lady, I have loved you."

"Such pretty chivalry, sir."

"I am always in your debt." I wrapped my arms around her and kissed her. Her lips answered mine, though soon enough she put a hand against my chest and pushed me softly away.

" 'Tis no debt, sir." She smiled at me gravely. "Had I known your strength, I would not have healed you so quick."

"Lady." I searched her face a long moment, unwilling to believe she spoke in jest. "God willing, I will return soon. Do you stay at Camelot?"

"Unless my father calls for me."

"This matter." I made a wide gesture. "At least it brought us together." I drew a breath, almost unwilling to say it. "I know you mourn Sir Agravain's death."

"I never loved . . ." She stopped, and so did my heart. "At least Lancelot has not killed both of you." She took my hand in both her own. "Pray God you come safely back, Sir Michel."

I kissed her again, sure at last of her love. She put an arm about my neck and held me till we both were breathless. And then I knew it certain, that for her heart I would forfeit my liege to Craon and even my debt of Merlin, as easily as Lancelot gave up his of Camelot. Never more would I doubt the force of love.

The way to Joyous Gard was rutted and dusty, of the armies going to war. We met Sir John's cousin Olivier, with his half dozen knights and a score of footmen. His squire rode before us, the pennon of Brucombe bound to a raised lance, and as the little flag flew bravely overhead the ardor of war caught at us, and even the footmen, tired from their long tramping, stepped more quickly.

It was Vespers when we passed a small and pretty castle where Arthur's banners flew from the turrets.

"Castle Lonazep," said Olivier. "Joyous Gard is but a little farther." He waved a hand at the rich manors all about. "See how they bulge with harvest. I will raid them all, tomorrow."

We rode a thick wood where dust powdered the leaves and night already lurked among the shadows, and when we came out, Lancelot's castle stood half a league away, copper red in the lowering sun. It crowned a small rise, and a walled village lay beside it, and a line of willows marked the stream at the foot of its hill.

And just before us lay the king's army, men and animals, wains and paddocks, the whole camp broad as any city. Men's voices rumbled in the air like small thunder, brightened by laughter and the clatter of pots. Smoke rose through the still air from a hundred kitchens and the smell of cooking moved my stomach. The setting sun lit all the ranked pavilions, and at first it seemed no more than another, vaster tourney.

The king's tent stood at the center, and Arthur sat inside among his
knights, every one full-armed. Olivier bowed and recited his loyalty, and
the number of his men. Sir Gawain, now the king's marshal, put him
into the company led by Sir Bedevere.

"Thank you, Olivier," said the king. "I remind you, sir, and all of
you, this siege is not a war. The lands here are Lancelot's but you will not
disturb them nor their harvest. We come only to retrieve the queen."
Olivier could not hide his disappointment.

Arthur smiled at me. "Praise God you are healed, Sir Michel."

"Well healed, sire. And though I am Craon's man, in this matter I
offer you my arm."

"And I take it gladly. I would have you in my own guard."

Once more Gawain gave me a place in his pavilion. Several knights
of the guard slept there, yet the death of his brothers made the tent half
empty. "What huge mishap," I said to Gawain's squire, "that your
knight has no kin now, save Sir Mordred."

The man nodded sadly. "And for the souls of Sir Gareth and Sir Gaheris, he swears hatred of Lancelot forever."

But Gawain was too late. The worst was done. Lancelot, that would
not hear me, might have listened to Gawain. Yet Gawain would not
speak then, nor even at the queen's trial. Only now, three brothers slain,
did he swear his hatred. It would be a frightful matter, this feud between
princes.

In the long twilight I found Hugh at the paddocks, talking to other
squires. "Sir," he called. "The king has even pardoned Sir Briant and Sir
Laramort, for their arms in this war." I could not tell whether it was fear
or hatred that tightened my gut. "And they say Sir Almant is with Sir
Lancelot."

I looked at his eager face. "You remember I let Briant go?"

"Nor do I understand it yet, sir."

"Would his death return my sister's life?"

"Sir Michel, 'tis a matter of blood. Are you afraid?"

"I fear nothing, Hugh." But as I said it, I remembered Lancelot
speaking the same words. I walked out past the camp, alone. Away from
that rumbling assembly the evening lay almost quiet. A new moon hung
low in the west. Camelot knights ordered the night's guard and in the
stillness I almost caught their commands. Joyous Gard stood like a
shadow across the darkling meadows.

How long ago it had all began, under an evening sky much like this.
I listened for the song of a blackbird, but instead the scrape of drawn
swords sounded behind me. I turned. Two knights strode toward me. In
the evening gloom one had Laramort's pale face, and the other wore Briant's dark beard.

Twenty-eight

"He came like a spy from Joyous Gard," muttered Briant. "In the dark we could not know he was a friend."

"A very dear friend," said Laramort.

I wore my mail hauberk and carried a dagger, but had no shield or sword against their long blades. "Two swords 'gainst one dagger," I cried, " 'tis near as brave as four against a girl."

They came at me quick. I bellowed and flailed, and ducked between their raised swords. Briant's pommel banged the side of my head. My lunging dagger nicked Laramort's cheek.

"Damn," he cried, and clapped a hand to the cut. In the dusk his blood showed black as Rebecca's under the lopsided moon. Time flickered, the years vanished, I stood as Raven again, a boy before the king. His dagger lay to hand and I would kill them both.

Briant glanced at Laramort's cry. I hacked at his sword hand. As he flinched I shoved him against Laramort. They staggered together, and I stabbed at them, seeing nothing, hating them both. My point jabbed Laramort through his mail. I slashed at Briant again. They staggered back, parrying weakly, bewildered by my carelessness. A small voice in my head was Pierre's warning against rage, was René's warning of pride. I kicked Laramort hard in the gut. He dropped his sword. I bent to pick it up, Briant swung and missed, our blades rang as he parried my attack. I hacked again and caught an armored shoulder. He stumbled away. I turned to meet Laramort, but he was running from the field.

Squires were shouting in the camp. Knights ran up, drawn by the noise of combat, and caught Briant as he fled. Sir Bedevere appeared, and Mordred from the king's tent.

"They came at me with drawn blades." I waved the sword at Briant. "Laramort flees."

"Bedevere, send after him," Mordred growled, and without another word he led us to Arthur's tent. The king still talked to Gawain and his other captains. "Fighting?" he cried. "Cannot my knights save their ardor for the enemy?" And then he saw who we were. "Damn you, both of you. This damned thing." He stood, his face thunderous. "Briant of Marwood. Years past I sent you from Camelot. Now, within the day of my pardon, again you assault my forgiveness."

Briant raised his handsome face, that bore the thin scar I gave him at Sibyl's. "Sire, permit me my defense."

"My lord," I said, "he and Laramort came at me with swords."

"Is this true, Sir Briant?"

"It is, my lord, but . . ."

"Then you have no defense." The king lifted his voice that even those outside might hear. "Briant of Marwood, I would not have you in this camp after Terce tomorrow. I would not have you in Britain after Michaelmas. Six weeks, sir, to settle your affairs, ere I revoke your liege and seize your lands."

"My lord," said Mordred, "your army cannot spare such a fine knight." But Arthur scowled him silent.

Briant stared a long moment, yet when he spoke he said only, "As you are king of Britain." He turned and strode out the tent.

Arthur swung to me. "Two swords against one dagger; had I any doubt of you, Sir Michel, this ends it. I would not send you away, till this siege ends, but then you must go back to Craon." He clamped his mouth shut. "This feud poisons my kingdom."

Hugh washed the blood from my head and bound my wound, and I lay dozing in Gawain's tent when the knight came in, rumbling how ill it was we fought among ourselves.

"A feud, Sir Gawain." I sat up, despite my throbbing head.

"Damn you all for it." By the dim light of a rush candle his squire helped him take off his mail armor. "Stay close to the king tomorrow," he said. "I ride at our head, to answer the deaths of my brothers."

"A blood feud," I said.

"Princes of Orkney, murdered . . ."

"By the knight you'd say nothing against, a month past."

"God's name," Gawain roared, "were we not at siege . . ." But then he stopped. He knew well enough a score of knights might fall tomorrow, a hundred die before the end of it. He lay down and his squire blew out the light, but in the dark Gawain spoke again. "Guard the king well, Sir Michel de Verdeur."

"With my life, Sir Gawain of Orkney."

The king's guard was a score of young knights. We woke at first light, knelt in the cool dust to be shrived, and at sunrise paced full-armed before his tent. A red banner fluttered above Lancelot's castle. "Look," I cried, " 'tis a signal."

And that moment a man's voice cried out over the rumble of the camp, "They are here, they are in the wood, they attack."

A crowd of knights burst out the trees behind us. Each wore on his shield the red and white of Ganis. It was Bors and his cousins that drove straight through the camp, toward the king.

"Our horses," I bellowed at the squires. "Draw your blades," I cried to the guard. "Take the charge on their off side. Stand firm, they must not injure the king."

They fell on us like a storm, swords hewing, horses trampling. In the dust and clangor I hacked at whatever stood before me, man or animal. A knight fought next me, his red-gold hair unprotected by mail; we struck a horseman together, Mordred and I, and the knight screamed above us.

Their attack swerved away. One of Arthur's guard had been felled by a sword across his shoulder, but the rest were uninjured. Squires brought our battle-horses, and lances and helmets. We swung up quickly. They attacked again. My lance took a knight square in the helmet and drove him off his horse. I let him fall and charged another; there were footmen to deal with him. Bors himself gave me a great blow as we passed, yet he and his knights were outnumbered and fighting desperately.

I wondered Lancelot sent so few, when new horns rang and he came with his full army at a gallop, already halfway across the meadows. Gawain bellowed, marshaling his captains. Bors and his men fought with new strength. Another of our guard fell. Arthur sat his own horse, swinging his great sword. I hacked his opponent across the back, and the king hit him a huge blow to the side of his helmet. Another rode at Arthur and I charged to cut him off. Yet another appeared. My helmet rang under his blow. It was thus all the morning. We fought without respite. In a melee oft you might draw away and take a breath, but the king was under constant attack and not till midday did Lancelot sound a horn and draw off his companies toward the castle.

My head shrilled with pain. I gasped for breath and sweat burned my cut scalp and my sword arm shook with fatigue. The dead and wounded lay among tents and under trees, dragged from the field, and if Lancelot's retreat left his wounded our prisoners, that day I had no thought of ransoms.

The king, astride his horse, raised his visor and wiped his sweating face. He took a horn cup from a squire and drank.

"Praise God, sire, that you are safe."

"Sir Michel." He laughed, breathless. "We have done rare work this morning."

"My lord." Gawain galloped up. "We attack, soon as we are re-formed. I will not rest till I cleave that man's head."

Arthur nodded. "But in your hatred, good nephew, do not forget other men may need their ease."

I swung down and limped about, looking to the guard. We had another dead and three sorely wounded, but the rest stood at the king's pavilion passing an aleskin and gnawing loaves. Squires wiped our sweating horses and salved their wounds. Somebody's page handed me a bit of cheese and a slice of black bread.

"Gawain will attack," I said, chewing. "Stay close to the king."

Almost before I finished, Gawain's heralds sounded their horns. His company charged straight down the meadow, with Bedevere's just behind and then Mordred and the rest. Arthur spurred away and we had to ride hard to catch the galloping king.

Our charge caught Lancelot but half-prepared. Gawain drove straight at him but in the swirl and clangor they could not meet cleanly. In the midst of the fray the king lay about him with huge energy, and though knights of Ector's company made repeated drives at him, we battered them all away. The battle raged and shifted, yet Lancelot's army was sorely outnumbered and despite their skill we drove them steadily back. They made a stand at the wooded stream, where we fought long and hard, our horses tramping the shallow water, our blades hindered by willow boughs. At last they broke and sprinted for the castle. Gawain's exhausted company followed but a little way.

My ears rang in the sudden quiet. My throat ached from thirst and shouting. Night quivered under me, exhausted. Dizzy with fatigue, I drew off my helmet and could breathe again. Melees never tired me so, and this night there would be no hot bath nor any grand meal. Nor any company of ladies, though for a moment Naime's face stood before me, unsmiling and serious.

The guard, but a dozen now, rode slowly back across the trampled field, past the groaning injured. As we passed Lucan's knights I saw Balen slumped exhausted in his saddle. Sir Lambert had brought three knights from Denham.

He gave a weary grin, and turned to ride beside me through the lengthening shadows. "No champion's table for you, tonight."

"No," I said, still breathless.

But he cried out, "Oh, God," and drew up short and swung from his horse. A squire sat the trampled ground, holding a fallen knight. Balen dropped to his knees beside them. The arms on his shield were too battered to recognize, but Lambert's bloodied face lay deathly pale when Balen drew off the helmet.

"My God," he cried, "Sir Lambert." Tears streamed down his face. "He was the finest knight, I would have died for him. God's blood, that he must die in this damned cuckold's war."

It was true. I had no greater friend than Lambert of Denham. His house had always been open to me. He never spoke ill of the wound I gave him. He believed in John's dubbing, and stood at my side always. Staring down at his broken body, I remembered his homecoming, how his lady laughed that he would no longer tourney.

"Take him home." I wiped my own eyes. "Stand by his lady."

It was full dark, after the meal and the counting of the dead, when I stumbled at last into Gawain's tent. In the gloom a knight spoke, hoarse. "Good even, sir," he said, and the voice stopped me dead. The rushlight Hugh carried flickered on Briant's face. He sat a stool, blood-dark bandages on his head and shoulder.

"The king sent you away," I said.

He grinned, painfully. "Oh, I rode out at Prime, as he commanded. But what did I find, lurking in the wood?"

"It was you gave that cry?"

"Some say I saved the king today."

"It gave us a minute." I turned and staggered to my cot, and put my weary head in my hands. Briant. Had I killed him at Bramhill, Bors might have killed the king. Was this God's will? How could any man understand it?

Lancelot gained no advantage from his first day's attack, but lost as many as we, and with a smaller force it hurt him more. Still, next morning he appeared early, and we rode again to meet him. Gawain, leading us, thundered down the field against Bors. They met violently, and the crash of their lances unhorsed them both. Behind them all the companies stormed together.

The king rode again in Mordred's company, away from the most violent tumult. But when Gawain fell he stood in his stirrups and drew his blade. "God defend us," he shouted, " 'tis my best knight."

I galloped up beside him as he spurred his horse. "My lord," I cried, "pray you have care."

"Gawain has fallen."

"Sire, you will draw them to you."

"Gawain has fallen," he cried again.

I waved his guard to us and put myself on Arthur's right hand. He drove into the armies, now a violent thunderous mass, hacking his way through like a man crazed. I struggled to shield him, but Lancelot's knights saw his arms and attacked immediately. Arthur chopped at one of them, and I hit the stunned knight a second time. A great blow rang on my helmet. I turned to beat at my attacker. It was Lancelot.

I struck him hard as I could. Lancelot. My sword notched his shield, his reply stung my shield arm. Lancelot. I saw each move he made, strong enough to break me if I wavered. He parried so well I wondered if he, too, saw the coming blow. Lancelot. I had no time to think of fear, could only beat at him as he beat at me. Half our strokes failed, for our horses moved beneath us and other fights jostled us. Lancelot raised his sword again. I was half-deaf already from the clangor and shouting. Off balance, I swung under his guard, caught him sharp across the stomach. His shield wavered. I chopped his helmet, caught his weaker answer. He struck a blow that left my arm numb. My blade took another wedge from his shield. I parried a huge blow, stood in my stirrups to strike. He caught it with his shield. His answer nearly drove me from my saddle. My arm tired, my head swam. I slashed at the face of his helmet. He missed his parry. My blade drove into his visor. I had to jerk it free. The blow had stunned him. I labored his shoulders. Blood welled through his mail. I hit him hard as I could, but he raised his shield again.

"The king," a knight shouted.

I spun away, unthinking. Arthur slumped from his horse under Lionel's blow. My sword drove Lionel from his own saddle, but already Ector stood over the king, his blade at Arthur's throat.

"Now," he bellowed, "by Christ, I'll end this war."

Even as I charged I knew I failed.

But Lancelot's voice boomed over the noise of battle. "Ector, he is thy king, Ector. He made you knight, and all of us."

Ector paused. Lancelot leaped from his horse. He wavered himself, yet he bent over Arthur and helped him stand. We all stepped back, amazed and breathless at this chivalry, that in the midst of high battle, with only injury and death in mind, Lancelot saved his enemy. I could not deny my own admiration.

Arthur raised his visor. Tears ran down his bruised face. "God help us," he cried, though he gasped for breath. "Here is the finest knight of Christendom." He stared at Lancelot, and gripped his hand. "How I rue our dispute."

"My lord," Lancelot said, "I had no want of it." My blow had jammed his visor, and he drew off his whole helmet to show a face swollen and bleeding about the eyes. I had missed blinding him by a hairbreadth.

"My queen," said Arthur. "You hide my queen in that castle."

"To protect her from your death." Lancelot wiped his bleeding face. "Revoke your sentence, sire, and I restore her at once."

But the king's brow darkened again. "God's name, I will not." He raised his voice, though all about us the battle had gone nearly quiet. "Sir Gawain has fallen."

"He hath wounded Sir Bors," said Lancelot, "whom we would carry to Joyous Gard.

"And I take Gawain to his tent."

The king swung up and rode straight through the battle, between the bloodied and labored knights. I followed, close as I could. Gawain lay pale and half-conscious under a clump of trees, Bors' lance driven deep into his chest, the wound as serious as I gave Lambert. My anger flared, briefly. Lambert of Denham, that had recovered from my stroke but to die on this damn field, of the king's cuckoldry and Gawain's wrath.

"Go you well, fair knight," Arthur murmured. Gawain raised a silent hand as the squires carried him off. The king tugged at his beard. "Lancelot saved me. But never have I seen Lancelot so staggered. Nor his face so bruised. Who fought with him?"

"We met, sire," I said, and he turned and stared at me. "I had the advantage, sire, I thought to best him. But had I done it, Ector would have slain you."

"You thought to best him." He almost smiled. "But 'tis true, only he would have spared me."

Mordred galloped up, puffing, his horse lathered from the fight. "Sire, we have them now." Lancelot had turned his army back to Joyous Gard, though it lacked an hour to midday. "We will catch them," he cried, "ere they reach the stream."

King Arthur shook his head. "There will be tomorrow."

But that day brought rain and the next was Sabbath, and the wet persisted a long week till Our Lady's Assumption. The day I would have met Lancelot alone. But we had met already, and I had matched him. I remembered each blow, how hard he struck, how he wavered under my sword, how my own strength had wearied his. The whole camp knew of it. Some knights praised me for it, but many others glanced at me nervous, and even Olivier grew careful in my company.

*   *   *

Sir Gawain was soon healed well enough that we knew he would not die. The king had wished to send him to Camelot, but Gawain would go no farther than Lonazep. "This war," he grumbled, "it will fail utterly if I am not here to keep you at it."

Yet if Gawain's hatred did not waver, Arthur owed his own life to Lancelot and that nearly stopped the war. Lancelot no longer sallied from Joyous Gard. We encircled castle and town, and though the king at last allowed the taking of Lancelot's harvest, we made no siege machines nor any attempt to storm the walls. We sat in our tents drinking wine, or patrolled the fields armed and bannered. And every day I thought of my lady Naime.

So it went till Saint Giles' Day, and the knights' forty days were nearly done. Gawain had returned to camp, thin and angry, to argue that we must stand before Joyous Gard all the winter, that he would keep Orkney and every Scottish knight out of his own purse. But neither he nor the king could afford the whole army, and the rest made ready to leave.

It was the last gray hour of the day, and I rode back muddy and cold from the siege line, when a half dozen priests came trotting through the camp. I dismounted and followed them into the king's pavilion. The oldest, elegant in rich furs, spoke gravely to Arthur. Already the king frowned at his words. The pope, the priest said, heard of Arthur's quarrel with Lancelot. It distressed the Holy Father when Christian knights made war. He urged a truce. Lancelot must give up Guenever; the king must give surety for her life, and restore her station.

Arthur squirmed with anger. "My lord bishop, this is a matter of Britain, not of Rome."

The bishop shrugged. "Rome hath noticed it."

"Doth not the Book condemn adultery?"

"There were no witnesses."

Arthur leapt from his seat. "God save you, Rochester. It was Matins. What else might they have been doing at that hour?"

The bishop stood unflinching. "Sir Lancelot says it was an appointment, the queen wished to speak . . ."

"And the pope believes him?" cried Arthur.

"The word of a Christian knight." The bishop gazed at him. "Who saved your own life on the battlefield."

"God's blood, how I rue that." Arthur paced the tent. "A knight ought die killed by honorable foes, not saved by his enemy. And now for my immortal soul I must take back an adulterous wife."

"I have not spoke of excommunication," said the bishop.

"But you will." The king strode to him. "My justice condemned her, Rochester. My nephews are dead, war takes a score of my knights, destroys my Roundtable. But the pope would have me . . ." He glowered at the bishop. "Else British priests will not say Mass, nor shrive us ere we die."

The cleric held up a ribboned packet. "Here is his letter."

"I must take the queen."

"And make a peace with Sir Lancelot."

"My lord," Gawain burst out, "I will not have this peace. If you would, sire, you lose my homage."

"You see?" said Arthur. "Even my own knights hate this." The bishop did not answer. "Have you spoke to Lancelot?"

"We would go when we have your agreement," said the bishop.

"My lord." I stepped into their midst. "I am neither Camelot nor Joyous Gard, let me carry this word to Lancelot."

"Sir Michel." Arthur almost smiled, though even he seemed more earnest of me since my meeting with Lancelot. "Yes. Go. But I charge you, stay close to the queen till this matter be resolved."

Hugh bound a white cloth to a lance and rode before me. A thin drizzle had begun and the dusk drew in as we forded the narrow stream. A voice hailed us from Lancelot's battlements, where heads peered through the crenellations.

"I come under the king's truce," I shouted. "The pope doth require an end to this war."

"Wait there," called the guard, "where we can see you."

The rain increased. Our horses stamped and shook their heads, but the gate soon creaked open and we rode in under the tower.

Ector squinted at me as I dismounted. "Sir Michel de Verdeur. Welcome to Joyous Gard."

"I thank you, Sir Ector de Maris." A red-headed knight stood beside him. Rain dripped from his hood. "Sir Almant," I said, but he turned away.

"The pope himself?" said Ector.

"The bishop of Rochester, bearing a letter from Rome. I come with its import."

"Sir Lancelot waits in the Hall."

We walked quickly through the rain, across the crowded bailey between covered wains, sheds of raw wood, the smoking fires of footmen. Past a second gate more men were camped in tents against the high curving wall of Lancelot's keep. A strong door stood at the far end of the court, that opened past a stairway to the castle Hall. A great fire blazed at the hearth. A dozen knights talked together there, and Lancelot sat his high table. Bowing to him, I saw a new scar over his right eye.

"Of course I will meet my bishop Rochester," he said. "I will go now and you will escort me."

"The king desires I stay here, sir. With his queen."

He flushed with anger, and stood so quick his chair fell behind him. "Jesu. Not even a king's messenger may insult me." His knights rumbled where they stood.

"Sir, I bring only the king's wish."

"That puts you at the mercy of my wrath."

"Everyone speaks of your honor, Sir Lancelot."

He grimaced. "All save Arthur, king of Britain."

Women's voices sounded, coming down the stairs behind me. I knew it was the queen and did not turn to look. "The Holy Father believes you and King Arthur are the world's finest knights."

"Then, by God, let us battle. Let us meet, each his own champion." But he spoke in jest, his anger already past. "Heaven ought be happy to welcome such souls."

"The pope seeks to end this conflict, sir."

"Then I wait his word, and my bishop Rochester."

He glanced past me and smiled. Damask rustled as Guenever came round the table.

"Good Sir Michel." She smiled and took a place beside him.

I drew a breath. "My lady." After a month of camp life, of rain and mud, she looked more beautiful than ever, and even I might imagine her my courtly love.

"Sit you, sir." Lancelot pointed the seat opposite him.

"Sir, I thank you."

I brought the king's anger, yet Lancelot put me at his high table. At last I understood it, that his huge ability at arms made him both fearless and merciful. He neither envied nor hated any man, and his anger was brief as a summer storm. For this had Camelot's finest knights joined him, despite King Arthur. I myself, feeling the warmth of his smile, feared he might also entice me from the king. Could any man resist the kindness of his manner, the nobility of his broad face?

A server brought a silver cup, filled with wine. Lancelot passed it to me, that I might drink first. "Thank you, sir host," I said, before I gave it to the queen.

Another lady sat beside me. "Michel," said Naime.

Twenty-nine

The wine of Joyous Gard might have held a potion, so did my heart leap at her voice. I could not speak, my ears roared, my hands shook.

"I could not believe it was you." She put a hand on my arm. "Michel?"

"Lady." I gripped her hand with my own, and struggled with my tongue. "Dear Naime. How came you here?"

"My lady called." She nodded at the queen, yet did not take her eyes from me.

"Pray God," I murmured, "this matter of her be not settled for a month, that I may see you every day. And every night."

She raised her brows. "Do you besiege every castle?"

I blinked, caught by the memory of Matilde abed at Craon, that said the same. And still the courtly words came easy. "Only the most beautiful, lady, that is the one I desire." Naime smiled at me, and there in that beleaguered castle in the midst of war, love filled up my heart again.

The queen's ladies gathered in the Hall for the evening meal. Servants lay napkins before us, and little knives for our meat. The cup passed and I wiped it carefully for Naime. "Thank you, sir," she said, and pressed her leg to mine beneath the table. I could hardly think for it, nor keep my hands steady.

Famous knights took their places along the high table, and Sir Bors sat on my other side. "Sir Michel," he said, hoarse. He was thin and pale as Gawain. "Welcome to Joyous Gard."

"Sir Bors, I am pleased you heal. Sir Gawain mends, too."

"I am glad to hear it. And you, sir, how your strength grows, and your fame. Even Lancelot mentions it." He touched his own brow just where Lancelot wore my scar.

I swallowed, to subdue my pride. "Pray God we meet no more at war."

"The truce of the pope." He glanced at Guenever, his long face unhappy. "I fear this matter will not end so easy."

"Sir Gawain swears a blood feud of his brothers."

"And I will always defend my kinsman." He stared at me. "You are the king's man, now?"

"I am sworn to him, but only for this matter."

The cup passed again. Lancelot spoke to Bors. The lady Naime asked that I cut her meat. "How famous you have grown," she murmured, "that Bors and even Lancelot speak of you."

"And do you look at me more kindly, lady?"

"No more than ever, good sir."

"Then you know what I have ever desired."

She glanced at the hand I had taken. "This is no sport, sir. No sleeve worn on your tourney helmet."

I drew a breath. "I love you, lady. I wish not your color, if I have your heart." She did not speak for a dozen beats of my own heart, and then she put her other hand on mine.

All through that meal I felt happy as I ever had, as if there might be only love and we two, caught in some eternal flowering springtime. Always this castle spoke of love. Years past the place had sheltered the love of Tristram and Isoud, against the wrath of Isoud's husband Mark. Lancelot had named it Joyous Gard then, and now it held himself and Guenever, against Arthur. And myself and Naime against . . . But I did not know against what.

When the ladies had risen and only knights sat table, Bors leaned to me again and murmured, "Such a pretty lady."

"So she is," I said.

"You know her older sister is Elaine, who so witched Lancelot she got Sir Galahad of him?"

My head swam with wine. "Ought I fear her magic, too?"

He laughed aloud. "If I meant to give you warning, Sir Michel, I were much too late."

The tables were half empty when Lancelot stood. Knowing what I must do, I shook my head to clear it and went to him.

"The king has charged me to guard the queen, sir."

In the air between us there stood suddenly rain and winter and war.

But his fury came and went as a passing cloud. "Damn me, this matter doth transmute us all." He lifted his head and called his castellan. "Sir, this knight will sleep at the queen's door."

The old knight bowed, stiffly. "If you wish it, sir."

He led me up a stair and past a small chapel. The queen sat in her solar, lit by a small fireplace, with Naime and several others that looked up smiling. "This knight will guard you, madam," said the castellan.

Guenever flinched as if he struck her, and clenched her jaw and turned bitter eyes to me. "Are you now my king's cleric, sir?"

"I have his orders, lady." I turned to the castellan. "I would see the chamber."

He led me past their unhappy faces to an ample chamber half-filled with beds and lit by tapers, that smelled of apples. Another door stood in a far corner. "What is that?" I said.

"The servants' way."

"My esquire will sleep outside it."

"Good sir." He gestured at the beds. "Think you my lord comes here, among these dozen ladies?"

"Else she goes to him."

"Sir Lancelot stays in his keep, sir, across the bailey, under the eyes of sentries, through the night's rain." He stared another moment, before he clamped his thin lips and walked away.

The queen stood at the fire, her hands gripped tight. "Do you make me a prisoner, Sir Michel?"

"The king would have me close to you, madam." I looked at her door again. "Vespers to Prime."

"Yet the king wishes me back a loving wife?"

"Only he can speak of that." I watched the firelight on her unhappy face and kept my eyes from Naime. "You have been eight weeks in Joyous Gard."

"I had been eight weeks in Purgatory, save for Sir Lancelot." Her look was almost pleading. "Does no one take my side?"

"Many do, lady." So might I, save for the night of Mordred's ambush, for all the nights before Lancelot tramped the servants' corridor. She read my disapproval and closed her eyes.

In the buttery across the rainy court, Hugh sat among red-faced squires and drank their ale. He swallowed his laughter when I told him. "What must I do, sir? Slay her if she comes out?"

"Wave your sword, bang the walls, shout to wake the castle. Follow her if she goes past you. Do not injure her."

"But, if it's Sir Lancelot?"

"Then in God's name stay asleep."

He pushed away his mug. "If he does not kill me before."

"Lean something against the door, that will fall if it opens. Remember, give the alarm and nothing else."

"Oh, sir, I will remember that."

The ladies were retired when I came back. I knelt in the chapel to say my prayer for Giles. The solar was dark save the dying fire, and soon a servant came to bank it. I lit the stub of a taper against the gloom. The castle grew very quiet, though at long intervals sentries called on the battlements overhead. I opened a wood shutter and stared out at the night meadows. A pelting rain hid Arthur's siege fires. Praise God I slept tonight under a castle roof, and not in that cold and muddy camp.

I drew my blade, untied my sword belt, and leaned the empty scabbard against the chamber door. Just inside slept the queen. And Naime. My breath caught, but I gripped my heathen sword in the king's name and set a chair near the hearth.

I was fast asleep when the scabbard clattered and fell. The candle had burnt almost out, and in the sudden draft the flame leaped and died. The chamber went completely black. I stood carefully. She must pass me on her way.

The scabbard rattled again as she pushed the door. "Mary," she muttered, in a voice that did not sound like Guenever. I thought she must be nervous.

"Lady," I murmured, "go back to your bed."

There was a long silence.

"Are you a false knight, empty of courtliness?" Naime said.

My heart stopped. "Lady, I thought you were the queen."

"The queen," she muttered, "hath more sense than grope the dark for love."

I could not breathe. Here at last, her lips, her arms, her long legs, myself within that shaded field. Oh, God and Christ.

"Michel," she whispered, "where are you?"

"Lady." I cleared my throat. "Lady, think you why I am here, against Sir Lancelot, sworn to the king's honor and, oh my lady, mine own honor as well."

There was another silence.

"Oh, lady, despite my true love of you, and all my words at table."

She did not answer.

"Lady, I love you, but you must go back to your bed."

"Sweet Mother." She let out a long breath. "How I do weary of knights and honor."

"Lady, I . . ."

"Good night, Sir Michel." The door closed sharply.

* * *

Bishop Rochester came to Joyous Gard next morning. Lancelot greeted him in the Hall and I took my place near them, full-armed, hauberk and sword a weary weight after my restive night. The queen sat with her ladies at the fire, and Naime would not look at me.

King Arthur, said the cleric, would take Guenever and never charge her of events past. But he made no peace with Lancelot.

"Sir Gawain is adamant of his dead brothers, therefore the king gives you only truce, and thirty days to quit his kingdom."

"King Arthur sends me into exile?" said Lancelot. I had never seen him so pale. His knights rumbled their displeasure, and the queen put a hand to her throat.

"Else you stay here, and besieged."

"This is the pope's wish?"

"It is all the king will accept."

Lancelot sat frowning, as if he numbered his men, how long the siege might last, how he might attack the king again. It made me glad I had armed myself. But then he murmured, "Good Rochester, a knight cannot disobey his Holy Father, nor his liege lord." Guenever closed her eyes. He turned and stared long at her, ere he spoke again with a broken voice. "Tell the king I will bring my lady to Camelot, before Sabbath next. If he will not hear me, then I must take ship to my own lands, Brittany and Banioc."

The groans of his knights rumbled in the Hall. The queen slumped in her chair and Naime bent to her. Yet as she did she glanced at me and, though I disbelieved my eyes, almost smiled.

The rain had stopped, the day Lancelot rode out from Joyous Gard, and in the autumn sunlight he made a grand procession. Guenever rode beside him, both dressed in white robes broidered with gold. Before them went a dozen knights, clad in blue velvet. Naime and her other women followed, and then a score of knights, all in white. But in the midst of all their finery, I rode behind the queen in battered armor and a battle-stained surcoat. Hugh carried a lance upright with Craon's pennon, and my shield of dragon, tree, and raven, that still bore the marks of Lancelot's sword.

"I am Craon's," I had said. "I will wear no other livery. Nor, by King Arthur's order, will I ride apart from the queen."

Lancelot gazed at me sadly. "Will you ever forgive me?"

"Too many knights have died," I growled. " 'Tis but fortune that I am alive, and not dead at your hand, as well."

"The king would have burned her."

But I turned away, too furious to argue. Lancelot had no equal in battle. As a fighter I admired him as no other knight; even his new scar was but a mark of the wizard's gift. Nor could I deny his magnificent chivalry, that in the heat of battle saved the king. Yet that huge ability gave him an unwavering certainty, and he believed that if he never failed at battle, then every other act, whether in court or bedchamber, must be equally legitimate.

For years he dallied with his lord's queen, yet had no notion it might injure his immortal soul. Blind that he damaged king and Camelot, on his return his Sangral vows dissolved like salt in water. Agravain's jealousy he brushed aside. My own voice was but another saying what he would not hear. He killed all save Mordred at the ambush. He killed all save me at the queen's bonfire. A score of each side had died at Joyous Gard. For honor, for love, but more especially for Lancelot's eternal righteousness.

God knew I understood love's power. I had been a fool of it, often enough. But no matter what I did for love, I would not deny what I had done. I would not plead innocence nor claim it never happened nor say it was the fault of some other man's unwarranted wrath. Yet Lancelot, finally come to Camelot, stood in the great Hall before the king and spoke of nothing but his prowess.

"My lord, I did not seek that fight in the queen's corridor. My lady summoned me. I had only just arrived when Agravain and the others, full-armed 'gainst my single dagger, beat on her door and called me traitor and false knight."

"That is not so," cried Gawain, red-faced with anger. "It was Matins, you had been there hours."

Lancelot shrugged, smug in his knightly skill. "I defeated them all, sire. My victory proved their charges false."

Nor had he sought the deaths of Gareth and Gaheris. Only the threat to a great lady brought him to the field. He reminded the king, and Gawain and many others, how he rescued each of them, had saved their lives. He would found chantries, that priests might pray each day for those he had killed. He swayed the assembled knights, ladies watched with damp eyes, even the king was moved. But Gawain remained adamant, and in his fury challenged Lancelot to a combat the king could not allow during the pope's truce.

At last the king saw he must decide between the two of them. Remembering his wife seduced, his nephews slain, his army battered, his court divided, and his fellowship destroyed, King Arthur chose Gawain's anger over Lancelot's chivalry.

Lancelot, stunned and disbelieving, turned and went away from Camelot, and spent his last weeks in Britain dismissing his fiefs, giving to his knights castles and manors he held himself. I would have stayed at Camelot with Naime, to ease her anger, but Arthur decreed I ride with Lancelot everywhere, and see him gone.

We came finally to Southampton two days before Michaelmas. His fleet rocked on the waters of the bay, two dozen ships to bear his men and horses and the hundred Camelot knights that left with him. In the cool windy sunshine I watched Lancelot's own ship loaded. Red-headed Almant stood among his knights, and I walked to him and bowed. "Sir Almant of Damerel."

He squinted in the sun and put a hand on his sword. "Michel de Verdeur. Would you fight me yet?"

"Vows taken, vows forgot," I said. "Who knows which may foster good, which evil?" He frowned, not understanding. "We may meet, sir, when I return to Craon."

He stood very still. "I have no argument of you."

"Nor I of you, Sir Almant. Too much blood hath flowed already." I put out my hand. He shook it carefully, the act unnatural after all those years. "Go you well," I said.

"And you."

We both turned quickly away.

It was Vespers when the tide began to ebb. Lancelot walked the quay, unwilling to leave. "You will tell him I am gone."

"I will, sir."

"Tell him I love and honor him still. I would defend him 'gainst any man. You must tell him, if ever he has need I will bring all I have." Even now, sent away from Britain by an angry king, he imagined the brotherhood of knights still connected them.

"Goodbye, Sir Lancelot," I called, as he stepped into his ship.

He smiled. "God save you, Sir Michel. I will send to Craon to say how well you served King Arthur."

"I return soon enough, myself." I put out my hand. He reached from the boat and took it. His grip was very strong.

"And tell her," he murmured, blinking damp eyes, "tell her she still owns my heart."

Thirty

We rode up to Winchester through a clear autumn morning, bright as spring though it was October. Cattle grazed the stubbled fields, farmers cut drying reeds for thatch, honey peddlers trundled their carts from village to village. The sun shone warm on our robes, and Hugh made tunes on the pipe he bought in Southampton. It was finished. Lancelot had gone. His departure saved both king and Camelot, and surely I owed nothing more to Arthur. My liege to John called me back to Craon. Despite my love of Naime, in this bright autumn I might sail any time, follow Lancelot across the harrowed sea.

Certainly I had done well of Britain. I had gained a champion's tourney victories, ample battle ransoms, Giles' coin, Briant's horses, even my fame against Lancelot. I had founded Lark's chantry at Ryford's forest chapel. I had, after it all, fifty pounds of coin with the Jews of Winchester, and a hundred of armor and animals still at Denham. And yet I was but a small and lackland knight.

We rode in at Winchester's south gate at midday. A knot of laughing squires shouted to us that king and court made a grand feast that evening. "The sun shines," Hugh said, "the war is over." He looked about, grinning. "I've always fancied Winchester, sir. Just see that pretty lass. I wonder if her father's rich enough."

I laughed with him, yet in the sunny day and the happy city something dark edged my thoughts. This warm day was not spring. Winter came, inevitably. I turned aside to the cathedral. The chants of Sixte echoed in the old high nave. I knelt and prayed, not knowing why.

Up at the castle, porters unloaded wains in the sunlit court, hens cackled in cages, eels slithered in barrels, sturgeon shone in baskets. The songs of minstrels rang from the Hall, its shutters open to the fair weather, and the castellan appeared at the arched door and cried, "Welcome, Sir Michel, has he truly gone?"

"Gone at last, Sir Grummore. And where is the king?"

"In his chambers." He laughed and pointed at the old keep.

I glanced at the queen's casements. A month past, Guenever had stood on her bonfire, waiting the king's death. "And my lady?"

His smile faded. "She stops at Amesbury, among the holy sisters." He looked away. "The consolations of prayer, they say."

"God give her rest," I muttered. Naime would be there, too.

I walked into the keep's shadow and up its old stairs. Arthur sat with Gawain and Mordred and a dozen others, laughing over a cup. They turned smiling when the herald called my name.

"Welcome, Sir Michel," cried the king. "Give him the cup, he will be thirsty from the road." He had trimmed his beard, his face was fresh, his eyes were clear. "You have seen him away?"

"I have, sire. On yesterday's ebb."

"We saw he wears a new scar, and from your blade."

"He does, my lord." I touched my own brow, while a murmur of approval ran among the knights.

"Praise God he's gone," Gawain rumbled.

"Good sir," said Arthur, "let us hear no more of this."

"Nay, my lord, I will not cease, you will hear of it always till I meet him again, sword loud on sword."

"Brother," said Mordred, "pray, let us have peace."

"Damn you, they were brothers, too."

"Good knights," cried Arthur, "I would have no bickering between the marshal of my kingdom." He put one hand on Gawain's shoulder, and his other clasped Mordred's arm. "And my steward of southern Britain."

If the gathered knights murmured their pleasure at Gawain's title, Mordred's position sat less comfortably with them. Many thought him very young. Others said Orkney gained too much renown in Britain's court. All wondered if Mordred were the king's half-incestuous son. Yet when I looked about I saw none of them would speak of it. God's Name, had Camelot learned nothing from this war? Would the king's incest be as invisible as the queen's adultery? Almost I said it, myself, but then my eye found Briant among them.

The king saw my angry glance and understood its reason. "And from this day," he rumbled, "I will have an end of private feuds. Especially this, between Michel de Verdeur and Briant of Marwood."

Briant pushed his way forward. "My lord and king." He bowed deeply. "You have my knight's pledge of it."

At Sir Edmund's I had been unable to kill Briant. At Southampton I had shook Almant's hand. No man's death could resurrect the dead. My revenge had gone to ashes, yet it irked me that in Arthur's chamber and at his command I must give it up.

"Sire, this man killed . . ."

"God's blood," he rumbled, "I will have no more of it."

Then, I thought, by God, I will have my raven's fee for it.

"My lord, at your wish have I served you a year and more, have fought in your tourneys, guarded your queen, battled your enemies, served as your herald." I paused, that all of them remember it. "More than a year, though I am a man of John, baron of Craon." Arthur clamped his lips shut, knowing well what I would ask. "For this, sire, the manors of Craon in Blackmoor . . ."

". . . are the manors of Glastonbury and my father's prayers."

"My lord," said Mordred, "surely he deserves something. You have many vassal fiefs, recovered of knights gone away."

But I would take no other lands. "Sir John sent me to recover his manors, sire, and that only."

"And Craon may not have them. I have said it a dozen times."

"Then I will return to Craon." I bowed again. "And every man I meet will hear how Britain's king refused me."

"What?" he cried. "Do you threaten me?" His eyes flared with anger and my heart thumped at my own audacity. "You have not heard what I offer."

"The manors of Craon, sire . . ."

"At Astolat," said Arthur, "Clegis remains my castellan." He gave a hard smile. "But my constable has withdrawn. Astolat is a royal castle, its garrison a dozen knights and twoscore men, its income fifty pounds. If your valiant arm merits a higher place, Michel de Verdeur, your impetuous youth keeps you from it."

The knights about us murmured their approval. It was a royal position, and a clear mark of the king's esteem. A castle's constable was master of its guard, though with Britain at peace there would be little to do. He wished me here in Britain. And the wizard had said, be his man. Yet Astolat felt an affront, to Sir John as much as me.

"My lord," I said, "I thank you for your generosity. But I am a man of Craon, not of Camelot." The chamber went deathly silent. "I came to Britain for the manors of my lord John. I will take nothing for myself only." I bowed to his cold-eyed stare, praying he gave me a week to leave Britain.

The king watched me, tight-lipped. "Michel de Verdeur. Once of Greenfarm, of the demesne of Camelot. Mayhap a natural son to my sister Morgan." He glanced about. "My lords, what ought I do with this knight?"

"Away," most said, though several muttered, "Blackmoor."

"Even my advisors stand confused." Arthur smiled thinly. " 'Tis high insult to refuse a king's gift, yet your liege to Craon excuses it. Nevertheless, sir, do not delay your sailing overlong."

In the street of the Jews, Aaron answered my knock and led me up to their little chamber off the stair. Simon his uncle had come from Southampton, for the city was closed to them, and their ships and their foreign crews must put out from other ports. He complained of the king's tallage for his war against Lancelot, but I had thoughts only for my goods and coin, and how I might ship it all across the winter sea.

" 'Tis a great risk, so much coin aboard a winter ship," I said.

Simon raised his brows. "Buy manors here, sir, estates. There's many free with all those knights gone away."

"I have refused the king his post. I have said only Craon's manors will satisfy me."

Aaron nodded. "Well, sir, if you bring us the coin, we will give a letter for our cousins in Rouen, that they give you the same amount there."

"Truly?" I could but half believe him, yet I remembered Lambert's broken chest, and that on a summer voyage. "I will fetch it all soon, I would sail before All Souls'."

Almost I did not stay for the king's feast at the castle, save it was dishonorable to depart so quick. I took a seat far from his dais, and though there were minstrels and jugglers and acrobats, and much wine flowed with the abundant courses, and knights hailed the leaving of Lancelot, still a sense of gloom hung over the great Hall. It felt half empty. Many had sailed and many others, pleading manorial duties, had not come. And Guenever was absent.

Next day I set out for Amesbury, in company with Sir Aliduke and three of his knights. They all knew of my refusal of the king and though they said nothing, glanced at me curious. Once more I went as Craon's man, a new shield painted with John's dragon, my own green tree, my black raven. Hugh wore new green livery and carried Craon's white pennon tied to a raised lance. The sun shone warm on our winter robes. Acorns hung fat among the browning leaves of the oaks, and sparrows fluttered the stubbled fields. Here and there farmers had begun their winter plowing and the damp smell of earth delighted me, though Aliduke and the rest, knights of castle and town, took no pleasure in it.

For an hour that bright morning my worries eased, yet soon enough Naime's face went before me. I thought to ignore my liege of Craon for her, almost, and stay in Britain. Yet she frowned and muttered of Angevin inconstancy after Joyous Gard, and it came to me that, in part, her coolness fueled my own obstinacy with the king. If I rode to Amesbury thinking to plead my love again, in truth both the king's anger and my own sent me back to Craon. I could only hope we would part fondly.

As if it echoed my thoughts, the sky went dark over us and a chill wind tugged at our robes. "False summer," muttered Aliduke, "quickly gone."

The rain blew toward us like a gray curtain, that we met on the last hill above Amesbury. It fell so hard that when we came to the abbey court, water already puddled the gravel and sheeted from the stable eaves. It drummed angry on the shingles of the cloister roof, along the same way Naime had led me when we first met, a year past. In her chamber Guenever sat before a small fireplace, bundled in furs. Naime was among her ladies, bent over her broidery hoop, and did not look up as we came in.

The queen's face bore lines I had not seen before. Her beauty had a sharper cast, the bones of her cheeks were more clear, her eyes more tired. Yet when Aliduke bowed before her she smiled and her whole form eased. "Praise God, here is a knight I can trust."

"My lady," said Aliduke.

Her gaze darkened again as it fell on me. "Sir knight," she muttered, "bring you another message from the king?"

"No, madam. I come instead for your leave to say good-bye."

"Good-bye?"

Out the corner of my eye I saw Naime's head swing up. "The king," I said, "will keep the manors of Craon. Despite my petitions and my year of service."

"My lord offered him the constable of Astolat," said Aliduke, "but Sir Michel refused him."

"Did you?" said Guenever. For a moment her eyes shone and I caught a breath of her old vigor. "Did you, indeed? Yet he leaves you free to travel Britain?"

"He knows I leave soon, madam."

"We will be saddened when you go, Sir Michel." She gazed at me. "Mayhap I have a manor."

"Lady," I said, "forgive me, but I am Craon's liege man."

Guenever frowned, herself. "Chivalry," she muttered.

That evening at table the abbey's steward sat me with Naime. But though I praised her beauty, though I told of Lancelot's going and of the king at Winchester, though I cut her meat and wiped the cup, she would not speak. Against that sullenness I could not think how to progress, and not till the second courses were finished did she turn and mutter at me, "You would have killed her."

"My lady, it was the king . . ." I stopped, hearing myself pleading another man's anger. I thought I was forgiven of that, for she had healed me, after.

"Had not Lancelot rescued her," she said.

"Who but Lancelot brought her to that bonfire?"

She plucked at her bread. "My lady finds the world joyless without him." Her eyes were suddenly damp. "And now you leave."

My heart beat. Might she love me yet? I took her hand. "Lady, I love you, and your tears pierce my heart."

She drew it back. "I found it stout-armored against love."

"Naime, pray let us not repeat that night at Joyous Gard."

"It was thy notion." She looked away. "The king's command. Thy knightly honor."

Beside the fire a minstrel began to sing, of love and heartache.

"I have been weeks away, and every night I cursed myself of it. But now beside you I forget everything but love."

"Once more, thy Angevin flattery."

The minstrel strummed his psaltery and sang of his lady's bright eye, her round bosom, her hard heart. The taperlight on my own lady's cheek stopped my breath.

"Dear Naime, how may I say it? I love you."

"Do you, sir?"

I imagined a small softness in her voice. "I would be thy vassal, thy servant."

"Good sir, I do not ask it."

The minstrel sang of his lady's sharp tongue, his own bewilderment.

"I must sleep in the lodge, outside the cloister gate."

"This is a nunnery, sir."

I took her hand again. She did not draw it away. "Lady, pity me, I have lost my heart and with it all my liberty."

"What you lose, sir, I do not have."

"But it is yours, lady. Whether you wish it or no."

My lady of high beauty, sang the minstrel, my lady never yielding.

I drew a breath. "Whether I wish it or no."

"Once more," she murmured, softly, "this empty courtesy."

I lifted her hand and pressed my lips to it, and she watched me under lowered lids. "Dear lady, I love you. More than life."

Within her ebon tower, cried the minstrel, hath she chained my heart.

"Why ought I believe you, sir?" But there was no edge in her voice now, and her lips were almost parted in a smile.

"My lady." I took her both her hands and kissed them again. "Somewhere in this place, is there not somewhere?"

"You are so sudden, sir."

I felt my cheeks hot and my breath short. But now she truly smiled, and her bosom was rising, her eyes glistened. She stood and turned and went along the chamber, out a farther door. I followed, through a darkling passage and up a turning stair to a dim chamber where curtained beds stood against tapestried walls.

"Sweet lady." I pulled her to me.

"At least," she said, "tonight you do not shield yourself with armor and honor."

"Lady." I kissed her. She wrapped her arms around me. We kissed again. The chamber swam around us. We staggered against a curtained bed and onto its high broidered cover. We had no time to remove our robes, but swept aside only what was needful.

"Oh, sweet knight," she whispered, and wrapped her long body about me and took me in.

It had been months and I was very sudden, but I would not stop until again and yet again. At last she pressed a hand to my chest. "Dear Michel, spare us both, this is no nightlong melee."

"Lady, I love you."

"At last I believe it." She took my face in both her hands and kissed me. "And I love you, Michel."

"You have enchanted me," I said. "Since we first met, here at Amesbury."

"That day you could only see the queen."

"Lady, 'tis not true."

She kissed me again. "Ah, chivalry."

For the span of that hour all the world's troubles vanished. And though I must leave her soon enough, go out through the winter cloisters and the rain-filled night, neither wet nor cold could damp my smile and I slept without dreaming, though at first dawn I imagined she came to me again.

I was gnawing a loaf in the visitors' refectory when Hugh appeared. The queen sent for me, and I wondered at the early hour.

Her chamber felt cool and dim after the night's warmth. Only a few ladies sat with Guenever, and Naime was not with them.

"Sir Michel," she said, "Aliduke tells me there were but few knights at Winchester. That many sailed." She closed her eyes and I kept myself from touching her to ease her sorrow. "That many others kept away. The king noticed, and he will think." She stopped again. "Who can tell what he will think? But he is not, surely, much pleased with me. I wonder will he ever forgive me."

"My lady, I am certain he will." Though I doubted it would be soon. "May I do you any service ere I leave?"

Her face eased. "Though I regret your going, Sir Michel, I pray you might carry letters to Brittany."

"I will, madam," I said, without pleasure. They would be letters to Lancelot. "Before All Souls'." I drew a breath. "And, I pray you, forgive me of that day on Camelot's meadow."

"The king and his law." She glanced away. "Britain's law. Against courtliness. Against love."

"But, my lady, does not the king also love? Think you, how would you feel were you him?" And once again I must rue my tongue.

She went abruptly pale. Her face might have become stone, and for a dozen heartbeats she did not move. At last her jaw unclenched and her brow smoothed, though the energy of her anger that lingered made her as beautiful as before. In the chamber around us her ladies breathed again.

"Michel de Verdeur." She stared at me. "Always I wonder, is it folly, or true wit?"

I took a breath myself, as I bowed to her and begged her leave. Naime had come into the chamber while we spoke, and now she turned and went before me into the abbess' cloister. I hoped to read love in her face, but she did not smile or even look at me.

"Good morning, my lady, I love you with all my heart."

She tossed her head, annoyed. In her furred robes she looked the king's daughter, that I had forgot for a night. "Last night I believed you would stay in Britain."

"Lady, I am a landless knight, man of a foreign lord, object of the king's displeasure. You are a noble's daughter. . . ." Several ladies passed us silently, their eyes watching every move. "Naime, would you walk in the garden?"

She drew her furred mantle about her shoulders. A pale morning sun lit the bare paths, where a few last bees nosed among shriveled herbs, hoping for blooms and finding none.

"Foolish bees," I said, "to think sunshine makes it spring." She sat a cold stone bench, and I beside her. "I love you, my lady." She stared at me a moment before she turned her head away. "Dear Naime, last night you said you loved me." Still she looked away. "I must go, today, for my coin and my belongings."

"And then to Anjou," she muttered, "but had you taken the king's offer."

"Would then your father revise his intentions, that you might marry me, and not go soon yourself into a nunnery?"

She shook her head. "Oh, Michel, come back soon. The queen goes within the month to Wallingford and Reading. And London for Yule with the king. We will not return to Amesbury till Candlemas."

I had thought her eyes hazel, but that day beneath her tears they were the color of the autumn sky. I took her hands and raised them to my lips. "And you go with her?"

"As long as the queen wishes. And my father."

Her sadness wracked my heart almost more than my own. "The queen would have me carry letters to Lancelot. Mayhap," I said, knowing it could not be true, "mayhap I will bring his reply."

She shook her head. "You return to Craon." She turned away. "Where, I doubt not, some lady yearns for you." She closed her eyes and dropped her head.

"Naime," I said, "since we met I cannot even remember Craon. Since that day even the queen's beauty is no match for yours." I swung off the bench and knelt before her in the cold damp gravel. "Lady Naime of Corbin, always will I be your knight."

"My knight," she whispered. "Always will I remember you."

I bowed over her knees a long moment, my own heart filled with ache and delight, before I stood and drew her up and kissed her till she softened in my arms. "Always you have my love, Naime."

"Always I am your lady." She kissed me once more, before she laid a hand softly on my chest and pushed me gently away.

Hugh's voice called, under the cloister arches. A king's herald, muddy from the road, strode toward us. "Sir Michel de Verdeur, my lord Arthur would have you at Winchester."

"He calls," said Naime. "He will keep you here." She gave a smile as bright as I had ever seen. I took her hand and kissed it again, and she almost laughed as she turned and walked under the arches of the cloister, into the nunnery. Just where she passed a rose vine entwined a pair of columns, as if its fragile stem had the strength to bind the polished stone.

"Sir Michel," said the herald, "the king is in haste. He sent me ere first light to overtake you."

"What does he want?" I asked, "does he call all his knights?"

"Only you, sir."

"Then I come. Hugh, see to our baggage and our horses. We leave, sir, soon as we may."

Thirty-one

All the long way to Winchester I saw Naime's smile and felt her kiss, and the gentle press of her hand as she turned away. I wondered at the power she held over my heart, for if her cousin witched Merlin, God knew she did the same to me. And yet, so ensnared, I felt only happiness. The captured wizard, surely he must feel the same.

As we rode, the early sunlight faded and the rain began again, and by the time we tramped the gravel of Winchester's court we were chilled and sodden. I strode up the stairs to the king's audience chamber, the high dim space damp and wintry, and knights and clerics clustered about a glowing brazier warming their hands. Sir Grummore spoke with Sir Bedevere, Camelot's chamberlain, and when the page announced me they looked up, surprised.

"Where have you come from?" said Grummore.

"Amesbury, sir. The king called me."

"He has been closeted since midday with our bishop."

Very soon, as if the king waited my arrival, another page came to lead me up the winding stair. Arthur's bedchamber was new painted, its walls green with gold figures. Logs blazed in the fireplace, and rain beat on the glass window.

"My lord," I said, bowing.

"Sir Michel," said the king. "Come, warm yourself at the fire." A servant handed me the cup of heated wine.

Bishop Aymer was a round and sturdy prelate, much like Stephen of Angers. "Sir Michel," he rumbled, "your fame goes before you."

"Thank you, my lord."

"How is my lady Guenever?" said the king.

"Very well, sire. Though . . ." Arthur watched me search for words. "Though she is still worried of your humor, my lord."

"The king hath forgiven her all," said the bishop.

Arthur's expression did not support Aymer's words. "We have been speaking of the mage," he said.

"And still I protest it, sire," the bishop grumbled.

"My lord," Arthur growled at him, "stay or go, as you will."

The bishop twitched and muttered, but kept his place.

Arthur turned to me. "Merlin has been my guide, Sir Michel, all my life. He raised me in my youth, and after I was made king he appeared and counseled me, though oft in strange disguise. But now, for a dozen years . . ." For a moment he stared into the fire. "I saw him last at Ulfius' watch. When he spoke to you. And since again, you say. But never to me." He voice died away.

I recited the mage's appearances, Camelot, Winchester, Craon, Saint Michel's mount. I wondered he did not give Arthur something like my knight's seeing, save there was no easy gift to aid a king.

"And now, Michel, I send you to find him."

"The mage?" I gaped at him. "Sire, I cannot summon him, no one can, you know well he appears of his own whim."

He would not hear me. "I send you specially to old and pagan sites. Tintagel. The forest Perilous. Elamet. 'Tis said Sir Bagdemagus saw him prisoned beneath some faerie stone in Cornwall. Though we cannot ask where, the knight is at Banioc." Arthur shut his eyes briefly. "Avoid Christian places; the lady that witched him can have no power over holy domains."

"The Lord God hath power over all creation," said the bishop.

"Were that true, sir . . ." the king began, before he stopped and turned back to me. "Ride far, Sir Michel, nor stop till Easter, when I return to Camelot. Britain needs his counsel urgently."

"Britain's fate lies in God's hand, sire," said the bishop.

"My lord Aymer," Arthur growled.

They glared at each other a long moment, but I hardly noted their argument. I saw instead Arthur gave me an impossible task and without benefit, and though it delayed my leaving, I must ride the winter roads and not be with my love. "My lord, I go west for my goods and coin. I return to Craon ere winter close the ports."

The king stared at me, unable to believe I refused him.

"Sire," said the bishop, "this knight hath too much fear."

I shook my head. "It is not fear, but futility. We both know it, my

lord, that every knight of Britain might search for him, yet the wizard
may be found only if he wishes it."

"Have you," said Arthur, "no love of chivalric quests?"

It was my turn to stare at him. Almost I said, I am Raven, Greenfarm's brat. Almost I said, It was chivalry's failure that put me here
before you, dubbed a knight.

"Sir Michel, the mage speaks to you most, and latest."

Almost I said, If Merlin had counsel, he would give it. Yet of a sudden I understood the king. For all his reign Britain had been the world's
wonder, Camelot its moral center, Arthur himself knighthood's sum-
mit. Now it all collapsed. Everything failed him. He stood deserted by
his queen, by his best knight and a hundred vassals, even his mage no
longer spoke to him.

"Sir Michel," he said. "You must travel every way, broad or narrow.
You must visit every pagan stone, every ancient barrow and magic
spring and shadowed wood. Britain is desperate."

In truth Arthur was desperate. He had nothing left save the guide of
his youth, a guide that spoke only to Greenfarm's brat.

"My lord," I repeated, "the mage appears at his own fancy."

"Sir Michel, I have nothing else."

"Then I will do it, sire. You must give a letter patent, that I may
stay at any castle, any abbey, any manor. You must repay any coin I use.
And, sire, no matter what the outcome, I leave Britain the fortnight
after Easter."

Hugh and I went down a road of mud and ruts and water, through the
blowing end of the storm. I had written yet another letter to Craon. He
will never give the manors, I told Sir John, yet I do this for his favor of
Craon and myself. But in truth I did it for the mage, that even in this
hopeless thing I might be Arthur's man.

On the second morning as we rode out from Astolat, a pale blue sky
showed among the hurrying clouds. At midday I turned aside to Denham, though I must wonder if another of Lark's knights waited at Giles'
ford, astride Ryford's way. Since Lambert's death the king had settled
Denham's wardship on Sir Kay, and I worried how that bitter knight
served Lady Margaret, whether he took so much he left her barren. But
the lady was well pleased, and as we sat that evening, said he took no
profit of her widowhood, even fostered her oldest son that was a dozen
years from manhood.

"A dour man, Sir Kay," I said, "but honorable." After, when the
lady retired and the other knights gamed in the Hall, I leaned to Balen's
ear. "And who will Margaret wed?"

"She is closest to Sir Robert." He nodded at Denham's steward. "But he is soundly married. And Francis is a devout cleric. Denham runs well, Sir Kay has a hundred worries, the lady seems uneager." He gave a quick grin. "She is ten years my senior, yet I woo her faithfully. So do the others. She keeps us all at bay."

I clapped his shoulder. "Pray God your suit will triumph. But think you, if Kay is the warder, then it is he you must woo."

He blinked at me. "God's name, Michel, you are right."

"I only wish my own future were so simple."

"How is my lady Naime?"

"She loves me. Completely and with high pleasure."

"Ah, wonderful." He smiled. "Yet she is Lady Corbin. More lofty even than my Margaret."

"How well I know it," I muttered. "And I am liege of Craon."

Next morning no knight stood at Ryford's ford, but a wooden cross instead. I stopped to mutter a prayer for Giles, and wonder who marked his grave. Past the little village with its puddled market, I stopped to gaze down the chapel lane to its winter-bare trees. I must come at Vespers, this winter, and hear her Mass.

At Greenfarm a new wooden fence surrounded the houseyard, and its puddles were now filled with river gravel. My father had built an ell on the house, and the byre now held two milk cows and a pair of oxen. I drew up and gazed at it all, at how prosperous they had become, before I turned and rode on into the winter chill.

Bagdemagus had seen Merlin, rumor said. The way to his Cornish estates was cold and bitter, for the steady winter rain soon turned to snow, and then to icy drizzle. His steward, that still managed the lands, could not say where his lord had seen the mage, or if he truly had. He led us out on the windblown downs, but every pagan cromlech stood rainswept and empty.

We went on to Tintagel and its windy rock, above a roaring ocean. After a chill night in the narrow castle, I stopped at an old chapel set amid a high-walled graveyard. A single ancient monk bobbed and muttered to a smoke-blacked crucifix.

"Merlin," he said. "How any man might call him wizard is beyond me. Caught by the whim of some silly girl."

"Caught by love, father."

"More the fool, then."

"Is he here, father, or anywhere about?"

"Of course not." Nor had he any notion save the bishop's, that Britain remained in God's competent hands.

Old ragged stones stood all along that blustery coast, in broken circles, or leaning against the constant wind. None who lived among them, neither peasant nor knight, had seen the wizard. Near the end of a clear cold day and not long after Yule, we came on an old straight way, Roman-built. It led us northward till the pale sun, declining in the west, lit the roofs of an old priory.

Hugh drew up and stared. "It's the place we stayed, René and me." His eyes went wide, remembering. "The night you were in her forest. Lady Morgan."

"Then tomorrow," I said, "we will find her castle."

Hugh paled at the idea, and next morning he rode close to me as we went out. The day was clear again, very bright and very cold. The forest trees spread their bare branches over our heads, and the wood seemed absolutely soundless. We found the way easy enough, though it was thick with fallen leaves, as if nobody had ridden there for months. The water of the lake lay flat and gray, and ice still rimed the edges among the reeds. A path led round it, very clear, that made us pause and glance at each other. It ran away from the lake into the wood, but soon enough another clearing brightened beyond the trees and, its form filtered through bare branches, a small high castle.

The sun shone cleanly on its pale stone, and on the winter grass of its greensward. We drew up and stared at it. Nobody was there. No banners flew from the pointed roofs, no guards paced the battlements, no horses galloped the winter meadows. Nor was there any manor nearby, nor fields or cotts. No farmers trundled loaded wains, no geese called after their girl, no doves circled the high keep. It stood isolate as a castle in a dream, yet the wooden bridge was lowered across its green moat, and the heavy gate stood half-ajar.

"At least," Hugh whispered in the wintry silence, "it's more than shifting lights."

"The king came here," I muttered. "She told him something. Enough that he agreed to that ambush of Lancelot."

God's Name, those six months seemed six years. I nudged my palfrey across the grass. His hooves drummed on the wooden bridge, echoed under the arched gate, rang on the shaped flagstones of the court. It was a rich castle, every roof slate, every window glass. Opposite the gate another great door stood open, and without a thought I rode under its high arch, and into the castle Hall.

"Sir," Hugh called.

I heard him dismount and walk in, but I urged my nervous animal around the dim space as if it were another courtyard. Benches and trestles were stacked against the kitchen screen, except one long table that stood the stone dais. It might all have been deserted years ago, save for the lingering smell of smoke and even food. Hugh, sniffing at it, bent and put his hand over the ashes in the central hearth.

"By God, sir," he cried, and leapt back, "it's still warm."

My breath stopped. A chill ran down my spine. I glanced around, certain somebody watched. Nobody stood in the minstrels' gallery, nor could I see a spy hole that might give to a chamber above, yet someone watched and I was suddenly aware I rode my horse here, like some rude untutored knight.

"My lady Morgan," I called. My voice echoed in the empty place and Hugh cowered in the doorway at the sound. "My lady, I seek the wizard Merlin. The king your brother sends me. He much desires the old man's wisdom. If you know where he is . . ." My voice trailed away. Were she the witch I believed, she knew it already. I stared about. She knew it, and this was her answer, a deserted castle, a knight who rode thoughtless in its empty Hall, a fire dying on its hearth.

This was her answer; not the flickering reminder of my beginning but this bleak image of the end. For another month it hung over me, as gray as the clouds of winter overhead. The country seemed haunted, again, and I was glad to stop at day's end at any priory or manor that offered light and human voices. At last, one cold midday we paused beside one last stone tomb, on a high hill above a broad wooded valley. The rain in our faces had begun to freeze. "There's nothing here, sir," Hugh muttered. "No wizard nor witch, sir, naught but grass and mud."

Merlin was not here. Neither grassy tumps nor stone-lined mounds restrained him. He was not here, nor there, nor anywhere we might look, and suddenly I understood that absence. It was love that prisoned him. His place of capture was no old stone ruin nor muddy hole underground, but the wide bright country of the heart. I had walked its heights, myself, its pleasant dales and fearful chasms. Sibyl led me there, and Matilde, and Naime captured me yet. But though it was the world's finest country, it lay nowhere in the world. Or more exactly it lay everywhere, and it was folly to search for Merlin among the rain and grass and empty hills.

"The country of the heart," I murmured. "We are five leagues from Amesbury, Hugh. There's little time ere dark to find my own heart's country."

He grinned at me under his dripping hood. "It was not my notion to stop, sir."

It was Candlemas eve, and in the abbey stables there were hardly places for our horses. The queen had arrived two days past, and Sir Mordred came today. A bright fire warmed the chamber where knights and ladies laughed together. Mordred sat next the queen. I could not see Naime.

Guenever smiled as if she were glad to see me. She was beautiful still, though cool and withdrawn, and the rare energy that once stirred me seemed vanished forever.

Mordred raised his red-blond head. "Well met, Sir Michel. I had wondered where I might find you." He shrugged that Merlin remained undiscovered. "Times are no longer simple, matters are no longer clear. The wizard's season passes. Certainly this matter of Lancelot is gone beyond his help." He shook his head, sadly. "My brother poisons the king's mind."

"Mordred," the queen said, " 'tis not so dark as that."

He stared at her long before he pulled his glance away. "Gawain would sail for Brittany at Easter." His voice was a little hoarse. "The king will not let him go alone."

Guenever closed her eyes. "My lord Arthur," she murmured, "gave me promise he would not battle Lancelot."

Mordred watched her again. "Even chivalry may sometime demand vengeance, my lady."

Her frown stared past us, as if she saw as far as Brittany.

"Where is King Arthur now?" I asked.

"Saint Albans," said Mordred.

Guenever nodded, her glance returned. "Soon we leave to meet him there. He will make a progress northward, to Ely and Lincoln."

"While I travel my stewardship," Mordred grumbled.

"Madam," I said, "pray you tell the king that I have not found the wizard, that I will search till Easter."

She nodded distantly. I bowed my leave of her. Naime had not appeared, yet all the rest talked and laughed, and the widow Agraine lifted her white head and smiled.

"Good Sir Michel, have you found him?" she asked.

I bent over her withered hand. "Where is she?"

She drew it back in mock anger. "Sir knight, what courtesy is this?"

"I am sorry, lady, it has been three months. . . ."

Agraine smiled. "Naime is with the abbess." She nodded down the room. "In her chamber. A letter came from her father."

I thought to go at once, knock on the door, burst into the chamber, but at that moment the abbess herself appeared. Heedless of courtesy I strode to her. "What of my lady, madam?"

She blinked at me. "Lady Naime has gone to the bedchamber."

I took the cramped steps two at a time. A maid sat inside, and among the ladies' canopied beds another was with Naime, comforting her.

"Lady," I called.

She lifted a tear-wet face. "Michel." She came to me open-armed. "Oh, Michel."

"Dear lady, why do you weep?"

She clasped me, and kissed me. "My father." She began to weep again.

I held her tightly. "Does he call you?"

Her mouth covered mine as if to stop all words, and I did not resist. At last she put a hand to my chest and drew a long breath. "My father. Though he is called a king, my father rules a small spare land. I am his youngest daughter, he has no dowry suitable."

"Lady, I would wed you with nothing."

She dropped her head, and shrugged her way out of my arms. We both knew it was impossible. "His letter." She drew a breath. "He gives me to Nuneaton, that like Amesbury is a convent of Fontevraud." Her voice had gone deathly calm. "Mayhap 'tis pleasant, a bride of Our Lord. The sisters here seem very happy."

I gripped her hands. "The queen, can she not help us?"

She shook her head. "The king comes to Kenilworth in the middle of Lent. Nuneaton priory is but a few leagues distant."

"I will travel with you."

"The king sends you to Merlin."

"Then, dear lady, we must love much and often, these few days before the queen departs."

"I am a nun," she murmured, her eyes downcast, "I am Christ's bride."

"Oh, my love, not yet. There are a few days left."

"Already they are passed," she answered.

For a time, angry and thwarted, I thought to journey to far Corbin, confront her father. I was a knight proved by combat, mayhap bastard nephew of the king. I traveled on Arthur's embassy, He had offered me a royal post, and were I to stay in Britain that would surely lead to higher posts, even into his own household. Once there, no minor king might refuse his daughter.

Yet for all my heart's ache, I remembered my vassal's oath to Sir John. That was the matter, clear. I might do what my heart wished, yet so did Lancelot and Guenever, that brought Britain to such a pass. I might follow my earthly desires, yet so had the knights who killed Lark. Only feudal vows and knights' honor, that word I had so grown to distrust, gave knighthood any virtue. Were I to fail that, I would be no better than Briant and the rest, and surely Lark's death had been in vain.

Thus I did not go to Corbin, but sat with Naime in a corner of the queen's cloister and spoke of my quest, that I did not think to ever find the wizard. She was silent a long moment, before she turned and gazed into my eyes with a look I could not understand.

"Despite love's boundless country," she murmured, "I am sure he is somewhere, Michel. You are his green knight, you must ride to Aven's Burgh, and Cerrig Duon." On her tongue the names echoed with age and mystery. "Gors Fawri. Boscawen-un. And Dyffryn Ardudwy."

"Lady, tell me where, I will go to every one. And then, dear lady, will I come to Nuneaton."

"Ah, Michel. Ever thy Angevin courtesy." She smiled, but kissed me sadly. "You will away to Anjou. Where other ladies will make you forget me, easily as you forget them here."

"Lady, I can never forget you."

She shook her head, and gave me another kiss. "And have you seen nothing else, all this winter?"

"Wind and rain, lady, mud and snow." I looked at her. "And Morgan's castle." She did not seem surprised. I told her of the untraveled path, the empty Hall, the still-warm fire. I said what I thought the lady meant by it.

"Then what meant her lights before, Michel?"

"That the truth of my parentage flickers dark and obscure. But now . . . now for Britain all is dim and empty and cold."

"Save the fire at its heart." And she kissed me again.

The queen departed on a morning of wind and fleeting sun. I bowed before her and swore again my loyalty, long as I should be in Britain. She thanked me soberly. I took Naime's hand, that shook slightly in my grip, and bent to kiss it. "Dear lady, how I envy Christ of you." She closed her eyes. Tears ran down her smooth cheek. I touched one, and put my finger in my mouth to taste the salt. She stared, and her own tongue touched her lips, and then she turned away.

Sir Mordred left that day, too, and we rode together as far as Sarum Castle. Sunshine blew quick across the open downlands, yet springtime felt a lifetime away.

"Very pretty, my lady Corbin. Almost as lovely as the queen." But something else furrowed his handsome brow. "In two weeks, Sir Michel, though the king be at Ely or even Norwich, heralds will go out from Windsor. Royal heralds, with letters patent. I travel to give warning of it. I ought not have stopped so long here." He looked away briefly. "King Arthur calls each vassal to Winchester, at Easter, that he have a thousand knights for his army."

"A thousand? 'Tis a massive host."

"My brother has persuaded him that Lancelot's long insult demands high retribution. They will sail Saint Mark's Day, the end of April." Again he glanced away. "I stay in Britain, of course. The realm must be served, I am his steward."

"But, Sir Mordred, Britain is not attacked. The Holy Father calls no crusade. The king breaks his own truce."

He stared at me, a blackness in his gaze I had never seen before. "You would do well not to speak of that, sir."

"I meant no affront, sir. But think you, will Sir Gawain kill Sir Lancelot?"

"Or be killed. My brother has lost all sense. This siege will be far worse than Joyous Gard."

"All for Sir Gareth and Sir Gaheris."

"And for my lady Guenever." At last he smiled. "That remarkable woman."

Yet despite Mordred's brightened eye and the sun's quick warmth, a chill crept over me. Clear in his voice I heard his brother Agravain. Agravain, whose jealousy of Guenever had led to siege, exile, his own death. Now, Gawain's hatred kept the matter afire and Britain would have a second war. And Mordred, the third of them, was in love with her. Pray God his desire might have a milder ending.

And then, remembering my own desire, of a sudden I wondered how Naime knew it, that Merlin had called me a green knight.

Thirty-two

My wizard's road brought me again to Denham, and Balen's grin and the lady Margaret's invariable hospitality. A letter from Craon waited me, written in William's quick hand that needed the help of Francis to reckon it. Sir John was unhappy I did not retrieve his lands. From the distance of Craon it seemed a simple matter. Of course I might seek the wizard, in courtesy to Arthur, but he would expect me at Craon soon after Easter. He thanked me that I refused the king's offer at Astolat, he would find a like place for me, on my return.

Étienne of Châteaubriant returned from Camelot's tourney with high praise of my victories, and John valued the renown they gave Craon, in Britain. Sir John had news himself, of a son Maurice, first of the lady Adele. Amaury and Clare had a boy christened Henry. And Philip and Matilde, just before his letter was sent, a girl named Marie.

God be praised, she had another child. And Philip was a father. The birth of children in Anjou eased my heart much, and made my return seem less troublesome. I wrote in answer how Britain came against Lancelot, that I must stay till the king were gone and ships could be had for passage. Were Naime not yet in Nuneaton, I thought, I would wait until that black day. And then it came to me, I must not leave till John Baptist's, that I take Rebecca's Mass at Ryford's chapel on the day of her dying.

I set out again in better spirits, and even the weather softened, as if spring would come early, that year. All the places Naime spoke lay in deepest Cumbria, or farthest Wales. They were ancient mounds or pagan shafts heaved up in empty fields, or stony passages open to the seaborne wind. At each I was told, keep away, 'tis the devil's domain, the gate to Hell. At none did I meet Satan, at none did I find Merlin, but at each I remembered Naime, and every day I rued the wizard's haunts lay so far from her.

The middle of Lent, the air loud with birdsong and all the hedges hazed in green, I rode again Bramhill's lanes and into Sir Edmund's courtyard. I had not seen them since Winchester, and the gray-haired knight welcomed me with his dour smile, and in his narrow solar Sibyl was large again with child. She smiled as I bent over her hand. She called Harold to greet me and I stared a long moment at the boy, proud how he had grown. Even the little one she had suckled now toddled among the ladies. She put a hand on her belly. "This one is Edmund's, truly."

"I am pleased to hear it, lady."

"Once you were not so exacting of courtly love."

It was true enough. "I have seen my lady Morgan," I said, though Camelot's wood seemed very far away.

"So Edmund heard. Are we truly cousins?"

"The lady made no answer." I stopped and looked away, remembering her grim and empty castle.

"Edmund also heard a tale you bested Lancelot at Joyous Gard."

"It was nearly true, lady."

"You did?" Her eyes went wide. "You defeated Lancelot?"

"I matched him; mayhap I had the advantage. He wears a scar." I touched my own brow, delighted to show her.

"We had not believed it." She stared at me almost frightened, before she went on. "I have not seen Briant in half a year. They say Sir Mordred fosters him." Her gaze grew worried. "Michel, he said he'd ever hate you, that you were a fool and a coward not to . . ." She glanced away. "To kill him when he was here."

"You begged me not." Briant's hate was no surprise, and her anxiety almost pleased me. "I have no worry of that knight, lady."

And then it was Thursday of Holy Week, the end of a long spring day, and the setting sun cast our mounted shapes against Winchester's gate. The king called his army. I had brought my armor to sell, four days from Denham by slow ox-cart through glorious weather, the bright season bursting all around. Balen rode with me, bringing Denham's scutage, warrant of Lady Margaret's loyalty.

At the castle Arthur and his gathered knights filled all the chambers, yet Sir Grummore found us space in dusty chambers over the gate. Balen delivered his coin. I strode up to the king's chamber, the space as lively that spring evening as it had been gloomy in winter. Arthur was not there, but a crowd of armored knights stood about, their mail gleaming in the torchlight, their voices rumbling of war. Mordred came to shake my hand. Sir Gawain, that I expected to be much pleased, looked aged and bitter, and growled at me that I did not sail with the king's army.

"Sir Gawain, my lord Craon might side with Sir Lancelot."

"Only scoundrels support that blackguard."

"Pray, sir, do not slander Sir John."

A passion darkened his face I could not understand. "See you this knight?" He raised his voice to the others. "See how he avoids valor? A vassal, he says, yet does he hasten to his lord? Once we believed him a knight of high chivalry, yet now he shows his true nature. A few ransoms at tourney, a little battle-fame." He looked as if he might spit on the rush-strewn floor.

I was tired from the road, and my own anger flared and my tongue would not be still. "God save us, sir, where is the valor in this pointless conflict? The chivalry in this stupid war?"

"Sir," he rumbled, "do not slander the king."

"I honor the king, sir." My voice rang on the stone vaults overhead. "If you remember me, Sir Gawain, I remember you as well. Once you had only praise for Lancelot. Once you reproved your brothers their feuds of him. Once you stood silent, unwilling to condemn his dalliance. Yet now, all damage done, all fellowship ruined, now you can offer only bloodshed."

"Damn you." He stepped toward me, a fist on his dagger. "I speak of knightly virtue. Naught but peasants misjudge that."

His words brayed in my ears. I could not let them stand. I remembered Gawain's strength, at Camelot's tourney, yet I drew myself up and thrust a hand at him. "Gawain of Orkney," I cried, "no man may say that of me. I will have my justice." Around us the chamber hushed. "I will demand it, of King Arthur."

I turned and strode out through their echoing silence. I could but pray God, against his strength, I might injure Gawain very quick.

At Simon's door, a squire in Camelot's livery held two palfreys, and men talked upstairs. I had sent my Denham ox-cart to the street of the Jews, that he give me a price on all of it.

"Knights?" I said to Aaron, "buying arms?"

He nodded. "Without coin, and only promises on their lands."

It was Sir Lucan, Camelot's round-faced butler, that called his squire to fetch a hauberk. "Sir Michel," he said, as I climbed the narrow stair, "go you with us to war?"

"I am here to sell, Sir Lucan."

"Damn, wish I'd known. Rather have bought from you than them."
He did not even lower his voice, but smiled and patted his ample stom-
ach. "But I think you are a bit slender. Do we see you at the castle, Sir
Michel?"

"After Vespers, Sir Lucan." Clearly he had not heard of my argument
with Gawain; the thought of it stopped my breath.

Simon bowed him out the door, and only when we sat together did I
notice how the Jew had aged. His black hair was gone half white, and he
had to squint at the bit of paper that listed my armor. He reckoned it
sixty-three pounds. He would sell all he could before the king sailed.
But, he said, I must store my coin at the castle. If the king announced
another tallage, they could not keep my silver separate from their own.

He drew a tired breath and rubbed his eyes. "You stay in Britain,
sir?"

"Till summer." I watched his lined face. "Why do you ask?"

He glanced out at his garden. "Arthur is a hard king, sir, but he does
protect us. Who will guard us when he leaves?"

They were only Jews, usurers, sinners in God's eye. Yet I owed them
much. Even my life. I drew a breath and reached to grip his hand. "I may
not be often at Winchester. But if you have need, send to Denham, or to
Nuneaton."

At the castle court hoofbeats clattered on the gravel as another dozen
knights rode in, come for the king's army. The queen had just arrived,
too, and one of her pages dodged among the horses and cried out, "Sir
Michel, my lady would speak with you."

In the dim solar, ladies in travel cloaks stood weary among the clutter of chests and bundles. Guenever sat beyond them, at a casement open
to the soft evening, her cloak and wimple removed while a maidservant
brushed her unbound hair, bright against her black robe. The fatigue of
journey lined her face.

"My lady," I said, bowing, "you sent for me."

A servant came with a cup of wine. She took a sip before she spoke.
"I called, and then I heard your dispute of Gawain."

Sir Aliduke sat beside her, drooping tired. "The king is very angry of
it, Sir Michel."

"And I as well," said Guenever, though she spoke mildly.

"Lady, I could not allow . . ." I thought to argue Gawain's words but
another notion had come to me. "Think you, madam. If I injure Sir Gawain, there will be no war."

They stared at me. "My lord the king," muttered Aliduke, "will sail
in two weeks, Saint Mark's Day. His army is called, his fleet is assembled. He will not stop now."

"But this is Gawain's feud."

Guenever shook her head. "Arthur hath not forgiven Joyous Gard."
She gnawed her lip. "He will go, even without Gawain."

"And leave Sir Mordred as justiciar," Aliduke said.

I lifted my head at his words. Mordred, as justiciar, to rule in Arthur's stead. It did not surprise me, truly. "But has not the king named a
successor? Were he to . . . to die in this war?"

"Constantine, son of Cador." Aliduke drew a weary breath. "Duke of
Cornwall and cousin to the king. But Constantine sails with the army."

Guenever gazed out the casement. "How I rue it, that God gave us
no son." We both stared, at the curve of her cheek and the fall of her
hair. Fleeting as the spring breeze through the window I felt again the
physical delight that once shone always about her.

Aliduke drew a long breath. "Lady, do not fret." He turned to me,
his face blank. "Sir Mordred has been most attentive to my lady, but she
. . . Let us say she seeks friendship with other knights that stay in Britain."

"Madam," I murmured, "always you have my arm and sword."

"Thank you, Sir Michel. And I will pray for you, even against Gawain." She glanced past me. "But here is another lady."

I turned. There stood Naime. I must have staggered.

"I keep her with me still," murmured Guenever. "I pray her father
and Our Lord will both forgive me."

I hardly heard her. I strode to Naime and took her hands and kissed
them, and without a word she led me to the next chamber and a dim
corner where we embraced till we could not breathe. All about us noisy
servants assembled beds.

"Lady, you are here."

"Michel, why do you challenge Gawain?"

"He said I was a peasant."

"Ah." She glanced away. "Praise God for knightly honor."

I drew her to me again. "Is Gawain undefeatable?"

"Oh, Michel." She leaned against me. "Must there be nothing to life
but blood and battle?"

"And love and jealousy, and hatred and revenge and war."

She drew a shuddering breath. "When the king leaves . . ." My kiss
made her pause. "When he leaves my lady will stop at Amesbury. And I
with her."

"Then, lady, I will be always at Amesbury, too." I laughed, thinking
how the fortunes of love swung to and fro. I kissed her again. A maid
passed with a lamp, and its light moved on Naime's cheek. My heart
stopped at her beauty, at my love of her, at my desire. Praise God I found
again the country of my heart.

"Amesbury is a nunnery," she murmured. Tears shone in her eyes, made bright tracks down her face. She pushed herself gently away. "Will I be able to heal you, Michel, after you meet Gawain?"

If I had forgot my challenge in her arms, it fell on me all the heavier as I crossed Winchester's court. I might have muttered with worry, for grooms and pages stared at me. And in the king's chamber, that rumbled with knights' voices, everyone fell silent when the herald announced me.

"God defend us," Arthur cried out. "Wherever I am, there you are to dispute my knights. I ought banish you this very night." Even the taper-light seemed to bend under his anger.

"My lord, I must . . ."

But he had turned on Gawain. "And damn you, sir, that your folly imperils my campaign."

"Sire," Gawain said, "a hasty word . . ."

Arthur stood and paced the chamber, while every knight watched him. "I will have no fight."

I clenched my jaw, unable to let it die. "My lord, think you. If I be a true knight, then I have clear affront of Sir Gawain. If I be false, what of my contest with Sir Edmund?" He glowered, but I kept on. "God gave me victory in Angers, where John of Craon dubbed me. God gave me victory at Camelot, and since, fame and many ransoms. I have met and equaled even Lancelot." I paused, that they all remember. "I have given much service, to yourself and to the queen. Who might do these things save by Our Lord's will? Would He permit them, were I not a true knight?"

"Sire," Gawain rumbled, "let us battle. Tomorrow morn."

"There will be no combat," Arthur said.

"Sire," I cried, "I have the right of challenge."

"There will be no combat."

It was an ancient privilege. The chamber muttered that Arthur withheld it, and I could see him thinking even as he stared them down. "I will call the lady Morgan," he growled. "She will settle this matter at last." He summoned his castellan. "Sir Grummore, send you to bring the lady here, before Saint Mark's Day."

"As for you, sir." He glowered at me. "If you would fight, then sail with us. There will be more than you want, at Banioc."

For a week his army grew, till it was a thousand knights and twice as many footmen. Their pavilions stood ranked on the river meadows, the smoke of their fires rose constantly, their sound was a high wind in old trees. War's excitement lit both castle and city bright as the springtime,

and promised adventure, glory, and revenge. After Easter the army
began to move, like a giant waking to the spring, with the rattle of harness and the smell of horses, the shouts of carters and the dust of the
road. It was all so exciting that, remembering the morning we rode from
Sir Amaury's to Saint-Georges, I thought to go thus again, bright, impatient, on the road to war. But then I remembered Angers. And I remembered Joyous Gard, and the stink of battle, the ache and gush of
blood, the screams of men dying.

King Arthur had called me to him in the castle. Robed in my
courtly best I followed a squire up his turning stair again. A new tapes-
try hung the wall of his private chambers, and he sat beneath the opened
glass window. Once again the bishop of Winchester was there, and two
knights, Sir Kay and another, lean and tall and blond.

"Sir Michel," said the king, "you could not find Merlin."

"I could not, sire." I told the places I had searched.

"God keeps him hidden," Bishop Aymer murmured.

The king frowned. "Sir Michel, you know I leave Britain in the
hands of my steward, Mordred of Orkney."

"I have heard it, sire."

"If Merlin should appear, you must tell him at once."

"Of course I will, sire." Yet even as I spoke I felt my own hesitation
at Mordred's new post. "Though it is my intention to sail for Craon, sire,
after John Baptist's."

His eyes went suddenly cold when I spoke the date, and in his red-
blond beard his lips made a hard line. Behind me Sir Kay growled, "He
has made a chantry, sire, for that damned girl."

"I know it," Arthur muttered.

"Sire?" Aymer raised his brows. "You rebuke a holy chantry?"

I could not conceal my smile. They remembered Lark, and for king
and seneschal both, that saint's day would be always hers.

Arthur turned away, his jaw clenched, and thrust a hand at the second knight. "This is Constantine, duke of Cornwall. I have named him
my heir. If I should not come back from Banioc . . ."

Constantine looked much like Sir Amaury, if harder and more powerful, yet there beside Arthur he seemed not great enough to be a king.
"My lord," I murmured, "all Britain prays for your safe return." He
brushed away my conventional words. "But sire, I have still my challenge of Sir Gawain."

"God's beard," Arthur cried, "you are annoying as a . . ." His eye fell
on my broidered tabard. "As a cursèd raven, damn you."

I bowed deeply. "My lord, I seek only your justice." It was a small
thing, like something tossed into a thicket, yet when he admitted his

memory of Lark, and then saw me as Raven, he gave me all the fee I might ever ask. "I thank you for your kindness, sire, and pray God for success in Brittany. Mayhap we will meet in happier days."

King Arthur's eyes blazed with anger, yet ever the knight of high courtesy, he gave me a grim nod. "So do I pray, Sir Michel."

The knights sent for Lady Morgan returned on Saint Mark's eve, without the lady. We all knew that if she wished, they would find her at once, else they might search forever. I was not her child, yet she would not deny me. Camelot must believe I was a true knight.

King Arthur sat Winchester's great Hall that last evening, and with him his high knights, Gawain and Lucan and Constantine and Kay, each wearing polished mail and a new tabard broidered with the crowns of Camelot. Beside them were Mordred and Aliduke, and Guenever in a gown of pale samite. The king announced his war, and Mordred's office. We stood and raised our cups, and made the gray stone echo with our cries of Godspeed, of victory and safe return.

And when at last we rose from table, I walked to Sir Gawain. "Good sir, pray let us not part enemies."

"Hasty words, spoke in anger." He ran his fingers through his iron-gray hair. "Nor will the lady come to judge between us."

"I would relent my challenge, Sir Gawain."

"And I my words, Sir Michel. How I wish you sailed with us."

"You will not give up your feud, sir?"

"I am sworn to revenge my brothers."

"And how many brothers will you kill for them?"

"Damn you," he rumbled, but gave a grim smile and gripped my hand. "I will hear no more of this. Let us praise the king's judgment, that kept us from killing each other."

"Would the king had such sense of his own lady, Sir Gawain."

He barked a laugh. "Ah, young Michel, none of us have any sense with the ladies." He glanced a moment toward the queen. "We have each of us our green knight's wife."

"Sir, what do you mean?" I muttered, suddenly bewildered.

"When you'd rather lose your head, than lose her heart."

I stared at Gawain. Must I lose my own head, that I keep Naime's heart? In truth, I had already. The wizard had called me green, when I was but a soft spring leaf. And still I was. Gawain watched me. I muttered good voyage, and turned away confused.

Balen, grinning, seized my arm. "I'm to Denham tomorrow." He led me out to the evening court. "You must come, Michel, on Rogation Sunday. I take a wife." He gave a happy laugh. "My lady Margaret." I clapped his back, laughing myself, delighted his news overshadowed my befuddlement. "All the rest courted the lady," he said, "but I remembered your words. I argued myself to Sir Kay." He struck a pose. "Look you, sir, 'tis Balen, banneret of Denham."

The rains of spring began the day King Arthur left, and castle and city went suddenly hollow under the steady falling water. A week after, the day the queen would leave, it was still raining. Naime and I had spoke each day, yet each day she sent me soon away, as if she would separate herself from all the world. I could not be angry. I knew not what to do, save I could not stay at Winchester when she left. That morning I had our own horses saddled, for Astolat or somewhere, and crossed the puddled court to take my leave.

Guenever sat unhappy among her baggage, and when I bowed she glanced away. "Good Sir Michel, I feel a widow here at Winchester. Nor can I go to Camelot, for there I would remember . . ." She shut her eyes as if in pain. "I would keep to myself at Amesbury."

"Yes, madam. May I come and serve you there?"

"I take only Sir Aliduke and his few knights." She shook her head, as much in sadness as refusal. "But in the love of your lady, Sir Michel, I pray you do not forget me."

"My lady, no one who has met you can ever forget you."

She stared at me a long moment. "Go you well, good sir."

"God defend you, my lady."

Naime waited at the door. She took my hand as we went slowly down the turning stair. "Come often, Michel, she will not send you soon away."

"It is you, lady, that send me hence." She dropped her head, but I pressed on. "Oh, my lady, I would take you anyway, beyond all the world."

Naime raised her eyes, almost smiling. "Oh, yes, Michel. But Lancelot no longer shelters lovers at Joyous Gard. Nor at Banioc, besieged by the king. And would your own lord, at Craon?"

"Lady, I would keep you always from Nuneaton."

"Dear Michel, I must be the queen's. Or God's."

"Naime, how I love you."

She lifted her lips to mine. I clutched her, breathing the scent of her hair. We held each other as if we might stop time, we kissed long and again. I would not let her go but she pushed a hand against my chest, and did not look back as she climbed the stair.

The rain fell bitter on me, in Winchester's court, and when I ducked under the dripping stable eaves I had not the voice to speak. Hugh and I swung up without a word and rode to the castle gate. Under its heavy arches Sir Mordred came clattering in, a dozen knights close behind. He drew up and lifted his sodden hood.

"Sir Michel, do you leave us?" He voice rang on the stone. I saw Briant behind him, glaring at me, and pale Laramort. What did Sir Mordred, I wondered, with these among his knights?

"Sir," I cleared my throat. "Had I known you returned I would have waited your leave."

"You have it, sir. But where do you ride?"

"Astolat, sir," I said. "Denham."

"Sir Michel, those manors you petitioned, the old king's prayers . . ." He looked at me, unblinking. "I must be certain Glastonbury keeps them well. Would you ride to Blackmoor for me?"

I nodded at him, surprised. "I do it gladly, sir."

"Thank you." Still he did not blink. "As justiciar I have dominion over all Britain. Lands, fiefs, manors. It would please me to satisfy my friends."

I gripped my reins to cover my amazement. Did he offer me John's manors, or did I only imagine it? I drew a breath and said, "I hope always to be your friend, Sir Mordred."

"God be praised such knights remain in Britain." He gazed past me, his voice softened. "And is my lady still here?"

"She is, sir, though she leaves today for Amesbury."

"How it grieves me that she goes." Once again he stared at me. "Thank you, Sir Michel, if Lancelot kill my uncle and Britain make me king, ought I not have his queen as my own?"

This time I had to cough to hide my astonishment. "Pray God, Sir Mordred, the king comes safely home."

"Of course, Sir Michel. Of course."

Thirty-three

Soon enough we heard that king and army were landed safe in Brittany. They marched to Lancelot's manors, ravaged his lands, laid siege to his city of Banioc. Secure within his castle, Lancelot refused to give them battle, though Gawain paced at the closed gates, hurling insults, and the king built engines for the assault.

I rode to Blackmoor, as Mordred wished. The manors, that still I thought Sir John's, were indeed well kept. The winter wheat stood lush and green in the broad fields. The spring barley was new-sprouted, the houses well-thatched, the farmers amply fed. Those I spoke with seemed pleased their lord was Glastonbury's abbot and not some king's knight. If the rents were high, at least they were steady, and not dependent on the whim of their lord or the tallages of the king.

The whole way I chewed on Mordred's words. He had been very plain, that if I lieged myself to him I could have these four manors. Yet surely if I took them, I would find myself ranged against the king when he returned. And never had the wizard said, be Mordred's man. Mordred tempted me, who was but a small knight. What must he offer bannerets, and earls and barons? And he had been very plain of the queen, as well. I had seen his love clear enough at Amesbury, yet now I wondered if he might desire Guenever because she was Britain's queen, and not for herself alone.

From Blackmoor I went again to Camelot, riding across its booming drawbridge in a heavy rain. It amazed me how the castle had changed in so little time. The place I remembered as almost magic now seemed empty and deserted as a tomb. Weeds scummed the water of the moat. Grass sprouted among the cobbles of the great court. The groom that took our horses grumbled they had little hay and no oats, that the king took everything against Lancelot. Both Kay and Bedevere were gone to Brittany, and Laramort rode with Mordred and there was no knight-steward to keep the castle.

I strode up through the rain toward the inner bailey and the king's keep, thinking, somewhere I had seen all this. The church door stood ajar, despite the weather. Out the corner of my eye I saw a tall man inside next Ulfius' tomb, his hand laid on the carved figure of the old knight. I had gone past half a dozen steps before I understood I knew that figure, knew it very well. I turned back. The church was empty.

"Merlin," I cried. My voice echoed among the dead tapers.

I put my own hand to Sir Ulfius' statue. No warmth lingered on the stone arm. But I had seen him, truly, and suddenly I felt like Arthur, the night of Ulfius' watch. A dozen years past had Merlin left the king abruptly, his magic wisdom withdrawn, Arthur's own wit all Britain had anymore. Now it was me he abandoned. Like the king I must find my own way, no matter where it led. I drew a sudden breath, for I had remembered it was Morgan that showed me Camelot, deserted. What *did* the old man do?

"Merlin," I cried again. Of course there was no answer.

And then, as if to ease all my dark worries, the hawthorn bloomed white for Rogation. Meadows shone yellow with cowslips. Thrushes called in the budding hedges, nervous of their young. And Denham village had decked itself in blossom.

Farmers laughed at their house doors, already red-faced from ale. At the manor Lady Margaret curtsied to me, happy, and only Balen frowned with worry. We sat over a wine cup, in wedding robes too warm for the bright day, while he described a banneret's life: manors, reeves, his manorial court, villages, hundreds, sheriffs, knights, stewards, tithes to the bishop of Wells.

"And Mordred calls a high council at Winchester, a week from today. But I'll plead my nuptials, the need to settle my new estates."

"And your new wife," I said, "that brings you four children."

He nodded, seriously. "All very sturdy. But the heir of Denham will be my own son, born nine months from tonight."

I laughed at him. "Oh, quick and puissant knight."

He managed a small grin. "God save me of your Latin. But, Michel, there is another letter from Craon, not three days past."

Again William had written it, and again I struggled with his hand.

Sir John deplored Arthur's war. He swore he would not aid Lancelot, though that knight had sent Craon a letter that spoke highly of me. His missive had contained another, a small sealed parchment that John sent on to me.

The queen's name was written on it.

"What will you do?" asked Balen.

"Take it to her. Naime is there." I looked at him square. "I have sworn to the queen as long as I am in Britain.

He nodded. "And she has Denham." At last his face broke into a hearty grin. "Sir Michel, I command you, you must stay after the Sabbath and ride with me my manor's bounds. I would have you show high and proper envy, for the new lord of Denham."

A crescent moon hung in the trees beside Amesbury's river, the evening Hugh and I came again to Amesbury. I rapped at the abbey's heavy gates and called my name, and at last a grumbling porter swung the portal open. Guenever sat in her taperlit chamber. The old widow Agraine waved at me, but Naime was somewhere else.

"Welcome, Sir Michel," said the queen, her voice weary.

"Madam, I have a letter from Craon. And within was this."

She took it, and read the name, yet for a long moment she seemed loath to open it. "From Craon?"

"From Banioc, lady. Sent on by Craon."

Her eyes lit. "Banioc," she murmured, and stood and walked quickly away to her bedchamber.

Agraine motioned me to a place beside her. "How very good to see you, young Sir Michel. How long it seems."

"And you, lady. But where is Naime?"

She gazed at me silently. "A Black priest came for her. Sent by her father, that was very impatient, the monk said."

"A monk? Not a friar?"

"A Benedictine. A thin, pale man, his face haggard from excesses of the spirit." The old lady touched my hand in sympathy. "Rogation Sunday."

I had been at Denham, toasting Balen. I shut my eyes, and waited for my heart to fail.

Guenever was there, smiling. "To all my ladies Sir Lancelot sends greetings." They murmured, pleased. "Close besieged by the king and insulted by Gawain, yet he is loath to fight." She sat her chair again. "Thank you for bringing it, Sir Michel. And your lord, for sending it. In truth I had small hope to hear of him."

"I wish, my lady, there were happier news here."

She caught my strickened tone. "Ah, Michel, I am sorry. She was a great comfort."

I drew a breath. "Madam, does the king write?"

"He sieges Banioc. He asks of Mordred."

"Sir Mordred sent me to Blackmoor. I stopped at Camelot."

She almost flinched at the name. "Mordred makes Winchester his seat." They all avoided Arthur's Camelot now. "He comes every Sabbath, to talk of nobles, the kingdom, the news from Brittany. And all the while he looks at me as if he were a stricken calf." She smiled without humor. "I might think he courted me, if ever he spoke of love."

"It is always on his mind," I said. "He means to have you, madam, however it may be."

Her eyes snapped open. "Does he say this plain, sir?"

"Plain enough, lady."

"Does he think you might tell me?"

"I think he does not care."

She stood, her eyes glittering. "Sir Michel, once I asked your loyalty."

"And still you have it."

"But, sir, would you defend me of this justiciar?"

I had no hesitation. "Lady, you have but to ask."

"Then, Sir Michel, ride you to Winchester, speak to him close, that you discover more his mind of me." She paused. "And of the king."

"I will do it, lady." I was almost thankful of the crisis.

As we crested the last hill Hugh pointed to a dark cloud rising over the city. It was a kitchen afire, a common thing in cities. The smoke bloomed and grew, and by the time we reached the gate it seemed whole houses must be aflame. But it was not my worry and I had turned toward the castle when cries rang out. A half dozen dark-robed people fled out the gate, pursued by a shouting crowd. A yellow mark flashed on one black sleeve.

"Jews," muttered Hugh.

I turned and thrust my palfrey between them and the noisy mob, bellowing, "Way, make way."

"Christ, what do you?" a man shrilled. "Get out our way."

I stood in my stirrups. "What do you?" My sword glinted, and the flat of it against his head staggered him.

"These damn Jews," another shouted. The rest dodged away.

"The king protects them," I cried.

"The king is gone to France or somewhere."

"But his knights are still here." I swung my sword above their heads. "Get back in your city, damn you all."

They shouted and cursed and milled about, but soon straggled back inside the gate. Hugh came up behind me, his drawn blade bright in his hand. "Good lad," I said. He made a sour face.

"Kind sir knight." A Jew with a bruised cheek clutched at my stirrup. "Thank you, sir." The others cowered nearby. I wondered that Winchester's constable failed them.

"Are those your houses burning?"

"Aye, sir."

"Aaron ben Abram, how is he?"

"It's a stone house, sir, he's wet his thatch."

"Hugh," I said, "keep your blade out. We will visit Aaron." The Jew next to me paled, not understanding.

I laid my sword across my pommel. The crowd jeered as we rode in the gate. Flames snapped and flared at three houses in the Jewish street and a larger throng made a wide circle away from the heat. I drove my horse through them, to Aaron's next the burning houses, and drew up beneath his windows. I had to shout several times before a shutter inched open.

"Sir Michel?" His voice rattled with fear.

"Are you safe, Aaron?" I could see only half his pale face.

"We are, sir. But a woman and her child died next door."

"Keep back," cried Hugh, behind me. He waved his sword at an advancing clot of men. "Back, damn you."

"We are men of Winchester," they yelled. "The city has the king's charter, we are free of demesne and tithes, of bowing to damn knights like you."

"Free to murder the king's subjects?" I shouted.

"The king's off on his damn war." One spat on the street. "That we pay for, while these damn Jews build stone houses with our coin. We'll burn them, every damn one of them."

"You will not." I nudged my horse forward, my sword pointed at him. They retreated before me. I growled down at them and pressed them farther. There were a hundred in the street and more crowding in, enough to overcome me easily, and Hugh and Aaron and all the rest. But only if some were willing to die.

I backed my horse again. "Aaron, how many are you?"

The shutter rattled. "Thirteen," he murmured. "My family and Simon's. We took in a neighbor."

The crowd began to rumble. Hugh shouted at them again.

"Get out of our way, esquire," growled another man.

I rode at them. They stopped again, but now they would not retreat. Several waved long sticks, and one had an actual pike. The new leader wore dried blood on his butcher's apron, and the cleaver glinting in his hand frightened my horse.

"Do you truly want to die?" I asked him.

"You would not kill a citizen for a damn Jew."

"I would kill any man for the king's laws."

They began to move again, circling our flanks.

"Stop," I cried. The mob paused. The butcher and the armed men stood before us, but those at the sides were unarmed.

"Sir," Hugh muttered, "I'd not die for a few damn Jews."

"I will charge left," I murmured aside to him. "It's the thinnest part. Follow me through. I'll not hold you, after that."

"Sir . . ."

I kept my voice low. "I'll turn and drive their rear. They'll not be so brave when their blood begins to flow."

"Talk, talk," cried the butcher. "There are too many of us, sir knight. You can go now. Or you can die."

"Sir," Hugh muttered, "I can't leave you here."

"Then you must chop, lad. Hands, arms, faces, heads. And never worry what you cut."

I watched their circling mass and prepared to charge, but at that moment shouts rang out and, praise God, mounted knights appeared at the end of the street. They swung their blades and pushed their horses grimly through. Pike and sticks disappeared, and the butcher vanished in the throng.

"Where have you been?" I asked the leading knight.

He spat in the dusty street. "Are we not here?"

"After a dozen beaten, two killed, three houses burning. Had I not happened here it would have been the whole street."

"Mayhap." He spat again. "These have failed Sir Mordred's tallage." Aaron opened his shutter carefully, and the knight turned on him. "Jew, if you anger the men of Winchester, the castle cannot protect you always."

I stared at him. "Mordred sets another tallage?"

"Sir Mordred is angry at this narrow tribe and their claims of poverty. He will deal with them when he returns for his council." The knight glanced at the burning houses. "What does it matter, a few Jews? If they're gone, nobody can collect their usury." He pulled his horse around and rode away.

Men had come out the other houses with water buckets, and hooked firepoles to pull down the burning timbers. Aaron, pale and shaken, opened his door. "Sir Michel, thank you." He led us inside. "Thank you, sir. I believe Heaven watches over us."

The families huddled in his cramped solar, with women and children I realized I had never seen before. "We must go tonight," Simon muttered.

"There's no time to pack, before dark," said Aaron.

"And tonight begins Sabbath," the neighbor said, hoarse. He was a small thin man, crouched in one corner with his wife and daughters, and unable to keep his gaze from my sword.

"Today is Friday," I said. They might not have heard me.

"We'll leave tomorrow," said Simon, "soon as the gate opens."

The neighbor spoke up again. "The Torah says keep holy . . ."

"Let's wait, Uncle," Aaron said, "till after the Sabbath."

"If they come tomorrow they will break down the doors." I half drew my sword, and the neighbor shrank away. "I might stop them on the stairs, but they will light the straw in your stable."

"The house will burn." Simon waved his hands. "Us with it."

"But the Sabbath," the neighbor complained, "God says . . ."

"If I rest this Sabbath," Simon growled, "I rest forever. I did not bring my family from Southampton to die in Winchester."

"Perhaps they won't come back."

"Perhaps the sun won't rise. We'll go to Astolat, to Ezra."

"Astolat is two days away," said the neighbor.

"Ten leagues," I said. "I will take you there." They stared a moment before they let out a sigh, though Hugh frowned and looked away. "You must go the whole distance in one day. I will bring two more hackneys tomorrow morning, at first light. Load your own animals heavy, but remember they will have a long day."

Thirty-four

Simon and the others glanced worried over their shoulders, and pushed their laden animals at a steady pace. By midmorning we were halfway to Salisbury. The old road ran straight out of the forest and down to a narrow stream, where farmsteads clustered beside the fording. Here I had met Merlin as my drunken friar. Today a knight sat his horse alone in the stream, letting the animal drink. I thought for a moment he was the mage, till Briant turned and looked at us. He had let his beard grow, and its dark line made a handsome frame for his face. He stared at us and the train of animals, and burst out laughing.

"Behold. The famous knight, become a leader of Jews."

I drew up at the water's edge. "You ride without a squire?"

"I ride hard for Winchester. I carry news of Banioc."

"What news?"

He smirked at me, pleasure instead of hate on his face.

"What news, damn you?" I growled.

He pulled up his horse's head and stepped the animal a little away. He raised his voice like a herald. "King Arthur and Sir Lancelot," he cried, "have met in single combat before Banioc Castle." He crossed himself, and my heart stopped. "The king is defeated and slain. Sir Gawain maintains the siege."

My mind floundered at the idea. "How do you know this?"

"Letters are come from Brittany." He drew a packet from his cloak. "I met them at Weymouth."

Arthur dead. I could not believe it. "Was there no herald?"

Briant hesitated. "Of course. But I ride before him. To Winchester and Sir Mordred."

"What was the herald's name?" If I worried of the messenger I might forget the news.

"A young knight." He paused. "I can't remember."

Arthur, dead. I would not believe it. The Jews muttered behind me, frightened. Yet something of it had not the ring of truth. Briant did not mourn, nor did he rejoice. He might carry news of Banioc's weather, not the death of Britain's king.

He had nudged his mount up the bank. "Briant," I called out, "I never gave oath against killing you."

"What?" he cried. "Do you imagine I am afraid?" Hatred bloomed at last across his face. "Twice you might have killed me, but your peasant's fear prevented it." He spat on the road. "By God and Christ, when this matter is done, when Mordred is king, then will I hunt you down, then will I revenge the deaths of good knights." He sat a moment staring, before he pulled his horse around and cantered quickly past the Jews, toward Winchester.

Arthur, dead. Even Briant's threat could not distract me from that. Arthur dead, Mordred crowned, it meant Guenever pursued. I thought to send Hugh to her at once, but the Jews carried more coin than a single sword could defend. We pressed on to Salisbury. Nobody at the bishop's palace had heard Briant's news, nor of a king's herald. I prayed them send a messenger to Amesbury.

We reached Astolat just as the sun was setting, and our clatter in the Jews' street brought Ezra and his cousins out of their house. The large man had lost weight, care lined his thick face, and his pretty daughter stood next him, a hand on his arm as if she feared him ill. He puffed raggedly as he looked up at me.

"Here, at last, the one Christian knight in all Britain."

I shook my head. " 'Tis a debt I have owed for years, Ezra. Since old Abram, in Winchester. Since you, at Caen."

Ezra reached to take my hand. "None of us could understood why Abram did it. Thank heaven he did."

"Yes," his daughter said, "thank you, sir,"

"I am Michel," I said. "What is your name?"

"Rachel," she murmured.

I smiled at her. "And what of that young man of Astolat?"

She put a hand to her mouth, and dropped her head. Ezra frowned. "He met an unfortunate end, traveling from Southampton. A pity he had no knight to guard him."

Once more I had forgotten it, that these were Jews. I shook my head. "I am sorry, Ezra. And for you, Rachel."

In Astolat's castle Sir Clegis made me welcome at his table. His household sat around him for the evening meal and when I told my story they all went pale and muttered and made their signs. Clegis knew nothing of it, but said that small Astolat would be among the last to hear. My own doubt of Briant seemed foolish, something I clung to for hope of the king, and at first I did not speak of it.

"Sir Mordred will be king?" his wife asked.

Clegis shook his head. "Arthur had named Constantine."

"Then we must expect him within the week," I said, "come to claim his throne."

"Sir Mordred," Clegis said, "has called a great council at Winchester, three days hence."

I remembered Balen spoke of it. "He called it," I said, "as if he knew when he would need it. But think you, Sir Clegis, if Constantine does not soon arrive, might this news be false?"

"What do you mean, sir?"

"Only that I do not trust the messenger."

He raised his brows. "Any such letters must be sealed with a king's seal. Only Mordred in all Britain has one." He gazed away, thinking. " 'Tis true enough he covets the crown. I will speak to my friends on the council, but I fear our justiciar has wooed to himself half of Britain's lords and barons."

Sir Clegis rode to Winchester the day after the Sabbath. The queen's mission might send me with him, save she knew already that Mordred as king would have her his queen. Now she needed knights, and I stopped at Astolat to practice arms. Two days later a herald returned. The council had accepted the letters. Mordred would be crowned in Winchester's cathedral, Whitsun morning.

"That's but four days," I said, unbelieving. The herald nodded, grim. All was in place for a coronation. By calling his council Mordred had brought together all the bishops, and every noble save those fighting Lancelot.

I sent Hugh hurrying west to Denham. Guenever needed every friend, despite Balen's married happiness. He did not return till late Saturday, but brought Balen with him and two of Denham's bachelors that were now his own. Balen scowled at me. Were it Briant carried the letters, of course they were false. I was a fool to have waited so long.

Next morning was Sabbath and Whitsunday itself, yet we set out full-armed, helmets and shields on our saddles, our squires leading destriers. We came to Amesbury in the long summer dusk, where once again the abbey gates stood closed. The chants of Compline came faint from the church. I rapped the thick wood and called my name.

"The queen's not here," the porter cried, over the gate.

"Where is she, then?"

"Winchester. Sir Mordred called her."

"Damn," I said. "Then let us in, I must speak to the abbess."

It was true, the abbess said. The queen had gone at Mordred's summons, his letter written to be almost a proposal of marriage. "Ere she left, my lady swore she would never wed him." She shook her head sadly. "But I do not see how she can refuse."

She nodded at my notion that, were the king dead, Constantine would have come already to claim the throne. She would send her own letters, of Mordred's enterprise, to the army before Banioc.

"And we must ride to Winchester tomorrow," I said.

Balen stared at me. "Against Mordred?"

Just then the porter shuffled in. " 'Tis another at the gate, lady. From my lord Aymer, bishop of . . ."

"Then let him in," she cried.

The young cleric puffed as he bowed before the abbess, unused to long riding. Sir Mordred had indeed been crowned, that day and at midday Mass. But the news he brought was of the queen, that she had left for London two days before, that she went to arrange the wedding, to have dresses sewn and minstrels hired.

We would not believe it.

"This wedding," I muttered, pacing, "when is it?"

"John Baptist's. 'Tis but three weeks." A spark flared in my mind at that date, as if Mordred were now one of Lark's knights.

But the abbess protested against it. "The lady hath sworn her life against this marriage."

"Then," I said, "we must ride instead for London. At first light, quick as we may."

"And two of my sisters must go with you," said the abbess, "for her spiritual resolve. They are her close cousins."

"Lady, we cannot wait on a slow wagon."

"Then, sir, they will ride their own palfreys."

I need not have worried. Both were daughters of high nobles, sent like Naime unwilling into the nunnery, and rode as well as we. And on the way the lady Martha, a plain woman with a bright tongue, diverted us with tales of falcons she once had, and how they would stoop the birds we saw.

Late the second day we came to Westminster's royal abbey, beside its wide river. London lay another half league eastward, past rich estates and little villages along the curving riverbank. The sun was setting behind us when we rode down to a murky ravine and the wooden bridge that spanned it, just before the city wall. The rough planks boomed under our mounts. At its far end a sergeant stood within the old gate, shading his eyes.

He did not move despite our horses. "Full-armed, sirs? Pray you stop outside. Blackfriars is just there, on Holborn hill."

"We come for the queen," said Martha. "These knights have sworn her liege."

"The queen?" He gave a quick grin. "Then come in, sister." He pointed over his shoulder. "White Tower's away at the east end. You've heard she's shut in?"

"Shut in?" I said. "What do you mean?"

"Locked herself in. Against Sir Mordred."

"By damn," cried Balen, "that was her notion."

The sergeant laughed grimly. "But go you soft, sirs, there's knights standing afore Beauchamp Gate."

"They will not stop us," I said. We paused to loose our blades and take up shields, and I rued we had no time to rest our wearied horses.

London was as crowded as Winchester, though five times bigger and that much more noisome. The rutted street led up to a grand old cathedral on its dusty square. A market spread out beyond, though most of the stalls were empty now. The streets were full of rubbish, and the houses leaned over the way. Cobbles rang where we forded a little stream. It seemed a long half league before we saw a wall beyond the crowded roofs, and then the high square keep, its whitened stones yellow in the sunset.

"The Tower," cried Martha, and nudged her horse forward.

But beyond the last houses a knights' pavilion stood in the open field, a crossbow-shot from the nearest gate. A score of footmen in Mordred's red and white scrambled to their feet when they heard our horses, and their shouts drew a knight out the tent.

He squinted at us and raised a hand. "Sirs," he cried. "You may not pass."

"We bring two holy sisters," I called. "For the queen."

"And four armed knights," he said.

"Good sir, let us in." Martha pushed forward and we followed her closely. "We are the queen's companions."

"Sir knight," I shouted, hoping to be heard at the gate beyond. "We come in truce, we would enter peaceably, let us pass."

"Alas, sister, and good sir knight." He made a mocking bow. "You chance upon a siege."

Three other knights had come out the tent. The footmen shifted toward us, their pikes uncomfortably close. The heads of guards showed on the wall above the gate. I turned to Balen and the others crowded behind me. "When I draw," I muttered, "do you also. Keep the ladies in the middle, make sure the battle-horses get through, let nobody stop us."

"Sir knight," cried Martha, "I am the queen's holy confidante."

"Sir," I called again, "we come in memory of the king."

"The king?" he cried. "The king is dead, sir. We have a new king." He laughed. "Though his queen doth shut herself up till their wedding day."

"Then at least allow these holy ladies passage."

A squire came out the tent, carrying their sword belts. The knight who spoke turned to take his. I cried out, drew my own blade, and spurred past Martha. The footmen gave a shout, but we caught the knights unprepared. The first had his blade but half out when I chopped at his arm. My horse drove against a second and bowled him over. The third swung his blade too late and I hacked his mailed shoulder.

"To the gate," I cried, "beat on it, call out to them."

The ladies galloped close behind me, and then squires and knights. The footmen ran at us from both sides, but we sprinted our way through them. At the castle gate the defenders had the small wicket open. The nuns ducked quickly inside, and we leaped from our horses and turned against the oncoming pikes.

"Now." Balen swung his sword. "Who wants an early grave?"

The crowd of them straggled to an uncertain stop.

Behind us the squires had got the horses in. "Quick," Hugh cried, "hurry, sir."

We backed into the castle, and though our retreat roused the footmen, the guards inside slammed the gate in their faces.

Sitting in her painted chamber in the old Tower, the queen was very pleased to see us all. Once again her bright smile warmed and moved us. "Praise God you came safe through my siege. You remind me there is still honor in Britain, though I had feared it lost."

I bowed over her hand. "Madam, no one may refuse your need."

We made eighteen knights under Sir Aliduke's command, two score footmen and a dozen Flemish crossbowmen inside London Tower. We arrived just in time, for the next morning Mordred's captain began his siege in earnest. He brought up a catapult, two dozen knights and three score footmen. Despite our arrows he rolled a warshed up against the western gate, and after a single day of thunderous pounding its iron-headed ram broke down the heavy door. It was all very new to me, this defense of castles. I worried that, the first gate destroyed, we must retreat to the high tower and its inner court. But Aliduke only nodded grimly, pleased that we had a smaller perimeter to defend, and a stouter second gate.

The whole castle was a rough square, one side along the river, and Tower and inner bailey standing at the southeast corner. Mordred now controlled the outer court, a practice field and kitchen gardens to the west, and to the north an old chapel of Saint Peter's, and castle stables we had emptied of animals and straw. Our second gate opened at a corner next the Tower. Aliduke put our Flemish crossbows on its high strong battlements, where they were little bothered by catapult stones, and made it hazardous for anyone crossing the open ground below.

If that defense kept Mordred's men away from the second gate, still they managed to bring the ram and its shed against a corner of the inner wall, hidden from the keep by the angle. The heavy blows began again, deep as thunder, that now seemed to shake the Tower itself. We could not let it stand, and on the third morning, in the dim gray light before sunrise, we burst out the gate in full force and swept them away, demolished the ram and burnt its shed.

That day Mordred himself appeared on the tower over the outer gate, come to direct the attack. He set more catapults to stone the keep. He built a warshed from the western gate halfway across the outer court, and there began a tunnel to undermine our wall. One dusky evening under a summer rainstorm he sent a dozen knights, and a score of footmen with axes, against the inner gate itself. The rain and the dark and their heavy shields protected them well, while they hewed at the wood. But we opened it, without warning, and hacked at them as they spilled inside. Bleeding and crippled, most fought their way out, and fled through the storm. Our pursuit went as far as the shed, where we routed the miners and set its timbers afire, that smoldered all the night under the soft rain.

That sally ended Mordred's active siege. Even the catapult stones stopped falling. Still, he kept us encircled and sent each day a herald, praying Guenever come out, promising her the kingdom. Each time she answered she would die rather than be his queen. We might have lasted months, yet after a week of stalemate his force decamped. We stood the Tower's high battlements, shaded our eyes against the summer sun, and saw them crossing the river on the new stone bridge. They were marching south.

Aliduke laughed, for the first time in the whole siege. "God's blood, who might draw him off, save Lancelot, or the king?"

And it was true. Within the hour three London burgesses appeared, picking their way through the wreckage of the outer gate. One cupped his hands and shouted up to us. "God be blessed, lady. King Arthur is alive, he lands today at Dover."

Thirty-five

The king returned. Britain was saved. We cheered and hugged each other. We threw open the gates and took the burgesses up to the Hall and plied them with drink and meat. Yet Guenever sat the high table deathly pale, and when Aliduke raised his cup to toast the king she put a hand to her throat and shut her eyes.

"Lady," said Aliduke, "why this dismay? Our king returns."

"The king comes." Her voice shook. "Lancelot spares him. Mordred will not." She glanced around at us. "Here are twenty knights, dear Aliduke, valiant as the world's best. But they cannot last forever."

"All Britain rallies to the king, my lady."

She would not be comforted. "The knights who besieged me, are they not loyal to Mordred? The barons Mordred has enriched, are they not loyal, too?"

"Dear lady, the king will prevail, and all will be right with Britain again."

"So pray we all, Aliduke." For a moment she closed her eyes again. "God knows my lord Arthur is a chivalrous knight, who would never fail his honor."

Aliduke shook his head. The rest of us glanced at each other. The king returned to Britain. Of course he would defeat Mordred and come again to Camelot.

But the queen would not be eased. "I fear he loves me no more. Even Gawain, once my greatest champion, is become my sternest enemy." She raised her head, and grief marked her beauty. "As you are my knights, so are you Arthur's. He needs you. I send you to him. Tomorrow."

"Ah, dear lady," we murmured.

"I keep but Aliduke." Her eyes found me. "And Michel."

"Lady," the others cried, dismayed.

"Two knights," she said. "Two ladies. A priest and two sisters. I go to Amesbury, to take there Holy Orders. Save only that the king wish me as his queen again."

The early sun glinted on the roofs of the Tower. Our knights gathered in the outer court, full-armed and anxious for the road, and Balen and I stared at each other a long moment. We clasped our hands tight. "Damn the queen's mood," he muttered, "we ride to victory."

"God go with you," I murmured.

They had swung up on their mounts, when a herald rode in through the broken gate. He came from Dover. Arthur and Mordred had fought the day before, and though the king won each side lost many knights. "Alas," he cried, "the greatest was Sir Gawain of Orkney, that died at Vespers of an old wound reinjured."

The very light of morning seemed to dim around us. "Go you quickly," cried the queen, "he needs you even more." They rode out, silent. In the church monks sang a Mass for Gawain's soul, and for Britain. Sir Aliduke knelt beside me, muttering, "We shall all be dead, ere this thing is done."

We ourselves set out early the next day. The guard at Ludgate told us Sir Mordred massed his army anew, to battle the king on Barham Down. "God save us, will they fight every day?" cried Guenever.

"Till one is destroyed," Aliduke said.

We rode in plain cloaks that covered our arms, hoping the queen might be taken for some minor lady. We draped our destriers to hide their lines, and the laden hackneys, for she took all her gold and coin. Aliduke kept us to narrow lanes, and we went from abbey to priory and came to Amesbury at Vespers on the third day. I looked for Naime before I remembered where she was. Only four women sat the abbess' chambers, and even old Agraine had gone away. They knew nothing of king or Mordred, save that Arthur had been victorious again on Barham Down.

Early the following morning Aliduke and I rode out through a steady rain, he to Winchester and I to Salisbury. Old Sarum Castle stood just above the city. I rode up to the gate and called my name, but the guards would not let me in. Two great armies moved nearby, their issue undecided, and the constable opened his castle to no one.

"Where is King Arthur?" I shouted through the drizzle.

"He moves west toward Camelot," he answered, and did not call him king. "He has every knight from the war, and hundreds more flock to him. He stops for tomorrow's Sabbath a half dozen leagues past Salisbury." Mordred, he said, had a larger host, though few had seen battle; he assembled opposite Arthur. The knight looked down at me and drew a breath. "They agree to parley. Pray God they do not fight; it would be a huge combat."

"Who would win, sir?" I called.

His answer took a long moment. "The king, so we pray." Even then he did not say which was his king.

At Amesbury the queen paced the dripping cloister arches. Her face went pale and hard at my news. "Do you remember, Michel, that once I imagined a time without war?"

"I remember, lady." It had been among the pagan stones, a league west of the abbey, where she had spoke of hope and delight till sadness overcame her. I watched her besieged by that same sadness now, and knew there had never been a woman like this. Despite my love of Naime, none could be more beautiful, more desirable, more vulnerable.

Yet her eyes were dry and her mouth grim, when she asked, "And would you leave me, Sir Michel, for the battlefield?"

"Sir Mordred must not prevail, lady. I go for your defense."

"Yet had I kept the lady Naime, you would stay with me."

"Madam, if she were here, how much more must I defend my knight's honor, and the king's."

"Honor." Her whole form sagged, and tears stood in her eyes. "Why is it the honor of knights is always the enemy of love?"

I did not answer her. We both knew it very well, that love and honor were become the mortal enemies of Camelot.

The rain had blown away and the morning stars shone overhead, when Hugh and I walked to the abbey's church. A choir of nuns sang Lauds in the echoing nave, while in a dim side chapel the priest shrived us for the road, and for the battle.

Sir Aliduke waited at the shadowed stables. "God go with you." He shook my hand. "Almost I regret my staying."

"Good sir," I said, "you must keep the queen well."

We rode out the abbey gate and up through the town, to the open ridges above long valleys still blurred with fog. The sun slid up above the eastward hills, very bright in the crisp morning. It glittered on the guards' pikes on the walls of Sarum, but down in Salisbury thick fog still murked the city streets, and our hoofbeats echoed in the empty ways.

Fog, I thought, remembering Camelot, remembering Angers. As we rode the damp empty market a one-eyed beggar stared at my armor. "What king do you follow, sir knight?"

"King Arthur, of course."

"Of course." He spat in the damp dust. "Battle tomorrow, they say."
He grinned sourly. "Hundreds dead. Good pickings."

I hauled my palfrey to a stop. My dagger glinted before his ugly face.
"By God, anyone I find scavenging is a dead man."

"Dead yourself, most like." He eyed my blade. "I'll remember that
pretty thing."

I slashed at him. He dodged away. Still blind with anger I led us
down the wrong street, that ran past clerics' houses and mason's sheds
into the cathedral close. A crowd of murmuring priests were gathered in
the mist before the great church.

"Damn," I muttered. "We'd best go out and around."

" 'Tis Sabbath, sir," Hugh said, "and John Baptist's eve."

John Baptist's eve. Dear God, in the confusion of this war I had forgot. Tonight I must be at Greenfarm, at Ryford's forest chapel, to hear
Lark's Vespers. John Baptist's. The scream of the hare, the lopsided
moon. It was a dozen leagues. If I turned at this moment and rode hard,
I might arrive in time. But never could I come to Arthur by tomorrow
morning.

"I've never seen such a cathedral, sir," Hugh said.

God help me, that I must choose between Arthur and Rebecca, between Camelot and Greenfarm. But then I saw that long ago I had already made my choice. That summer day in Camelot's Hall I had stood
beside my father. Take the horse, I had said.

"Sir Michel?" Hugh called. "There's no battle today, sir, we have
time aplenty."

Kings and prophets carved in stone stood beside the doors, that
would soon be raised to their niches. Salisbury Cathedral. How long ago
had bearded Jubal and frail Eudes led me into this high stone place.
Hugh opened a door and once again it rang with priests' voices, as it had
that far morning when I had been so young and unafraid. When the
death of Lark still lay so fresh in my heart.

We had ridden four leagues south, staring into the sun for the dust of
armies, when a small company of horsemen crested the next hill. I drew
up and shaded my eyes. It was Sunday, but were they king's knights or
Mordred's, I must meet them armed. I swung down from my palfrey.
Night shook his head and snorted when I settled on him. I hung my
shield across my shoulder and my helmet over the pommel of the saddle.

They were four of them, each with a squire. Their banner was Mordred's white and red.

"We meet battle a day early," I said to Hugh. "Guard yourself
against those squires."

He did not answer, but strapped on his iron cap.

A grassy meadow sloped down toward them, and I drew up at its top. If they came at me they must charge up it. Against four I needed every advantage I might get. They rode close together, one blond and one sandy-haired, one with a trimmed black beard and the last with a pale face. I stared, unable to believe it. Here was Briant once again. And Laramort.

They drew to a halt at the bottom of the slope. Briant shaded his eyes. "By Christ and heaven," he cried, "here again this filthy churl."

The others I had seen before. The blond, who was Arnold of Chester, shouted up at me. "Do you ride for King Mordred?"

"He is not king, sir."

"He hath been crowned at Winchester."

"And we are each his liege." Briant grinned. "He hath given me four manors in Blackmoor Vale, that were Glastonbury's."

Damn Mordred, I thought.

"But you ride away?" I called. "Do you flee Arthur?"

"It is Sabbath," Arnold said. "King Mordred sends us to Salisbury to fetch the bishop."

"Though on the way we are free to kill rogue knights." Briant tugged at his reins and his horse pranced nervously. He muttered something to them, and they glanced at me again.

"Let us meet tomorrow," I said, "on the field of battle."

"If you defend Arthur, you do treason to King Mordred," said Arnold. "We must take you captive if you defy us."

Briant muttered and shook his head, and then without warning he stood in his stirrups, bellowing, "Damn you all, this damn chivalry." He pointed at me. "That is a farmer's brat who has lived too long." He leaped down and strode to his battle-horse. "Who has killed too many knights." He grasped his shield and helmet, and seized a lance from his squire. "God help me, I pray the dung-heap bastard is not shrived, that my blade through his peasant heart will send him screaming into Hell."

The others followed him, arming and mounting, but more slowly. Laramort said nothing and I saw how he hung back. I strapped on my helmet. I was strangely unafraid, though I thought, Four of them, and I with a single lance. The memory of Lancelot rose before me, Lancelot at Winchester, that had unhorsed five knights with a single lance. Lancelot, the greatest fighter I had ever seen. I might not match him, but pray God I had learned something from him.

They muttered at each other who would do what. Still Laramort sat his battle-horse a step away from the others. I gripped my shield, lifted my lance, and drove at him.

He saw my charge. He lowered his lance in answer. His horse struggled as it came up the slope. His shield bobbed. More clear than ever I saw his coming swerve. His lance skidded away. My own hit his shield high, the point gouged wood off the top, drove against his helmet and into his eye-slot. He dropped like a stone from his horse. His fall nearly pulled the lance from my hand.

For the briefest moment I regretted him dead so suddenly. But there were three more. I turned Night quickly. The rest had lowered their lances. Arnold, on the left, was least prepared. I drove down the slope at him. My lance caught his shield solid and rammed him backward off his mount.

I turned. Briant rode at me. We met hard. His lance broke a corner off my shield and gouged my arm. Mine glanced away. The last of them was almost upon me. The force of our meeting broke his lance. Arnold, unhorsed, had got to his feet. I ought have run him down, but I charged instead at the knight whose lance I had just broken. He slipped my point off his shield and his sword hammered my helmet as we passed. My ears rang. I galloped against Briant hard as Night would go. I stood and my lance punched him sprawling away over his horse's withers.

One dead. Two unhorsed. Night began to labor from the sudden turns. I charged again at the last mounted knight, who had come up to shield Briant. My rush surprised him, he waved his sword and pulled up his horse's head, dodging away. My point drove into the animal's neck. Blood spurted and the lance was pried from my grip as we passed. Briant stood just beyond, his sword raised. I saw the blow but could not swerve. Reaching up, he chopped my unshielded side. The force of it half knocked me from my saddle but I felt nothing more until, turning Night again, the pain struck. My chest flared, my arm ached, I could not breathe.

I drew my sword despite the agony. Arnold waited with his own. He dodged to my off-side, but I saw it and caught his blow on my shield. My backhand chop took his neck just beneath his helmet. He stumbled and dropped his blade and fell. But the pain of that swing made the sunlit day go dim as evening. Night's every step made me gasp. I clutched at my pommel with my good hand. My shield almost dropped away. And then I remembered, at Winchester, Lancelot had been worse wounded.

I pulled Night around. Arnold lay unmoving. Briant was running for his battle-horse, and as I rode up dodged behind the animal. My weak chop nicked the withers of his horse. The animal screamed and kicked and Briant had to dodge away.

"Damn you, squires," he cried, his voice muffled in his helmet. "Where are you? This is no polite joust. Kill him."

I rode straight at him. I saw he would dodge but I could neither lift my blade nor control my horse. Night, trying to swerve, sidestepped into him. Briant fell, and as he did a hoof dug into his side. He shrieked in pain.

Four knights, I thought, hazy. Now squires came at me. I got my sword up, two-handed, despite the pain. The first lad would not meet me. The second tried to parry my blade with his own. My blow fell on his upraised arm. He screamed, and the others veered away. I heard more hoofs. The knight on the wounded horse had got his animal into a canter. Somehow I caught his raised sword with my shield. He lifted his blade again but here was Hugh, charging past, that hit him on the rear of his helmet. It stunned him, but his backhand answer drove Hugh out his saddle.

Christ, young Hugh. Still I could not parry. The knight chopped at my helmet and half deafened me. I dropped my blade hard as I could between the ears of his injured horse. The animal staggered and the knight's blade wavered. Gasping, I swung at the eye-slot of his helmet. I chopped at his gut and saw him shudder. Breathless with pain I drove my point against his neck and thrust him sideways out his saddle.

I could not move anymore. Hurt paralyzed me. A fire roared in my chest so I could not breathe. My right arm shook, though I could feel nothing in it nor even lift it. The squires circled like young wolves, only half-brave. Briant struggled to his feet, his drawn sword as support. Hugh sat up, and I prayed he was not badly hurt. I let go my shield and gripped my sword left-handed. I climbed down from Night, and then had to clutch his mane and pant in agony. Briant still leaned on his blade. Blood oozed from under his helmet. He gave a rasping cough.

"Bastard peasant," he gasped, "that murders horses, injures squires."

He lifted his sword weakly. I hacked at his helmet. He staggered and fell, sitting on the dusty earth. Hoofbeats sounded. I had forgotten the squires, and I could do nothing but dodge, a step away and back again. The first missed me, but the second's blade clanged on my helmet. My weak answer took his horse on its hindquarters, and his animal skittered and fell.

I bent over Briant and pulled away his helmet. He had vomited blood, that still frothed from his mouth. His nose bent slightly, a thing I had not noticed since the day I saw him in Ryford's lane. He did not open his eyes. "Peasant bastard," he gasped, and raised his sword. I gripped my own with both hands. At first I could barely lift it, but then and for one swift moment I moved as if uninjured. I raised the heathen blade and screaming from pain and long fury I dropped the sword on him. Briant shuddered like a tree under a woodsman's ax. His neck parted like a log under that ax. There was blood everywhere.

I had no strength. I turned, wavering, gasping for breath, consumed by pain. Briant's squire stared at me wide-eyed behind his injured mount, as if he could not believe what I had done. The others crouched over the whimpering lad with the broken arm.

Hugh staggered toward me. His swollen face bore a pattern of moon-shaped cuts from the knight's gauntlet. He glanced away from Briant. "You bleed, sir." He pointed at my side.

"My ribs are broken."

He helped pull off my helmet. Sunlight fell upon me, staggering as pain, brighter than I had seen for years.

"You have killed all four, sir."

"Only three, Hugh. Praise God they had unwilling squires."

"I meant, the four you sought."

All four. It was true. All four of them. I had my revenge. Here at last, on this day and in this empty country, it was finished. Briant, Laramort, Giles at Ryford wood, Orsain at Pouancé. I almost laughed, despite my pain. I had killed all four. Dear Rebecca, I answer your blood. Despite myself.

Hugh wrapped my ribs and made a sling for my right arm. The squires went to their dead knights, removed their helmets, and made their holy signs. My lance point had mangled one whole side of Laramort's face; the rest was even paler in death. Arnold lay nearby, his neck broken, a scream frozen on his lips. And Briant. God, how I killed Briant.

The last knight sat the trampled grass, still unable to rise. His squire took off his helmet and mail hood, and bandaged his bleeding neck. "I am Johan of Wells," he said, hoarse. "Michel de Verdeur, are you farmer's brat or Morgan's bastard?"

"You must yield, sir," I said, though I carried no sword.

"I yield. To the bastard, not the peasant."

"And I accept it, sir."

He glanced about. "You have killed good knights today."

"That I would have rather met on the battlefield."

"There will be no battle." For a moment he held his breath against his pain. "Arthur had sent to ask a truce when we left."

I stared at him. "A truce? Then why attack me?"

"It was Briant. He recognized you afar. He said he had sworn to kill you. Nor would Laramort refuse." Johan took another breath. "We all knew your fame of Lancelot. But we wanted the fight. Especially if there would be no battle." He smiled grimly. "And by God, there were *four* of us."

Thirty-six

Of a sudden I did not know what to do, nor where to go. The sun shone warm overhead. Light clouds hung in the blue sky. Half deaf from the clang of battle, I imagined the world completely silent, save for sparrows calling in the meadow.

Hugh and the others took up the dead and wounded. We found a hermitage in the next valley, shaded by old oaks, where the monks bound and salved our wounds. I gave the prior half my spoils, that he offer the dead a Christian burial, and succor Johan of Wells till he was healed. He shook his head at it.

"Fighting on the Sabbath."

I smiled at him. "And John Baptist's eve."

Aching in every joint, I knelt in the little chapel and prayed for all the souls killed by my heathen blade. The blade that I had sheathed at Briant's death, that I might never draw again.

The king asked his truce. I was sore injured and much wearied, and if Arthur did not battle I had no haste to find him. We took the midday meal in their refectory. I lay on a shaded bench in their cloister and fell asleep. The sun was two hours from setting when Hugh woke me. The side of his face had gone purple. My right arm was stiff, and the hurt in my ribs nearly kept me from climbing on my palfrey.

The monks pointed us our way, and we rode without haste through the pleasant easy country. After another league we came to a long fertile valley, where wheat stood tall and green in the broad fields. A thin haze might have stood beyond the next hill and my ears imagined distant horns, but when we drew up to listen I could hear nothing. We rode past a small manor house where curtains blew at open casements, but nobody looked out them. A group of cottages made a little village. Chickens scratched the road and geese clattered in one houseyard, but there was no sign of people.

Hugh stared at me. "Where are they all, sir?"

My heart stopped. "Oh, my God, I have a fear . . ."

We found a rutted way between the fields, and rode up the long hillslope quick as my hurt would allow. Yes, there was a faint horn, and distant shouts, and the clang of swords.

"God defend us, Hugh, they are fighting."

A little wood crowned the rise. Peasants clustered under the tree shade, so many they must have come from miles around. They shrank away as we rode past, and drew up under the last oak. The air beyond shone gold in the lowering sun. A wide valley lay below us, rich with sown wheat, its fields curving away to the bottom and then up a farther hill. At first it seemed a wood, too, for there were logs scattered about as if a great storm had uprooted every tree, broken every branch. But then some trunks moved, and armor glittered in the light and horses wandered limping, and tattered banners fluttered. Rooks cawed and vultures circled overhead, and suddenly I heard the screams of dying men.

I caught my breath. Here had been two great armies, each a thousand knights. Where were they now?

In the distance a single horn rang. Horses galloped, dust swirled. Iron clashed on iron. Dear God, they still fought.

"Hugh," I cried, "we must find the king."

We rode carefully down the slope. Knights with lances broken in their gut lay staring at the sky, among shredded banners that might have been the king's. A score of corpses sprawled broken in the grain, knights of both sides. A little way beyond, a half dozen wounded men gasped with fatigue. Two sergeants stared up at us, that wore Mordred's colors but had not the strength to challenge.

A smell like winter filled the air. No, not winter but winter's eve, the stench of slaughter in the days before winter fell. We rode through the stink of blood, of flesh and bowels and death, and winter coming chilled that summer's evening, a long black winter without a hope of spring.

A little marshy stream flowed at the bottom of the fields. The wounded lay thick there, groaning and writhing, half already drowned in the shallow water. Just beyond rang the clatter of arms, and the cries of battling knights. The three or four that still guarded Arthur were attacked by half a dozen. They dashed together, half paralyzed with fatigue. They screamed and hacked at one another, and fell dying from their horses. The whole vast unthinkable battle had shrunk now to this tiny skirmish.

A battered knight cast away his broken shield, lifted his sword, and galloped at the king. He was Mordred. I spurred my horse to outflank him. But Arthur saw him coming, seized a lance and charged his own tired mount.

"My lord," I cried, "beware."

I might have shouted down a well. Mordred lifted his sword. Arthur charged unwavering. When they met, his lance drove through Mordred as through a sack of grain, and I saw a yard of it emerge from Mordred's back. Their wearied horses stumbled to a halt. But Mordred kept his saddle, despite his violent wound, and with a face savage with pain raised his sword two-handed over the king.

"My lord" I cried, "let go, back away."

The handle of Arthur's lance had become entangled in his tattered surcoat. A man less weary would have got away, but as he struggled Mordred dropped his blade on Arthur's helmet with a huge crash. They fell together from their horses.

I rushed to them, hardly feeling my own hurt, and swung down and knelt over the king.

"Here," said a voice, "you." Sir Bedevere wavered above me.

We cut the straps and drew away Arthur's helmet. Blood gushed from the wound. Mordred's blade had dug through steel and scalp and skull, and beneath the flowing blood Arthur's brain might have lain exposed. My hands shook as we bound his head. His hair, red-gold when he sailed to Banioc, was now streaked with white. Red blood, white hair, the colors of both Lancelot and Mordred. God's mercy, this best and finest king.

Camelot was slain.

Sir Lucan stood over us, one hand clutching his stomach. Blood ran through his fingers. He had killed Mordred's last knight, but it cost him dear.

"Is there nobody else?" I said.

"Everyone is dead." Lucan spoke through clamped teeth.

A thousand knights. A storm worse than the hardest winter to uproot all these trees.

"What happened?" I said. "Why did you fight?"

Bedevere stared at the king. "We drew up for battle. Both sides, despite the Sabbath. The king sent a flag of truce. We thought it was received. Then somebody." He waved a faltering hand. "Some knight drew his sword." Tears ran down his dusty cheeks. "God knows why."

"To kill an adder," Lucan muttered.

I ought have come sooner. But it was the Sabbath, I had defeated four on my own field, I could have done no more here.

I turned and stumbled away. Not everyone was dead. A hundred footmen, perhaps, still staggered the field. But every knight had fallen. My eyes blurred with tears.

Camelot was truly slain.

"There, sir," said Hugh. "Denham's colors."

What had been a swirling fight was now but broken men. Balen lay unmoving, and when Hugh drew off the helmet his face showed no mark of pain.

"Take his dagger," I said, "we'll give it to his lady Margaret."

Arthur woke, though I hardly believed it. He struggled up on one elbow and scowled at Mordred, dead beside him. "I would go from here," he said, in a voice I did not recognize. "I would not die with men I hate."

Bedevere pointed down the valley. "There is a chapel, sire. Not a mile away."

I sent Hugh for their horses. We got the king into his saddle after a great effort. I ached everywhere, but I thought Arthur felt no pain at all. We rode him between us through the battlefield. It took till dusk, for he would ever stop and peer down at the dead, and mutter their names. We found the colors of Bramhill and there lay Edmund, too old to joust but not too old for war. And another widow made.

"God defend us," cried Arthur, "how many have we killed?"

We had no answer. Camelot had slain itself.

The chapel was long deserted, but we found a hermit's straw pallet for the king. Lucan sat beside him, pale and much injured. I sent Hugh for water at the weedy spring. Bedevere prayed at the moss-grown altar. Even the priests were killed or fled, and the king had no one to sing a Mass for him.

I had brought a loaf from the hermitage but only Bedevere was hungry. Lucan could not get enough to drink.

Arthur woke. He stared around with bloodshot eyes. "Who is this?" His voice was very weak.

"Michel de Verdeur, sire."

"Michel de Verdeur." I could see the memory return. "Michel de Verdeur. Morgan's bastard. Or so my bastard claimed."

"Sire?" I said.

"Mordred." The name seemed acid in his mouth. "Bastard prince of Orkney."

Christ save us, even that rumor had been true.

"Sir Michel de Verdeur. Merlin spoke to you, but not to me." He cleared his throat and his voice strengthened. "And then, he would not even speak to you." He gazed at me, though I wondered what he saw. "Michel de Verdeur. The manors in Blackmoor. They are yours."

I knelt and took his shaking hand. "Sire."

"I give them to you. Not to John of Craon. To you."

"Thank you, my lord." I could not refuse him now, though it failed my liege to Craon.

"They are yours. With all these dead." He paused, wavering. "There will be many others. But a canon of Glastonbury must sing my father's prayers." He drew an uneven breath. "Another must pray for me. Every day. You will endow these things."

"I will do it, sire."

"Michel de Verdeur." He was silent again. "How well you fight. I remember you at Joyous Gard, you will soon be fine as Gawain." His voice broke. "Ah, dear Gawain. And Lancelot. My best kinsman. My best friend. I could not stop their feud. I had no wish to stop their feud." He drew another breath. "She was my wife, given me of her father Leodegrance. I thought to kill Lancelot at Joyous Gard myself. Would that Mordred had slain him that night. By God, she was a beautiful bride."

He fell silent. Lucan slept. Bedevere fidgeted.

My ribs throbbed. "The queen is at Amesbury, sire."

"Amesbury."

"She would take Holy Orders, save you wish her as your wife."

He closed his eyes. "Oh, how I wish her. She is always my wife. But this." He moved an unsteady hand. "All this. Do you know, Sir Michel, all this is because she is my wife? Because she is so beautiful. So beautiful." He breathed for a moment. "No woman ought be so beautiful. Our Lord ought never make such a beautiful woman, that only His Sangral might divert us. And then for only a little while." His eyes opened. "But it will be long ere I need a wife, Sir Michel." He shut them again. "Very long."

"My lord," said Bedevere, "we will carry you hence, we will find the best physicians."

"Bedevere, you know where I must go."

"Sire, we must hie to Salisbury."

But Arthur slept again.

It was midnight when his voice shook us from our drowse. In the black night cries sounded from the field, and muttering voices and deep grunts. "What is it?" said the king, nervous. "What happens to my good knights? Lucan, go and see."

"I will go, sire," I said, standing.

But Sir Lucan, smiling in his pain, put out a hand. "The king's wish," he said. He struggled up and shambled out.

After a long while he came back. " 'Tis the wounded, my lord," he said, "their men no longer care for them." He drew a hoarse breath. " 'Tis the scavengers, that rouse the dying as they rob them." He paused again. " 'Tis the swine rooting, eating everything not armored."

"Oh, God," said the king.

"There is no one to protect them, sire."

"No one? Oh, Lucan, what have I done? Pray help me stand."

I stepped forward and gripped Arthur's hand, but already Lucan had raised the king's shoulders. Arthur leaned on him as he stood. Lucan gave a loud sorrowful cry, the chapel filled with the stench of bowels and he fell gasping, a froth at his lips. His belly had failed at last.

"Ah, sweet knight," cried Arthur, "have I killed you, too?"

Lucan did not answer.

"Soon enough," Arthur said, "we will all be dead." He looked at Bedevere. "I must go. You know the way."

"Yes, sire."

"I will stay, my lord." I held him upright with my good arm. "I will bury Sir Lucan at dawn." I clasped him near as a brother and when he blinked at me, death looked out his eyes.

"Good," he said.

"My lord and king," said Bedevere, "Sir Michel must come, too. It needs all of us to move you."

Once more Hugh brought our horses. He rode ahead, his drawn sword across his pommel. Bedevere and I kept on each side of the king and he fell asleep as we went, and woke with a start, and fell asleep again. Only the summer stars lit our way. I wondered that Bedevere knew the country so well, for the road seemed to come and go as fitfully as the king's strength. We rode all that brief night and when dawn grayed the sky we paused on a hilltop. The earth had changed to sand under our horses' hooves, and far away over the tops of pines lay the wide cool line of the sea.

We found at last another chapel, built of dark stone. A broad lake lay nearby, black and mirror-still, the last stars glittering on its face.

"Here," cried Arthur, suddenly awake.

"Just a little more, sire," murmured Bedevere.

The way sloped down to the edge of the pines. Rough grass ran out to a narrow beach. Pale waves curled upon the strand.

"Here," said Arthur. The three of us got him from the horse and laid him on the scented needles.

"There," said Arthur. But he pointed to an empty sea, and Bedevere and I looked at each other, our eyes wet with tears.

"Here," said Arthur. He raised his sword. "Bedevere. The lake. Throw this in."

"Sire?" said Bedevere. "Excalibur?"

"Into the lake."

Bedevere shook his head, frowning. But he lifted sword and scabbard and belt, and trudged up the slope again. Of course I knew the stories, how Merlin had shown the young Arthur a magic lake, how a lady's arm came from the water holding that great sword. But I always thought it must have happened somewhere mysterious, in magic Wales or distant Ireland. I could not believe it was here, beside this easy brightening ocean.

"Sire," I said, "does the Lady of the Lake dwell here? Is she truly Nimue, who witched the mage?"

But Arthur slept again.

Anxious as I was of the lady, so was Bedevere anxious of the blade. The king asked what he saw when he threw it away. Bedevere had seen nothing and Arthur, knowing he had failed, sent him again. The lady, I thought; she who gave it must receive it back. But Bedevere did not understand, and when Arthur sent him a third time I went instead. I found Excalibur where he had hidden it, in a niche in the chapel wall. For a moment I thought of throwing in my own blade, but that must go to Abbotsbury. I threw Excalibur far as I could. As it was in the air I glanced away. When I looked again the surface of the lake lay smooth as ever.

"What did you see?" asked the king.

"The lady," I said. It was almost true. For shadows made, fleetingly upon its dull wall, the face of Naime within the chapel. Bedevere stared at me, unbelieving.

"There," said Arthur.

And dark upon the growing dawn a sail moved. A ship tacked in to shore. We clasped our hands under the king, despite our hurts, and carried him out from the trees, out under the high bright sky, across the strand crunching under our boots, out to the edge of the waves. Three ladies stood on board, each dressed in deep mourning, each beautiful as a queen. The keel ground upon the shingle and the sailors backed the sail, and they leapt from the ship and came wading through the shallow waves, their gowns wet to the thigh.

"Ah, brother," cried the dark one, and bent and kissed him.

She was Morgan. Her dark eye rested on me one brief moment. I bowed to her, unable to speak. They lifted him between them and carried him to the ship. The craft drew away, quick as it had come. I stared after it, incredulous.

"How did they know?" I asked, but tears streamed down Bedevere's face. "Where do they take him?"

"Avalon," he murmured, and wiped his eyes. "The isle of apples. And of spring."

But I smelled again the stink of slaughter. "And only God Himself may know, if spring will ever come again."

Bedevere could not contain his sobs. He turned and strode back through the trees. I heard him mount his horse.

"Sir," I cried, "where do you ride?"

He gave no answer, but spurred away up the slope.

Hugh waited with our own horses, the dawn bright in his eyes. I climbed stiffly on my palfrey. Even more than after yesterday's battle, I felt light-headed and confused, as if I woke in a strange new place and knew not what to do, nor where to go. We rode slowly under the pines. A cuckoo called, three notes instead of two, as always after John Baptist's. This morning, years ago, Lark died. This day I had sworn to kill her knights, and almost I believed I had wished it, that in the end her death would shatter Camelot.

We came again to the dark chapel. I thought it deserted, yet two figures stood there, a man and a tall young woman. They raised their heads, she drew back the hood of her cloak, the new sun moved on her face, soft as lamplight.

"Dear lady." I stumbled from the horse, my hurt unfelt.

"Sir Michel," Naime murmured.

I went to her and took her hands.

"You are injured, sir," said the man.

I knew the voice. It was my drunken friar's. It was the old man at Craon, the lad at Michel's mount. Almost, it was hers. I turned and stared at him. In the newly brightening day he was both old and young, weary and alert.

I bowed. "Good wizard, what do you in this empty place?"

"The same as you, Michel de Verdeur. To see the king to Avalon."

"And had you no magic to keep him here? Memories enough of old Ulfius, but no word to Arthur that he save himself?"

The shadows deepened under his brow. "Not even kings are free of fate."

"It was not fate," I said. "Camelot has slain itself." He did not argue. I saw in his eyes a sorrow so deep I had to glance away. "But my fate is to be always a green knight."

"And so you should remain, Michel de Verdeur."

"And my fate, dear lady, is to love you always."

"Michel."

"The king has given me the manors in Blackmoor. If I stay in Britain I have hopes of many more. I would woo you, Naime, though you be a king's daughter."

"You will be a great knight, Michel." She frowned and looked away. "But I have told you of my nunnery."

"Lady, your father cannot . . ." Then suddenly I understood, could not deny what I had always known. She was Naime and Nimue, both. The Lady of the Lake. Merlin's bane, yet always his. She had witched us both. "Naime," I cried. My sudden tears blurred her face. "Oh, my dear lady, how?"

"Spells work in many ways, Michel, and the greatest are the least expected."

"But lady, you and I . . . can this never be undone?"

Merlin spoke behind us. "Your love hath nearly broke it."

"Lady." I could barely see for weeping. "If you come to Camelot we might . . ."

"Alas," she said, "they will see no more of me at Camelot."

I took her hand and kissed it. "Then will I follow you to the farthest shore, across the sea . . ."

She drew me close. "Oh, Michel, you know you cannot follow." She kissed me on the lips, and very long. "Good-bye, sweet Michel."

Even now I feel it, the hand she put to my chest, the soft pressure that was not a push but a lingering touch even she was loath to break. She had done it many times, yet never with such finality. I would have reached for her, taken her and held her, save I could not lift my hands to clasp her, nor move my feet. She turned and walked into the chapel. Merlin bowed and followed. To my streaming eyes they moved like shadows, and then I could not see at all. My heart ached, as if burning tongs levered it from my chest. I gasped for breath. I could not swallow. The world roared in my ears, another storm come to blow me away, with all of Camelot.

Blind as a headless man, I put out a hand and found my horse. Aching in every joint, I pulled myself into the saddle.

"They have gone, sir," Hugh murmured. "King. Wizard. Lady."

I turned toward his voice. The light of the new sun flooded my eyes. The world stood around me once again, dense and solid and unyielding.

Hugh gave a small laugh. "And where go we, Sir Michel de Verdeur?"